T0095511

THE GABRIEL CHRONICLES

Book 3—The Superiors

Also written by Dennis Flannery:

The GABRIEL CHRONICLES
Book – 1 – The Beginning

The GABRIEL CHRONICLES
Book – 2 – New Home

The GABRIEL CHRONICLES
Book – 3 - The Superiors

The GABRIEL CHRONICLES
Book – 4 – Sharkra

Lenny

THE GABRIEL CHRONICLES

Book 3—The Superiors

DENNIS FLANNERY

authorHOUSE®

AuthorHouse™
1663 Liberty Drive
Bloomington, IN 47403
www.authorhouse.com
Phone: 833-262-8899

Published by AuthorHouse   10/11/2022

ISBN: 978-1-6655-7319-1 (sc)
ISBN: 978-1-6655-7318-4 (e)

Print information available on the last page.

Any people depicted in stock imagery provided by Getty Images are models, and such images are being used for illustrative purposes only. Certain stock imagery © Getty Images.

This book is printed on acid-free paper.

Because of the dynamic nature of the Internet, any web addresses or links contained in this book may have changed since publication and may no longer be valid. The views expressed in this work are solely those of the author and do not necessarily reflect the views of the publisher, and the publisher hereby disclaims any responsibility for them.

CONTENTS

Author's note

This science-fiction novel is not based totally on conflict, as most are; rather, it's based on the lives of human colonists as they progress on their new planet. Most of the science fiction in this and the previous novels in the trilogy is based on scientific fact or generally accepted theory.

The Gabriel Chronicles, the last of the trilogy, tells the story of the extraordinary lives and adventures of exceptional men and women. The following explanatory notes are for the benefit of those who have not read the first two novels.

SLF (pronounced "self") stands for synthetic life-form. At the beginning of this novel, there are just three SLFs living on the planet Gabriel: Vance, Troy, and Gary.

The *Norman* and the *Marian* are starships built on Earth for the sole purpose of colonizing another planet. The *Norman* is a single sphere one hundred meters in diameter and contains twenty decks. The *Marian* is made up of five such spheres, each the size of the *Norman* and connected to the others by large corridors. The *Marian* looks similar to a giant jack in the children's game jacks. The *Norman*, piloted by the SLF Vance, left Earth in the year 2030. The *Marian*, piloted by the SLFs Troy and Gary, left Earth 415 years later, in 2445.

Stasis is a state-of-the-art method of putting living beings in a frozen hyper-sleep. The colonists in both the *Norman* and the *Marian* were transported to Gabriel in stasis. Those in the *Norman* remained in stasis for four hundred years while Vance seeded the planet Gabriel. The colonists of the *Marian* remained in stasis for just forty years before arriving at Gabriel. When SLFs go into stasis, they simply turn themselves off for whatever period of time they wish.

Vance Youngblood is a retired SEAL captain. He is of average height and powerfully built, and he has an olive complexion, menacing dark eyes, and wavy black hair that starts low on his forehead. He is highly intelligent and clearly not a man to be on the wrong side of. Vance provided the planning and security for the WGC before becoming a SLF and captaining the *Norman* from Earth to Gabriel.

Troy and Gary, Earth's last leaders, headed the World Guidance Council (WGC). They became SLFs in order to pilot the massive starship *Marian* in escaping Earth before a massive asteroid destroyed it.

Troy is medium height and slender, with short-cropped brown hair and brown eyes. He looks and acts like the CEO of a large corporation.

Gary is a tall dark man with curly salt-and-pepper hair and dark eyes, and he possesses an excellent scientific mind. He was second in command of the WGC in the years prior to Earth's destruction.

Alexander Gabriel is tall, blond, and handsome, with striking blue eyes and an average build. Alex was the main protagonist in the first novel in the trilogy. He was the driving force in creating the WGC five hundred years before Troy and Gary were born.

Teddy is as warm and caring an individual as can be found. He is a born entertainer and a lifelong friend of Alexander Gabriel; he appears in all three novels.

Dale Isley is a small, tidy, good-looking man. He has brown hair and a manicured beard and is considered one of the greatest minds in history. Among his many accomplishments, Dale invented Isleium, the substance the SLFs are made of. He designed the weapon that allowed the WGC to take over all of Earth's governments and enforce mankind's conformity to the new laws imposed by the WGC. Among his hundreds of designs and inventions was the propulsion system for the *Norman*, which was also used more than four hundred years later on the *Marian*.

The planet Gabriel has six continents: the North Pole and South Pole, which are uninhabited; the Vast Continent, the largest; the North Dumbbell and South Dumbbell; and the Ring Continent, where the planet's colonization began.

There are three other alien races in the novel *Gabriel*, the second in the series. The Vout are an advanced race. They are tall, thin, hairless, friendly, and somewhat boring. They were the first to befriend the humans. The Malic are short, hairy, ugly, and vicious. They attacked the humans of Gabriel, which resulted in a short war that killed two dozen humans and all but four of the Malic. The Yassi are short, cute, hairless, and delightful. They are more technically advanced than the humans and Vout and became fast friends and allies. Their starships are stunningly beautiful. The Yassi woo in lieu of clapping or whistling.

Aside from the two main human starships, the *Norman* and *Marian*, there are smaller ships called runabouts, both large and small. There is nothing fancy about these ships. They appear to be little more than stylized boxcars with pontoons. They are the workhorses and are used as transports of supplies and personnel. There is also a beautiful shuttle built by the Yassi and gifted to the humans of Gabriel.

Home-Bay is the original colony of Gabriel. It's located on a beautiful bay on the west side of the Ring Continent.

It was decided early on that for those on Gabriel, the days, months, and years had to be adjusted to sync with the actual length of days, months, and years of their new planet. The time the planet Gabriel took for one revolution on its axis was divided into twenty parts, resulting in twenty hour days. Gabriel orbited its sun every two hundred of these days, so that became the length of their year. Those two hundred days were divided into ten parts, resulting in ten months containing twenty days each. The months were simply named Mo-One through Mo-Ten. A date of January 5, 2018, on Earth would read as Mo-One 5, 2018, on Gabriel.

The first book in the trilogy follows the life of Alexander Gabriel, a brilliant investment broker who is shot back in time to begin his life over starting at age eight. It tells of his accumulation of a vast fortune over the ensuing decades. He uses his massive wealth and the assistance of three other exceptional men, each with a unique area of expertise, to change the world.

The second in the trilogy, *Gabriel*, continues the story of three of these four men. Dr. Isley creates a substance that allows him to build natural-looking prosthetics, giving amputees around the world functional, lifelike limbs and paralyzed people new functional nerves. Years later, he takes this incredible technology to its ultimate conclusion. He builds a complete synthetic life-form, a SLF. The synthetic body and brain are designed to accept the complete intelligence, personality, and abilities of any human. Vance Youngblood became the first SLF.

With Alexander Gabriel's money and Dale Isley's brilliance, the WGC builds a colossal spaceship designed to take a small number of colonists to a distant planet. The SLF Vance Youngblood captains the ship. He alone, over the next fifty years, develops the planet Gabriel, making it suitable for human habitation.

Alexander Gabriel and Dale Isley appear as holograms in this and the novel *Gabriel*. Their intelligence, personalities, and appearance are stored in the starship *Norman*'s computers.

PROLOGUE

Vance had a small smile on his face as he entered the beautiful shuttle, a gift to the humans of Gabriel from the Yassi. *That's the last stop,* he thought. *Now I'm going to my island.*

Just over a month ago, on the hundredth anniversary of the colonization of Gabriel, Vance, by design, had come out of his self-imposed twenty-year stasis. He could not and would not miss the celebration. These were his people, and his people were his life. For the past month, he had attempted to visit every town and colony on the planet; he'd missed few. He loved visiting with old friends and meeting those younger than twenty years old—those who had never seen this man, this extraordinary SLF, the father of their wonderful world.

From an altitude of fifteen kilometers, he spotted his island. *There it is.* A big smile spread across his face. *It's greener and denser,* he thought as he banked the shuttle and headed to the west coast of the island. *It's been twenty years. Plants grow.* He smiled again as he took in the expanse of his paradise. At a length of forty-two kilometers and a width about half that at its widest point, it was a large island but not the largest on the planet. However, to Vance, it was the best.

He could see a large, beautifully designed cabin made of river rock and log through the trees on the shuttle's right. "There's our home," he said aloud, as he'd said many times to his beloved Lara. He slowed the shuttle and settled quietly on the expansive lawn that extended from the home's large front deck down to the rocky bank of the Lara River. His brow furrowed, and he looked out the window of the shuttle. *Somebody's been caring for this place.* He nodded in appreciation.

Less than a minute later, Vance exited the shuttle with a fair-sized duffel bag in each hand. He stopped when his feet hit the grass, and he took a deep, appreciative breath. *Ah, smells like heaven.* He smiled again and headed toward his home.

He managed to open the door without dropping the duffels and continued inside. He set the duffels down and looked around the living room. *This is exactly as I left it twenty years ago. Exactly. Hmm.* He looked toward the bedroom, half expecting Lara to come out and greet him, but there was only silence. His heart sank a little. He turned and walked into the kitchen and immediately spotted a note stuck to the refrigerator door: "We're in section three. Please join us."

Who's we? he thought, and then he shrugged. *Okay, I'll do that.*

He headed to the back door on the far side of the kitchen. The wall on the right side of the door had a row of pegs holding a small array of umbrellas, gloves, and hats. He smiled as he spotted his old straw hat still hanging on its peg. His smile faded as he saw that the peg next to it was empty. After a moment, he reached over, took his old hat off the peg, and put it on before opening the door and walking out.

Section three was where he and Lara, many decades ago, had released the first of the gorillas—Kong and his ladies—and they could occasionally find them and their progeny there as the years passed. Over the years, more gorillas of varying genetics had been introduced.

Section three was a delightful two-kilometer walk up the river from their home. Over the decades, the trail had become a well-established walking path. For about half its distance, the path bordered the Lara River; the rest meandered through a thick forest. Vance was a hundred meters inside section three, when he heard some activity coming from a clearing up ahead.

As soon as he entered the clearing, he spotted a young woman in her late teens intently hammering some siding to a shack of some kind. She was a tall, slender young lady with olive skin and short dark hair under a bright red scarf.

I don't know this person, he thought.

The young woman didn't see Vance approaching and continued to give the piece of siding some serious whacking.

From Vance's left came another noise. He turned just in time to see another young lady walk into the clearing about thirty meters away. She was carrying a baby gorilla on her hip. She stopped when she spotted Vance, and then she slowly slid the little primate down, setting it gently on the ground. Her eyes never left Vance's as she released the small ape.

"Oh, Jesus," Vance said softly.

This young lady had long red hair under an old straw hat. Her eyes sparkled as she started walking rapidly toward Vance.

"Hi, hon. Welcome home," she said, smiling brightly.

Hi, hon. Welcome home. Her words reverberated in his mind several times before he repeated quietly, "Oh, Jesus."

Vance stood stunned. His synthetic brain wasn't prone to malfunctioning, but this scenario stopped it in mid-thought. There, just a few meters away and closing, was the love of his life—his two lives. *What did she say? "Hi, hon"?* He remained dazed and simply stared at the lovely apparition as she approached.

The young lady continued to close the gap between them. She stopped half a meter in front of Vance, slowly removed her straw hat, and let it fall to the ground. Tears of joy glistened in her green eyes as she looked up into his; a smile remained on her face.

Vance's mind slowly began to function, and his first thought was *They should have told me.* His next thought was *Oh my. Oh my!*

Vance continued to stare at the stunning apparition, an exact copy of the only woman he'd ever loved. He smiled slightly as he regained his voice. "You knew I was coming?"

She nodded. "They contacted me earlier and gave me a heads-up."

Vance was silent for a moment before saying, "They didn't extend me that courtesy." His smile faded a little.

"Alex and Dale—" She paused for a brief moment. "They insisted I call them by their first names." Her eyes got a little bigger. "I can tell you it took a couple of months before that became natural."

Vance's smile returned briefly as he nodded in understanding.

"They were quite concerned about how to handle this situation." Her expression became more serious. "You are very dear to them. They wanted to make our meeting as wonderful for you as possible."

That put the smile back on Vance's face. "Of course."

She returned the smile and continued. "My studies made me aware of this island—your island—so I mentioned it to them. They jumped on the idea, so I can assure you our meeting here was well thought out."

Vance's smile broadened. "I'm sure it was." He looked deep into her eyes. "Is your name Lara?"

She nodded quickly.

Vance could sense the longing in the young woman. He knew her as he knew himself. She was the same woman he had left on Earth centuries ago and the same woman who'd been taken from him twenty years ago. This was not a stranger. He took off his hat and dropped it next to Lara's. "I have always loved you, you know?"

Waiting not a second longer, she threw her arms around his neck and kissed him.

Lara had been preparing for this meeting for more than a month, since the first centennial celebration of the planet Gabriel, which was the day Vance Youngblood had come out of his self-imposed twenty-year stasis. However, that past month hadn't been the beginning of her preparation.

Two years ago, when Lara was seventeen, she and her surrogate mother, Sonia, were summoned to the bridge of the *Norman*. In that meeting, with three of the four councillors of Gabriel, she was informed that she had been cloned for the express purpose of being Vance Youngblood's companion. Her first reactions were fear and bewilderment, but after taking a few moments to clear her head and process the initial revelation, she was exhilarated. She, like all citizens of Gabriel, knew of Vance Youngblood. He was the father of their world. Everyone knew from early childhood that the SLF Vance had, over a period of four hundred years in planet time, single-handedly developed their planet. All the trees, plants, grasses, animals, fish, and fowl were a result of Vance Youngblood's efforts.

Knowing she was to be his woman, she began to study. She read everything written about him and watched all the available videos of him, dating all the way back to his days on Earth. In the beginning, she marveled at the size of the man. He was short by Gabriel's standards at under two meters, but he had a remarkable body. His chest and arms were heavily muscled, but his shoulders were legendary. They were massive. He was a handsome man in a way. He was square-jawed, with a smallish, sharp nose; intelligent dark eyes; and wavy dark hair that began low on his forehead. All in all, he looked formidable.

Lara studied hundreds of hours of Vance and the original Lara interacting on the distant and now extinct planet Earth many centuries ago. She watched videos of Lara, the first clone, and Vance mingling with the citizens of Gabriel. The two had been inseparable for fifty-eight years until Lara's death at the relatively young age of seventy-six.

The young Lara clone had never met Vance, but she knew more than anyone the deep love Vance and Lara had for each other. She not only knew the facts but also could sense the deep emotions of her predecessors. Without ever meeting him, she acquired a profound love that was impossible to explain.

Vance and Lara sat next to each other, holding hands on their leather couch. Vance had a bemused look on his face while he and Lara engaged in conversation with Alex and Dale on the viewer.

Alex said with a slight smile, "Are you pissed at us?"

"I was for a brief moment, but that passed quickly." Vance looked at Lara and then back to the viewer. "You did what you did out of compassion for a friend."

"I was hoping that would be your conclusion," said Alex.

"I knew it would be," added a smiling Dale.

"Then did we do the right thing?" asked Alex.

Vance nodded. "I cannot thank you enough."

Alex smiled. "Are you coming back to Home-Bay?"

Vance looked at Lara and smiled. "Not for some time, probably quite a while. We have a lot to learn about each other." Vance looked up at the viewer and smiled broadly. "Don't call us; we'll call you." With that, the viewer went blank.

CHAPTER 1

BACK TO HOME-BAY
MO-FOUR 2, 100

Vance guided the exquisite shuttle through the cave's mammoth entrance and into the starship *Norman*'s flight deck and settled it gently on its pad. In less than a minute, its hatch dropped down, and Vance and Lara exited to a cheerful welcome from the flight deck crew.

Vance was instantly aware these people were not surprised to see Lara with him. *The word has gotten out*, thought Vance. *They know about Lara.*

After greetings all around, they headed to the elevator hand in hand. Down they went, arriving on deck twenty a few seconds later. As they walked down the exit ramp, they were again greeted by the enthusiastic welcomes and congratulations of two dozen or so Gabrielites who had been occupied with various chores inside the *Norman*'s vast cave. Vance's smile didn't diminish as he shook hands with the well-wishers. He beamed as he observed Lara maintaining a radiant smile as she warmly exchanged handshakes and hugs with all of her lifelong friends.

The greetings did not abate as they casually walked out of the cave and toward Vance's historical home across the river. It was a perfect day, and many residents of Home-Bay were out for strolls around the bay. Their walk home, which normally would have taken ten minutes, took them nearly a full hour. They didn't mind. To the contrary, both thoroughly enjoyed the interactions with their fellow Gabrielites. Vance glanced at Lara as they approached their home.

She's as happy as I am, he thought. *We are soul mates and have been since we met on Earth so long ago. She is a new Lara but the same Lara.*

Vance's Home-Bay home had been impeccably cared for over the past two decades while he lay in stasis. It was exactly as he had left it, as was the case with their island.

Lara had, for the previous two years, been given full access to his home. Alex and Dale had wanted her to be completely comfortable with her surroundings before she and Vance returned to Home-Bay. They hoped that to Vance, nothing had changed except the obvious. This Lara was nearly sixty years younger than her predecessor, but that meant little to Vance—he had his Lara back.

A week after Vance and Lara had settled in, they were watching a news program featuring amateur news anchors Bob and Brandon.

To fill the half-hour broadcast, Bob and Brandon had to use just about everything going on around Gabriel, and considering the total population of the planet was just under thirty thousand, it took some effort to keep the program interesting.

"Teddy would have been great at this," Vance remarked with a little melancholy.

"Without question," said Lara. "If he did the news, everyone on the planet would watch. That's a certainty."

"But these guys do a great job," Vance said.

"Yes, they do."

Within a minute, a knock on their door caught Vance by surprise; for someone to show up at his door without an appointment was unusual.

Vance paused the program. "Well, I'll go see who's come a-calling," he said with a colloquial accent and a smile.

Lara smiled and nodded.

Vance patted her on the knee, got up from the couch, and headed to the front door. He opened it with a flourish.

There, standing on his porch with his soft brown eyes and a huge smile, displaying his legendary bright white teeth, was Teddy IV.

This Teddy was the second clone born on Gabriel and the fourth Teddy overall. Teddy III had been born in the sixth year of the new Gabriel calendar. He, after a lifetime of entertaining all on Gabriel and thousands of visiting Vout and Yassi, had passed away at the age of ninety-four during the first year of Vance's twenty-year stasis, just over nineteen years ago. A day after Vance had come out of his stasis, he'd been told of Teddy's passing. He'd taken the news hard and grieved alone at Teddy's grave site. He'd been there for more than three hours.

Vance's great affection for Teddy started in Earth date 1983 at the Gabriel Mansion in Newport Beach, California. Jason Gould, the second chairman of the WGC, had predicted a calamity when Teddy and Vance met for the first time, but that didn't happen—quite the contrary. Their instant compatibility came as a complete shock to those who knew both. Their personalities could not have been more different. At that time, no one knew a more stoic, humorless hard case than Vance Youngblood; he rarely smiled and never laughed. One look at Vance convinced all but the terminally stupid that he was a man not to be trifled with.

On the other side of the coin was Teddy. No one had ever known a warmer, funnier, kinder, gentler, or more entertaining person. Everybody wanted to be around Teddy.

Somehow, these two divergent personalities hit it off and became instant friends. As their friendship grew over the next two years, Vance's association with Teddy changed his personality to an extent no one would have thought possible. He became a softer, more caring person. One could depend on hearing his deep, heartfelt laughter whenever Teddy was around. When the original Teddy was killed by skinheads on Earth in 1985, some suspected Vance was responsible for all five of the punks' gruesome deaths, but nobody ever acted on those suspicions.

Prior to Teddy's imminent death, in those saddest of days, Alex had the doctors at the hospital remove and preserve some of Teddy's DNA. Human cloning at the time was not possible, but Alex knew it would be in the future—he would see to it. Twenty years later, Teddy's first clone was born to surrogate parents. He became a famous entertainer like his predecessor and provided geneticists with valuable data on the question of nature versus nurture. It was this Teddy, the second Teddy, who had said a sad goodbye to a departing Vance just before he left Earth aboard the *Norman* in 2030, and it was this Teddy who was at Alexander Gabriel's side when Alexander died in December of 2043.

There, standing on his porch, was Teddy IV, an identical copy of the previous three Teddys.

Vance was momentarily stunned, and his face lost all expression. Teddy stood his ground and maintained his brilliant smile. Within ten seconds, Vance had Teddy in a bear hug that threatened the young man's continued existence.

"Good evening, sir," Teddy managed to squeak out.

Vance did not reply. Had he been capable of tears, they would have been flowing. He held on for a full minute before releasing young Teddy and then stood back a pace to take a better look at his beloved old friend in a new body. He said nothing.

"I see ya still have the strength I've heard so much about," said Teddy as he rubbed his shoulders, took a couple of deep breaths, and made a few goofy stretches.

"Teddy. My God, we have a new Teddy." Vance finally laughed with joy and appreciation.

Vance's reaction was clearly pleasing to Teddy, and his expressive face was lit with delight. He nodded enthusiastically. "Yes, sir."

"You don't call me sir. We're friends; you use my name." Vance again grabbed the hapless Teddy and locked him in another huge hug.

"Sir, Vance, you're killin' me here." This time, his face and voice displayed exaggerated discomfort.

Vance waited another few seconds before releasing the squirming young man.

"This huggin' is gonna take a little gettin' used to, if I live long enough," Teddy said in mock seriousness. Then he smiled broadly.

Vance returned the smile and laughed. "You'll live—get in here." Vance stepped to one side to allow Teddy access to his home.

"Yes, sir."

Teddy squeezed by Vance and then stopped and half turned as Vance closed the door.

"Well, go on," said Vance as he gestured down the hall.

Teddy turned and continued down the short hall before it opened to the spacious living room.

"Hi, Teddy," said Lara with a big smile as she jumped up from the couch and walked rapidly over to Teddy. She threw her arms around his neck, gave him a hug, and kissed him on the cheek. Teddy retaliated in kind.

"Hi yourself," Teddy replied. "I'm grateful to know Vance's strength hasn't rubbed off on you." He released her.

"Apparently you two know each other," said Vance with a big grin.

"Pretty much grew up together," said Lara.

"Of course. You're about the same age and were brought up in the same town. How could you not?"

CHAPTER 2

FIRST MURDER
MO-EIGHT 13, 100

Vance and Lara divided their time between their home on Home-Bay and their island. At the moment, they were at their home in Home-Bay, sitting out on the deck that overlooked the Vance River and the town of Home-Bay on the far side.

Vance cocked his head. He'd heard something Lara hadn't.

"I'll be back," he said as he patted Lara on the knee and stood up.

"Vance, are you near a viewer?" said a voice as Vance walked into the living room.

"We were out on the deck. What's up, Alex?"

"Had an incident up north."

"What sort of incident?"

There was a pause before Alex answered. "Murder."

Vance remained silent for several moments before answering. "Shit! Shit! Shit!" There was a short pause. "Be right there. Have a runabout ready for me."

"It'll be ready when you get here."

Ten minutes later, Vance walked onto the *Norman*'s bridge. "Who, why, where, and when?"

"The logging community up north is where. A young man named Reg Whetrume is apparently the villain. The when was last night, and I have no idea as to why. Tom Sullivan was the victim."

"Oh no," said Vance, his grief apparent. "I know Tom and his family. Shit!" *One of the few places I didn't visit*, he thought. *Damn it.*

Vance said nothing for a few seconds before continuing. "Whetrume? Big kid. His parents are wonderful people. God damn it!" Vance was sad and furious at the same time. "I'm heading up north." With that, he turned and headed to the elevator.

It was a cold, blustery day as Vance's small runabout landed in the designated clearing just a short walk from the community center. As he exited the craft, he was met by four men of varying ages, all dressed warmly with heavy hooded coats. Vance didn't require a coat at that temperature; it had to be much colder before the temperature affected his SLF body.

Jack, the eldest of the four, was well known to Vance. They had been acquainted for sixty years. He was one of the *Marian's* original colonists. Vance knew the other three young men as he knew all on the planet—not well, but he was aware of their lineage, occupations, and where they lived.

"Jack, it's nice to see you again," said Vance as they shook hands.

"You too, sir. Been a long time."

"Too long."

Jack turned to the three younger men. "I'm sure you remember Joe, Pete, and Isha."

"I do, but it's been ten years since I've seen them. Just kids then." Vance smiled. "Grown into men now." He extended his hand to each one and greeted them by name.

The three younger men were clearly awestruck and probably somewhat intimidated. They'd been in their early teens when they last saw Vance and probably hadn't fully appreciated who he was, but they certainly did now. No matter what else happened that day, they had a story to tell for the rest of their lives.

"Let's head over to my office," said Jack. "Get out of this cold for a while."

"Lead on," said Vance.

Once inside the modest building, the four men removed their coats and hung them on hooks by the door. Each stood behind a wooden chair, leaving the one comfortable-looking padded chair in the center for Vance. He noticed the courtesy and took the seat. The others followed his lead. The fireplace on the west wall was putting out a delightful warmth. It reminded Vance of his home on the island of Mariana back on Earth. His mind shot back to sitting in front of such a fire with Lara long ago.

His attention quickly returned to the present. "Well, let's hear the story."

"Yes, sir. It's a sad one, I'm afraid," said Jack.

"Murder usually is."

"Never been a murder on this planet," said Jack. "This is hitting the people here hard. They're shocked. They're confused."

"It's going to hit everybody on Gabriel hard. It's a sad day," said Vance sincerely. "Nobody other than your community and the councillors at Home-Bay are aware of what happened. When we get it sorted out, we'll make the announcement."

"Yes, sir."

"So go on."

Jack paused for a moment, gathering his thoughts. "Reg Whetrume has always been a bit of a bully when he's drinking. He's a big guy and knows his size intimidates most."

"Already I don't like this man," said Vance.

"Yes, sir, and you're going to like him even less in a minute. Last night, there was the usual gathering of people in our community center, which doubles as a tavern. It's a nice place to spend an evening with friends, shoot some pool, and have a beer." Jack choked up a little and stopped talking for a couple of seconds before continuing; he was clearly deeply distressed by what had happened. "It was just a normal evening, but Reg was being particularly obnoxious and, for reasons known only to him, was picking on Tom Sullivan. Tom is a fair-sized man himself but a truly friendly person. Everybody liked him. Maybe that's why Reg was on him—envy."

"That's what most believe," added Joe.

Vance nodded at Joe in acknowledgment of his contribution.

"Nobody wants to be around Reg when he's drinking, but he's a decent person when sober," added Pete.

"That's right," said Jack, "but Reg was drinking more than usual, and the more he drank, the more obnoxious he got. A few people left the center early because of it. And as I said, he was giving Tom a hard time. We could see that Tom was starting to get pissed, but he held it in for quite a while."

"I think Tom's lack of reaction was mistaken as fear by Reg, so he kept at it," said Isha.

"That's about the time Reg roughly pushed Tom out of the way as he was heading to the bar for another beer—nearly knocked him over," said Joe.

"I think Tom would have taken Reg's abuse all night if Reg hadn't pushed him. No one likes to be shoved."

"No, they don't," said Vance.

"Tom spun him around and punched him in the face. Reg went down on one knee but made the mistake of getting back up. He charged Tom like a bull. Tom hit him square on the nose real hard. Reg went down again and was unconscious." Jack gathered himself for a second. "I've never seen anyone knocked unconscious before. Thought Reg might be badly hurt." Jack stopped talking again. "Tom walked away and sat at the bar. You could see he was real upset—now we all were. Tom had his back to Reg, probably thinking the fight was over; I sure did. But Reg woke up in a minute or so and took a couple of minutes to clear his head. Then he did something nobody expected. He walked over to the fireplace, picked up a chunk of firewood, calmly walked up behind Tom, and hit him with all his might on the back of his head. I think it killed Tom instantly."

"The son of a bitch," said Vance.

"Yes, sir," agreed Jack and Isha at the same time.

Vance said nothing for a moment while he sorted his thoughts. "Was Tom married?"

"Yes, sir. Just for a few months. Penny is her name, and she's a beautiful young woman."

"I think she's still crying," said Joe sadly. "She saw the whole thing."

"That cowardly bastard."

"We feel the same," said Pete.

All five men sat quietly for a moment. The four northern men all knew Vance's history. Everybody did. They knew the history of what he'd done to the evil men on Earth. There was little doubt Reg had a horrible future in store.

"Where is Reg now?"

"After running out of the tavern, he went to his house and picked up a hunting rifle and pack," said Pete.

"He took off," said Isha. "Headed into the south woods."

"Shit! That's going to complicate things."

"Reg's a good shot too," added Joe.

Vance took a communicator out of his pocket. *"Norman,"* he said. "Alex here."

"Get a fix on Reg Whetrume for me, please."

"Give me a second," said Alex.

The five men sat quietly until Jack broke the silence. "What's going to happen to him, sir?"

Vance took a deep breath and let it out slowly. "On old Earth, we would have executed him—and I haven't ruled that out." Vance paused for a moment. "Does Reg have any children?"

"Yes, sir, two boys and a girl."

"What kind of woman is his wife?"

"Cindy is a delightful person. She's been a wonderful mother. Their three kids are well behaved, polite, and good students," Jack answered. "Reg, as far as I know, has been a good father."

That information doesn't jive with the bastard's actions, thought Vance. "Can Cindy manage her life here without Reg?"

Jack said nothing for a few moments and then said sadly, "Not really, no, sir."

"We'll move her and her children to Home-Bay. There will be plenty for her to do there. She'll be comfortable."

"Yes, sir."

"Got him," said Alex over the communicator. "Looks like he's just about eleven kilometers south of your position. On your screen."

"Which of you is familiar with the south woods?"

"We all are, sir," answered Jack.

"I just want one man to accompany me while I go pick up Reg. Who would be the best for that?"

The three young men looked at one another for a moment before Jack answered. "I think Isha would be your best bet. He's our best woodsman."

"Isha it is."

"Thank you, sir." Isha was clearly delighted.

Joe and Pete had the dignity not to show too much envy.

Vance showed the communicator's screen to Isha. "Here's where we need to go."

"Yes, sir, I know right where that is. It's an old logging camp."

"Any place close we can land the runabout?"

Isha thought for a moment. "Not really, sir. That area is filled with new-growth timber mixed with a lot of old-growth stumps and slash."

Vance nodded. "Okay, let's take a hike."

The five men got up and filed out of Jack's office.

"Need to pick up a few things. Isha, follow me. You other men prepare some place we can put Reg for a day or two."

"Yes, sir."

Vance turned and started walking to the runabout as Isha followed. Once there, he opened the rear hatch and climbed in. He opened a cabinet, removed a backpack, and then opened a second cabinet and took out a small public-address system normally used to direct or give information to crowds. The whole system weighed only a kilo. He opened a third cabinet and removed a small-caliber carbine. He handed the carbine and PA system to Isha, stepped out of the runabout, closed the hatch, and slipped on the backpack.

The two headed south on a well-traveled gravel road. After a half kilometer, the road turned west, but an older, overgrown dirt road continued south. Isha gestured toward the south road, and they took it.

Vance looked around at the thick growth of pines and firs. Had the circumstances been different, he would have been thoroughly enjoying himself. The many smells of the forest produced a wonderful bouquet. He remembered flying over the area in a large runabout while broadcasting the seeds that had created this magnificent forest. That had been more than five hundred years ago in planet time.

It was soon evident that Reg had taken that road. His boot prints were clear, and they continued to see flattened grass and broken foliage along the way.

After a few minutes of silence, Isha spoke. "Sir, is it all right if I ask you some questions?"

"Sure, what's on your mind?"

"I'm curious about old Earth. I've read a lot of the history, but frankly, I find it difficult to believe some of what I read."

Gabrielites were naturally curious about the planet they came from. History was one of the subjects nearly everyone found interesting.

"Such as what?"

"Violence. Everybody understands that the human population on Earth was extremely violent. It is documented in just about every history book. Was it as violent as history describes it?"

Vance continued walking but did not answer the question right away. "Before the WGC took over the Earth's governments in the year 2010 Earth time, evil had a strong grip on the world. Throughout the ages, man's inhumanity to man has been well documented. Violence seemed to become more prevalent as the centuries passed, but I'm not sure that was the case. It's true that as the population grew, more and more people were maimed or killed by other people, but I'm not sure the actual percentage changed. The communication and the reporting of horrible events became more sophisticated, more widespread, and faster. What you've read probably gives the impression that the majority of humans were violent. That is not true." Vance stopped speaking for a moment as they hiked side by side up the road. "I would guess that less than ten percent were bad people, while the vast majority were decent people who were victims or just stood by and did nothing while the evil people took advantage of and terrorized others in a multitude of ways."

"Were there a lot of murders?"

"A lot, yes. I don't know the numbers, but I would say an average day on Earth would produce a couple thousand murders, maybe many times that on any given day."

"What?" Isha stopped dead in his tracks with a look of disbelief on his face.

Vance stopped and turned toward him. "You have to keep in mind that there were more than seven billion people on the planet. Eighty percent were living in poverty and half of those in wretched poverty. They had to scrape and fight and sometimes kill to even feed themselves and their families."

"Eighty percent. How could that be?"

"It's very complicated. I suppose if you read the history of mankind from every angle, you would begin to get a clue. The short version of the cause—and, subsequently, the effect—was overpopulation. Millions of people crammed into tight spaces. The living conditions of hundreds of millions of people were so horrible that they almost defy description. These people had little or no shelter, little food, and no clean water or air. Diseases killed millions every year. Women living in such conditions would have eight or more children in the hope that one or two would survive."

Vance looked over at Isha and could see that he was deeply affected by what Vance was telling him. Vance continued. "These poor people knew this was their lot in life. It would not get better for them, and that was the worst of it; they had no hope. Human life in such places had little value. Such places became the breeding grounds and recruitment centers for evil men to build their armies. The people were taught to hate, and they were taught to kill. They had nothing to lose."

Isha paid close attention as they continued to walk.

"The biggest contributor to the evil in Earth's most recent history, before the WGC took over, was a single religion. The worst evil came from governments and countries that were controlled by that religion. Their zealots murdered millions in the name of their God."

"What?" Again, Isha stopped. "Millions?"

"It's hard to believe even for me. How could such evil be allowed to happen?" Vance nodded in the direction they were going and started walking.

Isha followed. "How?"

"They were allowed to continue because of inaction by the populous. The innocent, peace-loving people didn't stop them, and because of their lack of action, they became irrelevant. That was the underlying cause of just about every atrocity and war throughout Earth's history."

"Why didn't the leaders stop them?"

"In many cases, the heads of governments were the instigators. In other cases, the governments were too weak or frightened to stop the evil people in their countries."

"I don't understand that."

Vance smiled a little. "I know you don't. You were born and raised in what just about everybody on Earth would have considered a paradise."

That caused Isha to smile. "I think it is too."

That pleased Vance. "Good."

The two walked on for a few seconds before Vance continued. "All governments were corrupt in one way or another, in a great variety of ways. There were no exceptions that I'm aware of. Some were pure evil, and I don't say that lightly, while others were self-serving to the detriment of the governed and every level in between."

Isha remained silent in thought for a full minute as they walked. "I've read there were two hundred separate countries on Earth."

"That's about right. Some formed; others merged over the centuries."

"Do you think Gabriel will eventually split into separate countries?"

"Absolutely not. Not while I'm alive."

Isha nodded enthusiastically.

Vance smiled. "Here on Gabriel, we are one people with one language and one common culture, and we have constant communication. We are, in effect, just one big, spread-out town."

Isha nodded in understanding. "We are. That's true."

Isha remained quiet and thoughtful. Vance said nothing as they continued their hike. He waited for the next question. He liked this young man. He liked that he wanted to know about things that, understandably, most people on Gabriel had little interest in or went out of their way to avoid.

Isha was ready with another question. "How many people do you and the other councillors want to have on Gabriel?"

"We have set a tentative worldwide limit of three hundred million and city limits of one hundred thousand, but that may change as time goes on."

"Really?" That surprised Isha. "That's a lot of people."

"It is compared to what we have now, but I assure you that it will never seem like too many. This is a big planet. We have four temperate continents, hundreds of large islands, and thousands of smaller ones. That many people scattered among the towns and cities will not seem crowded. We calculate that a populous that size will be able to provide everything we need as a civilization."

Isha's brow furrowed. "How are you going to control the population?"

"Hopefully it won't come to that. We have one culture, and it is and will remain made up of highly educated, intelligent people. Everyone will know the goals for a couple of centuries before the population reaches three hundred million. Eventually, families will probably have no more than two children." Vance paused for a moment. "But that's a long time from now."

Isha nodded. "It sure is."

"Here, we have the opposite challenge. We have too few people." Vance smiled. "In the beginning, we had only nineteen humans on this planet. That number was growing at a nice pace when the *Marian* arrived and brought five hundred more to enhance the gene pool. Now we are at about thirty-four thousand—way too few to become a true civilization."

"How many make up a civilization?"

Vance returned the smile. "I don't know. I suppose that is subjective, but for me, I think one million is enough." Vance paused. "I can see the day when many will rise up and demand that the population be allowed to exceed our limit of three hundred million."

"You think so?"

"Take my word for it."

"But—"

"I suggest we change the subject for now. We are centuries away from such a scenario."

Isha nodded. "Yes, sir."

They walked for another fifty meters before Isha had another question. "Have you ever killed an innocent human?"

This question took Vance by surprise, but he hesitated for only a moment before answering. "Yes." After a brief pause to gather his thoughts, he continued. "When you're a soldier at war, you are required to kill the soldiers of the opposing army. That's your job. It was kill or be killed. I strongly believed my country's form of government was worth fighting for and, if necessary, dying for. The United States had the greatest freedoms the world had ever known, and because of those freedoms, it had the highest living standard in the world. The poor in the US lived nearly as well as the wealthy in many nations. Unfortunately, the US began fighting wars for the wrong reasons—not to continue the country's way of life but sometimes for hidden political reasons. The United States began changing over the decades. Government became too big, too powerful, too clumsy, and too corrupt. It began taking away the freedoms that had made the country great. As freedoms were taken away, the country started to collapse while the government became even more powerful and more corrupt."

Vance looked at Isha. "The men I killed were, for the most part, innocent. They were ordered by their superiors to fight, as was I. But after the WGC takeover, we stopped that. There were no more wars."

Neither said anything for a few moments, and then Isha posed his next question.

"How did you feel when you killed someone?"

Vance had hoped this question wouldn't come up. "The first time was a terrible feeling. Guilt, regret, and empathy hit my mind hard and fast. It was nearly debilitating to me, as it probably was for most." Vance paused for a moment. "But the second time wasn't as bad, and so forth. I became hardened because I couldn't afford to feel the horror, sadness, and self-loathing. I blocked those experiences from my mind as best as I could. Some blocked the horror better than others. I was one of the lucky ones. I was able to block those memories and feelings."

The two had been walking in silence for a couple of minutes, when Isha stopped and held up a hand. "Camp's just over this hill, sir," he whispered. "Just a couple hundred meters."

Vance nodded as he stopped walking. He turned and took the carbine and PA system from Isha. "You wait around here. Find a place where Reg won't see you, in case he gets by me and heads this way."

Vance could see the look of disappointment on Isha's face but said nothing.

"You don't want me to grab him if I can?"

"I do not. Can't afford to lose a fine man like you. Already lost one."

That statement placated Isha some, and he smiled. "Yes, sir."

"I'll whistle when it's safe for you to come over the hill."

Without another word, Vance started walking up the road alone.

Once on top of the hill, he could clearly see all five small buildings. They were in better shape than he'd expected. He took cover behind a large pine stump and set the carbine on top of it. He slipped off the backpack, opened it, and took out a sophisticated pair of binoculars. He made a couple of adjustments and raised them up to his eyes.

The binoculars had a number of features, and infrared imaging was one of them. He scanned the buildings one by one, starting with the closest. In the third building, the largest, he spotted Reg. Other than being in shades of red, the image had great detail. From where Reg was located, Vance could tell he wasn't on the lookout for visitors. He was lying down in the middle of the building.

How did his genes get to this planet? Stupid bastard thinks we can't find him.

Vance scanned the surrounding area for the most advantageous spot from which to proceed. Once he'd decided, he put the binoculars' strap around his neck, slipped on the backpack, picked up the carbine and PA, and headed to his left.

In about fifty meters, he came to the spot he had chosen. It was about thirty meters in front of the cabin. A pair of pine stumps were located close together and created a V shape. He set the carbine on one of the stumps, put the PA next to it, slid off the backpack, and set it on the ground. He retrieved the carbine, tested it for aim and fit to his shoulder, and then put it back down. He picked up the PA, switched it on, adjusted the sound level, and put the mic to his mouth while watching Reg through the binoculars.

"Reg Whetrume, this is Vance Youngblood." He could see Reg quickly sit up. He didn't move for a few seconds before he jumped up, grabbed something, and headed toward the back of the building.

"If you try to run, I will put a hole in your leg."

That stopped Reg in his tracks. He turned toward the front of the building and stood still.

Vance assumed Reg was not only panicked but also confused. He smiled. *What are you going to do, asshole?* he thought.

Reg stood there for a full minute, not moving a millimeter.

"Put the rifle down, Reg, and walk out the front door."

Reg remained stationary for another thirty seconds and then turned toward the back of the building and moved a couple of meters before stopping again.

"If you touch that back door, you'll be one-legged."

Within two seconds, Vance could see Reg throw something, and he assumed it was the rifle. Reg started walking to the front of the building. He stopped on the far side of the door. "How do I know you won't shoot me when I come out?" he yelled.

"You don't, but I guarantee I'll shoot you if you don't."

Reg stood motionless for a few seconds before accepting the inevitable. "Okay, I'm coming out. Please don't shoot me."

Reg opened the door but did not walk out for a few seconds. Vance assumed he was building up his courage.

"I'm so sorry!" he cried out as he walked out to the front of the building. "I was drunk; I didn't know what I was doing. He was my friend. I didn't want to kill him."

Vance said nothing as he stood up from behind his cover and walked toward Reg, holding the carbine casually in his right hand at his side and the backpack in the other. He set the backpack down, put two fingers in his mouth, and whistled loudly. Then he turned his attention to Reg. "You are going to suffer for what you did."

"But—"

"Shut up," Vance said, cutting him off.

Twenty seconds later, Isha came running over the hill, and he didn't stop until he was standing alongside Vance. He was breathing rapidly.

"Isha," said Reg pleadingly.

"Don't you talk to me, you rotten turd pile."

Vance smiled inwardly. "Isha, I've got some tape in the backpack. Get it out, and wrap it around Reg's wrists in the back and around his mouth. I don't want to hear anything he has to say either."

When Isha had finished binding Reg's wrists and roughly wrapped the tape around his mouth, Vance motioned toward the path leading back to town.

As the three entered the community a couple of hours later, they were joined by Jack, Pete, and Joe.

"Got a storage shed all set up for Reg," said Jack.

"Lead on," responded Vance.

A silent three-minute walk got the six to the shed.

"Cut the tape off this man," Vance said to Joe.

"Yes, sir."

Joe ripped the tape off Reg's mouth first, and immediately, Reg started pleading with his ex-friends. "I'm sorry—really sorry. Please don't let this man kill me."

"Shut up!" screamed Joe.

"But—"

Joe slapped Reg hard. "Shut up, you shit. You killed my best friend."

The slap split Reg's lip.

Vance assumed that was probably the first time Joe had hit someone in anger. It saddened Vance that this horrible situation had caused violence to replace the natural gentleness of the man.

Joe spun him around, cut the tape off his wrists, and then shoved Reg into the shed. Jack stepped over and shut the door. There were no locks, but Jack had installed sturdy steel hangers on either side of the door to hold a heavy board. He slipped the board into place.

Vance nodded in approval and then addressed Jack. "Take me to Tom's wife. I need to talk to her for a bit. And I'll want to meet with Reg's family. They'll be in bad shape."

"This way, sir," said Jack, and the five headed south toward a neat row of tidy log homes.

"That one is Reg's home." Joe pointed at the home on the far right. "And this one is Tom's." He pointed at the home just in front of them.

Vance nodded. "Okay, you three can get back to your families. I thank you for your help."

"Yes, sir," they responded in unison.

"Isha?"

"Yes, sir?"

"I enjoyed talking to you. You're a fine young man. You would make a fine history teacher. You have the mind for it."

"Oh, thank you, sir. I can't tell you how much this day has meant to me."

Vance smiled, nodded, and walked to Tom's home.

After spending two hours consoling Tom's wife and meeting with Reg's family, Vance was heartbroken. He hadn't felt this sense of grief, empathy, and rage since the loss of twenty-three Gabrielites in the battle with the Malic a half a century ago. Both families were devastated. Reg's wife was in shock, and his children couldn't stop crying. It was all Vance could do to remain calm as he tried to comfort them. This was not his area of expertise.

"I suggest you and your children accompany me back to Home-Bay," said Vance. "We'll find you a nice situation to be in and raise your children."

"Yes, please. I can't stay here. I couldn't look my friends in the eye anymore." Cindy broke down and bawled.

An hour later, per their prior arrangement, Reg's wife and children met Vance at the runabout. Their friends and neighbors had helped them pack all of their belongings. The bystanders shed tears as the family's possessions were loaded into the cargo bay and the four Whetrumes boarded the craft.

Vance shook hands with Jack. "I'll be back in a couple of days to pick up Reg."

"He'll be ready, sir."

Vance settled the Whetrume family into two large staterooms on the *Norman*, staterooms the original nineteen colonists had used while their homes were being built around Home-Bay. Once that was done, he went directly to the bridge. Troy was there, talking to Alex and Dale.

"I'm back," Vance said as he walked to the captain's chair.

"I don't envy the trip you took," said Alex.

"Ditto," said Dale.

"Unfortunately, this will become a part of our history. It was bound to happen sooner or later. It's just that it was so stupid. No reason at all. It broke a lot of hearts."

"Including yours and ours," said Alex.

"Yes, it did," said Troy. "I made an announcement about twenty minutes ago on the news program, telling what happened up north."

Vance nodded. "Thanks."

"On a bit of a plus side, we have Reg's wife and kids set up with a fine family in Seaside."

"Oh, that's good. Again, thank you."

The small community of Seaside was located on the western side of the Ring's massive inland freshwater sea. It was about 470 kilometers over the mountain range east of Home-Bay. The area had become known for its freshwater fish. The community supplied most of the trout, bass, and salmon for Home-Bay and other areas on the west coast of the Ring.

"Being uprooted and moved to a different environment will be tough on the kids for a while," said Alex.

"It will be, but they'll adapt," said Troy. "It's a fine place to live."

"How about Tom Sullivan's wife?" asked Dale.

"She's chosen to stay up north. She has lifelong friends and some family there. She's a capable young lady," said Vance. "She'll be fine in time."

"I'm sure she will," said Alex.

"We're not going to execute him," said Vance out of the blue.

"Really?" said Alex. It was his turn to be surprised.

"No, sir. His children and parents asked me not to, and I said I wouldn't. I won't go back on my word. And above that, I'm sure Reg didn't mean to kill Tom. But he did cause his death and will suffer for it. And frankly, I'm having trouble emotionally at the thought of killing a human being. If he were a threat to others, it would be different, but with what I have in mind, he will never again be a threat."

"You have softened, my friend," said Alex sincerely.

Vance nodded. "I have."

"What are you thinking?" asked Troy.

"Maroon him on the Malic island."

"Oh?"

"That's a steam bath down there," said Dale.

"Yes, it is." Vance had a trace of a smile. "He'll probably think he's in hell for a while."

The next day, the small runabout flew out of the *Norman's* flight deck and headed north.

After landing in the northern community, Vance was again greeted by the same four men. After greetings, the five of them walked to the storage shed.

"Reg giving you any trouble?" Vance asked.

Jack smiled. "Tried to get away when we opened the door to feed him. That didn't work out too well for him. Joe here smacked him with an ax handle."

Vance smiled. "Good for you, Joe."

"My pleasure, sir."

When they arrived at the shed, Pete lifted the hefty board off its supports and opened the door.

"Is there a place in camp where we can put him so everyone can take a last look at this murderer?"

"There's a big oak tree dead center, sir."

"Good. Get some suitable chains, and we'll put him on display and let the camp's people say what they will to him before I take him away."

"Yes, sir."

Vance addressed Reg. "You, follow me."

"No, I will not. I have a wife and children here. I'm not leaving."

Vance smiled a little. "First off, your wife and children are no longer here. They've been moved to a nice place. So are you going to come peacefully, or do you want me to come in there and aid you in your exit?"

Reg didn't move, nor did he look at Vance.

"You four might want to stand back a pace or two," said Vance as he walked into the shed.

As he entered the shed, Reg quickly stood up and took a defensive stance. He was a good deal taller than Vance and maybe thought he could take him. When Vance was in striking range, Reg swung his right fist at Vance's head. Vance ducked; grabbed Reg by the crotch and shirt front; and, in one motion, flung the startled and now screaming Reg out the shed door, where he landed face and chest first eight meters beyond. It looked as if he'd been shot out of a cannon.

"Holy shit!" said Joe.

"Oh my God," added Isha.

Pete said nothing. He just stood stunned. Vance was as quick and powerful as they had always heard, but seeing him in action put new meaning to *quick and powerful*.

Reg was in a heap in the dirt, groaning in pain while trying to regain his breath. He was clearly done playing tough guy.

After pausing for a couple of minutes to allow Reg to regain his breath, Vance walked up to him and booted him in the ass. "Follow me."

Reg did not hesitate. Considering the pain, he got up as quickly as he could, and he had to walk quickly to catch up to Vance. The other men followed, smiling.

Nearly the entire community was milling about in the camp center when the six men arrived. The citizens quickly fell in behind the six as they walked down the center of the street. When they reached the large tree, Pete and Joe, without hesitation, wrapped a small-diameter chain around Reg's wrists and ankles and then around the tree, bolting it securely on the far side. Reg remained silent, his eyes cast down.

The crowd was quiet. Just a few mutterings could be heard.

"Stay here, and keep an eye out," Vance told the young men. "Grieving people can be unpredictable."

"Yes, sir."

"Jack, why don't we go visit with Reg's parents and Tom's wife again?"

"Yes, sir. That's a good idea. They are wonderful people. And they're sure hurting."

An hour later, when the two returned to the center of the small community, Vance was surprised to see that only the three men he'd left guarding Reg were still there.

"Just a few called him some ugly names," said Pete. "Most were crying and said nothing."

"They just turned their backs and left him after a few minutes," added Joe.

That's good, thought Vance. *They shunned him. Interesting.*

The runabout landed in a small open space bordering a small creek that flowed down from the high hills. The creek would supply Reg with fresh water and fish.

It was hot and appallingly humid when Vance and Reg exited the runabout. A steam bath would have had trouble competing with the weather on that part of the planet, and Reg had been born and raised in nearly opposite conditions. As an offset, the heat and humidity made for a lush island. The Malic had not wasted the many seeds and cuttings provided to them, and they'd done a surprisingly good job of planting and nurturing them in the few years they had inhabited the island. There was a profusion of tropical fruit trees, such as banana, papaya, avocado, and mango, and all manner of edible plants. There were a great variety of birds, including those of the peacock family, which provided a tasty protein, and there were monkeys and small pigs similar to javelinas, which further provided meat. If Reg was at all resourceful, he wouldn't go hungry.

Vance walked back to the cargo bay, removed a large crate, and set it on the ground.

"In here is everything we think you'll need to survive. Don't waste it."

Reg was already bathed in sweat as he looked around. "You're just going to leave me here?"

"Yes." Without another word, Vance turned around, entered the runabout, and left.

CHAPTER 3

THIS 'N' THAT
MO-ONE 12, 101

Vance's face displayed a slight smile as he rode up the elevator to the bridge deck of the *Norman*.

"Good morning, gentlemen," Vance said as he stepped off the elevator.

Troy, the last chairman of the WGC and the captain of the *Marian*, was sitting in the captain's chair. He quickly stood up. "Captain on the bridge," he said, displaying his great respect for Vance.

The life-size holograms of Alex and Dale were displayed four meters in front of the captain's chair.

"Nice to see you, Vance," said Dale.

"Welcome back, my friend," said Alex.

"Vance, this is your chair. Please." Troy gestured toward the chair.

"Thanks, Troy." Vance walked over and sat.

"All's well on the home front?" asked Dale with a big smile.

Vance returned the smile. "If you're talking about Lara, she's perfect. It's as if all of my Lara's memories were transferred to her. She seems to know everything about us. Occasionally, she'll ask for details on some past experiences—but not often. It's amazing and uncanny. It's wonderful."

"You know her," said Alex. "She was a reporter on Earth. It's her nature to investigate, and investigate she did. When we told her she was to be your woman, she spent the past two years studying everything about you and the previous Laras."

Vance returned the smile. "I'm sure she did."

"Nice to have you back in that chair," said Dale.

"Don't get too used to it. I don't plan on spending much time here."

"You've spent all you need to," said Alex.

"I'm thankful I'm seldom needed here anymore. Hopefully no longer required."

Alex said nothing for a moment. "You hadn't been needed here for a long time until Tom's murder."

Vance shrugged. "Troy could have handled it."

"Not like you did, sir," said Troy.

"You've been the single most required person in the history of Gabriel," said Alex.

"I might add something that is well known and universally agreed upon," said Troy. "Without you three and Jason Gould, there would not be any humans in the universe. If any one of the four of you were missing from the equation, all would have been lost."

"That's true," said Dale.

"Agreed," said Alex. "We all had a part to play."

"At any rate," Vance said with a smile, "if I get bored, I'll go out and stir the pot some."

"You do that," said Troy.

Alex changed the subject. "I assume you're ready for a briefing as to the state of the planet?"

"I am."

Dale began by providing statistics on Gabriel's population growth, food production, infrastructure, and a dozen other comparatively mundane subjects. He finished by reviewing the planet's ongoing labor-intensive projects.

"It still amazes me that these bright people are so willing to work hard at what those on Earth would have considered menial to skilled labor. They are, by all accounts, quite happy," remarked Vance.

"Physical work is only work if you don't like doing it. Most hobbies require physical labor of one sort or another," said Alex.

Troy smiled. "People like working with their hands; it's relaxing to the mind and good for the body."

"There is some work that still requires assignment," said Troy.

Vance nodded. "We knew some jobs would be a pain in the ass, but the products are needed. There's no choice here."

"Everybody understands that," said Troy.

"And most of these labors are getting easier," said Dale. "Automation is replacing much of the hardest and dirtiest work."

Alex looked at Vance and smiled. "I might point out, my old friend, that you spent five decades on this planet, working with your hands to develop Gabriel. And you worked just about every minute of every day without help. That might be considered mind-numbing work."

Vance smiled. "It wasn't for me. It was exciting. I was creating something of great value. It gave me a wonderful sense of accomplishment." Vance paused for a moment. "And I would point out that I don't tire."

"Noted," said Dale.

Vance was reflective for a moment. "What else have we got?"

There was silence for a moment before Alex spoke.

"Well, there's something new in Taupo Bay."

"Taupo Bay—I've always liked that place." Vance nodded in approval. "Reminds me of Home-Bay in the early years."

"I suspect that most of the future villages and towns will resemble Home-Bay in many ways. It's a place that all others will be compared to, clearly a role model," said Troy.

"All the towns and settlements so far have been near oceans, bays, and rivers. Always on the water," said Alex. "My home in California was on Newport Harbor."

"I remember that home—stunning place. That's where you lived when we first met," said Vance. "That's where I met Teddy."

The conversation stopped for a moment. It was likely they all were reflecting upon their experiences on old Earth.

Troy broke the silence. "Taupo Bay is located in one of the prettiest locations on the North Dumbbell. Great natural harbor."

"And they've become nearly self-sufficient over the years due to excellent management," added Dale.

"So what's happening in Taupo Bay?" asked Vance.

"The mayor, Ian Henderson, seems to be starting a movement of sorts."

"A movement?"

"It's not like an ancient religion but kind of feels like it could head that way. For the past couple of years, Henderson has been tapping into the *Norman*'s and the *Marian*'s computers to study all the theories written about intelligent design. And a few months ago, he began holding local seminars on ID. He's gathering quite a following, and he's just requested permission to hold one here in Home-Bay."

Vance shrugged a little.

"We three have talked about this possibility for centuries," said Alex, "so I don't have a problem with his lectures."

Vance said nothing for a second. "I don't have a problem either, but I am curious about his possible motivations or end game."

"You're a cautious man," said Dale.

"With age grows wisdom, they say." Vance looked at Alex. Vance was the only one who knew the story of Alex's life in the decades before the forming of the WGC. It was the single most incredible story he'd ever heard, and had he heard it from anyone other than Alex, he would have called bullshit. However, because Alex had told it, he knew it had to be true. He'd never repeated it to anyone, not even Lara, but the story all but pointed to the existence of a superior intelligence—not necessarily God but a far-advanced intelligence of some kind.

"I know we three are open to the idea of some sort of intelligence far greater than ours," said Alex as he turned toward Troy. "Any thoughts on the subject?"

Troy seemed surprised by the admission. "I'm a bit of an agnostic, but there are times when I look around and see the beauty and incredible complexity of the universe and the beauty of nature, and I wonder how all of this could be by chance, by natural selection, evolution, or mutation."

"It's truly a mystery," said Dale.

"The true atheists can give excellent arguments and facts in favor of evolution, mutation, and natural selection, but they just can't explain the beginning," said Alex.

"That's it. How did it all start, and what holds it all together?" added Dale. "We know everything—save black holes, neutron stars, and the like—is made up of nearly empty space. Somehow, this empty space is given form and texture, seemingly held together by some sort of inner gravity." Dale paused for a couple of seconds. "The thing is that many forms of this infinitesimal matter are given intelligence to one degree or another. It just boggles my mind. It seems we are made of little more than a thought."

Wow! thought Vance, and he quickly glanced at Alex and Troy. He could see they were as impressed with what Dale had said as he was. Dale, he knew, was considered the most brilliant human in history. Yet his incomparable mind could not begin to comprehend how these seemingly impossible physics worked.

"If all of this boggles your mind," said Vance with a smile, "I may never think about it again; that would be a complete waste of time."

Alex and Troy nodded in agreement.

"Interesting to note that we have never questioned or discussed religion in any form with either the Vout or the Yassi. I wonder what their feelings are on the subject," said Alex.

Vance smiled to himself. *Those two wonderful groups of beings have made our life on this planet so much easier.* "Next time they're here, I'm going to bring it up," he said.

Alex and Dale nodded in agreement.

"So we'll let Henderson hold his lecture?" asked Troy.

"Why don't we have him visit us and give his pitch?" said Vance. "If it makes sense, we can schedule time on the viewer, maybe after the evening news, and let everybody hear what he has to say."

"The average IQ of Gabrielites is approaching one hundred forty—forty percent higher than that of old Earth. A higher IQ begets a greater curiosity. I'm sure our citizens will be quite interested in what Henderson has to say."

Vance smiled. "Okay, I'll invite him to come talk to us."

The other three nodded in agreement.

"What else is going on?"

"Gold," said Troy.

"Gold?" Vance said.

"Yes, sir. Our allotment of a kilo per person per year cannot be maintained indefinitely due to the population growth. Presently, there are fewer than thirty-five thousand people on the planet, but in another century, there will be hundreds of thousands." Troy shrugged. "There won't be enough gold."

Dale came into the conversation. "Adding to that, as the years pass, mining enough gold has become more challenging for two reasons. First, we have only one mining laser."

"We can order another one from the Vout. I'm sure they will be willing to sell us a new one," said Alex.

"If we're in agreement on this, I'll contact the Vout and have them start construction on a new laser," said Troy.

Everyone agreed.

As Troy explained the challenges ahead concerning gold, Vance thought with pride that from the beginning, starting with the Vout Lakes, they'd designed the mining in such a way that they were able to create something of value to man or beast at the extraction site after the gold was exhausted—lakes and ponds in most cases and canals, streams, and roads in others, plus shelter caves in each community. *Had there been shelter caves in all our settlements, we wouldn't have lost so many of our own in the battle with the Malic,* Vance thought with sadness.

"Those facts aside," said Dale, "we have to begin basing the distribution of gold on annual production. The production divided by the population at the end of each year will determine how much per capita can be distributed. It's as simple as that."

"Right now, the barter system is still a large factor in providing goods and services. Gold is used for major expenses and, of course, is the only currency used to pay for products brought by the Vout and Yassi," said Alex. "The time will come when we will need to bring the WEC into play."

"The WEC." Vance smiled. "I haven't heard of that name in hundreds of years—world economic currency. It never occurred to me that we might someday have to print money."

"No paper money. It's too easily manipulated, and it has a short life span," said Dale.

"We came to the same conclusion decades ago on Earth," said Troy. "We have four presses aboard the *Marian* to strike coins. We also have the machinery and smelters to process whichever metal we choose into the proper form for striking. And we have hundreds of brand-new stamp dies for six denominations of WEC coins and five for bars."

"Eleven different denominations?"

"Yes, sir. One-cent, five-cent, ten-cent, twenty-five-cent,

fifty-cent, and whole WEC coins and bars of five, ten, twenty, fifty, and a hundred WECs," said Troy.

Alex nodded in appreciation. "You colonists from the *Marian* thought of things that didn't occur to those of the *Norman*."

Troy smiled. "Just following your lead. You of the *Norman* didn't miss much. But some bright young woman noticed that coin presses were not on the *Norman*'s manifest."

"Excellent," said Alex.

Vance thought for a few seconds. "I'm assuming you three and a few others have been giving this quite a bit of thought."

"We have," said Alex.

"Alex, if you think this is the way to go, that's what we'll do." Vance gave a big smile. "I have no business even being in this conversation. Economics has never been my long suit."

Alex nodded. "We'll keep you informed."

Vance nodded and paused for a moment. "What else do we have?"

"A couple of days ago, we received a communication from a Yassi ship that I'd bet a WEC or two you will find interesting," said Dale.

"Let's hear it."

"They dropped by the Byuse home planet, Rime, to see what the Malic are up to."

He had Vance's full attention. "Is that so?"

Vance hated the ugly little Malic. They'd caused the deaths of twenty-three Gabrielites, all of whom had been close friends and loved ones. Among the dead was the first human born on Gabriel, their beloved Adam. At the time, nobody had known that prior to attacking Gabriel, they had attacked the starship *Marian*, leaving it crippled and adrift in space. Had it not been for the Yassi coming across the *Marian*, that ship, its advanced technology, and more than five hundred colonists from Earth, including Troy and Gary, would never have been heard from again.

"Yes, and apparently, our dear friends the Yassi were quite surprised by what they found."

"Such as?" asked Vance.

"It seems the Malic have changed their ways to a great extent. The Yassi reported no detectable signs of any weapons manufacturing or any indication of aggressive behavior at all."

"Are you sure they were on the right planet? The planet whose intelligent populous, the Byuse, were all but completely destroyed by those rat bastards? They effectively killed the hand that fed them," Vance said, half joking.

Dale smiled. "I suspect that knowing the Yassi, they were."

"And the Yassi's probes clearly showed that the Malic have dramatically changed in appearance. They looked clean, their garments were colorful, and they no longer sport those big canine teeth."

"Really?" said Vance, surprised. "What was it—about forty-seven years ago that the Yassi returned the three rat bastards and their newborn to Byuse?"

"Forty-six years, yes," said Dale. "At least three generations for them, probably four."

"Their culture must have made a dramatic shift to cause them to pull or cut their canines. Those, as I recall, were a great source of pride."

"The Yassi think it is possible that returning the Malic clean and defanged set a trend and changed their culture," said Dale. "They also think the Malic may have considered our treatment of them extremely kind and may be trying to emulate us."

Vance was incredulous. "Kind? We destroyed their ships, probably killing close to a thousand. Only four survived that short war. We blew one of those four into hundreds of small pieces, cut off the fangs of the remaining three, and marooned them on a steamy island. If they think that's being kind, they ought to see how we treat people we like."

Everybody laughed.

"But we didn't beat or kill the remaining three," said Dale. "We showed them how to wash and provided a place for them to live that was to their liking. Their society probably considered that very kind indeed."

"That, combined with the fact that they don't have any more warships or means to travel and plunder other planets, may have added greatly to a massive cultural shift," added Alex.

"A bar of soap may have changed an entire culture—remarkable," said Troy.

There was a pause in the conversation.

"Other than those notable items, everything is running quite smoothly," said Dale.

"I think we should have you give a state-of-the-planet address in the near future. Mainly to inform our citizens of the gold situation," Alex said.

"Troy, since you're overseeing Gabriel, do you want to make the address?" asked Vance.

"No, not now that you're out of stasis. You are the leader of this planet. I simply fill in when you're out." Troy smiled.

Vance nodded. "I appreciate that. You set up a time, and we'll get it done."

MO-FIVE 8, 101

Ian Henderson walked onto the bridge of the *Marian* at the agreed-upon hour. Vance, Troy, and Gary stood to greet him. After they all shook hands, Troy suggested they move to the conference room located just off the bridge.

"We will have Alex and Dale join us via hologram," said Gary.

"Thank you," said Henderson. "I was hoping to talk to all of Gabriel's leaders."

The four men took their seats at the small board table, putting Ian Henderson at the head. Each had a recording pad and a glass of water.

Once settled in, Gary said, "All set."

"Alex, Dale," said Vance.

Instantly, both men appeared as holograms at the end of the board table.

"Nice to see you, Ian," said Alex.

"Ditto," said Dale.

"I'm delighted to be here. And I want to thank you all for allowing me to present my studies and beliefs to you."

"We have been talking about the possibility of a superior race for a long time," said Vance. "Hearing another point of view on the subject will be, at least, refreshing."

"Please proceed," said Alex.

Henderson nodded and paused for a moment. "To start, if you were asked by a blind man to describe a Vout, Yassi, and human, you might tell him that each stands upright and has two eyes, two ears, two arms, two legs, five toes on each foot, and four fingers and a thumb on each hand. The blind man, at this stage of description, would have to conclude that all the species were identical, would he not?"

Everyone nodded in agreement.

"Then you would go on to describe the differences. The Vout are a head taller than humans; the Yassi are a head shorter. Both the Vout and Yassi have no hair at all, whereas humans have hair in various places on their bodies. The Vout and Yassi vary little in overall appearance, whereas the humans vary a great deal in size, shape, and coloration."

None of the five listening to Henderson said anything.

"There are, of course, other differences. The Yassi's and Vout's planets are farther from their suns and therefore have less light. Consequently, both races have larger eyes and less skin pigmentation than do humans. It is noteworthy that there was a great deal less variation in appearance among the colonists who arrived aboard the *Marian* than among those who arrived on the *Norman*."

"That's for sure," said Vance.

"The humans aboard the *Marian* had had five hundred more years to evolve, meld together, and gain in physical size and IQ. We know that the average IQ on Earth just before its destruction was thirty points higher than it was when the *Norman* left the planet."

Dale smiled. "But not thirty points higher than those humans who came to Gabriel aboard the *Norman*."

"No, sir," Ian said quickly. "Actually slightly lower than those original colonists."

Vance smiled. "Thank you. I assume the improvement, if you will, of humans is an example of natural selection. The best, brightest, and most adaptable would naturally attract mates with the same attributes. Birds of a feather."

"Without question, yes, sir."

"Go on," said Alex.

"One might conclude," Henderson said, "based on these facts alone, that the Vout's and Yassi's civilizations are a great deal older than that of the humans and that we humans will, at some time in the future, lose our individual distinctions."

"I would find that boring," said Vance. "But it is something we might keep in mind and possibly try to circumvent in the future."

"We might want to consider selective breeding or genetic engineering to maintain individualities in the future," said Gary.

"It's worth looking into," said Dale.

"I've noticed that the offspring of the *Marian*'s colonists, when mated with those of the *Norman*, certainly have more physical variations," said Vance.

Alex smiled. "Someday, desirable mates may be chosen because of their distinctness."

"Wouldn't be surprised," said Dale.

Henderson went on describing the similarities and differences between the Vout's and Yassi's home planets. "It is interesting to note that the native trees, bushes, and plants on Vout grow considerably taller than similar plants on Gabriel due to their planet's weaker gravity. The same Vout plants and trees, when transplanted to Gabriel, become stunted or, in some cases, cannot survive at all. It seems they are too frail. The reverse is true on Mahyu, the Yassi home planet. There, they have shorter, stockier plants and trees due to their stronger gravity. Mahyu plants and trees grow taller on Gabriel and seem to thrive."

All of this is common knowledge, thought Vance. *We have many alien plants and trees on Gabriel.* Vance smiled to himself. *And everybody is aware of that.*

"Evolution is the answer," Henderson said. "Adaptation and mutation on a universal scale."

He's advocating evolution? Vance was surprised at the apparent turn away from the subject of the presentation.

"The intelligent-design hypothesis has been argued for more than six hundred years. The argument against intelligent design always turns to evolution, adaption, and mutation. And there is undisputable evidence that evolution is a fact. I personally believe evolution, in all of its forms and branches, is wholly responsible for the vast variety of life in the universe. But just how does this evolution nearly mirror itself from planet to planet and solar system to solar system?"

Henderson paused and took a sip of water. "How is it that on planets light-years apart, plants and animals have evolved independently for hundreds of millions of years yet can be described as the same to a blind man, with just superficial adaptations to fit their environment?"

Henderson had everyone's attention. He let his last question linger for a few moments and then said, "Some ancient religions taught that a god created all things and that man himself was created in the image of his creator. According to some ancient religions, the entire world was created in seven days." He smiled. "No one that I'm aware of continues to believe anything like that."

Henderson stopped and quickly reviewed his notes before looking back at the five men. "It is inconceivable to me that nowhere in this vast universe exists a far more advanced race of beings. It is impossible for me to believe that a far superior race exist does not exist anywhere in the billions of galaxies, trillions of star systems, and quadrillions of planets. In fact, there could be hundreds or thousands of such races—living beings who, for the sake of this argument, may have been in existence millions, if not tens or hundreds of millions, of years longer than we have. I suggest that these beings became superior because of the very same evolution that affects everything in the universe."

Henderson paused again to let that thought settle in.

I'm impressed, thought Vance.

"What will be the gains in IQ, knowledge, and wisdom for the Vout, Yassi, and humans in a million years? What presently unimaginable feats will we be capable of?

"How would we, as an example, create life on millions of distant planets if we so desired? Would we visit each planet and personally seed and nurture all living things, as you did, sir, here on Gabriel? I think not." Henderson looked at Vance and nodded acknowledgment.

Vance returned the nod.

"Maybe a far advanced or superior race might simply set adrift in space a variety of molecules and cells carrying DNA capable of adapting, morphing, and mutating to suit its environment."

"Adrift in what?" asked Troy.

Henderson smiled. "Good question. The answer, in my opinion, is most likely comets and asteroids. It has been assumed for centuries that much, if not most, of the water on planets has come from these celestial bodies. I'm suggesting that with water may have come the cells of life. The comets would not only transport such cells but also provide them protection. The cells could be locked in ice that may have an internal temperature approaching absolute zero. They could drift for millions or billions of years through the universe, galaxies, and star systems."

"Are you suggesting that a superior being planted cells in a comet with the hope that one day it would become part of a planet and the foundation of all life on that planet?" asked Troy.

"I am suggesting that it is possible a superior being may have, in fact, seeded millions or tens of millions of comets in such a way. Such a feat might not be difficult for such beings. They might not care one iota whether or not just a miniscule percentage of the seeded comets actually took root in a hospitable environment. The law of probability would dictate that only an infinitesimal percentage of such comets would merge with an ideal planet. Over the eons, many would simply evaporate in their exposure to stars; others might collide with a stars; and most would still be adrift, looking for a home. It may be something akin to a message in a bottle tossed into a vast ocean in the hopes that someday it would wash ashore and be found." Henderson paused for a moment. "Time, I suggest, may mean nothing to such beings. Time is infinite."

Henderson paused again for a few seconds while he glanced at his notes. "Putting evolution aside for a moment, I ask the following question: Where did it all begin?"

Vance smiled. *Now we're getting to the nut cuttin'.*

Henderson smiled broadly. "And I don't have the slightest idea."
What?

"If, in fact, these superior beings seeded the universe, where did they get the seeds? Did they design the seeds, and if so, who or what designed their seeds? And so forth.

"I have been interested in the possibility of intelligent design for many years, and other than the hypothesis I've just presented, which to an extent can be considered intelligent design, I can't even come close to explaining the beginning. How did the universe begin? The big bang theory is just that—a theory. Was the entire mass of the universe at one time contained in an object the size of Gabriel or smaller? If so, where did that mass come from? Was it always there in one form or another?"

The discussion went on for another half an hour, with Henderson answering all of the questions asked by the five.

When he'd finished, Vance said, "Ian, that was clear, concise, and well put together. Makes one think."

"Thank you, sir."

"If you would like, we suggest you take time after the evening news to present your thoughts to the rest of the planet."

"I'd love to do that."

"You pick a time, and we'll be sure that all know to watch."

CHAPTER 4

COMET
MO-EIGHT 14, 101

Vance had just finished his annual inspection of the *Norman* and had just sat down in the captain's chair, when Dale's hologram appeared on the bridge.

"What's up?" asked Vance.

"Just received a communication from the Yassi."

"What are our little friends up to?" Vance asked with a smile.

"Well, they've spotted a comet heading our way."

Vance shot up from his chair. "On a collision course?" His mind instantly went to Earth's destruction by a massive asteroid in the Earth year 2478.

"No, but it may get as close as three million kilometers. They are taking a few more days to plot its trajectory, distance, and time but believe they are within a few percentage points of being correct. They have remarkable technology."

"They don't feel we're in any danger, do they?"

"Not at this point. They say the comet will enter our solar system in approximately twelve years and be visible to the naked eye in about thirteen. Because of its size, they also hypothesize that it could affect our gravity and weather."

"I like the weather the way it is."

"Everybody does," said Dale.

Two days later, as Vance and Lara were on their daily walk up the Vance River, Vance got a call from Dale.

"Hello, my friend. News?" said Vance.

"We just received an update on the comet from the Yassi."

That got Vance's attention, and he stopped walking. "Good news or bad?"

"Mostly good. Their original estimate of the comet's trajectory turned out to be within a five-thousand-kilometer margin of error, so it doesn't have any chance of hitting us."

"The bad news?"

"Well, it's the size of the thing."

"How big?"

"Half the mass of Gabriel. It's essentially a small, rocky ice planet, and it's traveling at just over forty-nine thousand kilometers per hour. It will continue to accelerate as it approaches the sun."

"That seems fast."

"That is fast. It's nearly ten times the average speed of known comets, asteroids, or meteors," said Dale.

"Could it be natural?" asked Vance.

"Oh yes," said Dale. "Some of the physics in space are much more astonishing than the speed of this comet. Just because we haven't seen or recorded such phenomena doesn't mean they aren't there."

"So what are your thoughts?"

"I'm concerned more about the comet's effect on our gravity than I am about weather patterns. This comet will affect the tides and possibly cause our tectonic plates to shift."

"That would cause earthquakes?"

"At the very least."

"Shit!"

"There's more. It could also affect our moons' orbits, causing one or all three of them to—" Dale quit talking for a moment before continuing. "You get the picture."

MO-NINE 4, 101
CROSS-COLONIZATION

Vance looked at the other five participants sitting at the large table and nodded to himself. He was meeting with aliens from two other planets, something that, during his life on Earth, had happened only in science-fiction movies. *I would have never believed it possible.* He smiled at the thought.

For the first time in more than five years, the Vout, Yassi, and humans met together aboard a Yassi ship, which was presently in geosynchronous orbit over Home-Bay.

Vance and Troy represented Gabriel. Captain Toul and First Mate Gib represented the Yassi, and the Vout's representatives were Captain Viin and his second-in-command, Oot.

The Yassi vessel was awe-inspiring, as were all the others the Gabrielites had seen. That particular ship's mass was nearly that of the *Marian*, making it enormous, and its beauty was indescribable. The Yassi had once said the beauty of their ships didn't necessarily aid their function, but neither did it hinder it. The beauty of everything in the Yassi's lives was of paramount importance to them.

The six in attendance were meeting in an exceptionally appointed dining area off of the bridge of the extraordinary ship. They had been meeting for two days to develop a plan to make certain the continuation of their individual species. The knowledge of Earth's destruction and the impending close encounter between Gabriel and a massive comet gave all three races cause for concern. They understood that a natural phenomenon could destroy any of their home planets, but they'd developed no significant plans as contingencies, besides a few admittedly feeble ideas regarding evacuating their planets.

"So we are in agreement?" asked Vance.

"We are," said Toul.

"Agreed," added Viin.

"Then we will start the process," Toul said.

The three races had just agreed to accept, as permanent autonomous residents, the other two races to their respective planets. The Vout and Yassi planets already had colonies of Byuse, and now each would add two more races. Each planet would have four races, so if any of the home planets were destroyed, they would be assured of their species' survival.

After traveling to and exploring each of the seventeen islands offered by Gabriel's leadership, the Vout and Yassi each picked an island that best suited their requirements. As it turned out, both were in the southern hemisphere's cooler zone, and they were fairly close together, just more than eight hundred kilometers apart.

Both islands were partially developed, with basic vegetation, birds, and animals, and the lakes and rivers were stocked with fish. To augment the existing development, the Vout and Yassi brought a great variety of their native plants, animals, birds, and fish to introduce into their new environments. They wanted to establish these living things before they left the initial meeting on Gabriel, so when their colonists arrived in approximately four years, a slightly altered ecosystem would be in place to accommodate their needs. Toul and Viin also asked permission to bring ten Byuse couples from each of their home planets to be part of their new colonies on Gabriel.

Vance did not hesitate to agree. He had only seen pictures and videos of the Byuse but was aware of their high intelligence and peaceful temperament.

"They will be a welcome addition," Vance said, smiling. "Do we have another language to learn?"

"No, they speak English fluently," said Toul.

"Will they desire a separate island?"

"No. They will be part of our communities."

"I have no problem with that. Ten couples in each colony won't make much of a dent in your diverse societies."

"No dents. The Byuse are like us." Viin smiled. "Quite dull in comparison to the humans and Yassi. Both of our races will benefit from exposure to the Yassi and human cultures. It may even vitalize our personalities." Viin paused a moment and then smiled brightly. "Maybe not."

The humans and Yassi were caught off guard for a moment. A Vout had attempted humor. The four laughed heartily.

"Good one," said Vance.

"A very good one," said Toul.

Viin continued to smile. "Thank you. Now I'm sure we will benefit from living among you."

"In four years, we will have our people ready for their voyages to your home planets, and we will have the infrastructure completed for the settlements on your islands," said Vance.

"Excellent," said Toul. "We'll be doing the same for the humans and Vout."

"We are pleased," added Viin. He paused for a moment while gathering information via his earpiece. "Your computers will be receiving our infrastructure requirements within minutes."

Vance nodded in acknowledgment.

Toul looked at his computer screen. "You now have ours."

Vance smiled. "It will take the humans a little longer to put together the last of the details."

Viin and Toul returned the smile.

"Certainly no hurry," said the personable Toul. "We will be spending a few weeks planting our essential vegetation and establishing some of our indigenous wildlife. And of course, we'll be selling our products to the Gabrielites while enjoying the company of our human and Vout friends." His countenance changed a little. He appeared to be a little uncomfortable.

Vance noticed the subtle change. "Is there something more you wish to discuss?"

Toul paused for a couple of seconds. "I hope what I am about to ask will not be taken badly."

"I can't imagine you asking anything that would offend."

Toul smiled. "We want our own Teddy."

The request took Vance and Viin by surprise.

"How's that?" asked Vance.

"Is it possible to include an embryo containing a clone of Teddy to accompany the human colonists so that one day a Teddy could be born on our home planet, Mahyu?"

Vance had not anticipated this question. "That is an interesting request," he responded. "My first thought is to ask Teddy what he thinks of the idea. My second is if we have enough embryos to assure us of always having a Teddy here on Gabriel."

"Legitimate questions," said Toul. "And I would be willing to wager there will be more thoughts coming. We will, of course, accept any decision you make."

CHAPTER 5

MALIC ISLAND
MO-EIGHT 10, 103

The small runabout settled quietly on a clear area in front of a small but nicely put-together log cabin. The cabin hadn't been there the last time Vance had landed in that spot. He noticed that the logs used to build it were about half the diameter of those used to build homes on the Ring Continent, but he knew pine and fir trees did not grow in this climate. Vance guessed it was made of teak or maybe mahogany logs, trees that he himself had seeded on many tropical islands centuries ago. The area around the cabin and all the way to the small creek was tidy and well kept.

Well, this is a surprise. The man has managed to make a silk purse out of a sow's ear. Vance unbuckled his seat belt, stood, and turned toward the passenger cabin. There sat an attractive woman in her early thirties with three children, two boys and a girl. The boys were eleven and twelve, and the girl was nine. All three were big for their ages, dressed nicely, and well groomed. The four of them had been living with an elderly couple in the town of Seaside for the past two years. Cindy, Reg's wife, an excellent tailor, had secured a job in a local apparel store, and she helped her host couple with household chores. It was a symbiotic relationship.

"Cindy, are you ready to see your husband?"

"Yes, sir, as ready as I'll ever be," she said with apparent anxiety.

Vance knew Cindy was apprehensive about the meeting, but her children had been begging her for more than a year. She'd finally agreed and contacted Vance.

Vance looked at the children. "Ready to see your father?"

"Yes, sir," the older boy said quickly. The other two nodded enthusiastically.

"Well then, let's get out there and see if we can find him."

Vance pushed a button, and a hatch lowered out from the side of the runabout and onto the ground. Vance led the way out, followed by the children and their mother.

Because it was a different season, the heat and humidity were somewhat less than they had been when Vance was there more than two years ago, but it was still considerably warmer than the four were used to.

They walked the short distance to the cabin, up two steps, and onto a small porch. Vance knocked. There was no answer. He knocked again, but still, they heard nothing.

He called, "Reg!"

There was no response.

"Reg!" This time, he yelled.

Vance pulled out his communicator. "Dale, can you tell me where Reg is at this moment?"

"One second. He's about half a kilometer to the south and heading your way fast."

"Thank you." Vance turned to the family. "I believe if we just walk down and sit on that bench by the creek, your father will be along shortly."

The more Vance looked around, the more impressed he was at what Reg had done there. He had created a little park of sorts. All vegetation in the area was trimmed and pruned. He had placed boulders across the creek to create a small dam, which backed up the creek for about sixty meters and created a pleasant sound as the water poured over and through the rocks.

Within a minute, the children, being children, asked Vance for permission to walk around and explore the area.

"That's up to your mother."

Vance could see Cindy was getting more nervous as the seconds passed, and she was now constantly wringing her hands and looking over her shoulder.

"Yes, you can, but keep us in sight. Don't wander off."

"Yes, ma'am," said the older boy.

The three took off together and headed upstream. The boys

picked up smooth stones as they walked and skipped them across the shallow pond behind the dam. The girl picked up a large mahogany leaf and set it afloat.

Vance looked at the woman. "You're doing a fine job raising your children, Cindy. You should be proud."

"I'm proud of my kids; they're wonderful. I'm—" Suddenly, Cindy shot to a standing position. Her eyes were wide.

Vance turned to see what had startled her; it was Reg. He appeared out of the heavy foliage, walking quickly toward his children. As he walked, he dropped what looked to be a small bunch of bananas on the ground. The children were occupied with their play and hadn't yet spotted their father.

"Sammy, Tim, Elsa," Reg said loudly as he approached the children.

The oldest boy turned quickly, smiled broadly, and ran toward his father with his siblings right on his heels.

Reg had a big smile on his face and tears running down his cheeks as he dropped to his knees and put his arms around Sammy and then expanded them to encompass the other two.

"Oh my God. Oh my God," he kept saying as he hugged his kids. "You've grown so much. Oh God."

Vance and Cindy stayed put while the touching reunion continued.

Vance hadn't seen this warm, loving side of Reg. It gave him pause, and he momentarily reflected on his decision to maroon Reg on Malic Island.

Reg was sporting a full beard, his hair was long and pulled back in a ponytail, and he was probably five kilos lighter but looked healthy and fit.

After a couple of minutes of hugging and kissing his children, Reg looked at Vance and Cindy. He waved, picked up little Elsa, put her on his shoulders, took the boys' hands in his, and walked rapidly toward his wife and Vance.

When he was within a few meters of the two, he let go of his boys' hands, lifted his daughter off his shoulders, and stood her on the ground. "Thank you, sir," he said sincerely. "Thank you."

Vance nodded once without saying anything.

Reg's eyes went to his wife. "Hi, lovie," he said softly. "I've missed you so much."

Tears streamed down Cindy's cheeks as she opened her arms and hugged her husband.

"I'm going to walk upstream a ways while you two catch up." Without another word, Vance walked past the family and headed up the creek at a substantial pace.

Vance kept himself entertained by taking a hike into the rain forest along a path that he figured must have been established long before Reg arrived. *The Malic blazed these paths,* he thought. The humid heat didn't bother Vance. He could feel it, but it didn't make him uncomfortable. He enjoyed hiking and seeing the vegetation he had planted long ago. He stopped many times to look high into the canopy, marveling at the height of the teak and mahogany trees. They were thin, straight, and tall, maybe fifty meters or taller. In the more open areas, the fruit trees grew in abundance.

Vance soon came across an area where he assumed Reg had logged the teak for his cabin. There were a dozen stumps sitting over about an acre. *How in the hell did he get the logs back to his place?* Vance knew hardwoods were a great deal heavier than pine or fir, and he knew Reg had no power equipment. *Gotta ask him.*

Two hours later, Vance emerged from the same path Reg had used a couple of hours earlier, and he could see the family was enjoying their time together. Reg had pulled up a couple of short teak stumps for the boys to sit on, while he, Cindy, and Elsa sat on the bench by the creek. They were enjoying some fruit while talking and laughing.

When they spotted Vance, all activity stopped.

They're wondering what happens next, Vance thought as he approached the four.

"Looks like you're having a good time."

"Yes, sir," said Tim with a big smile.

"We are," agreed Cindy. It was obvious she had relaxed a great deal.

Vance nodded in understanding. "I want to have a little talk with your father," he said warmly to the kids.

They all nodded but looked a little frightened at the same time.

"Reg, walk with me."

Reg immediately stood. "Yes, sir."

Vance turned and started downstream. Reg patted all three children on the head, kissed Cindy on the forehead, and hurried to catch up to Vance.

When they were out of earshot but not out of view, Vance motioned toward a couple of large boulders. "Let's sit for a moment."

"Yes, sir."

"Reg, I'm impressed with what you've done here. You've made it your home. I've known men who would have given up within a month of being stranded on an island like this and possibly been dead by now. So you've shown me something here. Also, I can see that your family loves you. That tells me you've always treated them with love and kindness—frankly, not what I expected to find."

"I understand why you would believe otherwise," Reg said sincerely. "I've thought a lot about my history in these past two years. I believe I was a total asshole outside of my family from my early teens on. I was always big, and I became a bully. There are a lot of big men on Gabriel, and none are bullies that I'm aware of. I've concluded that I have a character flaw, maybe a bad gene." Reg looked back upstream and saw his children playing happily together in the distance. Cindy continued looking downstream in their direction. "I love my family." Reg started to tear up.

"I know."

"I can't thank you enough for bringing them to me. I—" Reg stopped talking for a moment before managing to choke out, "I thought I would never see them again."

Vance said nothing for a minute or so. He was drumming his fingers on the rock he was sitting on. *Damn, this isn't as cut and dried as I thought it would be.* Vance looked back up the creek. He could see Cindy and the three children watching him and Reg. He now realized he had caused not only Reg to suffer but also his wonderful family. *Damn, damn, damn.*

He turned and looked at Reg. "It was my intention to make this just a short visit for the benefit of Cindy and your children. But I'm having second thoughts."

"Yes, sir?"

Vance could see Reg was puzzled. "Do you have enough provisions to make your family comfortable here for a week?"

Reg smiled. "Oh yes, sir. We can make do. You can be sure of that."

"I have a few things in the runabout that will be of some help—blankets, emergency rations," said Vance.

"I can't begin to thank you for—"

Vance cut him off. "You are here for a reason. You took a fine man away from his family and friends forever. They will never see him again because of you."

"Please believe me, sir. What I did to Tom hurts me more than the punishment I have been given. Not a day goes by that I don't think of what I did to that wonderful man and to his wife, family, and friends. Their loss is forever, as you said. If it were possible, I would exchange my life for his."

Vance said nothing.

"I have asked myself why many times a day. I have no rational answer."

Vance knew Reg was telling him the truth about his guilt and feelings. He was impressed that Reg never used the excuse that he'd been drunk at the time, although that had been, without question, a major factor.

Vance had heard all he needed to hear. He stood. "Let's get back to your family."

The two stood and started walking back. Vance glanced at Reg and saw him smiling at Cindy as they closed the gap between them. He could see the puzzled expression on Cindy's face.

"I'll hang back and let you tell your family what's happening."

Reg was so choked up all he could do was nod at Vance.

A few minutes later, Vance joined the family. "Let's go get the supplies we talked about."

"Yes, sir."

A short time later, Vance was in front of the runabout's hatch, receiving hugs from Cindy and the children. He knew they were sincere hugs of gratitude. He knew without a doubt he was doing the right thing.

"I or someone will be back in a week to pick you up," he said to Cindy. "In the meantime, enjoy yourselves." With that, Vance entered the runabout, lifted off, and headed for Home-Bay.

Fifty minutes later, Vance walked onto the bridge of the *Norman*. "Alex, Dale."

The two holograms appeared in front of him.

"How did it go?" asked Alex.

"Not what I expected."

"How so?"

"I took Reg for a total asshole—a self-centered, overbearing bully. But that's not what I saw on the island."

"No?"

"No. He transformed the living area of the island into something quite nice. If it weren't for the horrendous weather, it would be a nice place to spend some time."

"Really?" said Alex.

"Yes, but that's not what impressed me. It was how much his family loved him and how much he loved them."

"You didn't expect that?"

"No, I guess I thought they would fear him. I assumed he would be a domineering bully at home. Thought his children and wife would be a little afraid of him. But that was not the case. Not at all."

"And?" asked Dale.

"I left the family there for a week."

"And?"

Vance smiled. "And I'm going to move Reg to Seaside to be with them."

"Really?" said Alex and Dale in unison, their surprise evident.

The town of Seaside was a picturesque place sitting at the back of a small natural harbor on the massive inland sea at the center of the Ring Continent. The area of the inland sea was ten times greater than that of the dry land. The weather in Seaside remained temperate most of the year, with rainfall of about half a meter per year. The sea itself was rich with life and contained a great variety of fish. Wildlife flourished in the surrounding mountains and valleys. Seaside's population had increased steadily over the decades because of those great assets and the spectacular beauty of the land.

The townspeople were mainly fishermen and had been since the first colonizers settled on the scenic little bay more than a hundred years ago. They supplied most of the freshwater fish for Home-Bay and other smaller communities on the west coast of the Ring.

Two weeks later, Vance was on the bridge of the *Norman*, talking to Alex and Dale. "As you know, Cindy and the children have been living at Doug and Terri Lambert's home in Seaside. Their home had four empty bedrooms after their children grew up and moved out."

"Yes, we know," said Alex. "Wonderful, warm-hearted couple."

Vance nodded. "Over the past two years, they came to love Cindy and her children but were reluctant to accept Reg into their home."

"Understandable," said Dale.

"I had a long talk with them, and after telling what I now believe about Reg, I managed to convince them to give Reg a chance." Vance smiled. "The entire Whetrume family is now in Seaside."

"And?" said Alex.

"Had a little blowback from the townspeople."

"I'll bet," said Alex. "I would think that most were surprised Reg lived more than a minute after being found by you."

"Yeah, that seemed to be the case," Vance said. He seemed a little hurt by this.

Alex smiled. "You are not the same man you were when we first met."

Vance nodded. "You're right. But I occasionally look back at myself—how I was and how I viewed the world around me—and I admit I feel a little ashamed. I was a hard-ass with little compassion or empathy for anyone." He smiled a little. "I like myself better now." He paused for a second. "And you two and, particularly, Teddy had a lot to do with that."

"I'd give Teddy most of the credit," said Alex.

"No doubt," said Dale.

"So how did you leave it with the townsfolk?" asked Alex, getting back to the subject.

"They, for the most part, are willing to give Reg a chance."

"Good of them, all things considered," said Dale.

"Reg has the potential to be a model citizen. Hopefully, in time, the town will come to accept him completely."

CHAPTER 6

THE COMET IS VISIBLE
MO-THREE 12, 113

Vance was concentrating on the viewer in front of him. On the screen was the image of the massive comet the Yassi had discovered. Vance's face displayed great concern. *Jesus*, he thought. The comet had been visible to the naked eye at night for the past month, and every night, Vance spent some time watching it on his viewer.

"You watching that comet won't make it go away, ya know?" said Lara.

"I know." He turned off the viewer and turned toward Lara. "Let's go to bed."

Vance's concern was growing as the days and weeks went by. He wasn't alone in his concern. Dale was keeping close tabs on the comet also.

"In another month, it will be visible during the day," Dale had just told him.

"And in less time, it could start affecting Gabriel," Vance said.

What's it gonna do? he asked himself over and over.

The next day, Vance joined Troy, Alex, Dale, and Ian Henderson on the bridge of the *Norman*. After thirty minutes, Henderson was concluding his request.

"So," said Henderson, "I'm hoping you will consider sending a probe to the comet."

Vance, Dale, Alex and Troy all looked at each other and nodded.

"I think we are all in favor of doing just that," said Dale. "Your hypothesis has enough validity to convince anyone that letting this opportunity go by would be imprudent at best."

"I can assure you all, Gary would insist this be done," added Troy. "This is right up his alley."

Henderson's expression displayed his delight. "I can't tell you how much this means to me. I've held this belief for nearly as long as I can remember."

"We may not find any trace of viable DNA," Dale said, "but that doesn't mean that all comets are, shall we say, barren."

Alex smiled. "I cannot imagine any race of superior beings, no matter how advanced, being able to seed every comet in the universe."

"All this seems almost beyond the limits of imagination, but so many important discoveries have been," said Dale.

"I'll of course be disappointed if, in fact, the comet is sterile, but I agree with you, sir, that it is unlikely all comets contain DNA."

"Then it's agreed?" asked Alex.

"I not only agree, but I insist," said Vance with a smile.

"Put me on the yes side," added Troy.

Vance smiled. "Okay, to that end, we need to start building and equipping a probe with the tools necessary to drill, extract, and analyze the ice within the comet."

"I'll get a team on it right away," said Dale.

MO-SIX 6, 113

The comet, which the Gabriel council named Yassi in honor of their discovery, had been visible in daylight for just shy of a month before Gabriel began experiencing tremors in various places around the planet. Most were located on or close to the continental plates and were fairly mild, but they had been increasing in severity as the weeks passed. So far, the property damage was minor, but Dale feared that would not continue.

"The damage is mostly frayed nerves," quipped Vance.

"Including mine," said Troy.

Dale's concern was proving to be a reality. The comet's gravity was starting to pull Gabriel out of shape.

"These tremors are going to become a great deal more severe as the comet comes closer," said Dale. "I recommend storing survival gear, such as food, water, blankets, and fuel, in the shelter caves."

"I don't know if I'd want to be in a cave during an earthquake," said Vance.

"Not during an earthquake, no," said Dale, "but it's possible that existing volcanoes will become more active, or new ones might be created. The real dangers will be the destruction of homes in an earthquake and ash fallout from volcanoes. People may need shelter."

Vance nodded. "Okay, we'll put out the word to get the caves stocked with all the necessities."

As the days went by, the tremors began shaking the areas above where the tectonic plates came together. Homes and structures along those fault lines began showing some damage. So far, the damage was minor, and no injuries were reported, but the amount of steam blowing out of existing volcanoes increased by a factor of three.

Within a week, all of the shelter caves contained enough supplies to keep the citizens alive for up to a month. Pets, such as dogs and cats, were not a problem; they would accompany their families into the caves. However, livestock, such as cows, pigs, horses, sheep, and goats, were another matter. There wasn't enough space or food for them. They would have to fend for themselves.

A week later, a large runabout entered a high orbit around Gabriel. Aboard the vessel were Dale's grandson Tony, who had been made the project manager, a brilliant young engineer named Tomoki who'd designed the mechanical functions and launching system for the probe. Vance would be the pilot, and an ecstatic Ian Henderson, who'd been invited along for the ride, completed the crew. The small probe, less than four cubic meters in total size, sat in the runabout's hold. Tony and Gary were in pressure suits, making a last inspection before preparing to open the outside hatch.

Using a modified rail gun, the probe would be shot like a bullet out of the runabout's hold. The probe would lead the comet as a bullet led a moving target. The probe's thrusters could make slight adjustments in the trajectory but the shot had to be nearly perfect; there was little room for error. As the probe approached the comet, thrusters would slow the probe, guide it to a predetermined landing spot, and then, hopefully, provide a soft landing on one of the comet's vast ice fields.

The countdown began as soon as Vance had the runabout oriented properly. There was no one more qualified in runabouts than Vance. He'd spent fifty years in real time seeding Gabriel with them.

"We're ready," said Vance. "The comet's in the crosshairs."

Tony and Tomoki made the final inspections and adjustments to the rail gun and then backed off to the far side of the hold.

"Fire when ready, sir," said Tony.

"Launch in five. Four. Three. Two. One."

The probe shot out of the runabout at a thousand meters per second.

"Whoa," said Tony. "Couldn't even see it go."

"Let's hope I'm a good shot," said Vance as he turned the runabout and headed back to Home-Bay.

Ten hours later, Vance, Tony, Tomoki, and Ian Henderson, along with the holograms of Dale and Alex, were in the *Norman*'s lab, keeping close tabs on the dozen or so monitors situated on a large wall on the far side of the room. They, along with the citizens of Gabriel, watched as the probe's cameras continuously sent pictures as it rapidly approached the comet and then slowed. Six minutes later, it landed within ten meters of the desired spot.

"Well done," said Dale.

"You are a great shot," said Tony.

"Piece of cake," said Vance.

"Let's take a look around," said Dale.

A command was sent, and the probe's cameras began taking a panoramic shot. The pictures sent back revealed a startling landscape. The landing spot was an immense plane of ice strewn with large, jagged boulders of varying colors. In the distant background, they could see a ridge of rugged, surprisingly tall mountains. It was not a hospitable place; it looked cold and desolate.

"Jesus, that's a nasty environment," said Alex.

After twenty minutes of observing the remarkable landscape,

Dale sent another command to begin drilling into the ice. The probe's telescoping drill could only reach a depth of twenty meters, so that would have to suffice. As the drill descended into the ice, the tailings produced were sucked inside the probe for analysis.

Half an hour later, the probe began transmitting data.

"Holy microbes!" said Dale. "We have life on comets."

Ian jumped up from the stool he was sitting on. "Please say that again."

"You were right, Ian. There is life on comets. A lot of life."

"Yes!" yelled Ian. "I knew it."

"Wow," said Dale as he continued absorbing the stream of data. "We have bacteria, viruses, and microorganisms full of DNA. That comet is a virtual cornucopia of life."

Henderson sat back down on the stool. His relief and joy were infectious. A brief look at Henderson was all one needed to enhance his smile. Henderson was one happy human being.

"This data is going to take quite a while to analyze, but at first glance, I'm seeing some very unusual DNA. This is very exciting."

A week later, Dale was giving a report to Alex, Vance, Troy, Tony, Tomoki and Ian.

"On that comet, there is DNA of which we have no record—DNA that would produce a life-form completely alien to anything we have imagined."

"This was not expected," said Alex.

"No, we were hoping for, at best, single-cell animals, maybe bacteria, but not a DNA string a great deal more complicated than that of a human."

"What?"

"That's right; there are nearly three times the double-helix pairs contained in humans."

"Wow, too bad we decided not to retrieve the probe and return it to Gabriel. We could have studied it more closely or maybe even grown whatever it was designed to produce," said Troy. "We could send another probe and bring some of that DNA back for study."

Dale shook his head. "I think we're probably better off keeping that DNA off our planet."

Gary looked puzzled. "That surprises me, Dale. I would think your curiosity would make you jump at the chance to study a new life-form."

"I believe this one would scare me."

"Really?"

Dale nodded. "Let that life find another planet to colonize."

"You're the boss when it comes to this sort of thing," said Vance.

"Agreed," said Alex.

Dale remained silent for a moment. "On the long-distance side," he said finally, "the comet will be at its closest proximity in about a month. That's when the poop will hit the fan. Then, in another month or so, its gravity's influence will start to abate."

Vance looked at Dale. "But it will return, will it not?"

"Yes, in two years, after it orbits the sun and heads back into deep space, but its return trip will keep it about one and a half million kilometers from Gabriel. At that distance, it will be much less visible, and it should have little or no effect on Gabriel."

"So far, the weather has not been affected," said Troy.

"Not yet," said Dale, "but if volcanoes start spewing massive amounts of steam and ash, it will be."

CHAPTER 7

FIRST EARTHQUAKE
MO-SEVEN 12, 113

A mild shaking woke Vance. "What the hell?"

"What's happening?" asked Lara as she too awoke.

"Earthquake," said Vance as he sprang out of bed.

He had barely gotten his pants and shoes on before a much bigger jolt hit. The noise sounded like several freight trains passing at the same time.

"Shit! Lara, get outside—now!"

She didn't have to be told twice; she grabbed a wrap and ran for the door. Vance was on her heals. The shaking was so bad that they bumped into the hall wall twice on their way out.

The earthquake settled down about the same time they were away from anything that could fall on them.

After a full minute, the tremors subsided completely. "Can we go back in?" asked Lara.

"Better not. Let's wait for—"

Another jolt hit with even more severity than the first. It would have knocked Lara off her feet had Vance not had his arm around her waist.

The quake calmed down to mild tremors, but the tremors were in a nearly constant rolling motion and weren't subsiding.

"I'll be right back; don't move," said Vance as he released Lara and ran into their home. Fifteen seconds later, he came back out with a communicator in hand.

"Alex, Dale," he said.

"Been trying to get ahold of you," answered Dale.

"We've been outside, taking in the night air," quipped Vance.

"I'll bet," said Alex.

"Send out an alert to tell everyone to stay away from anything that can fall on them," Vance said.

"Already done," said Dale. "We told them to wait for an all clear from us before they return to their homes."

"Good. We need to get the *Norman* out of the cave."

"They're preparing to do just that. And as you will see, the *Marian*'s bridge crew is taking her to a height of thirty meters."

"Yes, we see her, and here comes the *Norman*."

Vance and Lara could see the *Norman* moving out of the cave at a height of three meters. From their point of view, it looked as if it were on the ground. After clearing the cave, it rose to twenty meters as it moved to the spot where it had touched down the first time it landed on Gabriel many centuries ago. Vance had a strong flashback as he watched the huge orb from across the river. It was quite a sight, with the *Norman* hovering in the foreground and the *Marian* hovering in the background.

"That's kind of surreal," said Lara.

"The size of the *Marian* alone is surreal," said Vance.

The tremors abated slightly before stopping completely. Vance and Lara watched the huge ships for another five minutes before they headed back into their home, concerned about what damage they might find. Some artwork on the walls had fallen. Dishes and such had come out of the cupboard and broken on the counters and floor. The windows on the west side were shattered, and an inside wall was off kilter. The home itself looked to be sound and still perpendicular. Most homes were built of logs and were of a modern design, which created a somewhat flexible yet safe structure.

Dale's voice came over the communication system. "Vance?"

"Where was the epicenter?" asked Vance.

"The Pearls."

"I'll be there soon."

Vance sat in the captain's chair, staring intently at the viewer. The satellite images showed massive amounts of steam shooting out of the ocean about 150 kilometers south of the southernmost of the Black Pearl Islands. It was a dirty-looking steam made up of ash, magma, and blistering-hot salt water. The images of this new volcano and the new one forming on the Vast Continent were transmitted around the planet. Everyone could see what was happening to their world.

The viewer displayed a steam cloud rising out of the ocean just off the coast of the North Dumbbell. As the image and title changed to the South Dumbbell, right at the continental plate, they could see steam vents had opened just off the southern coast. The image changed again. This time a great deal closer, it showed the volcanoes of the Black Pearl Islands. The volcanoes that weren't completely dormant were starting to spew more steam and ash, but it was the south end of the massive chain of volcanoes that had their attention. Huge amounts of steam boiled out of the Vast Ocean ninety kilometers south of the southernmost volcano.

That day, Gabriel had experienced the first big earthquakes since the planet was colonized. On old Earth, some of the quakes would have been credited as 8.8 or higher on the Richter scale. The largest was centered twenty kilometers north of the northernmost volcano on the Vast Continent. A sudden and huge eruption at the epicenter of the earthquake gave birth to a new and violent volcano. Thousands of rocks ranging in size from baseballs to enormous boulders were blasted from the planet's crust, with some landing as far as thirty kilometers from the site. The shock waves from this massive upheaval could be felt for three thousand kilometers, all the way to the east coast of the Vast Continent.

"This is serious," said Dale. "The earthquakes and volcanoes aren't necessarily the problem, since there is little that can be horribly affected in that part of the continent. The problem is the ash."

"How big a problem?" asked Vance.

"The ash could bury the edible grasses and plants for thousands of square kilometers. And that could cause mass starvation for tens of thousands of animals."

"Will there be enough ash to do that?"

"Don't know yet. We're still getting data from the satellites, and we've got a crew on the way to the area. We'll know a little more in a few hours. In a few days, we should have a clear picture."

Lara walked onto the bridge. "Too scared to stay alone," she said with a small smile as she walked over and kissed Vance on the cheek.

"I should have brought you with me. I'm sorry—very insensitive of me."

"No problem, big guy," she said with a big smile.

"If I can interrupt," said Dale.

"Oops," said Lara. She quickly turned, walked to a close-by seat, and sat.

Vance smiled.

"The data we're getting now shows the new volcano has just about stopped spewing ash and is now ejecting magma." Dale paused for a moment as he studied the data flowing in from six satellites and the newly established ground instruments. "A lot of magma."

The intensity continued to increase as the days went on. New steam vents opened up on the four major continents. So far, none had been discovered on the North Pole or South Pole continents.

Jesus, thought Vance as he watched the viewer switch from one continent to another. *This has got to stop.*

The following week, Dale was giving a report to the gathering on the *Norman's* bridge. "There is some fairly good news coming in from the Vast's new volcano. It comes in three parts. First, the wind in the region has been very light. The ash cloud isn't blowing east nearly as far as we originally thought it would. The ash is heavy and is dropping within fifty kilometers of the new volcano.

"Secondly, that part of the Vast is experiencing its normal dry season, so most of the grazing animals have moved south in their seasonal migration. That, of course, takes the predators with them. The loss of life will be nominal. Lastly, the volcano itself is already more than five hundred twenty meters tall and growing."

Vance was, at the moment, transfixed on the Satellite images showing massive amounts of steam shooting out of the ocean 90 kilometers south of the southernmost of the Black Pearl Islands. It was a dirty looking steam, made up of ash, magma and blistering hot salt water. "The chain of ten Pearl Islands is in the process of becoming eleven," observed Vance.

"That's right. Nothing above sea level yet, but at this rate, something will be poking its hot head up in the not-too-distant future," said Dale. "When it does, the ash that is now mixing with water and falling back into the ocean will be free to travel a much greater distance."

"It's below the southern island, so if the prevailing wind doesn't shift north, Home-Bay shouldn't be affected," said Vance.

"That's correct," Dale said. "But if the wind direction stays as it is, the good farmland two to three hundred kilometers south of us will be hit."

"If the winds head south, little damage will be done, and just some uninhabited islands might be affected."

The images of this potential new volcano and the new one forming on the Vast continent were being transmitted around the planet. Everyone could see what was happening to their world.

"There doesn't seem to be any let up in the new volcano's activity," said Alex.

"To the contrary, the eruptions are growing stronger and may cause more new volcanos.

"The comet is doing what you feared it might," said Alex.

"It is. Its gravity is pulling our planet out of shape, causing a shift in the tectonic plates."

"Any way to tell how long this will go on?"

Dale said nothing for a moment. "Right now, the comet is as close to us as it is going to get. It's exerting as much force as it ever will, but I think we're in for a lot more shaking before it tapers off completely."

"What are the chances of more volcanoes popping up?"

"Excellent, I'd think. The North Dumbbell's northwest side has been pretty active in the not too distant past. The South Dumbbell's southern tip is also vulnerable. But if nothing occurs for the next few months, we may get past it."

"How about the poles?"

"There has been no data coming from satellites concerning them, so I'm assuming there is no activity. But time will tell."

MO-NINE 18, 113

The new volcanoes started to settle down. The volcano on the Vast Continent had grown to more than two thousand meters and was still spewing magma, but it was just a small hill compared to the giants in that chain of volcanic mountains. At its present lava flow, it would take decades, if not centuries, for the new volcano to gain that much height.

The new volcano at the south end of the Pearls had risen to 180 meters above sea level and remained active, but like the volcano on the Vast, it no longer was ejecting ash, only magma. The steam cloud caused by molten lava pouring into the ocean was so dense at times that it completely obscured the new volcano. However, the steam wasn't sufficient to have an effect on the planet's weather.

Another new but smaller volcano erupted about two kilometers off the shore of the northwest corner of the North Dumbbell. It quickly rose above the ocean but settled down within a week.

Yet another small volcano made its presence known on the southern tip of the South Dumbbell. This volcano seemed to be content just spewing a massive amount of steam. The continents of the North Pole and South Pole seemed to be unaffected by the comet's gravity.

The comet Yassi was pulling away from Gabriel as it continued its journey. It was now only dimly visible at night and soon would be out of sight altogether. It would continue in its orbit around the sun before starting its long trip back to deep space. In four years, it would become visible again to Gabriel, but this time, the tail would be leading the comet, and because of its elliptical orbit, the comet would be much farther from Gabriel as it left the solar system.

CHAPTER 8

VOLUNTEERS
MO-ONE 15, 114

Vance walked onto the bridge of the *Marian*, where about a dozen people were busy at their stations. It was the nerve center of the ship, a ship so diverse in its capabilities that it operated much like a small town. The bridge crew's main duties were to monitor and coordinate the ship's various sections.

When Vance was spotted, the word was given, and all stood at attention.

"As you were," Vance said as he walked through the bridge to the far side. The crew returned to their respective duties.

As Vance approached the door on the far side of the bridge, it quietly slid open. "Good morning, gentlemen and ladies," he said as he walked into the room.

"Good morning, sir," answered the nearly two dozen people in the room as they stood. Along with Troy and Gary, the remaining twenty were divided equally between young men and women.

"Please sit," said Vance.

The twenty young people in the room had been chosen from three hundred who had volunteered, and these twenty had become well known to Vance over the past few months. He had spent a great deal of time with them and their families, making sure all were aware of what their decision would mean to their futures.

"Sir," said Troy as he motioned toward a vacant chair.

Vance walked over and sat. "I assume you've worked out the timing?"

"We have," said Gary.

The meeting's purpose was to finalize plans for the ten couples to board the Yassi ship bound for Mahyu. The human colonists and their descendants would become permanent citizens of the Yassi home world. They would be the first humans to leave Gabriel, and the planet was abuzz with the news.

It was agreed that the colonists would hold their population to no more than a few thousand; their mission was not to populate a planet, as Gabriel's original twenty colonists had done, but to ensure the continuation of the human race.

Among the several attributes required of the colonists was a stout body. The gravity on Mahyu was 5 percent stronger than on Gabriel. A slight body would not be able to adjust as well as a heavier one. As it turned out, two of the volunteers were related to Vance himself. Four were direct descendants of the original *Norman* colonists, and the rest carried the genetics of the *Marian* colonists. In addition to the twenty, Gary had volunteered to accompany them to Mahyu.

Gary was the only one making a round trip. When he returned aboard the next Yassi ship, he would give a firsthand report on how well the colonists were settling in and what their previously unforeseen needs were. In addition, Gabrielites had a great deal of interest in the planet Mahyu itself. They had seen hundreds of pictures and videos of it, but an onsite account from Gary would provide more perspective. The drawback was that the planet Mahyu was 2.7 light-years away, and Gary would not return to Gabriel for at least eight years. As he was a SLF, the time wouldn't affect him personally, but it would make a difference to those on Gabriel; they would miss him. He and Troy had been best friends since their college days. After college, Troy had gone into politics, and Gary had gone into science. Both were highly gifted in their chosen fields and had ended their careers at the WGC, Troy as chairman and Gary as chief science counselor. Gary was a brilliant scientist and had provided invaluable assistance to hundreds of complicated projects on Gabriel.

A LITTLE HISTORY
EARTH YEAR 2477

Immediately after the discovery of the massive asteroid that would collide with and destroy Earth, emergency construction was ordered for three colossal starships. Had there been more time, many more ships would have been built, but even construction of three was considered folly at the time.

The new ships were designed to take as many humans as possible out of harm's way and transport them to planets suitable for colonization. The basic designs for the ships were already stored in the computers. The plans were based on the centuries-old *Norman's* design, which turned out to be a major contributor to the success of the enormous undertaking. The ships had to be completed and launched within fourteen months, or all would be lost.

Gary, being the chief science counselor, immediately became the driving force behind the construction of the ships. Within a week of the discovery of the impending asteroid strike, Gary ordered SLF bodies to be built for him and four other scientists and engineers. He needed himself and these highly gifted individuals to be able to work nonstop twenty-four hours per day until the completion of the project. To that end, dozens of technicians began working around the clock, designing and building the SLF bodies.

Gary's SLF was completed in under thirty days, an impressive feat in and of itself. The other SLFs were completed within the following two weeks. As a bonus, these scientists' and engineers' human bodies would not be affected by the transfer of their intellects to the SLFs, thus allowing the originals to continue working on the massive project. The creation of the five SLFs proved to be another major factor in the project's success.

The extraordinary worldwide effort paid off. The ships were ready in just under thirteen months. During the construction, one more SLF body was prepared for Troy. The human bodies of Troy, Gary, and the four other SLFs would remain behind with their families and friends to suffer the fate of all life on Earth.

The fifteen hundred humans chosen to take the trips were the best the planet had to offer, as had been the case with the colonists aboard the *Norman*. All would remain in stasis for the entire voyage, and most would remain so until a suitable environment complete with food and accommodations could be provided on their new world.

The technology in all fields of human endeavor had greatly advanced since the *Norman* left Earth some five hundred years prior. Astrophysics had been improved to a point where astronomers had already identified dozens of planets within fifty light-years, all suitable for colonization. Of those dozens, two were determined to be the most ideal. They were in the Goldilocks zone of their respective suns, contained a mass within 2 percent of Earth's, and had an abundance of water and a considerable amount of vegetation. After a great deal of debate, it was decided that rather than putting all of their eggs in one basket, they would send the three ships to different planets. Two, the *Vance* and the *Alexander*, would head for the new planets, and the third ship, the *Marian*, would head to Gabriel.

Troy's and Gary's SLFs would guide the *Marian* on its thirty-two-year voyage to Gabriel. The four other SLFs would guide the two other ships. SLFs were the only beings who could spend the decades required to make the voyage to a distant planet. There was no other practical way.

In the Gabriel year 50, the *Marian*, just five hundred million kilometers from Gabriel, was attacked by the Malic and crippled. Because repairs could not be completed without outside help, the *Marian* drifted dead in space for three years before being discovered by the Yassi. Immediately after being informed of the discovery, Gabriel's leadership sent the *Norman* to intercept the *Marian*. Working together, the humans and Yassi managed to repair the *Marian* enough to complete her journey to Gabriel.

Everyone soon realized that if not for the Herculean efforts of Gary and Troy in fighting off the Malic's initial attack, everything contained aboard the *Marian* would have been lost. The five hundred humans and the gene pool they represented, along with thousands of human and animal embryos, would not have survived. In addition, the *Marian* was loaded with an enormous cache of machinery and technology as yet unknown to the human settlers on Gabriel. It was remarkable that those two SLFs alone had managed to kill dozens of Malic and drive off the rest. It was even more remarkable that neither of the SLFs had any law enforcement or military training. However, being SLFs, they were 50 percent faster and stronger than a human. Further, it was now known that the Malic themselves were not very bright. Virtually all of the technology they possessed was stolen. Even so, the remarkable tale of the two beings driving off hundreds would be told and retold in the millennia to come.

Gary was nearly destroyed during the battle. The damage to his body was extensive, including the loss of his left arm. With Gary effectively dead, Troy was now alone on a disabled and partially plundered ship. The fusion generators had been disabled by the Malic in their effort to steal them. The *Marian* was as cold as a crypt.

In the following days and months after the battle, Troy busied himself by throwing dozens of Malic bodies off the ship and repairing what damage he could, but finally, with little hope of ever being found, he shut himself off. Fortunately, the *Marian*, unlike the *Norman*, was equipped with a small lab designed to service and repair SLFs. After the technicians aboard the *Marian* were brought out of stasis, they were able to rebuild Gary to near perfection.

The *Marian*'s SLF lab meant a great deal more to Vance than it did to the other Gabrielites. Over the centuries, Vance had put his SLF body through a great deal of wear and tear. His synthetic skin had accumulated a multitude of cuts, scrapes, and stretches. His synthetic hair had thinned, and his Isleium muscles had lost some tone. Despite the obvious deterioration, Dale always marveled at how well the Isleium and SLF technology had held up, considering the extreme environments they had endured. Within six months of the *Marian*'s arrival, Vance had spent three full days being serviced in the SLF lab. Vance called it his "hundred-trillion-kilometer tune-up." At the end of that time, he came out looking like his original SLF, a human in his mid-thirties. He felt as good as new—better, actually. The SLF technology had improved considerably over the centuries. Among the improvements was the full sense of taste. A full day of the tune-up was dedicated to installing a new tongue and other receptors. In addition, a simple evacuation system was installed. There would be no need for digestion. The first thing Vance asked for was a steak, a baked potato with all the fixings, and an ice-cold beer.

YASSI COLONISTS
MO-NINE 12, 118

"What a day." Vance was taking in the great view of the river that bore his name and the bay, and he could see his home through the trees on the far side.

"Perfect," said Troy.

Gary smiled and nodded without looking at his two friends.

The three were having lunch on the rear deck of Carlon's Pup, a favorite spot in Home-Bay. From their point of view, they could see not only the bay but also the terminus of Vance River as it surged out of the bay into the Vast Ocean, mixing its fresh water with the salt of the ocean. It was a view Vance would never tire of. It was the first thing he'd seen when he exited the *Norman* more than five hundred years in the past. He had built his home on the low bluff on the other side of the river. It was the only home clearly visible from that location.

Vance turned toward Gary. "So everything's ready for the Yassi?" he asked.

"Yes, sir," said Gary. "Their ship will arrive in three weeks."

Vance nodded.

"They will disembark here in Home-Bay to a welcoming celebration," said Troy.

"They will stay here for five days to get somewhat acclimated to our culture, atmosphere, and gravity before heading to their island," said Gary.

A waiter approached. "Gentlemen, may I get you something else?"

"Another beer, please," said Vance.

"Same here," said Troy.

"I'm fine," said Gary.

As the waiter walked off, Vance said, "They've named it New Mahyu."

"I've heard," said Troy.

"How long will they be here?" asked Vance.

"They'll be here a total of eight weeks, two weeks longer than their normal visit," said Gary. "They'll be helping their colonists get set up in their new homes. While they're here, we'll retrofit the twenty stasis capsules on their ship—and fourteen on the Vout ship when they arrive."

Vance was pensive for a moment. "How long before the Vout colonists arrive?"

"Five months," said Gary.

"Assuming all goes well with the welcoming of the Yassi, we'll use the same procedures for the Vout," said Troy.

Vance took the last sip of his beer as the waiter approached with two fresh ones. "How are our volunteers doing?" he asked as he and Troy put the empty glasses on the waiter's tray.

Gary smiled. "They're doing as well as can be expected, considering what they are about to embark on."

"It's interesting to see the contrast in physiologies and personalities of our young colonists," said Dale. "The volunteers to Mahyu are stout and have outgoing personalities. The opposite is the case for those heading to Vout. Quite a stark difference, actually."

"I've noticed." Vance smiled. "Also, there were a lot fewer volunteers for Vout."

"A lot fewer," added Gary.

Both teams of human colonists had gone through extensive training in a multitude of areas, including medicine, farming, ranching, and building. The colonists would be not only self-sufficient but also responsible for training and teaching future generations. The Yassi and Vout, of course, would be available for any unforeseen emergency, but the intent was for the colonists to stand on their own.

Vance nodded. "We're going to miss you while you're gone, Gary. You're a tremendous asset here."

"Thank you. I hope to be an asset on Mahyu."

Vance patted Gary on the arm. "There is no doubt in my mind that will be the case."

MO-TEN 13, 118

The magnificent Yassi ship had been in geosynchronous orbit over Home-Bay for just shy of an hour before one of their wondrous shuttles flew out of a hatch and dropped down to the landing site.

As always, a large welcoming committee headed by Vance, Troy, Gary, and community leaders from the four continents greeted them, along with the ten couples who would accompany them back to Mahyu and thousands of citizens from Home-Bay.

The Yassi were a wonderful race of beings. They were warm, friendly, and fun loving and had an intelligence more advanced than humans', and true to their personalities, they were willing to share most of it.

They had chosen a large island with an area just shy of five thousand square kilometers, located thirteen hundred kilometers southeast of the Ring Continent. It was a beautiful island. It contained an abundance of rivers and lakes and a diversity of topography that would provide land for whatever the Yassi wished to do. This island lay in the southern hemisphere and, as such, was colder than humans preferred.

Over the past four years, the humans had built a residential area ready for the establishment of a Yassi community, including homes, sanitation, water, power, shops, medical offices, food-processing facilities, a restaurant, and a myriad of other accommodations, all to the specifications provided by the Yassi. Everything was designed to make the Yassi feel as close to home as possible. They were already referring to it as New Mahyu.

The Vout had chosen an island within a thousand kilometers of the Vast Continent and a thousand kilometers northwest of New Mahyu. Its climate was a bit cooler than that of Home-Bay but warmer than the Yassi island. The finishing touches were being put on. Other than the stronger gravity, the Vout would feel as comfortable.

For centuries, the Yassi and Vout had made the long journey to Gabriel to mine gold, tin, and other rare metals, but since humans had colonized the planet, their trips had become about more than just acquiring resources; Gabriel had become a port of call. It was an oasis in their long trek through space. They fully enjoyed the company of humans, and the humans felt the same toward them. Since the Yassi and Vout no longer had to mine gold or other metals, they instead brought with them hundreds of products to trade in exchange for the sought-after metals.

During the time the Yassi and humans engaged in purchasing and selling products, Gary oversaw the installation of the stasis capsules and a stasis bed for himself aboard the Yassi ship. Once that was done, they loaded and stored the supplies and tools the humans would need on Mahyu.

CHAPTER 9

BINARIES
MO-THREE 8, 121

"Vance, Troy, we'd like to see you at the *Norman*." Alex's voice was uncharacteristically distressed.

Within a few seconds, Vance made contact. "What's wrong, Alex?"

"Need you and Troy here ASAP. We'll fill you in when you get here."

"Be there in ten," said Vance.

"Ditto," said Troy.

The two arrived at the loading ramp within seconds of each other and quickly continued up to the elevator. "Four," Troy said before turning to Vance. "Any idea?"

"None," responded Vance. "But I know it's bad."

They spent the next few seconds in silence before exiting on the bridge of the *Norman* and hurrying over to the main viewer.

Dale and Alex each had an agonized look that Vance had only seen once before, on the day they'd begun taking the *Norman*'s colonists out of stasis. That day, they'd discovered the first of the twenty to be reanimated, Terri Diggs, was dead. In that moment, they'd feared that there would be no humans on Gabriel and that everything they'd done—the planning, the dedication, the centuries of work—had been lost.

"Oh shit," said Vance. "How bad?"

"Very," said Alex. "I'll let Dale explain."

Dale had Vance's and Troy's attention.

"For the past year, we, the Vout, and the Yassi have been closely monitoring a binary neutron star system that's just shy of two light-years from here," explained Dale. "It's within half a light-year from Mahyu. There have been some unusual readings coming from that sector of space."

"Binary stars aren't all that unusual," said Vance. "Seems to me we are aware of thousands of binaries. There are probably millions of stars orbiting each other that we're not aware of."

"That is correct on both counts," said Dale, "but the distance between these stars is narrowing, and their orbits have increased in speed. We believe the two stars are going to merge."

"I'm assuming that is not a good thing," said Troy.

"In our case, it may be as bad a thing as there is," said Alex.

"The problem is that Gabriel lies directly in the path of the rotational axis of the larger of the two," Dale said. "That star is rotating at nearly a quarter of light speed."

"How can that be?" Troy asked.

"We know of black holes that are spinning at half the speed of light. Physics on a massive scale," Dale said.

"Jesus."

"Go on," said Vance.

"When two binary neutron stars merge, they will send out gamma-ray bursts along the line of the rotational axis. You might think of it as a massive laser."

"This burst may hit us?" asked Troy.

"If we're not on the other side of our sun when it hits—"

"Just how much damage can it do?" asked Vance.

"A GRB can release as much gamma radiation in a few seconds as a star, such as our sun, releases in its entire ten-billion-year lifetime."

"What?"

"You heard right. A GRB is the most powerful radiation in the universe."

"What we don't yet know, and may never know, is what the beam width will be. It can be from two to twenty degrees. If it's twenty degrees, the energy that hits us will be significantly less, and the reverse is true with a narrower beam. But in either case, if we're not on the other side of the sun when it hits, we're going to be severely damaged."

"Just what kind of damage can this thing do?" asked Troy.

"A long gamma-ray burst would destroy the ozone layer and

incinerate the side of the planet that gets hit. That would result in mass extinction, food depletion, and starvation on the other side of the planet. Everything will die or be damaged—everything. Gamma rays will cause a chemical reaction in oxygen and nitrogen, turning what's left of our atmosphere into what used to be called smog on old Earth. There would be enough smog to block the sun and create a cosmic winter."

"Holy shit!" Troy said.

"When is this going to happen?" Vance asked.

"That we cannot pin down. Any time between now and six months—it's imminent. It may have already happened."

There was silence on the bridge for a few seconds.

"Shit!" Vance said.

"When it happens, it will take two years for the burst to hit us."

"Then we must evacuate the planet," said Troy.

"How, and to where?" asked Dale. "At best, we could save maybe a thousand if we retrofit both the *Norman* and *Marian*. We could put half of them in stasis, but we would have to feed the other half for at least four years while we traveled to Vout or Mahyu."

"There must be something we can do," said Vance.

"We are assuming the worst. That may not be the case. There is a thirty percent chance we will be on the far side of the sun when it happens and a four percent chance our moons will absorb some of the radiation if they are in the right place at the right time."

"Those are slim odds," said Troy.

"Way too slim," said Dale. "The Yassi are sending as many ships as they can to take as many humans off the planet as possible, if in fact there are any left alive after the GRB. But their closest ship is still six months out. And a message has been sent to Vout, but unless they already have a ship within a few months away, they will not be of any help."

"What if some areas of the planet are still livable?" asked Troy.

"That's not likely," said Dale. "The cosmic winter will eventually kill whatever is left alive."

Vance sat silently, almost in a daze, as the others continued their discussion.

"If, by chance, there are parts of Gabriel that are livable, we'll move everybody and everything we can as fast as possible to any such locations," said Alex.

Dale continued with his report. "The Yassi have placed a probe as close to the binary as possible. It is sending us constant data on the stars. But the data will be almost two years old when we receive it. The probe will send a signal to us at the second of the burst. Studies indicate that the GRB travels just under the speed of light, so at light speed, the warning signal will only beat the GRB by less than eleven hours."

Nobody said anything for a couple of minutes.

"What can we do about this?" Vance said, coming back into the conversation.

Dale and Alex looked at each other and then back at the two men. "Short of evacuating the planet?" Dale said.

"Yes."

"There are a few things we can do to lessen the immediate loss of life."

"Which are?"

"We could, as evenly as possible, distribute the population around the planet. That way, only those on the wrong side will be immediately affected."

"I don't like that one," said Vance.

"The better option is to use the deep caves that every community is trained to use in case of an attack. Anyone in the caves might escape the initial burst."

"I'm liking this train of thought," said Vance. "We'll intensify the evacuation drills. Everybody will need to be in a cave within an hour of the alarm."

"That's right," Alex said.

Troy, who hadn't spoken for the past few moments, said, "You have used two words that are of great concern."

Alex looked at Troy. "*Immediately* and *initial*?"

"Yes, sir."

Dale nodded. "That depends on the duration of the burst. A burst can be from ten milliseconds to several minutes. The longer the burst, the more the damage."

"Go on."

"A GRB caused by the collision of two neutron stars normally creates a short burst. A short burst is any burst under two seconds."

"Just two seconds?"

"Yes, but the few studies made on GRBs suggest that no two are alike. They vary in all sorts of ways."

"What if everybody survives the initial GRB? What happens next?"

"In the worst case, everything on the surface dies within a few months in a nuclear winter. Best case is that the GRB is wide-beamed and will not cause mass extinction. We would survive that."

"I don't think we need to go into the multiple variances right now," said Alex. "Suffice it to say we believe we should prepare for the worst."

"Agreed," said Vance. "To that end, I'm going to authorize an emergency alert right now. Let's see how long it takes the folks to get into those caves."

"Now?" asked Alex.

"Yes, right now."

"Done."

Immediately, loud sirens sounded in all of the communities of Gabriel.

"That should have everybody's attention. Cut the sirens for a moment, and put me on the channel," said Vance.

"You're on," said Dale.

"This is Vance Youngblood. This is a drill, but I want everybody—and I mean everybody—in his or her shelter ASAP. Shelter captains are to report to me when everybody is secure. I expect those reports within the hour." Vance turned back to Dale. "Hit the sirens again."

All five councillors remained silent for a few minutes while gathering their thoughts and waiting for the shelter captains to report in.

"On a different note," Dale said, breaking the silence, "the comet will be coming back into view at night in a month or so."

"Well, that's all we need," said a disheartened Vance. "More volcanoes and earthquakes."

"We won't have to worry about that. The comet will be more than twice the distance from us that it was on its first pass. It will have no measurable effect on the planet."

Vance sat back in his chair. His brow furrowed, and his hands came together close to his face. It looked as if he might be praying.

"You all right?" asked Alex.

Vance didn't answer. *Something's wrong,* Vance's mind screamed. *Something's wrong here.*

"Vance?" said Alex.

Vance suddenly sat forward in his chair. "Something is wrong here."

"What?"

"Why, after more than a hundred years on this planet, are we experiencing two huge natural disasters in a row? It doesn't make sense."

"Just coincidence. What else could it be?" said Dale.

"I'm not buying that. Something's amiss. I just can't put my finger on it." After another minute, Vance's mind returned to the action at hand. "How's the emergency drill coming along?"

"We've gotten a few reports from shelter captains. Most haven't checked in yet," said Dale.

Within another half hour, all the shelter captains had reported that everybody was secure in the caves.

"That's a good time," said Troy.

"It is, and I'm kinda surprised," said Vance. "Put me on the intercom."

"You're on," said Dale.

Vance nodded and then said, "First, I want to congratulate you on a fine job in getting to your shelter caves. There is room for improvement, but I am confident the shelter captains will improve on their performance. Secondly, I want to tell you why we went through this drill." Vance paused for a moment before telling the population of Gabriel what he had learned in the briefing. He concluded by saying, "In any scenario, we know that the caves will offer the best protection from whatever blast hits us, hence the drill."

When he finished, he looked at Alex and Dale. They both nodded in approval.

MO-FOUR 6, 121

"I'm hating this," Troy said suddenly.

"We all are," Alex replied.

Troy dipped his head forward and closed his eyes briefly.

"I would point out that those left behind may be the lucky ones," added Vance.

Troy looked at Vance. "Lucky? They may be killed outright, gone in one horrible flash."

Vance nodded. He understood Troy's emotional investment. He felt the same. The people of Gabriel were like their children, grandchildren, and great-grandchildren. He knew he couldn't provide much relief for the overall picture, but he possibly could provide a little relief from the guilt they felt at what they were in the process of doing.

"Let me ask you: Would you rather die in a flash or spend a month or two starving to death in a cramped space?"

Troy said nothing; he just shook his head.

"Is it time?" asked Vance.

"It is," answered Alex.

"Put me on."

Vance's image appeared on the planet's viewers. "We, your councillors, have designed a method of deciding who will stay on Gabriel and who will be aboard the ships in space during the GRB. It's something that must be done.

"We are going to have a lottery. However, not everybody will participate. Those in the lottery will be between eighteen and thirty years old. There will be two lotteries, one for females and one for males. There will be twice as many females chosen as males. The females will be chosen first, and if a female has a husband, he will automatically be included, along with their children ages twelve and under. Once it is determined how many spaces are taken with the first draw, we will begin the second draw. The second draw will be done one man at a time. If that man has a wife and children, they will be included, as they were for the females. So it will go until we have reached the maximum number of evacuees.

"If any of you can come up with a more logical or fair way of doing this, please let us know."

Dale's image appeared on the viewers. "The balance of Gabrielites will seek shelter in the shelter caves during the GRB. The caves will, we believe, offer a great deal of protection from the gamma rays. All humans will survive with little to no damage. The problem lies with the damage to the planet. Will it continue to provide a life-sustaining environment?

"After the GRB, we will be returning to Gabriel, and depending on the damage and circumstances on the planet, we will off-load as many evacuees as possible. We will not be able to sustain the populous aboard the ships."

Troy's image came on the viewers. "As you all know, we have human colonies on both Mahyu and Vout. Humans will survive no matter what happens to our cherished Gabriel."

BINARIES MERGE
MO-FOUR 20, 121

Vance and Lara were in bed when the sirens went off at 18:32 on a pitch-black night in Home-Bay.

"God, it's happened," said Vance as he jumped out of bed. "Get dressed, sweetheart."

"Oh no," she said as she jumped out of bed. Tears formed, and she began trembling, but she said nothing as she silently and quickly put on the clothes she had set aside for this moment.

Vance could see his beloved wife was terrified, and it broke his heart. *She's a brave woman,* he thought with pride. He also knew the entire population of Gabriel was terrified at that moment.

Vance had his jumpsuit on within seconds. While waiting for Lara to finish getting ready, he looked around with great sadness; he knew this might be the last time he would see their home.

The Yassi probe had sent the signal that the binaries had merged and that a narrow beam burst was on its way. The sirens' sound was both expected and feared. The humans on Gabriel were getting their eleven-hour warning before the GRB hit their beloved planet. Everybody headed for his or her assigned cave. Surprisingly, the citizens displayed little panic.

Gabriel was on the wrong side of the sun; it was going to be hit. The burst was measured at just shy of four seconds in duration. The moons would be no help; in eleven hours, they would have orbited to the far side of the planet. The GRB would be a planet killer. Gabriel's rotation would put the Ring Continent and Vast Continent directly facing the oncoming GRB. The North Dumbbell and South Dumbbell continents would be spared the direct blast.

The population of Home-Bay headed to the *Norman's* cave. Within the hour, the *Norman* was to leave the planet, along with the *Marian* and all of the runabouts and shuttles. All crafts were loaded with as many humans as they could carry. Nearly six hundred could go into stasis and be part of a long voyage to Mahyu. The others would be packed into every nook and cranny of each ship. The ships had time to make it to the far side of the sun, which would provide a protective shield. A total of 5,654 humans were being evacuated from the planet, just more than 10 percent of the population. In addition, 10 percent of the Yassi and Vout populations were evacuated with the humans. There were six Yassi—two couples and their two youngsters—and one Vout couple, plus their child. It was the fairest way to handle the situation.

Everybody understood that these 5,663 men, women, and children might not be the lucky ones. They might have no livable planet to return to. By necessity, most were to be off-loaded on Gabriel to survive as best as they could, while the balance, the number who could be fed and cared for, were to remain on the long and crowded journey to Mahyu.

Every available space aboard the ships, including the living quarters, the massive storage areas, the engine rooms, and the flight decks, was packed with humans. Even the bridge of the *Norman* held four families, tightly packed. Included in that group, at Alex's insistence, were Teddy; his wife, Colleen; and their three youngest, twin girls aged seven and a boy aged five. Because of the rules, their two oldest, aged fourteen and fifteen, were to stay behind. Naturally, it was a rule that Teddy and Colleen had a great deal of trouble coping with. Thousands of parents were suffering in the same way. Only children twelve and under could accompany their parents.

Vance's ready room wasn't large enough to accommodate anyone. It held his stasis bed, a shower, and a small desk with a viewer but had little open space; it was left empty.

Vance's face displayed great sadness as he gave orders to move the *Norman* out of its massive cave.

Once they were clear of the cave, he gave another order: "Take us to five hundred meters, Dale, and hold there. We'll wait for all the ships to gather."

"Yes, sir."

"What's the *Marian*'s situation?"

"They're lifting off now."

Vance nodded. "Put Troy on the viewer."

A moment later, Troy's image appeared. "Yes, sir?"

"We'll wait at five hundred meters until all the ships are here."

"Yes, sir." Troy was being formal.

Within thirty minutes, all space-worthy crafts, from the smallest runabout to the Yassi shuttle, had gathered around the two huge starships.

"Dale, open a channel to all ships."

"They are open now, sir."

"We will stay together at all times. Our speed will be that of the slowest ship. That speed, I am told, will allow plenty of time for us to get to the far side of the sun before the GRB hits." Vance paused for a brief moment. "Let's go."

The Gabrielites on the bridge would have been thrilled under almost any other circumstances. They were seeing Vance Youngblood in command of the *Norman*. This picture was depicted in every history book on the planet. Each and every one of them had heard stories about him all of their lives. Now they were witnessing it firsthand. If they survived, they would be the envy of all Gabrielites for years to come.

"Dale, are all of the ships keeping up?"

"Yes, sir, and they are all on our tail."

"Thank you."

An hour into the flight, Alex found himself paying close attention to Vance. He had never seen his dear friend so dejected, not even when they'd lost Terri Diggs, who was to be the first of the *Norman*'s colonists revived. She, as it turned out, had been dead for decades before the attempt to revive her. However, this rapidly approaching catastrophe would not result in the loss of only an individual or twenty colonists; it would result in the loss of all life on Gabriel. Gabriel would become a dead planet.

Even though Alex's complete intellect was housed in the *Norman's* massive computer and he had no physical body to lose, he was truly afraid for the first time since Islamic extremists had kidnapped and murdered his parents centuries ago on Earth. His protector, the toughest and most resourceful man he had ever known, seemed to have given up hope. Alex knew that Vance's inability to do anything to prevent this unparalleled disaster was at the root of his deep depression. He was completely demoralized by the fact that all of his people—all of the life he had planted, nurtured, and loved over many centuries—were going to be destroyed. Alex realized it was almost more than the heroic man could bear.

Lara too could see the change in demeanor of her beloved husband. In the years she'd been with him, he'd never displayed the dark mood he was in now, not even when the comet was causing vast damage on Gabriel. Her empathy and compassion for him overpowered the fear of all else around her. Her heart was breaking for him.

Dale had directed almost all available instruments, sensors, and telescopes to be mounted aboard the available spacecraft and satellites to monitor the oncoming GRB. He kept a few trained on the comet Yassi. Some technicians questioned the need to maintain surveillance of the comet, arguing that the data would be irrelevant, but Dale insisted they continue transmitting all data to him, the Yassi, and the Vout. "We may not have any use for the data, but the Yassi and Vout surely will." He did not say anything to anybody about what he was thinking. His speculation was simply too farfetched to make public. He was the only one who was interested in the where and when of the comet.

His continuing calculations indicated that the comet's orbit would, at some time in the near future, cross directly between the merged binaries and Gabriel. His calculations determined that the comet's size and mass, in the right place and time, would be sufficient to block the entire GRB from hitting Gabriel. The data now indicated that somehow, the comet would be within minutes of providing a shield for Gabriel.

He continually and feverishly checked the data coming in from the three locations. The pressure on his Isleium mind was enormous.

He could virtually feel the fierce pounding of a heart he didn't have. The random chance of an unusually large comet traveling at an unusually fast speed intercepting a GRB at precisely the right moment was zero.

Dale's magnificent brain suddenly went blank and stayed that way for two full minutes, overwhelmed with continuing data—impossible data—and then it all became crystal clear.

Holy shit! his mind screamed.

Had Dale been a human, he might have had a small breakdown from the shock of what had just become obvious. He quickly looked at Vance, who was sitting forlornly in the captain's chair. The likelihood that all was lost was dragging this tough man down hard. Dale had never seen him like this. Standing alongside the captain's chair was Lara. She hadn't left his side for a moment since they'd arrived on the *Norman*. Her demeanor wasn't much different from his. She was continually wiping tears from her eyes. Dale knew her tears weren't from fear of her impending death or the destruction of Gabriel but, rather, from sorrow, compassion, and empathy for her beloved husband.

It was difficult for Dale to maintain a level voice as he appeared on the viewer. "Vance, a private word, please."

Dale could see a slight puzzlement on Vance's face as he looked at the viewer, but he nodded once as he rose from the captain's chair and slowly walked toward his ready room. His actions looked to Dale like the halting movements of an old man. As Vance approached his ready room, the door slid open. After he entered, the door automatically slid shut as he walked over and slowly sat down at his desk. Dale's image disappeared from the main viewer and reappeared in front of Vance.

"What's up?"

"Gabriel is not going to be hit."

"What?" Vance asked quietly, clearly not grasping what Dale had just told him.

"I've been watching the orbit of the comet. It's going to be in position to shield Gabriel. Probably completely."

"What?"

Dale smiled. "We have somehow become, for lack of a better expression, the chosen people."

"What?" Vance repeated for the third time.

It was clear to Dale this was another incidence of Vance's Isleium brain locking up. Dale knew the only time that had happened to Vance had been twenty-one years ago, when he'd spotted Lara for the first time on his island, but this time was different for a myriad of reasons. There was no way the information Dale had just told him could be real. It was an impossible scenario. His mind could not process it.

Dale quickly recognized the problem because he had just been through a similar occurrence. "Vance, relax for a moment. Clear your mind as best as you can. Let me know when everything starts working."

Ten seconds passed before Vance blinked rapidly. After another few seconds of sitting motionless, he blinked again. Then he cocked his head a little as he looked at the viewer.

"You okay?" asked Dale.

Vance shot up to a standing position. "Are you shittin' me?" he yelled.

"I would never," said Dale indignantly. "Not about this."

Vance said nothing for two seconds and then replied, "No, no, you wouldn't. Sorry." He sat back down hard. His demeanor changed to cautious optimism. "How do you know we're not going to be destroyed?"

"I'm not a spiritual man and never have been, but I tell you without reservation that this comet has been sent to protect us from destruction. There is no doubt in my mind."

Dale smiled as he watched Vance's facial expression turn from that of a man about to lose his life and everything he loved to that of one whose entire world had been snatched from the grasp of death.

He could barely choke out, "You have all the data proving this?"

"I do not."

"Then how—"

"Because it could not be anything else. There is zero chance that a huge comet traveling at ten times the speed of any other known comet would have a chance in hell of being anywhere near the sector of space that is involved, let alone being within seconds of being in the exact right place at the right distance and at the exact right time. The only conclusion I can draw is that it is being directed by something far, far above our own intelligence. So taking all of that into consideration, I concluded that it will, in fact, shield us from the GRB."

"No doubt?"

"None whatsoever. As a matter of fact, I would go so far as to recommend that you turn these ships around and head back to Gabriel."

"I—"

"Vance, you should know that I would never, under any circumstances, state something like this without being absolutely certain."

A look of acceptance crossed Vance's face. The ensuing relief caused Vance to break down a little. He put his face in his hands and kept repeating, "Oh my God, oh my God, oh my God."

After ten seconds or so, Vance stopped and looked up at a smiling Dale. "I will never be able to thank you enough."

"I did nothing," said Dale. "I'm just reporting the facts, which would have become apparent to all of us in less than an hour."

"I desperately needed those facts, my dear, dear friend. I have never been so low."

"Well, you're welcome. Now I think you ought to get your ass up, go out to the bridge, and inform the human race that we will not be destroyed. There are tens of thousands of our people who believe they are about to die."

"I believe you should have the honor of doing that."

"No, sir. You are our leader, and you are just about everything to us. You must be the one to give this extraordinary news."

As Vance walked back into the bridge, he knew all eyes were on him. As he walked toward the captain's chair, he could see their facial expressions go from deep depression to cautious curiosity. His step had regained its spring, and his expression was notably encouraging. The two dozen faces on the bridge started to display a smidgen of hope. Lara's face displayed the most curiosity; her brow was furrowed, and her head was slightly cocked.

Teddy's expressive face displayed a myriad of emotions as he watched Vance walk with a spring in his step.

Vance took his place in the captain's chair. "Dale, put me on the intership public-address system and all viewers on the planet, if you please."

"I please." Dale smiled. "You're on."

Vance smiled broadly, and everybody on the planet, the *Marian*, the *Norman*, and the shuttles and runabouts saw it.

"Citizens of Gabriel, our dear friend Councillor Dr. Dale Isley has just informed me that our beloved planet—" Vance paused for a moment to collect himself. "Our beloved planet will not—I repeat, will not—be hit by the gamma-ray burst. It seems—"

The screams of joy and cries of relief drowned out whatever Vance was going to say and continued unabated. Vance understood and quickly stood to give Lara a huge hug and kiss. Then he joined in the celebration on the bridge. He knew the same reaction would be going on everywhere. The details of this miracle could wait for another time. Vance looked over to Teddy and his family and laughed. Teddy's expression of relief was priceless as he hugged and kissed Colleen and his young children.

Everybody's eyes were on the viewers. All of the instruments and telescopes that had been trained on the Yassi comet and the binary stars were now pointing to the same exact coordinates of space. The comet that had caused widespread damage and hardships on Gabriel four years ago was now to be its savior. How could that be?

The comet was not visible to the naked eye but was crystal clear to the hundreds of telescopes and cameras trained on it.

Vance had risen from the captain's chair and was now standing close to Lara, holding her hand. The large viewer on the opposite wall displayed the comet and its massive tail against pitch-black space. It was 2:48 when the GRB hit the comet straight on, as Dale had predicted. Where the comet was, a red dot began expanding at nearly the speed of light and, in a second, became visible to the naked eye. The enormous tail, now leading as it headed away from the sun, reflected the red glow in spectacular waves and flashes. After a few moments, the center of the red glow turned a striking orange and continued expanding. This went on for thirty seconds before an emerald-green color briefly took its turn in the center, leaving just a thin ring of green before a bright sky-blue color appeared in the center. Nobody wanted to blink. Nobody wanted to miss a second of the phenomenon. Even at that distance, the vision already appeared to be the size of a saucer held at arm's length, and it continued to grow. The center became black as the outer rings continued to expand rapidly. It was the most beautiful sight anyone had ever seen.

Within a minute and a half, the phenomenon had spread to encompass a quarter of the night sky, and then it began to fade. In two hours, it would be invisible to the naked eye.

CHAPTER 10

THE RETURN HOME
MO-FIVE 1, 121

Vance and Lara stood as the *Norman* approached its landing spot in Home-Bay. The viewer was focused on the thousands of people surrounding the traditional landing site. *There my people are,* Vance thought with a joy he had never experienced before. He looked over at Lara and squeezed her hand. She had tears in her eyes. He quickly looked around at his friends and loved ones on the bridge. There wasn't a dry eye among them. Teddy was standing next to Colleen; their children stood in front of them. They were just a couple of meters off to Vance's right. Vance's smile got even bigger when he looked at Teddy's expressive face. *That's what joy looks like.*

The *Norman* came down first and settled onto its traditional spot. The cheering of the crowd was remarkable in its enthusiasm and scope. Within minutes, the massive *Marian* dropped out of orbit and majestically settled onto its permanent spot on the south side of the gazebo park. The cheering crowd got even louder. To say it was a jubilant occasion would not have done justice to the mood of the Gabrielites. All of the remaining ships flew slowly in a V formation over Home-Bay to the cheers, clapping, whistling, and wooing of the crowd, and then the V split up and sped up as the ships headed for their place of origin to join the celebration with their loved ones.

The single large access ramp dropped down from the belly of the *Norman*, and five separate ramps lowered from the *Marian's* five interconnected spheres. Within seconds, the area around the ramps filled with hundreds of people welcoming home their lifelong friends and families. People were laughing, crying, or doing both at the same time. They had been separated for less than ten hours, but ten hours earlier, they'd been sure they would never see each other again.

After the landing, a few citizens headed back to their homes to care for pets and livestock. The vast majority stayed and continued celebrating at the impromptu gathering at the gazebo park in front of the *Norman*'s cave.

There were more than ten thousand people in and around the park, and more were arriving by the minute. Those who had stayed behind continued to mix with the evacuees, hugging and kissing just about everybody.

The last to leave the *Norman* were Vance and Lara. They walked down the ramp hand in hand while smiling brightly. The crowd quickly spotted them, and resounding cheers and applause went up, continuing for a full minute until Vance stopped and raised his hand with the palm forward. He held it there until the din subsided to a dull roar. Then, without a word, he and Lara joined the celebrants.

An aging John Carlon, who had remained on the planet inside the *Norman*'s cave, opened his pub to all. He had all the beer and other libations from his storage room placed in strategic spots around the park and gazebo.

The celebration went on for three days. From time to time, the celebrants would become exhausted and head home for a few hours' sleep before rejoining the festivities. It was a joyous time that would surely be a major part of Gabriel's history.

MO-FIVE 5, 121

Four days after the return to Gabriel, Vance was again in his captain's chair, and his demeanor was that of a man who was undeniably jubilant. Standing to his right was Lara, whose beautiful face glowed with serenity. Behind Vance stood Troy, smiling widely. Superimposed to Vance's left were the holograms of Alex and Dale, both clearly in tune with the others. This image was being broadcast throughout the planet.

Vance said, "Sitting here in this chair on this ship, on our beautiful, safe, and flourishing planet, is an indescribable joy I share with all of you." He paused for a moment, looked at Lara, and then turned to Troy, all the while maintaining a big smile. "We have made a decision that we're sure everybody will agree with. We believe that the date of Mo-Four 4, 121, the date that one celestial body intervened with another celestial body to save our world from total destruction, should become an annual Day of Thanksgiving, a day of sincere gratitude and appreciation for whomever or whatever saved our planet." Vance again paused briefly. "And a holiday to celebrate the continued existence of Gabriel."

An hour after Vance's address to the population of Gabriel, Dale made an observation. "That's odd," he said.

"What's that?" asked Alex.

"One of our satellites just picked up something in low orbit over northwestern Vast."

"Orbit?"

"Wait. It's gone."

"Big bird?" said Alex.

"I don't believe we have any birds with a twenty-meter wing span capable of flying to an altitude of one hundred twenty kilometers."

Alex nodded. "A glitch?"

"I don't like glitches."

Twenty-six minutes later, Dale said, "It's back." Thirty seconds later, he said, "It's gone again."

MO-ONE 16, 122

"It's going to be interesting when the Yassi arrive later today," Vance said to Lara while helping her make the bed.

"Can I sit in on the meetings?"

"I think we can come up with another chair."

Vance was a little surprised that the Yassi seemed slightly subdued when they exited their shuttle, particularly considering the welcome of thousands of Gabrielites who were anything but subdued; they were quite the opposite, in fact.

Exiting last from the Yassi shuttle was brightly smiling Gary. When the crowd spotted him, they gave a rousing round of applause, whistles, and woos.

Troy had his friend's back.

When the Yassi entered the meeting room, they were fully aware of what had happened. Their instruments and telescopes had recorded the miraculous event. During their trip to Gabriel, they'd remained in constant contact with Dale and a dozen other of Gabriel's scientists. All were trying to make sense of what had occurred. None could get past the obvious: an intelligent power they could not envision, let alone calculate, was responsible. But why would any such entity use its immeasurable power to save a small planet?

Sitting at a large boardroom-style table in the *Marian*'s conference room were the captain of the Yassi ship, four Yassi scientists, Vance, Troy, Gary, and Ian Henderson. Lara sat on a chair just behind and to the right of Vance. On the large viewer on the far wall were the images of Dale and Alex.

Henderson was a happy man. His belief in the existence of superior beings had been all but proven. His theories, along with the undeniable fact that superior beings must exist, were the talk of at least three planets.

But now they faced several questions: Who or what were the superior beings? Where did they live? How old was their civilization? Why did they save Gabriel?

"We," said the Yassi captain, Roun, "could not imagine such power existing in the galaxy. We can't even begin to comprehend such an advanced intelligence."

"We're all of the same mind here," said Dale.

Roun nodded and continued. "We have, in our past, deflected three small oncoming asteroids and one small comet, thus saving our planet from considerable damage. But that amounts to less than an amusement of the young compared to what has happened here. Guiding a massive comet—causing it to increase its speed, alter its orbit, and be in the precise place in the galaxy at the precise time needed to block the GRB—is far beyond our ability to comprehend."

"If it's beyond your ability, it's certainly beyond ours," said Gary.

Roun nodded in understanding.

"And they had to know, to a millisecond, when the GRB would occur," added Dale. "And they had to have that information at least fifteen years ahead of time. That technology alone is beyond comprehension."

Nobody said anything for a few seconds. Then Alex spoke.

"There are many who believe a god or gods sent the comet. Many believe it was a superior race of beings, and many now believe they could be one and the same."

"We can't argue against any of those theories. All are speculation, but none can be ruled out," said Roun.

"Agreed," said Dale.

Roun smiled. "We also agree that whoever or whatever saved Gabriel thinks very highly of either the human race or the humans on this planet."

"Or just the planet itself," said Dale.

"Another possibility," agreed Roun.

"I'd rather believe the former rather than the latter," said Alex with a smile.

The Yassi liked that one and laughed.

"We can't understand any of this, and maybe we never will," said Vance.

Dale looked pensive for a moment. "I wonder if this action on their part took a great deal of their resources and a great deal of planning or if it was an afterthought or maybe just something to do for amusement."

"That is an interesting thought," said Vance. "A scary one."

MO-TWO 14, 122

Alex's image appeared on Vance and Lara's viewer. "Anybody home?"

After a few seconds, Vance and Lara walked into view.

"We are," Vance responded. "What's up?"

"You're not going to believe this," said Alex with a facial expression that all but said he didn't believe what he was about to relate.

"What's that?" asked Vance.

"We just got a communique from the Malic."

"We did not," said Vance with some humor.

"We did, and what's more surprising is that the gist of the communique is that the Malic wish to welcome the Byuse back to their planet."

That surprised Vance. "Welcome the Byuse back?"

"Yes, and they would like us to present the proposition to the Yassi."

"That doesn't make sense."

"I agree. Why wouldn't they just go directly to the Yassi?"

Vance shook his head as if to clear it. "You have their proposal?"

"I do. It's complete, detailed, and rational and seems to be well thought out."

"Well thought out?"

"I know—that doesn't sound like the Malic."

Vance smiled. "Could this be an interstellar joke of some kind?"

"That would probably make more sense."

"I believe we should treat this with some caution. Maybe an intelligent life-form is behind this? Maybe setting a trap."

"Agreed. They have enclosed a picture of three of them that I think you'll find interesting."

"Really? If I looked like the Malic, I wouldn't be showing pictures."

"Take a look." Alex sent the picture to Vance's viewer.

"Oh my God." Vance was caught off guard. He quickly sat forward on the couch.

"Those aren't the beings I've seen pictures of," said Lara. "These are kind of cute."

"Sure not the beings that killed twenty-three of us. At least that's not what they looked like back then."

The image on the viewer bore little resemblance to the Malic who'd attacked the *Marian* and Gabriel. Either the Malic were trying to pull a fast one by substituting beings of a different species, or they had managed to, in just three or four generations, nearly completely change their appearance through selective breeding, gene manipulation, or both. All possibilities seemed way beyond their known mental capabilities.

The viewer displayed a picture of a male, female, and child. They were dressed in nice-looking clothes and had noses instead of just two holes in a flat face. Their eyes were still black but weren't as cold as they had been in the past. Their hair wasn't rusty red but dark blond, closely cropped, and confined to their heads. Their heads also had ears of a sort; they were small but distinct. There was no sign of the long, protruding canine teeth they'd been so proud of in the past.

"That physical change can't be possible in three or four generations—can it?" asked Lara.

Dale came into the conversation. "It's been sixty-eight years since their attack on us. The four we had here were returned to Byuse sixty years ago. Considering their gestation period is just under five months and they mature at about twelve years, that would easily give them five generations. If—and this is a big if—they worked out a program designed to completely change in both physicality and mentality, it may be possible to accomplish what we're looking at."

"That would be astonishing," said Vance. "I wouldn't give them credit for that much planning and forethought."

"Nor would I," said Dale. "But if they had just a few smart ones and those gained control of the populous, it might be possible to lead that stupid, savage race to a different path."

"Hmm," said Vance. "Why don't we ask the Malic for a few details? If they are sincere about becoming responsible citizens of the galaxy, then they should have no qualms about telling us how they managed to change their appearance, intellect, and attitude."

"That's a good idea. In the meantime, I'm going to transmit their proposal to the Yassi and Byuse on New Mahyu. I'm certain they will find it even more interesting than we do."

Vance smiled. "Wait until I get to the bridge before you send it. I want to see their faces when they read the proposal."

"Okay."

Vance looked over at Lara. "Want to take a walk?"

"Sure. This will be interesting."

Twenty minutes later, Vance and Lara walked onto the bridge of the *Norman*. Vance was in an excellent mood.

"Are we ready to give our friends the news?"

"They're waiting. We have their communication chiefs, along with the leadership of all three races."

"Good. The Vout will have a great interest in this proposal."

"Are you ready?" asked Alex.

"Let's see them."

The large viewer on the *Norman*'s bridge came to life. In split screen were the Yassi, Byuse, and Vout.

"We have some interesting news," said Alex.

CHAPTER 11

MUTATIONS
MO-THREE 18, 122

Vance and Lara were sitting on the trunk of a fallen tree at the edge of a clearing, watching a band of gorillas forage along a tree line some sixty meters away. Hiking around their island to watch gorillas was one of Vance and Lara's favorite pastimes. Seeing the young ones and babies was particularly enjoyable for Lara, but the adult silverbacks were more to Vance's interests. The gorillas on the island were used to Vance and Lara and rarely paid them much attention. Occasionally, they would approach within a few meters and sit as if the two people weren't there.

Dale's voice came over the communicator. "Vance, are you available?"

Vance took his communicator out of his shirt pocket. "We're out enjoying the gorillas. What's up?"

"Well, it seems the comet did not completely block the GRB, as first thought."

Vance stood quickly. "What?"

"Apparently, a razor-thin slice of the powerful ray just nicked the northwestern edge of the Vast Continent, just at the horizon."

"Damage?"

"Not too much as far as we know now. It might not have been detected at all had two young men from a small wildlife observation colony not decided to do some fishing. Apparently, as they pulled their small boat across the sand to the ocean, they came across hundreds of dead fish that had washed ashore. They quickly reported their discovery to Home-Bay. I sent a team to investigate."

"Okay, keep me informed." Vance put his communicator away.

The GRB had dealt a glancing blow right where the continent met the ocean. It had hit at an acute angle, causing it to pass through a great deal of Gabriel's ozone layer before reaching the planet. The ozone had managed to absorb a good percentage of the burst but not all of it. There was enough radiation left to do a great deal of damage. Dale's team found not only dead fish but also dozens of dead or dying small coastal animals. Most of the dead were nocturnal and had been out in the open when the GRB hit in the dark of night. The few that somehow had lived through the GRB were horribly burned and maimed. The team now had the unpleasant duty of destroying all such animals they could find. The animals in the area that had survived were diurnal and spent their nights in underground burrows or caves. Unfortunately, after further tests, they determined that if the GRB had hit at the moment of or within a week of conception, the burrow and cave dwellers had a high percentage of mutations or outright death of their offspring.

On the night of the GRB, the small observation community, including the young fishermen, had taken shelter in the deepest of the dozens of small natural caves the assault of the ocean had carved into a cliff face over the ages. Unfortunately, the walls and ceilings of the caves didn't have the high gold content that the man-made caves in other parts of the planet had, and consequently, their protection from the GRB would have been marginal. They might have, in fact, been exposed to a nonlethal dose of gamma rays.

Vance had just walked onto the bridge of the *Norman*, when a call came in from Home-Bay's head of the OB-GYN clinic, Dr. Jen Aidery.

"Sir," she said, "first, before I start, may we have Dr. Isley and Alex Gabriel in on this conversation?"

"Of course. Dale, Alex," he said, and the two holographic men appeared. "Dr. Jen asks that you two be in on whatever she is going to tell me."

"Good morning, Jen," said Alex.

"Good morning, sir."

"How are you today?" asked Dale.

Jen paused a beat before answering. "Been better, sir."

"What's up?" asked Vance.

"Two days ago, I was called by John Hendrick, head of the observation colony in northwestern Vast. He asked me to come to their colony concerning a recent birth. It was an unusual request, so I knew he had a valid reason to call me. I arrived here yesterday."

"And what did you find?"

"We have a situation with two new births here."

"Uh-oh," said Vance. His mind instantly shot back to the date of the GRB; he did the math. It was just shy of nine months after the GRB.

"What sort of situation?" asked Dale.

"Mutations."

"Oh no," said Vance.

"Yes, sir, I'm afraid so."

"How are the mothers doing?"

"They're fine—no physical problems at all."

"That tells me there may be emotional problems."

"That's certainly possible, yes, sir." Jen continued her report. "I probably wouldn't have said anything or been too alarmed had it been just the one baby, but last evening, I assisted in the birth of the second, and she has mutations."

Vance said nothing for a moment. "What are the conditions of the babies?"

"Their conditions are fine. They're very healthy, in fact."

"But?"

"They both are not quite—" Jen stopped, clearly trying to find the right words to describe the infants. "I was going to say they're not quite human, but that would be incorrect. They are, of course, human. But they're different."

"Different?"

"Their bodies are a normal size, but their heads are bigger by just shy of fourteen percent. Their hearts are also a good deal larger than normal, and their blood pressure is correspondingly high. Their eyes are very large." Jen paused for a moment. "And their fingers are longer than normal."

"Both have the same mutations?" asked Dale.

"Yes, sir, nearly identical as far as we can tell at this moment."

"That doesn't make sense," said Alex.

"No, it doesn't. Not even a little," agreed Dale.

"Who are the parents?" asked Vance.

The young ob-gyn smiled a little. "The one who had the boy is your second clone's granddaughter, Amelia. Obviously, she is the same relation to you."

Vance smiled. "I know her well. How is she holding up, considering?"

"She has the Youngblood toughness; she's handling it."

"She's a strong woman both mentally and physically."

"Yes, sir."

"The other?"

"Clair. She had the baby girl."

"I believe she has about the same relation to Alex as Amelia has to me."

"Just one more generation," Jen said.

"Yes, that's right. Pretty young woman. How's she doing?"

"Not quite as well. She has a great strength of character also; she's just a little higher strung."

"The fathers?"

"The two young men who came across the dead fish. Charlie is Amelia's husband, and Sonny is Clair's. I have a little more information," said Jen, "not that it will answer this puzzle."

"What's that?"

Dr. Jen seemed a little embarrassed but continued her report. "Apparently, both couples, after hearing the GRB would not hit Gabriel, decided to have a celebratory roll in the hay, as they say."

"Not out in the open, I hope!" exclaimed Vance.

"Oh no, sir. They were in separate caves—by themselves at the time."

Vance rolled his eyes a little. "Okay, good."

"As close as I can calculate, the GRB must have hit within hours of conception."

"That still—" Dale paused in thought for a moment. "That possibly explains mutations but doesn't explain identical mutations."

"That's my thought too, sir."

"Can we see the infants?" asked Alex.

"Yes, sir. Just give me a second."

Jen stood, walked out of view for a few moments, and then returned, pushing a bassinet made of clear acrylic. She lifted the head end of the bassinet to an angle that allowed the viewers to clearly see the babies lying side by side on a soft cushion.

"Oh my," said Alex.

"This is interesting," said Dale.

"Holy crap," added Vance.

There on the viewer were the two babies, and they were different. It wasn't that their entire heads were bigger. Their faces were normal sized, but their craniums were noticeably larger—not huge or grotesque, but the difference was apparent nonetheless. Their eyes were significantly larger. The infant girl's were a striking blue, the same color as Alex's, the result of a recessive gene that went back at least four generations. In addition, she had fine white hair no more than a millimeter long, whereas the boy had dark eyes and dark hair that was a great deal longer and thicker.

"The boy has your coloring, sir," Jen remarked to Vance.

"And the girl has mine," said Alex.

"Interesting," Dale said. "I'm pulling up their parents' DNA. Jen, get the babies' DNA."

"Yes, sir."

Both babies had their eyes open and were looking directly into the viewer.

"Are they looking at us?" asked Vance.

"Normally, I would say no, as they are too young to see anything but shades of light and movement, but these two seem to be able to actually follow movement quite well. More like infants at a month or more."

"Interesting," said Dale.

"The clarity of their eyes is also unusual. Babies' eyes are usually clouded for a couple of months to the point that sometimes it's hard to tell what color they are going to be. It's especially true of light eyes, but it's not so with these two."

"Interesting," said Dale again.

"How are the parents reacting?"

"Confused and anxious, I would say," answered Jen. "But they are not rejecting these babies. Both mothers expressed a desire to nurse."

"Good."

"Is there any reason not to let these youngsters be raised in a normal manner?" asked Alex.

"At this point, no, sir."

"Jen, I would like you to put together a protocol for the parents to monitor these two on a weekly basis, if not daily," said Dale. "I want to know everything about them as they grow."

"Yes, sir," said Jen. "Height, weight, coordination, and strength."

"And mental acuity," added Dale. "That's the most important— mental acuity."

"Yes, sir. I'll put together a protocol and run it by you for any additions or changes."

Dale was pensive for a moment before saying, "Thank you."

"Tell the parents I plan on being there tomorrow morning and would like to spend a little time with them," said Vance.

Jen smiled brightly. "Yes, sir, I'll do that. They'll be pleased."

"Thank you for your report, Jen. Let us know if anything unusual comes up."

"Yes, sir."

With that, the connection was broken.

Vance and Alex looked at Dale. Alex spoke first.

"What do you think of all this?"

"It's the fact that they both have the same mutations that bothers me. The odds of that happening are astronomical." Dale paused for a moment. "Just like so much that has been happening around this planet for the past few years."

"You think there is a rat in the crackers here?" asked Vance.

"I don't think it's a rat," answered Dale. "Certainly not a rat."

Alex said nothing but was paying close attention.

Dale turned to Alex. "Other than your clones, I haven't seen your unique eye color come up in any generations."

"It's a recessive gene for sure."

"It will be interesting to see if she gets your olive complexion when she's exposed to the sun."

"The boy seems to have my coloring," said Vance.

"Yes, he does."

"Could it be possible it was another entity, not the GRB, that created the mutations? Maybe using the GRB as a cover?" asked Vance.

"That, my dear friend, is an interesting question," said Dale. "That could explain the identical mutations."

"It could, but it certainly opens up a lot more questions. Maybe even more disturbing questions."

"Yes, it could. Hold on," said Dale. "Getting the DNA from Jen. Give me a minute or two."

No one said anything while Dale studied the DNA now uploaded into the ship's computer.

After a minute or so, Dale turned to the others. "Well, the mutation is clear in both babies, and they are identical. The DNA of each contains hundreds of additional base pairs."

"Whoa," said Vance. "How many base pairs are there normally?"

"Just over three billion."

"Oh."

"I've never seen this arrangement of chromosomes," Dale said. "This is interesting. Both Sonny's and Clair's DNA are a close match to yours, Vance. That makes them a very close match to each other. Subsequently, their offspring's DNA is even closer to yours."

"Really?"

"Yes, sir." Dale continued to study the DNA records. After another minute, he looked at Alex. "By golly, the same is true of Charlie's and Amelia's DNA in relation to yours, Alex. So again, the baby girl's DNA is close to yours. The effect is nearly the same as a mating between a brother and sister."

"That's an unpleasant thought," said Vance.

Dale smiled. "Not incest, sir. There are probably many people on this planet who have closely related genes. Yours, Alex's, Jason Gould's, Teddy's, and, to a lesser extent, mine have always been somewhat more desirable than an unknown's. A slightly higher percentage of couples have been choosing to breed with either our clones or offspring of our clones. There has been no harm in it up to this point."

"Should we be curtailing such a practice for the future?"

"Not really, no."

"Would the effect on the DNA in this case be like the mating of distant cousins?" asked Alex.

Dale nodded. "Yes, and clearly, in this case, the DNA merged to that of distant relatives, namely you and Vance."

"Well, that more or less explains the coloring but not the mutations."

Dale's face showed some reservation.

"Dale?" said Alex.

"It's just that there are too many coincidences, and I'm not a big believer in coincidences."

The three said nothing for the next few moments. Then Alex said, "Vance, I recommend you take Teddy with you tomorrow."

Vance's brow furrowed for a moment before he smiled. "Got ya."

Midmorning of the following day, Vance, with Teddy in the copilot's seat, arrived over the community located in the northwest corner of the Vast Continent. Before setting the runabout down, they flew a slow circle around the area. From altitude, they could see the four beautifully designed log-and-stone homes and a larger building a hundred meters to their east. The homes sat more or less in a row about fifty meters apart on the western edge of a large, grassy field. The field ran along the top of a cliff that looked to be eighty to a hundred meters in height. All of the homes were within thirty meters of the cliff, which provided them with a spectacular view of the ocean. The open field extended back about half a kilometer east of the homes and ended at a thick forest made up of pines and firs, along with a smattering of hardwoods.

A large creek flowed out of the forest and meandered through the field before becoming a waterfall that flowed over the cliff and into the ocean ninety meters below, just to the south of the homes. From their altitude, Vance and Teddy could see that the field was divided into eight separate pastures by high-tech electric fences. The pastures were divided in such a way that the creek ran through each one.

Very nice, thought Vance. The setup reminded him of what had been done with the rolling hills south of Home-Bay many centuries ago. Three of the pastures held domesticated animals for food, and one held horses, which were used for transportation into the forests and plains beyond. The other four pastures were designated for studying and treating various wild animals.

Vance set the runabout gently down on the designated space, and within a minute, the two exited the craft.

Three men, including Charlie and Sonny, the young fathers of the unusual babies, greeted them.

"Welcome back to our little part of the planet, sir," the older man said as he held out his hand.

Vance shook his hand. "John, it's nice to see you again. As you can see, I brought my old friend Teddy with me."

"Teddy is always welcome here—and, I suspect, anywhere on the planet." John held out his hand to shake Teddy's but got a hug instead.

"Great to see you again, John," Teddy said with a bright smile.

Vance looked at the young men. "And here are the proud fathers of the newborns."

The two young men stepped forward. Both wore half smiles on their faces. Vance observed that they were a little uncomfortable and anxious.

Vance shook hands with the closest. He had Alex's blond hair and complexion. His eyes were blue but not the color of Alex's. "Sonny, you have grown some since I last saw you."

"Yes, sir, it's been a few years."

Vance turned to the other young man. "And, Charlie," he said as he took his hand, "you've filled out."

Charlie was a little more relaxed than his best friend and smiled broadly. "My wife is a good cook. Spoils me, I'm afraid. That and I've got a lot of Youngblood genes in me," he said with some pride.

Vance smiled. "I have those genes and a wife who spoils me too. We're lucky men."

Charlie's smile got bigger. "Yes, sir, we are."

"I don't believe you two have ever met my dear friend Teddy."

"No, sir, we haven't, but we have seen all of his performances."

It was clear the two young men were delighted to meet Teddy. Other than Alex, Dale, and Vance, Teddy was the most famous person on the planet.

Teddy didn't wait for further introductions. He first grabbed Sonny and gave him a warm hug. "Great to meet you, Sonny." Then he did the same to Charlie.

And the everlasting link is made, thought Vance, smiling inwardly.

"I can't wait to see the expressions on the girls' faces when they see who's here," said Sonny.

Vance looked around. "The area looks beautiful. You folks are doing a great job."

"It's shaping up, yes, sir."

Vance nodded in appreciation and then made an exaggerated gesture of sniffing the air. "Smells like Home-Bay."

"Different ocean, same smell," John said.

"Why don't we head over to my place?" said Sonny. "Dr. Jen, both our wives, and the babies are there. And John's wife too."

"Great. Lead the way."

As the four men entered Sonny's home, the four women stood up to greet Vance. Vance had known them all their lives.

The women's eyes immediately shifted to Teddy.

"Oh my God, it's Teddy!" John's wife, Mako, exclaimed, nearly screaming. The two younger women quickly joined her in expressing their surprise and glee.

Vance laughed. "I always lose my audience when Teddy is around."

Vance turned to Mako. She had been one of his favorites since she was a little girl. She was small and delicate, which was unusual for a Gabrielite, but she had a delightful personality, quick wit, and infectious laugh.

"Mako, it's wonderful to see you again." Vance took her by the waist and lifted her high above his head, as he had many times when she was a youngster. She laughed joyously, as did Vance and the others in the room. That simple act took much of the tension out of the situation. Vance set Mako back down and gave her a gentle hug. She hugged him back.

"I forgot how big around you are," she said with a smile.

"I haven't changed a bit," he kidded.

"Not for a very long time, I think."

Then Teddy began doing his thing. "Hey, Mako," he said to his old friend before he put his arms around her waist, hugged her, spun her, and gave her a kiss right on the lips. She giggled and kissed him back.

"Hey!" said John in mock shock.

Vance smiled as he walked over and hugged Sonny's wife, Clair. "Hi, kid. How are you holding up?"

"Not too bad, sir, considering."

After the greetings and Teddy making everybody laugh, the tension in the room dissipated. It was the first time anyone had seen Amelia smile since the birth of her son.

"We appreciate you coming all this way," said John.

"It isn't a problem. We're anxious to see the babies," said Vance.

"Yes, sir," said both mothers at the same time.

"They're in the next room," said Jen. "This way."

Vance and Teddy followed the young doctor, and everyone else trailed behind.

The sun shone through the large windows on the east side of the room and onto the two bassinets. Both had shaded tops that kept the sun off of the infants. Vance walked to the first one, the one with the blue blanket. "May I pick him up?"

"Sure," said Charlie.

Vance reached down and carefully slipped one hand under the baby's head and the other under his bottom. He lifted the infant up and put him to his chest with the baby's head just under his chin. "What's his name?"

"Shem," said Amelia.

"Shem?"

"Noah's first son. We found the name in the old Bible. Thought it might be appropriate. Firstborn after the flood of radiation."

Vance nodded in approval. "Well, it's a nice name. Shem it is." He moved the baby to arm's length, taking care to support the head, and smiled.

Shem seemed to look intently at Vance for several seconds. Then he smiled.

"He likes me—or he has gas," said a smiling Vance.

"Gas, I'm guessing," said Teddy with a serious face.

Everybody laughed again.

"That's the first time I've seen him smile," said Jen.

"Me too," said Charlie.

Amelia nodded once in agreement. Her face clearly displayed that she was uncomfortable with the situation and somewhat edgy.

"Well, I'm flattered." Vance pulled him back to his chest. "Does he act any different from other babies his age?"

"More alert maybe," said Charlie. "Doesn't cry—never once."

"That's abnormal for a baby his age," said Jen. "One might

assume he is somehow mentally deficient. I've read about cases of such abnormalities on old Earth. We've never had one here on Gabriel."

"Are you saying that Shem is disabled mentally?" asked an alarmed Amelia.

"Oh, hell no, not Shem," Jen quickly answered. "Quite the contrary. As far as I can tell, Shem's all there and then some in the brains department."

"Oh, okay. You scared me for a second."

"I'm sorry. I could have phrased that better," Jen said.

"I'm a bit sensitive right now, with his malformed head and all." Amelia paused for a second and watched Vance rock her son against his chest.

"I don't see a malformed head," said Jen. "A large head to be sure, but it's well formed."

"That's what I meant, I guess."

"There's a big difference," responded Jen.

Amelia nodded. "Shem doesn't cry, but he fusses when he's hungry, almost like he's angry. Kinda wish he would—" She quickly looked down and away in a failed attempt to hide her emotions from the others. It didn't take a great deal of empathy to see Amelia was deeply troubled by the condition of her baby.

"Not crying may not be normal, but it might be a blessing," Vance said, trying to make light of the situation. "And I might add that he takes much of his looks from my side of the family."

"He really does," agreed Jen.

"Handsome little guy," Vance added.

Everybody laughed.

"May I?" asked Teddy as he held out his arms.

Vance gently put Shem in Teddy's arms and stood back a pace.

Teddy brought the infant to his chest and rocked him back and forth for a full minute before bringing the baby up to his vision, and the two locked eyes. "Hi, Shem. I am so happy to meet you."

Shem immediately smiled again.

Everybody's eyes were glued to the two.

"Oh my. This youngster has a whopping spirit. I can feel it," Teddy said seriously as he brought Shem back to his chest and continued to rock him for a moment. He lifted him back to eye level and looked at Vance. "I sure sense a lot of you in this boy," he said. He looked back at Shem. "Let's have your old grandpa hold you again for a sec while I meet your friend." Teddy gently placed Shem back in Vance's arms, paused for a few seconds to study him, and then turned toward the other bassinet.

Vance smothered Shem between his massive arms and chest.

Teddy picked up the baby girl. "She's a lightweight."

"Yes, she's nearly a kilo less than Shem," Sonny said.

"What's her name?"

"Jarleth," Sonny replied.

"Nice. Unusual." Teddy looked down into the baby's startling blue eyes. "She is beautiful. Wow."

"You think so?" asked Clair. She flashed surprise at Teddy's compliment.

"No, I don't think so. Heck, just look at her. She's a stunner."

Tears began to flow from Clair's eyes. "But she's abnormal."

"Abnormal? Other than a slightly larger head, I don't see any difference between her and another baby girl, other than she's far prettier than most. As a matter of fact, I believe she's going to be competition for my wife in the looks department."

"But—" Clair stopped.

Jarleth smiled at Teddy while cooing a little.

"Jarleth smiles at everybody, but she really seems to like you," said Sonny.

"All the girls do," Teddy said with mock conceit.

"Yes, they do," said Mako while the three women in the room nodded in agreement.

Teddy smiled. "Thank you," he said humbly.

Everybody can feel Teddy's loving nature and warm spirit, thought Vance.

"Just look at those eyes. They're so startling that I didn't even notice the head size," Teddy said.

"But—"

Teddy raised Jarleth up to give her a gentle kiss on the forehead and then brought her to his chest and began rocking. "She's got a lot of love in her." Teddy kept rocking the baby. "And everybody around her is going to know it."

"But—"

Teddy looked over at Clair and smiled a little. "Do you consider the Yassi malformed or abnormal?"

Clair paused a second. "No, of course not."

"Well then, I guess I'll have to point out that the Yassi's heads are considerably larger than Jarleth's." Teddy smiled warmly. "And they sure don't have this baby's beautiful eyes."

Clair's eyes were getting misty. "Maybe I'm being overly sensitive about her appearance."

Jen smiled. It was the first time she'd heard Clair indicate that she might be unnecessarily concerned about the condition of her baby.

"I'd stack her against any on the planet. And"—Teddy paused— "she looks as smart as a whip."

"Yes, she does," said Sonny. "I've noticed that."

"Both of them do," said Mako.

Vance gently took Jarleth from Teddy, and before putting her to his chest, he tipped her back to see her face. He smiled. "Wow! You're a fine judge of beauty, Teddy. This is one gorgeous little girl. Her eyes are really hypnotic."

"I'll say. They're hard to pull away from."

Clair stepped forward. "Do you mind if I hold my daughter for a while?"

Clair cradled Jarleth so she could take a long, loving look at the infant.

"Oh my, she is beautiful, isn't she?" Tears started streaming from Clair's eyes. "Hi, sweetheart. Mommy loves you. I really do."

Jarleth gave her mother a big smile. Clair brought her daughter to her chest and sobbed.

The only dry eyes left in the room were Vance's.

Twenty minutes later, after they exchanged warm goodbyes, Jen escorted Vance and Teddy back to the runabout.

"You two are miracle workers," said Jen as she hugged Vance and then Teddy. "I can't thank you enough."

"Hey, piece of cake. All we did was point out their beauty and other assets, and their parents' natural love just took over."

"Well said, Teddy," Vance said before turning to Jen. "Apparently, you and Dr. Isley have developed a protocol to keep tabs on the babies?"

"Yes, sir. The parents have readily agreed. They want all the help they can get, and having Dr. Isley personally involved is of great comfort to them."

"He's definitely interested," Vance said. "We'll see you in Home-Bay, Jen." With that, he closed the hatch and took his pilot's chair.

"Just finished talking to Jen," said Dale.

"Ah, how are the babies doing?" asked Vance.

"They're starting to talk."

Vance paused briefly. "At six months?"

"Yes, and in simple sentences."

"Sentences?"

"Yes, sir. And it seems they like talking to each other more than their parents."

"Holy crap."

"It goes further. They do not like being separated from each other for longer than an hour or two. After that, they start raising hell."

"How are the parents handling that?"

"Not well at first, but Jen says they've been talking to the babies and explaining the problem with keeping them together. That seems to calm them some."

"You're kidding. They can be reasoned with?"

"So it appears. According to Jen, they have the intellect of two-year-olds but without the difficult attitudes normally displayed at that age."

MO-THREE 6, 123

"They're now reading," Dale told the other three on the bridge.

"Reading? They're only eleven months old," remarked Vance. "Beginning children's books, I assume."

"That assumption would have been correct two days ago. But they've moved on."

"Moved on to what?"

"As of earlier today, about a four-year-old level."

"Four years!"

Dale smiled. "Their learning curve is a bit steeper than the average."

"A bit?" Vance returned the smile. "How about their physical abilities?"

"Jarleth is a little behind babies of that age. She has a little trouble just sitting up."

"A lot of head to support," said Vance.

"That may be part of it, but it doesn't seem to affect Shem. He, according to his parents, is a bull. He's just starting to walk with the aid of whatever furniture is handy. Charlie reports that he is nearly tireless. As soon as he got the hang of walking, he tells me, Shem walked holding on to something for an hour or more nonstop until he collapsed from exhaustion. Then he slept like a rock, woke up, demanded food, and went right back to walking."

Alex smiled. "It sounds like the Youngblood genes are in full force and effect."

"For sure," said Dale. "Here is something else that stands out. Shem seems to look out for Jarleth. Amelia said she saw him try to help her sit up."

"Really?" said Troy. "That kind of thing is way ahead of the curve."

"Several years, I think," said Vance.

"It goes further. When she's sitting, he will sit next to her so she can lean on him. Remarkable for any child to do something like that, let alone a baby.

"Another odd thing. According to their folks, they will occasionally place their hands on each other's cheeks while looking into each other's eyes."

"That could be anything," said Vance.

"Yes, but there are so many unusual things with them," said Troy.

"I'll give you that. They've never been normal," said Dale.

"Your concerns about these two children seem to be becoming a reality," said Vance.

"Maybe," said Dale.

"I think we may have been colonized," said Vance with concern in his voice.

No one said anything for a couple of seconds before Vance spoke again.

"Not too long ago, we were talking about the possibility of a superior race in the universe, and now we're thinking seriously about whether or not we have, in fact, been colonized by such a race?"

"Hmm," Alex said. "Do you recall when we were discussing the reason such a superior race would bother to save a planet such as ours?"

"Like it was yesterday," said Vance.

"We speculated upon whether or not they liked the human race, or a few select humans at least, or maybe it was the planet itself they wanted to save," said Alex.

"I remember," said Vance.

"Now I'm thinking that it's probably a combination of everything but mostly the planet itself," said Dale.

"What brings you to that conclusion?"

"It's possible they want to expand their presence in the universe. To them, we have what might be a perfect environment. Their vision of this environment may or may not include us."

Vance's brow furrowed. "I believe that based on our history—and particularly your history, Alex—it's more than just our planet that something is interested in."

"That occurred to me too," said Alex. "That should be put into the mix as well."

"What are you two talking about?" asked Dale.

"I was about to ask the same question," Troy said.

Vance looked at Alex and raised his eyebrows. "It's up to you, sir."

It wasn't hard to see that Alex was conflicted. He said nothing for a full minute before addressing Vance. "I don't know if I can tell it."

"Do you want me to tell it?"

Alex shook his head slightly. "I think that now may be the time to share my story with these two."

Troy and Dale looked at each other but said nothing.

Alex looked at the two. "When I was forty-three years old, Jason Gould and I had a very successful investment brokerage firm. Our offices were located in Newport Beach, California." Alex smiled. "I'm going to be able to tell the story."

"Good," said Vance. "Continue."

Alex nodded. "During a spring ski vacation in central Oregon in Earth year 1997, I managed to ski into a tree, and I woke up lying injured on a wet street in Inglewood, California. The year was now 1962, and I was eight years old."

"What?" Troy smiled as if Alex were pulling his leg.

Dale said nothing but cocked his head a little.

Alex smiled. "You heard correctly. I was sent back thirty-five years in time and had to start my life over at eight years old."

"What?" Troy repeated, now clearly bewildered.

"Did you maintain your adult memories?" asked Dale, who seemed to be accepting the story. He'd known Alex for centuries and had never known him to lie about anything.

"Yes, I did."

Dale nodded as if it all made sense to him. "How did you handle that emotionally?"

"Not well at first, because of course, it was impossible. I assumed I had gone insane or suffered brain damage from the collision with the tree."

Troy sat transfixed. It was hard to tell what might be going on in his mind.

"I can't imagine how you coped," said Dale.

"It took about a week for me to force myself to accept the incomprehensible scenario and begin to play along with it. I believed at the time that the alternative would have landed me in a mental institution."

"I can't imagine how you managed to keep your wits about you."

"It was tough. The most difficult part was accepting my parents. They'd been killed in a plane crash six years before I had the run-in with the tree. But now there they were again, looking young, healthy, and happy. That was very hard for me to accept."

"I'm flummoxed here," said Troy. "How can this be true?"

"It couldn't be," said Vance. "But it is."

Alex nodded. "There are several major things to understand here. First, some entity managed to send me back in time, maybe using a different dimension or an alternate universe, a parallel universe. Who knows? It's seemingly impossible, but it happened. Second, I retained my memories, which, not coincidentally, included my investment knowledge of the future. Third, this knowledge allowed me to accumulate a vast fortune. Last but certainly not least is what was done with that fortune."

"You took over the world," said Troy.

"We took over the world," said Alex. "It was a team effort. It couldn't have been done without Jason Gould, Dale, Vance, and, of course, the fortune."

There was silence on the bridge.

"Had all that history not occurred, we would not be on this planet," said Vance. "There would be no human beings."

"My God!" said Troy. "My God."

Vance was staring blankly at his folded hands on the table. *Why would an entity want us here? Maybe they have a use for us. Maybe we won't like what they have in mind. Shit!*

"So," said Vance, "it's possible, maybe likely, that these superior beings have been guiding us to this time and place for centuries."

Alex nodded. "That has occurred to me."

"That might explain your history, Alex. And the history of the planets Earth and Gabriel," said Troy

"It might."

There was a long pause before Vance spoke up. "I suggest we get back to the scenario at hand."

Alex smiled. "The babies, possibly of these superior manipulators."

"We don't know that they are, in fact, the progeny of what Henderson calls the Superiors," said Dale.

"No, we don't," agreed Alex.

Dale didn't say anything for a moment. "They were conceived exactly when, or shortly after, the GRB hit this planet. They both have the same mutation. The odds of that happening are zero. It's statistically impossible. In addition, they seem to have brought forth the genes of two of the planet's most influential people—you two, Vance and Alex. That part could be a coincidence, but I wouldn't bet on it."

"I don't see how our genes would benefit them," said Vance.

"Great genes," answered Dale. "You two are special. In different ways, to be sure, but special."

"Agreed," said Troy. "SLF or not, Vance, look what you've done with this planet."

Vance shrugged.

"And, Alex," Troy said, "from what I've just learned, you were the chosen one all the way back in 1997 Earth time."

Dale nodded in agreement.

"Be that as it may, all of that history brings us to this point in time," said Alex.

"And the babies," said Vance.

"And the babies," agreed Alex.

"There is little, if anything, we can do to change whatever these unique children are going to do as they grow. We don't know if they are preprogrammed to perform a given set of tasks as they grow or if they simply will do whatever their intellect and circumstances allow or dictate.

"I'm concerned with what their role might be concerning us and the planet. If they are the beginning of a colonization, we could be screwed," said Vance. "Need to keep that possibility in mind as they grow."

Alex nodded. "I would point out that Teddy believes they are benevolent. He sees nothing but good in them."

"Teddy's opinion means a lot. There has never been a person who feels what's in people's hearts better than Teddy," said Dale. "Frankly, knowing how he feels about the babies removes most of my concerns."

"Okay, I'll remain the sole skeptic here. So what is to be done?" Vance said.

Alex smiled. "We let these two grow up with the support given all children on the planet. As time passes, I believe we'll be surprised, delighted, and maybe even occasionally frightened by these youngsters."

"That seems likely," Dale said. "I'm quite certain that talking and reading at this age is simply the tip of the proverbial iceberg."

"Maybe they are merely a product of evolution. Many changes in life-forms over time must have come from genetic damage, mutation, or alterations from an outside force. Could they be the random next step in human evolution?" asked Alex.

"Next step? A strong possibility. Random? Probably not."

Vance jumped in. "We need to keep in mind that the conceptions were a result of natural mating. But some entity may have tinkered with the seeds."

Dale nodded. "Maybe."

Vance smiled. "I was about to ask how in the hell anyone or anything would be able to do that, but on second thought …"

"Exactly. If they can protect us from a GRB, altering genetics wouldn't be a problem," Troy said.

"Here's another thing," said Dale. "Any beings capable of such a feat would clearly know that by producing two with identical mutations, we would speculate as we are now. And I suspect that too is part of their plan."

"Jesus, yes, of course," said Vance. "They let their cat out of the bag by blocking the GRB. They know that we know they exist. But either they don't care, or that's part of their plan."

"I think they do care," said Alex. "They want us to know. They want us to keep close tabs on Shem and Jarleth."

Dale nodded. "You're right. I doubt there is little, if anything, left to chance with these beings—and that's a little discomforting."

When Jarleth and Shem were just shy of their second birthdays, their families left the Vast Continent and moved to the Home-Bay area. Their parents felt strongly that they needed to raise their special children in a more social environment and that Shem and Jarleth would have a much better chance of developing normal social skills if they were around other children their age.

A few months after the move, Jarleth's and Shem's parents had babies born within a month of each other. This time, both couples had girls, and the babies were, to everyone's relief, normal in every way.

MO-FOUR 1, 125

Vance and Lara were enjoying the day, visiting shops and greeting friends in Home-Bay. When in town, they enjoyed having a meal at one of the town's four restaurants. Just as they left Lucy's, the newest café in town, they nearly tripped over Charlie, Amelia, Clair, and Sonny, who were out enjoying the day with their children. Their two infants were in small carriages, but Shem and Jarleth were walking beside their parents. The two three-year-olds instantly spotted Vance and ran over, raising their arms, clearly wanting Vance to pick them up. He obliged by picking them up at the same time, one in each arm.

"Well, what a pleasant surprise," Vance said, and then he kissed each one on the forehead. He noticed the craniums of both children had grown, as the rest of their bodies had, and remained exceptionally large in comparison.

Jarleth was still slightly small for her age. Her thick platinum-blonde hair had grown down to the middle of her back. Her olive complexion accentuated her outsized blue eyes, which were shaded with thick white eyelashes below fine white brows. She was, even at that young age, startling in appearance. When she entered a room, all eyes were drawn to her. Vance assumed that phenomenon would stay with her throughout her life.

Shem, on the other hand, was about average height for his age but heavier-boned and muscled. His thick, wavy dark hair was as the Youngblood genes commonly displayed, but rather than his hairline sitting low on his forehead, as those genes had consistently dictated, his hairline sat much higher, exposing his outsize forehead over his large, daunting dark eyes.

"Growing like weeds," said Vance.

"Yes, they are," said Clair. "Hard to keep Jarleth in clothes that fit."

Lara smiled. "Her clothes will be fine hand-me-downs for her baby sister."

"Already have our baby girl in hand-me-downs," said Sonny.

"How are you getting along in school?" Vance asked the two three-year-olds he was still holding.

"Very well, sir," said Shem formally.

Vance looked at Shem's parents for confirmation and got a nod from each of them.

"I love my classmates," said Jarleth with a big smile.

"Well, that's good to hear," said Vance, returning the smile.

Vance remembered Dale telling him that by his observations, the two played with their young friends more like adults would play with their children, and he said that even when playing with other children, Shem would rarely let Jarleth out of his sight. *He acts like a miniature bodyguard.* Vance smiled at the thought. *And he's not too subtle about it.*

Vance looked from Shem to Jarleth. Dale had told him that Jarleth seemed to take on the role of peacemaker and was good at it.

She has a loving nature, thought Vance. *Actually, she reminds me a little of Teddy at that age.* Vance smiled to himself. *Hell, Teddy's still that way.*

Vance remembered that the two had started school that year. "What grade are they in?"

Amelia smiled brightly. "Third."

"Our visitors are here," said Troy as the three-year-olds and their parents walked onto the bridge of the *Marian.*

Vance, Troy, Gary, and Teddy stood up to greet them. Alex's and Dale's holograms were also there. The two bridge crew members remained sitting at their stations, but their eyes were on the two youngsters. They had not seen them in person before.

Amelia and Charlie were in the lead, with Shem walking freely between them. Just behind were Clair and Sonny, holding Jarleth's hands.

Shem's head seemed to be on a swivel. He was taking in everything he could as they approached the center of the bridge. When his eyes came across the holograms of Alex and Dale, they lingered for a moment before continuing their scan of the bridge. Jarleth also looked around but not with the same intensity. She smiled at everyone on the bridge and, like Shem, lingered for a moment before smiling at Alex and Dale.

"Good morning, and welcome to the bridge of the *Marian*," said Troy.

"Thank you, sir," Charlie said first, followed by the others.

"Thank you," said Shem and Jarleth in unison.

Shem turned to look at Teddy. "Hi, Teddy," he said with a big smile.

Teddy walked over and went down on one knee in front of the little boy. "How about a hug?"

Shem didn't hesitate; he wrapped his arms around Teddy's neck, put his cheek on Teddy's, and held on for several seconds before releasing him.

Teddy smiled brightly. "That was a nice hug."

Shem then did something out of the ordinary. He put his hands on both sides of Teddy's face and looked into his eyes. His brow furrowed slightly as he removed his hands and turned to Vance. "Hello, sir," he said. "May I hug you too?"

Vance smiled. "I would be pleased if you did." Vance reached down, picked Shem up, and gave him a gentle hug before holding him out at arm's length.

As he'd done with Teddy, Shem reached forward, placed his hands on Vance's face, and looked into his eyes. This time, rather than looking a little puzzled, he nodded once and removed his hands.

Shem then turned his attention to the holograms of Alex and Dale. He looked puzzled as he glanced from one to the other. "What are you?" he asked.

"We are holograms of people who used to have bodies like you," said Dale. "A long time ago, we had our minds put into a computer, but not our bodies."

"We are able to think, see, and interact with people like you, but we cannot touch or hug," said Alex. "We miss that."

"I don't understand."

Dale nodded. "Someday you will. Right now, it's a little more complicated than you are able to learn."

"How long before I can understand?"

Dale's right eyebrow lifted a little. "Probably less than a year from now."

Shem said nothing for a moment, nodding. "Okay." He turned back to the others without another word.

They spent the next two hours giving the families a tour of the *Marian.* Everybody asked questions, with Shem asking the most. He seemed to gain intelligence as the moments passed. They finished the tour with a box lunch on the bridge. After that, the families gave hugs all around and entered the elevator.

As the elevator door slid shut, Teddy turned to the others on the bridge. "Wow, that was quite an experience."

"Yes, it was. Those two are hard to describe," said Troy.

"Shem has the brains and the brawn here," Vance said.

"He's a powerhouse. His spirit comes out in waves. I've never felt anything like it," said Teddy.

"And what a beauty Jarleth is," Troy said with awe in his voice.

"Inside and out," said Teddy. "Between the two of them, the bases are covered."

"Isn't it strange that no one has commented on the size of their heads?"

"Your attention is quickly drawn elsewhere," said Troy. "They are so dynamic."

"I believe we may be looking at the future leaders of Gabriel," said Alex.

Dale nodded. "They're like bookends—the same but different. Jarleth is the compassion, love, and reason, and Shem is the muscle and the brains."

"His strength of will and body may protect not only Jarleth but also, maybe in the future, the entire planet. From what, I have no idea," said Vance.

"That's a thought, but there is really no basis for thinking that," said Dale.

"But I suppose it's possible," said Troy.

"It's natural that we feel just a little more content and safe in thinking that the Superiors may have put them on Gabriel to shield us from something. Something powerful and dangerous," said Alex. "Whether or not that turns out to be the case doesn't matter."

"We've always assumed that whoever planted these two wonder kids also saved us from the GRB," said Dale. "Of course, that is simply more conjecture." He smiled. "Hopefully Gabriel's future will be devoid of any more horrendous threats."

"That is every bit as possible as, and probably even more likely than, any other scenario we've talked about," Gary said.

"Well, all I know is that they are wonderful children," said Teddy. "They are and will continue to be an asset to the planet."

CHAPTER 12

HERO
MO-SEVEN 7, 126

5:10

" What the hell?" said Reg as he sat up in bed. *Was that an earthquake?* He glanced at the clock on the nightstand. *A little early,* he thought, *but close enough.* He threw his covers back, swung his legs over the edge of the bed, and then paused for a second before standing up. Whatever had awakened him wasn't continuing. *Maybe it was a dream.* He looked over at Cindy and smiled; she was a sound sleeper.

He changed into his jumpsuit, put on socks and his work boots, and headed to the kitchen.

While waiting for the coffee to brew, he walked out onto their rear deck to take in the morning air.

The Whetrume home in Seaside was located a kilometer north of town. It was one of six homes located on the side of a hill overlooking a large gulch that had its beginning a hundred kilometers up into the forested mountains. From their rear deck, they could see the creek that flowed down the bottom of the gulch and emptied into the massive Ring Sea. There were thousands of such gulches and creeks surrounding the sea; they were the source of its fresh water. The volume of water flowing down the creeks varied with the time of year. It was the dry season in Seaside, and this creek was shallow and hardly more than a couple of meters wide.

Reg looked across the gulch. From his vantage point, he could see three of the dozen or so homes built roughly at the same elevation as his home. The thick pine and fir trees obscured the view of the other homes. The hill above those homes was a good eighty meters higher than on their side, leaving the boulder-laden hillside rising above them.

The vibration started mildly but was building in intensity.

"What the hell?" *Earthquake* was his first thought. "Shit!" He turned and ran back into his home. "Get up! Get up now! Get out of the house!" he yelled as he ran into his bedroom. Cindy was already out of bed. "I'll get the kids, and you get outside now," he said. As Reg turned back into the hall, both children were already on a dead run toward the front door; Cindy was now right behind them.

On top of the rapidly intensifying shaking came a thundering noise, followed closely by an enormous crashing sound. Within a few more seconds, the violent shaking subsided and then stopped altogether.

The family was standing on the lawn on the upside of their home. They could see their neighbors doing the same.

"I'm going to take a look around. You stay outside for a while."

With that, Reg walked around the gulch side of their home, checking for visible signs of damage. He took a quick glance across the gulch. The sun was just coming up, and the light was dim but not so dim that he couldn't see the damage to two homes directly across the gulch. One home was missing a small corner, and the other home looked half gone.

"What the ..." Reg's eyes quickly followed the dust-filled path to destruction down the creek. "Holy shit!"

There, lying at the bottom of the gulch, were dozens of massive boulders that hadn't been there moments before. They were mixed with hundreds of smaller rocks, broken branches, bushes, and splintered lumber. The boulders extended five meters into the sea itself. A few smaller rocks were still trickling to the bottom of the gulch.

"Oh shit," said Reg loudly.

"Oh my God," said Cindy as she approached Reg from behind.

Reg's eyes shot back to the damaged homes. "It's on fire." He spun to face Cindy. "Get ahold of everybody you can, and tell them we're going to need help."

Cindy cocked her head. "I can hear someone screaming over there."

"I know. Me too." Reg quickly kissed Cindy and headed straight down the side of the gulch, dodging trees while kicking up dirt and rocks as he went down at breakneck speed. The creek had been effectively dammed, and the water was starting to build up behind the boulders. Reg could see that the creek was already too high to wade across, so without hesitation, he turned to his right and started climbing the new boulder dam. He hit an unstable rock, and it gave way, throwing him off the boulders and onto the bank on his back. This momentarily stunned him and knocked some of the wind out of his lungs, but he didn't stay down for more than a few seconds before he was back on his feet, attacking the pile of boulders. This time, nothing slipped as he jumped from boulder to boulder and leaped onto the ground on the far side. He paused for a moment to catch his breath and look up the destructive path the boulders had created.

He had friends living in those homes—close friends. He began rapidly climbing up through the twisted and broken branches of fallen trees and over the tops of rocks and boulders that had not yet been dislodged. He climbed around a wall that lay half buried in the rubble, a wall he recognized. It was one of the kitchen walls of their friends the Hermans.

"Oh shit!" He and Cindy had spent many hours in that kitchen, drinking coffee and talking to their friends. He doubled his efforts to reach the damaged home. It was on fire.

Reg heard screams for help as he scrambled upward. He could hear people yelling from above and far below, closer to the sea. People were coming to help. *Hurry*, he thought. *Please hurry*.

He reached the Hermans' home, or what was left of it. The kitchen side was gone, including the dining room and most of the living room. The living room was where the fireplace was, and he instantly realized what had started the fire.

The entire home had been knocked off its foundation and was leaning downhill at a thirty-degree angle. It looked as if it could begin sliding down at any moment.

He didn't hesitate. He quickly climbed over what was left of the living room floor and worked his way over the steep incline toward the bedrooms.

"Lonnie! Carla! Can you hear me?" he yelled.

There was a muffled cry from the master bedroom.

"Carla?" he yelled back.

"Yes! Yes, I'm here!"

The light was improving quickly with the rising sun, and the rapidly growing fire lit the interior of the home; the smoke was becoming thick.

Reg felt as if it took minutes to reach the bedrooms, but it was only seconds.

The master bedroom's door was at the end of the hall, and Reg had to steady himself against a wall in order to keep his footing against the steep pitch of the floor. When he reached the door, he grabbed the handle and twisted. It turned freely, but the door didn't open. He put a shoulder against it and pushed, but it didn't budge.

"If you're close to the door, back away!" he yelled.

"Okay!"

Reg backed up a couple of meters and, with all his weight, sprang forward and gave the door a mighty kick just above the knob. It shattered, and he fell inside the room all the way to the back wall. The smoke was nearly solid above the two-meter mark, but the visibility was fair in the lower half of the room.

Carla was sitting on the edge of the bed, holding Lonnie's bloody head in her hands and crying softly. Reg didn't hesitate for a second. He scrambled across the floor, grabbed Carla by the hand, and started dragging her up the slope toward the door.

"No! Get Lonnie out first!" she screamed.

"I'll get him out, but you first." Reg continued pulling and dragging Carla toward the door. She quit resisting and began scrambling on her own. They went up the hall, across the upper part of the living room, through a hole in the outside wall, and out into the smoke-free air of the ground above the burning home.

"You stay here. I'm going back for Lonnie."

Carla's eyes suddenly got big, and she screamed, "Brock is home! Brock is home!"

Brock was their adult son. He lived and worked in Home-Bay but was home for a visit. In her terror, she had momentarily forgotten.

"Where?"

"Front bedroom! Oh God!"

Reg was already on his way back into the house. He had to grab the doorjamb of the front bedroom to keep himself from falling back into the master bedroom. He turned the doorknob. It resisted, but he put all he had into twisting it, and it broke loose. The door swung open and crashed into the wall.

The smoke was not yet in that room, and he had no trouble spotting Brock lying motionless against the downward-sloping wall. A dresser covered most of his torso. Reg slipped and slid down the floor, narrowly missing Brock's head with his boots.

"Brock! Brock, can you hear me?" he yelled.

He received no response.

Reg managed to reach under Brock's shoulders and pull him out from under the dresser. Then, with Herculean effort, he managed to get Brock onto his shoulder and climb back to the door.

A heavy rope suddenly snaked over the top of his boots. Reg looked up through the smoke and spotted a large man standing eight meters above him on the outside of the house.

"Tie that around him!" he yelled.

Reg didn't hesitate. He managed to off-load Brock and wedge him against the doorjamb. He grabbed the rope and tied it around Brock's chest.

"Pull him up!" Reg yelled.

Immediately, the slack went out of the rope, and Brock was hauled off the doorjamb. Reg guided Brock's ascent up the inclined floor all the way to the top, where three men had managed to rip away the remaining wall, leaving a clean ramp to the outside. The men pulled Brock to safety.

"Get that rope off him, and give it to me," said Reg as he gasped for air.

"You're not going back down there," said the big man.

"Give me the damn rope."

Another man quickly untied the rope and tossed it to Reg. He grabbed it and headed back down into the furnace that was his friends' home.

The smoke in the master bedroom was now only a meter off the floor. The sound of the fire roared in Reg's ears. The bedroom was being consumed. He could feel his jumpsuit starting to burn, but he scrambled to the bed, where he knew Lonnie was, and without hesitation, he tied the rope around his friend's chest.

"Pull! Pull!" he yelled.

Lonnie was pulled off the bed and onto the floor with a thud. They kept pulling as Reg painfully guided him as best as he could through the door and up the hall. They were just a meter from the outside, when the house, now nearly completely consumed in flames, suddenly tipped another fifteen degrees and started slipping down the steep hill. Reg lost his purchase and fell backward down the bedroom hall.

"Oh my God!" cried the big man in horror as the burning home gained speed on its trip to the bottom of the gorge.

"We've lost him!" cried another. "Oh my God, we've lost him."

Lonnie was now lying on his back on the ground that once had been under his front porch. The rope was still tied around his chest. He was breathing. Carla was by his side, holding his face in her hands. "Lonnie, wake up. Please wake up."

Two meters away, Brock was in a sitting position, coughing violently while looking around in a daze.

Cindy; her daughter, Elsa; and her youngest son, Tim, had managed to climb over the boulders where they entered the sea. From there, they ran up the community path along the shore to the path that led to the homes up the hill, one of which was on fire and leaning perilously downhill. Cindy's main concern was for the welfare of their friends the Hermans.

They were within thirty meters, when the burning home lost its grip on the hillside and plunged as an inferno to the bottom of the gorge.

"Oh, please, God. Let the Hermans be well," she said aloud.

"They must have gotten out," said Elsa.

"They'd better have," added Tim.

There were now about a dozen people at the site, all talking loudly and quickly.

Carla looked up just in time to see the Whetrumes coming up the path. "Oh Lord," she said as she quickly stood up beside Lonnie. Three neighbors, one of whom was trained in triage, were busy attending to Lonnie. After a quick glance at her still-unconscious husband, she started walking rapidly toward her friends.

"Oh, thank God," Cindy said as she approached Carla. "You got out. How's Lon—" She quit talking and looked past Carla and into the small crowd. "Where's Reg?" she asked.

Carla broke down. "He's gone!" she cried. "He saved us, and he's gone."

Tim and Elsa screamed, dropped to their knees, and doubled over in spasms of grief. Cindy looked at them as if she didn't understand what they were doing. She looked back at Carla. "No," she said. "I was just with him a little while ago." Her expression was one of puzzlement. "What do you mean he's gone?"

"He's—" Carla obviously couldn't say more. She instead pointed down the hill at the conflagration that once had been her home.

Cindy looked where Carla was pointing and just stood there staring at the burning wreckage. Then she started screaming.

6:33

Vance ran full tilt across the bridge that spanned the Vance River on his way to the *Norman*'s cave. Alex had given him the news of the tragedy at Seaside just two minutes before. He was heading to the cave to pick up a shuttle and head over the hill.

No, no, no, he repeated to himself as he ran. *How can this be?*

Few people were out and about at that time of day, and he saw only two Gabrielites as he entered the cave and headed up the *Norman*'s ramp. They spotted him before he saw them. For Vance Youngblood to be running to the *Norman* at any hour was cause for great alarm.

Vance went straight to the hangar deck, exited the elevator, and ran to the nearest small shuttle.

Twelve minutes later, he was circling the area of the disaster. He could clearly see the horrendous damage the landslide had caused to the hillside and the path of destruction all the way to the bottom of the gorge. He could see the remains of the still-burning home as it was being consumed atop the great pile of boulders. *Reg was in that house,* he said to himself with great sadness. He could see two dozen men fighting the small fires that the home had started as it crashed through the pines.

He turned the shuttle and headed to a landing site on an open beach a couple hundred meters north of the smoldering gorge. He exited the shuttle and ran to the crowd gathered at the bottom of the trail that led up to the homes.

"Oh, sir, we have lost Reg!" one cried out as Vance approached the group.

Vance nodded and stopped. "Who's in charge here?"

"Up there." A young man pointed.

Vance didn't hesitate to start up the gravel path at a dead run.

"Look at that," said someone in the crowd.

Vance tore up the path at an incredible speed, faster than most men could run downhill. He reached the top of the path in less than a minute and immediately spotted Cindy and her two children; he slowed to a fast walk as he approached them.

Cindy turned and hugged Vance as she continued to sob deeply. Vance said nothing, but tears filled his eyes as held her in a warm hug for several minutes.

He turned to her children and hugged them both at the same time. They cried together.

When they separated, Tim barely choked out, "My father is a hero. I'm so proud of him."

CHAPTER 13

COMING OF AGE
MO-TWO 4, 140

"Did you realize the wonder kids are going to be eighteen in less than a month?" asked Lara.

"God almighty."

"And of course, Jarleth will have her coming-out party."

Vance shook his head. "Where's the time go?"

Vance and Lara were hiking on their island. That morning, they headed west along the Lara River, a direction they seldom took.

"Look at that." Vance pointed toward a thick grove of mango trees up a low hill to their right.

"I don't—oh, I see them."

A family of orangutans were high in the branches of a massive tree, enjoying the ripe mangoes—a large male, a female, and two youngsters. One youngster was probably two years old, while the other was just a few months at best.

Lara laughed. "Doesn't get much cuter than that."

"They're even more laid back than the gorillas. They act like they don't even see us." Vance spotted a large boulder in the shade of a tree. He motioned in that direction. "Let's take a seat and watch 'em for a while.

After they made themselves comfortable, Lara continued. "Back to Jarleth and Shem."

"Okay."

"Did you know she's now taken an interest in medicine?"

"Good Lord," said Vance.

"Good Lord is right. She excels at music. Has a wondrous voice, is highly skilled at the piano, and has been writing music."

"And," said Vance, "a few months back, she began drawing. I've seen some of her art. She has an interesting and distinctive style. I think some of her sketches are already suitable for framing."

"*Wonder kids* is an apt description," said Lara.

Vance nodded. "Their individual interests are about as diverse as they can be. Shem's a powerhouse. He attacks with great vigor whatever subject draws his interest. His ability to absorb information and immediately put it to practical use is phenomenal. Science and engineering are definitely his long suits."

"And she's all about liberal arts," said Lara. "They have all the bases covered."

Vance nodded in agreement. "Look at that."

The two-year-old orang had the infant by the hand and was swinging it in an arc a good ten meters above the ground.

"If he lets go, that baby is going to get hurt," said an alarmed Lara.

"Here comes the mama," said Vance.

The mama quickly, for an orangutan, climbed down a couple of branches before swinging to the branch the two-year-old was sitting on. She reached down, took the baby by the arm, and lifted it to the branch. When it was secure and the two-year-old relinquished his grip, the mama gently pushed him away from the baby while chastising him loudly. Apparently, he got the message, because he worked his way to the end of the branch and buried his face in his hands.

Vance and Lara laughed at the sight.

MO-THREE 13, 140

Gasps, excited comments, and enthusiastic wooing from the Yassi and Vout were audible as Jarleth and Clair walked out of the cave and into view of those lining the pathway. Jarleth was radiant for her coming-out party. She was dressed in an exquisite self-designed gown reminiscent of an ancient Roman toga split up the sides to the hips. The gown was full length and made of a gold fabric like no other. It had been manufactured on Mahyu and purchased from the Yassi on their last trip to Gabriel. The material did in fact contain gold, which had been spun so finely that the individual threads were difficult to see with the naked eye. As Jarleth moved, the material seemed to flow and ripple as molten gold might. She wore high-heeled golden sandals with gold straps crisscrossing all the way up her calves. To top off her ensemble, she wore earrings, a necklace, and a bracelet made with brilliant blue stones set in exquisite white porcelain that resembled carved shells. The precious stones, which were nearly as hard and clear as diamonds, had come from the deep mines of the Vout planet. They'd been chosen because they were close to the color of Jarleth's eyes. Set against Jarleth's platinum hair, the effect was breathtaking. Her thick hair had been brushed back, and it came forward over her shoulders and nearly down to her waist, framing her face. Her radiant olive complexion required no makeup, nor did her eyes, which were a dominant feature that no amount of eye shadow could have improved.

Later that evening, Vance and Lara were out on their deck, reminiscing about Jarleth's coming-out party.

"I have never seen such a stunning woman in my life," said Lara.

"She was certainly otherworldly," said Vance.

Lara smiled. "Pun intended?"

"More or less, yes."

Neither said anything for a moment. Then Lara said, "She is like an angel."

Vance nodded in agreement. "Inside and out."

"Did you notice Shem never took his eyes off her while she went down the receiving line?" asked Lara.

Vance smiled. "I didn't—I couldn't take my eyes off her myself."

"The way he looked at Jarleth reminded me of how you look at me sometimes," Lara said as she squeezed Vance's hand.

Vance returned the squeeze. "Shem worships that young lady; he always has."

"Very unusual."

"Reminds me of us a hundred and sixteen years ago," said Vance.

Lara's smile widened. "I wasn't there, but I've watched the video a dozen times."

"Me too."

CHAPTER 14

IT'S REALLY BIG
MO-FOUR 20, 142

"Vance, Troy, Gary." Alex's voice came across their communicators at 14:00.

Gary was the first to answer. "Yes, sir, Gary here."

"Hold for a moment."

"I'm here, Alex," said Troy.

"Let's wait for Vance to answer," said Alex.

A few seconds later, Vance's voice came through. "What's up?"

"Why don't you head to the *Norman*, and we'll fill you in?"

"We're right in the middle of preparing our Thanksgiving meal. It's the twentieth anniversary." *My worst day ever and my best day ever,* thought Vance as he instantly remembered the threat of the gamma-ray burst and the comet blocking it.

"We know, but this is important."

"Are we being threatened?"

"Don't know yet. Something big this way comes, to misquote an old play."

Within an hour, Troy, Gary, and Vance were on the *Norman*'s bridge. Vance took the captain's chair, and Troy and Gary sat in chairs located on either side of him.

Alex's and Dale's holograms were to the side of the large bridge viewer, which displayed a section of the Milky Way galaxy's billions of stars.

"You have the floor," Vance said to Dale.

Dale nodded. "We have something approaching us from roughly the direction of the center of the galaxy. It's currently traveling at about half-light speed." Dale pointed at a large dot in the middle. "Right here."

Everybody's eyes were on the viewer.

"When did you spot it?" asked Vance.

"Just over an hour ago, but it could have been in our sensor range for weeks. Or it may have recently dropped to a speed that we could pick up in real time. We just haven't been scanning that sector of space, but there it is, and it's on a trajectory that will intercept us. I have notified the techs aboard the *Marian*, so they're tracking it also."

"So it's a ship?" asked Vance.

"Well, probably," Dale said with some doubt apparent in his voice.

"Probably?"

"It's the size that's throwing me off. It looks to be about five kilometers in diameter."

"Five kilometers? You mean meters?"

"No."

"Uh-oh," said Troy.

"Hold on," said Vance. "Maybe it's a group of ships spread out over five kilometers."

"Or maybe another comet," Troy said.

"No to both. If it were a comet, it wouldn't be coming from that direction, and it wouldn't be traveling at half-light speed. If it were a group of ships, they would have to be tightly packed, not spread out. I can detect no space between them. In my opinion, this is one ship."

"That's the size of a small city on old Earth," said Troy.

"Yes, but the volume inside a ship that size is equal to several cities. Its shape looks spherical."

"Big enough to be a world unto itself," Alex said.

"Being an old military man, I tend to see anything unknown as a threat. And this strikes me as a big threat," said Vance.

"It would be difficult for anyone to comprehend such a gargantuan ship without some trepidation," Gary said.

"I'll say," said Vance. "So how far out is it?"

"About five billion kilometers and closing."

"How long before it gets to us?"

"If it continues at the same speed, it will be here in less than a month."

"Could it be the Superiors?"

"That was my first thought, and it's still at the top of the list," said Dale.

"Or a different race of Superiors," said Troy.

"Now, that's a scary thought."

"So what's our next move?"

"I've no idea. We'll keep monitoring them and hope to God they're friendly."

"It occurs to me that maybe they are coming to check on our special ones—see how they are getting along with beings of a lesser intellect," Alex said.

"That crossed my mind too," said Vance.

"We've always assumed the Superiors who gave us Shem and Jarleth were also responsible for blocking the GRB," said Dale.

"Hopefully that's the case, and this is them," said Vance.

"Agreed."

"Maybe we're about to get the answers to a lot of questions."

"Mayb—it's disappeared!" said a surprised Dale.

The dot on the viewer was gone. Only a view of the billions of stars and galaxies remained.

"Shit!" said Vance.

"That's worrisome," said Gary.

"How can this be?"

"They know something we don't. It's hard to make anything disappear, let alone something that size."

"It just blinked out. Gone," said Troy.

Alex said nothing for a couple of minutes. "Maybe the Superiors have taken it out."

"Maybe," Dale said slowly while continuing to check his instruments.

"You don't think so, do you?"

"No. Had anything that size been destroyed, there would be a lot of debris. I can detect nothing in that sector of space. Nothing at all."

"This is disconcerting," said Gary.

"It was visible for just two hours total. Why?" Dale asked.

"Let's get Shem in here," said Vance.

"Why?"

"I don't know. Just a hunch. Probably nothing. I'm grasping at straws here."

Vance disliked unknowns more than most. To scientists, unknowns were a curiosity, a challenge, but to Vance, they were cause for concern and caution.

"Shem hasn't shown any precognition or telepathic abilities that I'm aware of," said Gary.

"I know," said Vance, "but we've spent the last twenty years believing that those two people were somehow connected to the Superiors. My thinking is that if there is the possibility of a connection, then we should be prepared."

Alex smiled. "That's better than grasping at straws."

"There might not be any connection at all, but it seems to me that their arrival will be about the same time as Shem's and Jarleth's twentieth birthdays," said Dale.

"It could be pretty close," agreed Vance.

Alex smiled. "So maybe they're dropping by to join the celebration?"

Even Dale laughed. "That's as good a thought as any other at this point."

"And a more pleasant one."

Thirty minutes later, Shem walked onto the *Norman*'s bridge. He was, at twenty, a little taller than Vance but not as heavily muscled. He was a powerful-looking young man nonetheless, and his manner was friendly and cordial, if not a little impatient at times. On many occasions, Alex and Dale observed that his demeanor was similar to Vance's on old Earth long ago.

"Good afternoon, sirs," Shem said as he walked onto the bridge.

"Ah, Shem, thanks for coming," said Vance as the two shook hands.

"I'm available to you anytime, sir. And I always enjoy being aboard this incredible ship." Shem greeted Alex and Dale and then shook hands with Troy and Gary.

"We have a dilemma—a puzzle, if you will."

"Oh? And you think I can help?"

Vance smiled. "I'm the only one who's given any thought to that possibility."

"If it's puzzling to you very smart people, I don't know how I'll be of any use," said Shem.

"You know we have always felt that you and Jarleth were somehow placed here by the Superiors."

"Yes, sir. That's never been a secret."

"Well, just under three hours ago, Dale discovered a ship heading toward us from the center of the galaxy."

"Really? I assume you've ruled out any known species and feel this ship may be that of the Superiors, or"—Shem shrugged—"I wouldn't be here."

"In a nutshell, yes."

Shem said nothing for a few seconds. "Tell me about the ship."

"Well," Dale said, "when our sensors picked it up a while ago, it may have just dropped to a speed we could detect in real time. Now I'm not sure that's the case."

Shem said nothing.

"The size is astonishing. It is five kilometers in diameter."

Shem's eyebrows went up as he slowly nodded. "That is astonishing."

"Here's something even more astonishing: a half hour ago, it disappeared."

Shem's big eyes got bigger. "Disappeared?"

"Just flicked out and was gone."

"Maybe it picked up speed again and went to time warp. That would make it undetectable."

"The acceleration to go to near light speed in the blink of an eye would be incredible," said Dale. "The power required to do that is beyond my comprehension."

Everyone on the bridge pondered that statement for a moment.

"Temporal dimension? Space-time shift?" asked Shem.

"Could be," said Dale, "but no experimental or observational evidence is available to confirm the existence of extra dimensions."

"That's true, but other than jumping to light speed, it's the only thing that comes to mind that might explain the ship's disappearance."

"Is it possible they are coming to visit us?" asked Troy.

Shem looked thoughtful for a couple of moments. "I don't know why, but I think that is a strong possibility." Shem paused for another second. "It seems likely that they would send a message before heading this way, if in fact it really is the Superiors."

"Maybe they don't think that way. Maybe they assume we'd assume they were coming to visit."

"Impossible to know what they are thinking. Their thought patterns and processes may be so alien to us that we'll never be able to understand them," Dale said.

"Shem, do you have any feelings at all concerning this ship?" asked Vance.

"No, sir."

"It's back," said Gary.

Everybody's eyes quickly turned to the viewer.

There it was, only this time, it appeared much closer.

"Uh-oh," said Dale.

The ship's shape was now distinctive. It was basically a slightly flattened sphere, reminiscent of an old-fashioned pincushion. The sphere was inside an external structure consisting of a massive framework of eight equally spaced ribs. The colossal ribs were connected at the ship's axes at the top and bottom. They were thinnest at the top axis, thickened as they wrapped around the equator of the ship, and then thinned again as they connected to the bottom axis. The ship itself was a brilliant gold color, but the exterior ribs were dark gray or black. The hull displayed no discernable features at all, not a seam or hatch. It looked like a huge golden glass ball.

"Holy cow," said Gary.

"Those ribs are more than two hundred meters thick at the equator," said Dale. "About twenty meters at the axes."

"Part of the propulsion system, you think?" Troy asked.

"I don't know, but it's certainly a spectacular-looking craft."

"That's five kilometers wide?" asked Shem.

"And just under five thick, not counting the ribs," answered Dale. "It's cut its distance from us in half."

"Had to go to near light speed to do that," said Gary.

"Hate to repeat myself, but that would be incredible acceleration," said Dale.

"It would have made it undetectable by the sensors," said Shem.

"And it would have gotten them to where they are now in a hurry," added Alex.

"How far out are they?" asked Vance.

Dale said nothing for a moment. "Less than two billion kilometers."

"They traveled three billion kilometers in thirty minutes?"

"Yes," said Dale. "That would be accelerating to near light and back down to half-light within that thirty minutes."

"Such acceleration and deceleration would crush any living thing to juice in an instant," said Gary.

"It certainly would if it were using our technology, but I'm betting these beings have figured it out," said Dale.

The five men were quiet for several moments while they observed the colossal ship.

"How would it be possible to create enough power to move such a mass at all, let alone to light speed in an instant?" Gary said.

"I'm assuming that's a rhetorical question," said Shem.

"It has to be. I wouldn't know where to begin," Gary answered.

Dale spoke up. "I believe when it disappears again, it will be here within an hour."

"You believe it will disappear again?"

"I'm all but positive."

"Shit!" said Vance.

"We could be in trouble," added Troy.

Shem turned to the others. "I don't think that ship is coming here to harm us."

"I agree," said Dale.

"You do?" asked Vance. "Why would you think that?"

Dale deferred to Shem. "You first."

Shem smiled. "Okay, thank you. If it were coming to harm us, why would it make its presence known for nearly three hours, long enough for us to speculate at length about its intentions and possibly set up defenses? Why then reaccelerate to something close to light, making it undetectable, causing us to speculate again about its motives and, frankly, worry about its incredible power and technology, only to drop back in speed again so that we can get another look at it before it arrives here?"

"Go on."

Shem continued. "I think they are announcing their intention to visit us in order to alleviate our fears. If a ship that size was to suddenly be in orbit around our planet, all sorts of panic might ensue."

"Perfect," said Dale.

Gary nodded in agreement. "That does make sense."

"I hope it does," said Vance.

"If we all concur that's the case, I think we need to inform the citizens right away," said Alex. "We don't want anyone surprised when it shows up."

Shem smiled brightly. It was a facial expression he didn't often use. "That could be exactly what they want us to do."

Dale also smiled. "Agreed."

After a few minutes of discussion as to how to present the coming event to the populous, the leadership group decided to give it to them straight, as they always had.

Alex smiled. "Ian Henderson is going to be one of the most interested people on the planet."

"No doubt," responded Dale.

"Go ahead and sound the alert. Let's get the people to their viewers."

A short blast of the planet-wide alert system was initiated, which was the signal that an important announcement was about to be made. A long and continuing blast meant to head to the protection of the caves.

They waited thirty minutes before Vance addressed the citizens of Gabriel.

"This announcement is in the form of a heads-up. We have detected a massive ship of unknown origin heading our way. We believe it to be friendly, and we believe it will be here in less than an hour, but that's just a semi-educated guess. You'll know when it arrives, because it will be quite visible. It is just over five kilometers in diameter. Yes, you heard it right: five kilometers. We don't know the purpose for its visit, but we don't perceive it to be a threat." Vance paused for a moment. "We'll keep you informed."

With that, the transmission ended.

Vance looked around the bridge. *Everyone looks as concerned as I am—except Shem*, he thought. *That's somehow calming.*

Seven minutes later, the ship disappeared. "There it goes," said Dale.

"Almost like it was waiting for that announcement," said Alex.

"I'd say that is just what they were doing," said Dale. "They were just over six light-minutes out, so they were clearly waiting for the announcement. This is getting more interesting by the minute."

Vance stood up. "Troy, Gary, Shem, I'm going outside to watch the sky. Care to join me?"

"A team of horses couldn't hold me back," said Troy.

"Let's go," said Gary.

"Keep your communicators on, please," said Dale.

"Will do," said Vance.

Shem said nothing but smiled while he followed the others to the elevator.

As the four men walked off the *Norman*'s ramp, they joined twenty or so Gabrielites hurrying out of the massive cave to see the coming phenomenon. Others who were either working in or enjoying the gazebo park joined them as they took positions on the expanse of grass. They looked to the sky. It was midmorning, so they weren't forced to look toward the sun. They didn't have to wait long.

It came in like a bullet. It started as a distant speck, and within seconds, it was at a dead stop over Home-Bay. It was like a fastball coming right at a person's head and then stopping a half meter from his or her face. Its appearance was so quick and startling that it seemed as if it were going to collide with the planet, and about a quarter of the people fell over backward from the surprise. Just about everyone screamed, yelled, or gasped, including Vance.

"Holy shit!"

There it was: a huge orb sitting stoically within a massive rib structure, in orbit above Home-Bay. It was impressive and stout looking. The *Norman*, with its hundred-meter diameter, would have appeared to be the size of a BB next to this ship's five-thousand-meter diameter. The *Norman* could easily have hidden behind one of its massive ribs.

"I've got to tell you," said Gary, "my heart is about to beat out of my chest."

"Oh my God!" said Troy.

"*Astounding* just doesn't say it," said Shem with a noticeable quiver in his voice.

"What the hell?" Alex's voice came over the communicator.

"I'll bet they did that on purpose," said Vance with a smile. "That was an attention-getter."

"It worked," said Gary.

"My attention is undivided," said Shem.

"Now what?" asked Troy.

"We wait," said Dale.

Surprisingly, Vance saw no noticeable panic from anyone, only excited conversations scattered around the area. *That's interesting,* he thought. *On old Earth, thousands of people probably would have been trampled in the panic.*

It didn't take long for people to start getting cricks in their necks from looking nearly straight up. As soon as one person found a convenient spot and lay down, it was just a matter of seconds before nearly everyone followed suit.

Vance nodded in approval as he sat on the grass next to the gazebo and lay back with his head in his hands. The other men did the same.

The hull of the ship was spectacular in its purity. There were no visible features; not even a hint of a blemish could be detected.

After five minutes of silence, Troy started a conversation.

"How many beings could be on a ship that size?"

"That would depend on the size of the beings," said Gary. "But for the sake of argument, based on the fact that all known intelligent species are more or less our size, I think a ship that size would have hundreds, if not thousands, of decks and levels. There are conceivably millions of beings residing within."

"Millions?" Vance was surprised at that estimate.

"Well, yes, how many floors or decks would a building five kilometers high have?"

"Ah." Shem was doing some mental calculations. "Something over fifteen hundred."

"Now, what if that building were five kilometers wide?"

The numbers were mind-boggling.

Still, the ship just remained in orbit. Its sheer presence was intimidating.

"The longer we lie here, the less of a threat I feel," said Troy.

"I agree," said Vance. "If they wanted to harm us, I think we'd already be goners. We would have no defense against any beings that could build a ship like that. Even if we fired a nuclear missile at it, its acceleration would take it out of range in a millisecond."

"Why do you think they're not making contact?" asked Gary.

"Maybe they're making preparations."

"Or maybe they want everyone to get used to their ship before disclosing the visit's purpose," said Shem.

Their conversation tapered off, and they continued watching the ship, along with every Gabrielite on their side of the planet.

"Gentlemen," Dale said, "we have activity on that ship."

Without the sensors and telescopes Dale had at his disposal, the four men lying on the grass outside the *Norman*'s cave wouldn't be able to detect any movement from that distance.

"What sort of activity?" asked Vance.

"An opening has appeared close to the upper axis."

"Big opening?"

"No. Maybe twenty meters square."

"Good. A big op—"

"Hold on; we have what I assume is a shuttle emerging from the ship."

Nobody said anything for a moment.

"Size?" asked Vance.

There was silence from the bridge of the *Norman*.

"About the size of one of our large runabouts. And it's heading down."

"What does it look like?"

"Like a small, slightly flattened orb—with ribs."

"Well, they're consistent," said Troy.

"Might have something to do with their technology—their propulsion system," Gary said.

Shem nodded. "Agreed."

"Vance, why don't you men head back in?" said Alex with concern in his voice.

"Okay." Vance paused for a second. "On second thought, I think I'll stay right here."

"Are you sure that's wise?"

"Just a feeling." Vance took his eyes off the ship and turned to the other three men. "Feel free to head back to the *Norman* if you wish."

Troy looked at Gary and then turned to Vance. "Gary and I are going to the *Marian*. There are a lot of techs compiling a great deal of data right now. We may need a lot of information soon."

"Roger that," said Vance. "Shem?"

"I will stay with you. I need to be here to greet these beings."

Vance looked a Shem for a moment, said nothing, and then turned back to the massive ship.

The shuttle came down slowly, much slower than the shuttles of the humans, Vout, or Yassi.

"I think we need Jarleth here," said Shem.

"Why?"

"Don't know. Kinda feel like that's the thing to do."

Vance didn't need further explanation. "Alex, get ahold of Jarleth. Have her join Shem and me out here by the gazebo ASAP."

"Will do."

Vance turned to Shem. "You're sure?"

"No, sir. Just a feeling."

Alex's voice came back on. "She's twenty minutes out."

"Damn," said Shem.

"The shuttle has stopped its descent," said Dale.

"Oh my," said Shem.

"What?"

"They're waiting for her."

Fifteen minutes later, Shem spotted Jarleth jogging quickly from the direction of the north bay, her long white hair in a ponytail trailing half a meter behind. She was nearly to the bridge spanning the Vance River.

Shem poked Vance and pointed at Jarleth, who was now halfway across the bridge.

"Good," said Vance as he spotted her.

She was dressed in a utility jumpsuit, the kind favored by most when performing tasks or work of any kind.

Three minutes later, her feet hit the grass of the park surrounding the gazebo, and seconds later, she was standing in front of Vance and Shem, breathing hard from the exertion.

Shem immediately took her in his arms and gave her a quick kiss. "Where were you?"

"Helping Mom plant some flowers around the house. We were outside watching the ship when Mr. Gabriel called." She looked at Vance and smiled. "Good morning, sir."

"Good morning, Jarleth." Vance returned the smile.

"The shuttle is moving again," said Dale.

Vance nodded slowly. "We're in no danger from these beings."

"No, we are not," agreed Shem. "They are us."

The alien shuttle's speed picked up quickly, and when it was within a hundred meters of the surface, it slowed and stopped, hovering just a meter above the ground—exactly where the *Norman* had first touched down on the planet more than five hundred years before.

"Damn," said Vance. "That's impressive."

"Those ribs are dark bronze, not black, as we thought."

The shuttle was as stunning in appearance as the mother ship. It didn't possess the stylized beauty of the Yassi ships and shuttles, but the globe in the center of the ribs was breathtaking. It looked extraordinarily smooth and polished. Like the mother ship, it was featureless but reflected everything around it like a mirror.

Quickly, several Gabrielites took their various recording devices, presently trained on the mother ship and re-trained them on the shuttle. The crowd in the park murmured excitedly, speculating about what would happen. Who were these beings? What did they want?

After a brief hesitation, Vance, Shem, and Jarleth began walking slowly toward the craft. Some of the crowd moved in behind them, while others moved toward the ship from different directions. They stopped advancing when they were within about twenty meters and stood quietly.

They didn't have to wait more than a few seconds before a ramp appeared, sliding silently out from the bottom of the featureless hull, and then a hatch noiselessly slid open above it.

Here they come, thought Vance.

"Good morning," said a pleasant voice from within the shuttle. "We are here to meet you, not to do any harm."

Vance hesitated for only a second before he took Shem's right hand and Jarleth's left and walked toward the shuttle's ramp. The people around separated to give them passage.

The three stopped at the foot of the ramp.

"Please come aboard," said the voice.

Vance looked first at Jarleth. Her expression displayed no trepidation at all. He looked over at Shem. He had a slight smile on his face as he met Vance's glance.

The three walked up the short ramp hand in hand. After they walked through the hatch, it quietly closed behind them as an inner door simultaneously opened, allowing the three to pass into a round room maybe ten meters in diameter. The room held no visible furniture or fixtures. The floor's surface displayed an intriguing design. A meter above the deck, extending a meter and a half up the walls was a window that wrapped completely around the room. They could clearly see all that was going on outside the shuttle. They could see the excited Gabrielites gathered around the shuttle, the gazebo, the mouth of the cave, and the Vast Ocean to the west.

On the far side of the room was a single being dressed in clothing similar to what a Gabrielite might wear for a formal occasion: black slacks, a white mock turtleneck shirt, and a high-collared button-less blue jacket. His shoes were black and looked to be made of leather. He was about Shem's height but quite slim. He had fairly broad shoulders, but unlike the Vout and Yassi, he had hair. His was white and cropped short, reminiscent of an ancient Roman style. His most striking features were his head and eyes. His head was proportionally the same as Shem's and Jarleth's, and his eyes were large and an unusual golden brown color. He was smiling.

"At last we meet, Vance," he said in the same pleasant, mellow voice that had welcomed them into the craft. "It has been a long time coming."

It took a few seconds for Vance to find his voice. "You know me?"

The alien's smile broadened. "Since the beginning of your existence."

Vance cocked his head and furrowed his brow as if the statement didn't make sense.

The alien ignored Vance's expression of confusion. "My name is Oruku."

"We cannot adequately express our feelings in meeting you,

Oruku," Vance replied after a pause. "I'm being remiss." He turned toward Shem and Jarleth. "I have little doubt that you know these two."

Oruku smiled brightly. "Since the beginning of their existence. They are one of the primary reasons we have come to visit."

The implication of that statement hit Vance with nearly a physical force. He backed up half a step. They'd assumed the Superiors had somehow planted Shem and Jarleth in the wombs of their mothers, but Oruku had made the same statement about Vance.

Vance's reaction didn't go unnoticed by Oruku. "We will discuss all that and a great deal more in the coming days, Vance. Please don't concern yourself now with your present thought. It will be answered to your satisfaction."

Vance's brow furrowed again. *How does he know what I'm thinking?*

Oruku smiled. "We don't read minds, Vance, but there is little else you would be questioning at this point."

And again, thought Vance, but he understood. Evidently, Oruku didn't miss even the smallest physical or facial expression. *He has extraordinary intuition, and he clearly knows me.*

"May I touch you three?" Oruku asked.

Jarleth did not hesitate. She crossed the space between them in four strides, put her arms around Oruku's neck, and gave him a warm hug.

"Wonderful, wonderful," said Oruku as he put his arms around her waist and returned the hug. "Wonderful."

Oruku seemed genuinely delighted.

As Oruku and Jarleth separated, he placed two fingers on each of her temples and looked into her eyes. "You are everything we have hoped for and, I think, much more than that. You are magnificent."

Jarleth reached up and put her fingers on Oruku's temples. "I know you," she said, displaying a little surprise in her voice. "You are me. You are Shem. You are some of Vance too."

Vance's eyebrows rose. *Some of me?*

Oruku nodded. "Yes, that's correct." With that, Oruku turned to Shem and held out his arms in an inviting fashion.

Shem crossed the room in three strides. He too embraced Oruku, who embraced him in return.

"You are the strength," said Oruku. "You are everything we

hoped for. You are, as is Jarleth, extraordinary." He touched Shem's temples with his fingers and looked into his eyes. "Wonderful. We are again extremely pleased."

Shem reached up, touched Oruku's temples with his fingers, and then smiled and nodded in acceptance.

Shem put his fingers on my face just like that when he was three, Vance immediately thought.

Oruku turned to Vance.

I wonder, thought Vance as he walked to Oruku and held out his hand.

Oruku smiled as he took Vance's hand and pulled him in for a hug. Oruku's physical strength surprised Vance, and it showed on his face. He returned Oruku's hug and stepped back a pace before putting his fingers on Oruku's temples.

He felt it. He could feel Oruku's spirit. It was indescribable. It was comforting. It was peaceful. "Wow," he said as he removed his hands.

"A new experience for you," said Oruku.

"Like no other."

Oruku pleasantly smiled as he nodded in understanding, and he placed his fingers on Vance's temples. "It is something we do to connect to another when we first meet or when we want to share a deep thought or emotion. It is called *Waoca*. In English, it translates as 'union,' 'accord,' or 'harmony.'" Oruku smiled. "Our Waoca tells me you are what we hoped you would be."

"Prior to today, our thoughts of you as Superiors had little resemblance to what you seem to be."

"We are aware of that," Oruku said. "We have been looking forward to this day for centuries."

"Centuries?"

"Yes."

Vance thought about that for a moment. "We have been referring to you as the Superiors." He paused for a second. "What do you call yourselves?"

Oruku smiled. "We are a collection of blended civilizations called the Arkell—or, roughly translated in your language, the Explorers. We are not superior; we are simply an ancient civilization by your standards and have accumulated massive amounts of intelligence and technology over a long period of time."

"How long?"

"You have theorized that there may be civilizations hundreds of thousands or millions of years older than yours, and you are right. From our first written word, more than seven hundred thousand of your years have passed."

"That is about six hundred eighty thousand years ahead of us."

"A little less, but that is essentially correct. Before we continue, I will tell you that we are transmitting all that happens here, and for the majority of our visit, to our ship." Oruku pointed to two small disks on his lapels. "These are cameras and microphones."

"Okay." Vance paused for a second. "Could you transmit to all of our viewers as well?"

Oruku nodded. "It is done."

"Thank you. That will save a lot of explanation later."

"For us as well. This visit will be monumental to our history. There is an extremely high degree of interest in your civilization and planet."

"Might I ask why?" said Vance.

Oruku nodded once. "We have three major motives and quite a number of other purposes."

Major motives? thought Vance. "Should we be concerned with your motives?"

Oruku smiled. "We know you, more than most, would be concerned about our motives."

"That's part of what I consider to be my job."

"And there is no other who could do it as well."

Vance raised one eyebrow but said nothing.

"As far as motives are concerned, we, the Arkell, have been observing humans for several thousand years, and we have chosen this time to make our presence known to you."

"Several thousand years?" asked Shem.

Oruku nodded. "This is a subject that will require a lot of time to explain and discuss. May I suggest that we put if off for the moment and stay with less complicated questions?"

"Yes, of course."

"Secondly, we wanted to meet Shem and Jarleth."

Vance was thinking what everybody else on the planet was thinking right then: *They are responsible for Shem and Jarleth.*

"You had something to do with their births, we're assuming?"

"We did. But again, we'll go into that in more detail at another time."

"And third?"

"We have, on rare occasions, caught a glimpse of another ship in this galaxy. We have tried to make contact to no avail."

"What sort of ship?"

"Its energy signature is similar to ours. Its size is bigger."

"Bigger?"

"Yes, we are sure of that, but this ship clearly doesn't want any contact with us."

"Why would that be?"

"We don't know, but when we have been able to track where it's been, we've discovered massive damage to planets, moons, and other large celestial bodies."

"What sort of damage?"

"Assets, such as minerals, water, and vegetation, have been stripped away with no apparent regard for the natural ecology. Two of the planets supported a form of intelligent life. One had most life destroyed outright, and the other was damaged to a point that much of the surviving life may not be able to continue."

"How advanced was this life?"

"Quite advanced. You could compare one planet's top intelligence to Earth's monkeys and apes and the other to your herbivores and various predators. There was a huge loss of developing life."

It was clear that Oruku was upset at the thought of such catastrophic losses.

"That ship could be a threat to us in the future," said Vance.

"Yes, that's certainly possible. We believe they may be as technologically advanced as we are."

"Uh-oh," said Vance.

"However, we have only come across this ship a great distance from here."

"How far?"

"Last we saw them, they would have been"—Oruku paused for a moment—"twelve light-years away from Gabriel."

That got Vance's attention. "Are we in danger?"

"We don't think so—while we are here. We have placed probes in place to monitor this sector of the galaxy."

"Sector?"

"Yes, we have designated three hundred eighty sectors in the Milky Way galaxy. Gabriel is located approximately in the middle of Sector 196. We will detect anything bigger than, say, this shuttle."

"How big—"

Oruku politely cut Vance off. "Being concerned at this moment is not necessary. We'll go into more detail on this subject at a later date."

Being a military man, Vance wasn't finished with questions concerning threats to their planet. "If you'll indulge me for a moment, I would like to ask two more questions."

Oruku nodded.

"Why do you believe they don't want to make contact with you?"

"We don't know, but as you can imagine, we have speculated about that for a very long time."

"Speculations?"

"One is that they might fear us. They may assume we have superior technology and weaponry. They may base that fear on their knowledge of our shields."

"Shields?"

"We analyzed their shields and found them to be a great deal weaker than what we employ."

"What about weapons?"

Oruku put his hand up. "Let's take this conversation up at a later date. We are in no danger at this time."

Vance reluctantly nodded in agreement.

"May I ask a question?" said Jarleth.

"Please do."

"Have you ever intervened in the humans' history?"

"We have, on rare occasions, intervened in Earth's progress. The civilizations have been, shall we say, occasionally altered." Oruku paused for a moment. "We will go into a great deal more detail on all subjects as our time here passes."

"How long do you plan on staying on Gabriel?"

"Two months or so, if you'll have us for that long."

"I suspect you'll be welcome for however long you wish," said Vance.

"We will try not to wear out our welcome."

Their use of English is perfect—not any accent, thought Vance.

Oruku turned his head to the right as a previously unseen door silently slid open. Two more Arkell entered the room. One was a male who looked somewhat like Shem, with dark hair and eyes. He didn't have the powerful Youngblood physique; his body was more like Oruku's. The other Arkell was a striking woman who looked enough like Jarleth to be her biological mother, with similar height, weight, and coloring, except for her eyes, which were close to the color of Oruku's. All three Arkell were of an indeterminate age. One might have guessed somewhere between forty and sixty.

"This is Janos." Oruku nodded in the man's direction. "And this is Nola," said Oruku. "You will find some things in common."

Jarleth immediately walked over and hugged the woman. Then she backed off half a pace and placed her fingers on Nola's temples. Nola reciprocated and did the same to Jarleth.

"Are you my mother?" asked Jarleth.

"A part of me is," said Nola in a soft voice similar to Jarleth's.

"Yes, I can feel it."

Shem smiled. "Clearly, Janos, you are part of me also." Shem walked over and hugged Janos, and then, following suit, he placed his fingers on Janos's temples and looked into his eyes. "Many of your genes are in my body."

"They are, and I am pleased." Janos placed his fingers on Shem's temples. "You are a splendid being."

Shem nodded once and turned his attention to Nola. He went through the Waoca with her as Jarleth and Janos did the same.

Vance smiled. "I'm now assuming that I have a gene or two in the mix here?"

Janos stepped over to Vance but did not hug him before preforming Waoca. "You are a synthetic life-form, and your feel is different, but we know you. You have maintained the spirit. It's been a long time since you were seeded—a very long time."

"Seeded?"

Janos nodded.

"May I?" Vance put his fingers on Janos's temples. "Remarkable. We are much the same."

"We have common ancestors." Janos smiled. "Your father of record was not your father."

Vance nodded. "I've known that since as far back as I can remember. He was nothing like me."

"But a man named Vincent Papas was," said Oruku.

"Vincent Papas?"

Vance had, from the time he was in his early teens, assumed his mother had had an affair. It hadn't taken him long to come to terms with it, and he was grateful. He had little use for the man who called himself his father.

"I'm Greek?"

"About forty-five percent," answered Janos with a smile.

"Five percent Arkell?"

"Exactly, yes. Your mother was half Irish and a quarter Native American, and the balance was German and Scottish."

"That's always been my understanding, yes." Vance stopped for a moment before asking his next question. "Why don't I have the same appearance as Jarleth and Shem?"

"Your father, Vincent, also didn't. Neither of you would have been accepted as a normal human being in those days. Your life would have been made miserable by the ignorance of the time. Because of that, the genes that contribute to your appearance were modified. Vincent's parents' human genes were exceptional, and because of that, we intervened in his conception. His genes became ten percent Arkell. Your mother's genes were also exceptional. The pairing of the two resulted in your birth."

Vance was stunned by the revelations. "I don't know what to say here."

Oruku smiled. "Vance, you will have more questions than most. Alexander will also have a great many. We will endeavor to answer all of them."

"Questions are flashing through my mind as we speak."

"And our answers will create many more," said Oruku.

Vance nodded and smiled. "As they just did. So where do we go from here?"

"We would like to visit Dale and Alexander in the *Norman*."

"Now?"

"Yes, please."

Vance was unsure how to proceed. "Let's take a walk."

"I will walk with you." Oruku turned to Shem and Jarleth. "Would you mind waiting here and spending time with Nola and Janos? They will give you a tour of this shuttle while answering some of your questions."

"Yes, sir," they said in unison.

Oruku smiled. "My name is Oruku."

"We will spend our time with Nola and Janos, Oruku," said Shem.

"Thank you." Oruku turned to Vance. "Shall we?"

As Vance and Oruku walked down the ramp and onto the grass, the gathered Gabrielites were surprisingly quiet. The expressions on their faces were of reverence and wonder. Vance looked back at the shuttle and still saw no sign of windows.

Vance and Oruku stopped when they stepped onto the grass. Oruku smiled as he raised his hand in greeting.

"This man's name is Oruku," announced Vance. "He is as dear a friend as can be found in the universe."

The crowd erupted with applause.

Oruku's smile broadened as he addressed the Gabrielites. "Thank you for the warm welcome. We are extremely pleased to be here on your beautiful planet. We will get to know each other as the days pass, but for now, we need to meet Alexander Gabriel and Dale Isley."

"May I ask Troy and Gary to join us from the *Marian*?" Vance said.

"Yes, please, we are anxious to meet both of them."

"I'm assuming they are paying close attention right now. Troy, Gary, would you care to join us in the *Norman*?"

With that, the two walked casually toward the *Norman's* cave. The crowd parted respectfully as they strolled comfortably up the path.

On Earth, a visit from an alien ship would have caused worldwide panic and chaos. But not here. Vance smiled at the thought. "I have a question."

"Ask anything."

Vance continued to smile. "Why did you bring your ship into orbit the way you did?"

Oruku smiled and nodded. "Because we knew you would love the dramatics of it. Humans, in our observations, enjoy risk—they enjoy an adrenaline rush, as you would say. Our arrival was designed to produce just that."

"I thought that might be the case. Well done, I might add. It will certainly be a subject of conversation for some time to come."

"Then we have succeeded in our effort."

Vance nodded. "Will we be able to visit your ship?"

"That is one of our wishes, yes."

"There are about eighty-two thousand people cheering right now," said Vance.

"We are aware." Oruku looked to his right. There, a hundred meters to the south, sat the *Marian*. "There's the *Marian*. What an outstanding sight."

Vance smiled. "We used to think she was a massive ship, being six times the size of the *Norman*, but now we know better."

Oruku nodded in understanding. He seemed genuinely enthralled as he and Vance walked up the paved path to the cave's entrance. His head moved constantly as he took in the sights of the gazebo park.

"This is simply delightful. To see Gabriel and walk upon its surface, feel its atmosphere, and smell its aroma is a delightful experience, an experience we have been looking forward to since your first landing."

Vance smiled. "You've been keeping tabs on us for a long time."

"In a manner of speaking, we have."

They said nothing for a few seconds before Vance continued.

"I'm delighted that you like our planet. I would think you have visited many worlds as pretty as ours or even more so."

"There are tens of thousands of planets in the galaxy that have extreme beauty in thousands of ways, but less than a handful come close to matching Gabriel's beauty of life in all of its forms. What you have done here is quite exceptional."

"Really? I would think that hundreds, if not thousands, of

planets that fit certain requirements for life as we know it would have been, over the eons, seeded and colonized with similar results."

"A few have, but generally, they have been seeded with a much narrower goal. In some cases, just enough to maintain a specific species or two. There are only four that were seeded and colonized similarly to yours; they are the exceptions."

"I don't know why that surprises me, but it does."

"We'll show you videos of dozens of planets before we leave, and we'll explain how they differ so much from Gabriel."

"That will be fascinating."

Within another minute, they entered the cave and headed to the ramp leading to the interior of the *Norman*. Oruku's head never stopped moving. It was obvious he was captivated by the experience.

"The *Norman*. The sight of it is nearly overwhelming to me."

"I'm surprised that such a simple ship by your standards has such an effect on you."

Oruku stopped walking and turned toward Vance. "Simple ship in a way, but it's extremely relevant and historical. Touch my temples."

Vance turned toward Oruku, reached over, and put his fingers on Oruku's temples.

The effect was overpowering. He could feel the emotions of Oruku—sheer joy, wonderment, gratification, and pride.

"My God!"

Oruku smiled. "Now you know a little of what your accomplishments have meant to us."

"A little? I'm amazed at your interest."

They continued their walk to the *Norman*'s ramp. Oruku stopped, looked up into the interior of the ship, and nodded to himself. "Shall we?"

"We shall."

Up they went, straight to the elevator. It was there waiting for them. They stepped inside, and the door closed.

"May we take a quick tour of the *Norman* before we visit with Alexander and Dale?"

"Of course. Let's head this way." Vance gestured to their left.

"We are very excited about this," said Oruku as the two headed off down a passageway.

Vance took great pride in giving Oruku a tour of the *Norman*. He was a little surprised at Oruku's great interest in what was, to him, antiquated technology. The two talked like old friends during the extensive tour of the ship. An hour later, they stepped onto the bridge of the *Norman*.

Oruku stopped and slowly looked around. "I am standing on the bridge of the *Norman*."

Vance knew that Oruku was talking not only to himself but also to 120,000 Arkell and 82,000 Gabrielites. Oruku's enthusiasm reminded Vance of Troy's reaction when he'd first realized he had come face-to-face with the historical Vance Youngblood and the *Norman*. It was a reaction he couldn't have imagined coming from a Superior.

Oruku's eyes came to rest on Troy, Gary, Alex, and Dale. He smiled briefly in recognition before walking straight to the two men and two holograms.

He stopped in front of Alex and Dale first. "Alexander, Dale," he said, looking from one to the other, "I am pleased beyond words to meet you both."

Vance had to smile. It seemed that both men had become tongue-tied. That wasn't out of the question for Dale, but he had never seen Alex in such a condition. However, after all, they were standing in front of a Superior. Alex found his voice first.

"I am nearly speechless, Oruku."

"As am I," said Dale.

"You two, along with Vance, Jason, and Teddy, have been the subject of tens of thousands of conversations over the centuries. It is I who should be speechless."

"That's quite humbling," said Alex. "You are certainly not what we expected."

The affable Oruku smiled again. "What were you expecting?"

Alex thought about that for a moment. "I can't answer for anyone else, but I expected a being a great deal more stoic—more godlike, if you will."

"That pretty much sums up my thoughts," said Vance.

"We can understand that." Oruku turned toward Dale. "Dr. Isley?"

"Frankly, I wasn't sure there would be any flesh-and-blood being at all. Or perhaps just a huge organic brain at the control of a vast network of computers and machines, or possibly beings that looked like insects. You could have been anything."

That caused Oruku to laugh, something he hadn't done before. "Dale, you have just amused and delighted a lot of Arkell." Oruku laughed again.

Even Dale smiled. "Wasn't trying to be funny."

"Oh, we know you, Doctor. That is what makes what you said so unexpected and amusing."

"Well, that makes me happy. I can't think of many times in my life when I have amused anyone. That's Teddy's department."

"Ah, Teddy. When can we meet him?"

"Soon, but when Teddy's around, there won't be much serious conversation allowed. So if you don't mind, I believe we would like to spend some time just talking with you," said Alex. "No offense, Teddy, if you're watching."

"I completely understand. We will meet Teddy at some other time."

Oruku turned to Troy, shook his hand, and then pulled him in for a hug. "It is a pleasure meeting you, Troy. Your leadership on Earth contributed greatly to saving a diversified gene pool and preserving most of the humans' advanced technology."

"Thank you, sir. I'm so dumbstruck right now. Don't know what to say."

"No need to say anything," said Oruku, "and my name is Oruku."

"Yes, sir."

Oruku smiled and turned to Gary. "Gary, the great scientist, we are pleased to meet you also." He shook Gary's hand and gave him a warm hug.

"Meeting you is an honor I will never forget, Oruku."

Oruku smiled and nodded once. "You all have many questions, and we will answer them as accurately as we can. Who wishes to start?"

Dale didn't hesitate. "May I ask how many are on your ship?"

"We maintain approximately one hundred twenty thousand people aboard our home ship."

"One hundred twenty thousand!"

Oruku smiled. "It's a large ship. That number allows us to comfortably maintain our civilization within the ship. All one hundred twenty thousand are watching and listening to us right now."

"That's quite intimidating."

"If I told you that all one hundred twenty thousand care for you deeply, would it be less intimidating?"

Vance smiled. "That does help—a lot."

"Would you like to sit?" Vance asked as he motioned Oruku toward the captain's chair.

"No, please. We would prefer it if you were sitting in that chair. Your sitting in that chair is part of the narrative we have maintained for a long time. If you don't mind, I'll sit here." Oruku pointed to one of the bridge technicians' chairs close by. "The Arkell on our ship would love to see you sitting there."

"Okay, sure."

"Good," said Oruku.

"I have a couple of questions that I believe are relevant," said Vance.

Oruku nodded. "We are ready."

"Okay," said Vance. "You refer to *we* quite often. Is that the royal *we*, or are there more than one of you?"

Oruku pointed at his left ear. "I have, when needed, hundreds of specialists who have access to information and technology on which I'm not completely versed, so when you ask a question that is out of my field of expertise, I will be given the correct information by the proper specialists."

"I see." Vance smiled. "So you are not omnipotent?"

Oruku returned the smile. "Far from it."

Vance nodded. "Okay, let's get to the questions."

"I need to ask the big question before I burst," said Dale.

"Did we block the gamma-ray burst, and if so, how did we do it?"

"Yes. You're quite perceptive."

"You're a scientist—one of the most brilliant we have encountered. That would naturally be your primary question."

"Thank you for the fine compliment. That's quite humbling."

Oruku nodded. "To answer your question, we did divert the comet to block the GRB. I will give you the short version of how we did it. I suggest you and our top physicist discuss the details at a later date."

Dale nodded enthusiastically. "Agreed."

"I will tell you that it wasn't child's play for us, as you have speculated might be the case. When our astronomers discovered the impending merging of the binaries forty-two years ago and determined that Gabriel was directly in line with the axis of the larger star, our top priority became saving your planet."

"That's astounding," said Gary. "Forty-two years ago."

Oruku looked at Gary and smiled. "We have fairly sophisticated technology."

All on the bridge laughed.

"I would like to point out that you saved our planet twenty years ago today," said Vance, "but I have little doubt you know that."

"It occurred to us, yes," Oruku said with a wry smile.

"What are the basics as to how you accomplished such a feat?" asked Dale.

Oruku nodded once. "It took a full month to calculate a practical way to block the GRB. After that, we spent months finding a comet the right size, makeup, and trajectory in the required sector of space and weeks putting the physics in place." Oruku paused. "I have to tell you we were near panic during this time. The thought of losing Gabriel and its inhabitants caused nearly as much consternation and anguish among the Arkell as the loss of Earth did."

"This is very humbling," said Dale.

"We have always assumed we were little more than a piece of dust in the vast universe, but now we are being told that we mean a great deal to others," said Alex.

"That certainly answers many of our questions," said Vance.

"We know that you had these far-reaching questions concerning the GRB. Who among us wouldn't?"

"We, meaning Dale and Shem, can get into a more detailed explanation at a later date," said Vance. "Why don't we get to some of the more mundane questions?"

"I'll start," said Gary. "How far away is your home planet?"

"We are two hundred sixty point four light-years from Gabriel at this moment."

"How long does the trip take?"

"It would take something under three hundred years, but we haven't been to our home planet in one thousand sixteen years."

"For one thousand sixteen years?" said Vance. "How is that possible?"

"Our ship is our home. It has everything we need or desire. You will see when you visit that the interior of the ship is nearly indistinguishable from an actual planet. We have farms, forests, lakes, towns—everything you have on Gabriel but on a smaller scale."

"Forests, lakes, and towns?" said a wide-eyed Troy.

"I cannot wait to see this," said Gary.

"How long did it take to build such a ship?" asked Dale.

"From the day of the beginning, two hundred three of your years."

"Incredible."

"It was a considerable undertaking."

"To say the least," said Dale.

"To add another dimension to this discussion, I will tell you that just more than thirty thousand years ago, we designed and built a ship, the *Geaalo*, to travel to the edge of this universe and into the next."

"To a neighboring universe?"

Oruku nodded. "It's a long trip."

"How long?" asked Vance.

"Two point three billion light-years, give or take."

"Two point three—"

"The *Geaalo* is a world unto itself, much like our ship—just somewhat larger. It will not return to this galaxy. Someday, in the distant future, it will be in a different universe." Oruku paused for a moment. "We have not heard from it in more than twenty-six thousand years and will never hear from it again. Millions of generations will live and die aboard that ship before it reaches the edge of this universe."

"How could a ship be designed to last billions of years?" asked Gary.

"That ship, like ours, is constantly upgraded or repaired. Worn parts are manufactured and replaced as needed. We have several decks dedicated to just that. We could, in theory, duplicate our entire ship in about half the time it took to build it the first time."

"Wow!" said Vance. "Do you harvest raw materials as needed from various celestial bodies?"

"Raw materials aren't needed too often. We recycle and remanufacture worn or damaged parts. In addition, we have a sufficient stockpile of materials on hand. If we run low, we will gather raw materials from various sources, as you suggested."

"A project, a voyage, that is designed to last at least two billion years," said Vance. "A little hard to get my mind around."

"Thinking outside the box comes to mind," said Troy.

"The records from those times, thirty thousand years ago, recorded that only a small majority of Arkell approved the project. It apparently caused some strife at a time when strife was only something to read about."

"Massive resources were required, with no possible reward for those left in this galaxy," Troy said.

"And resources from different inhabited planets were required to contribute to the project."

"And they objected?" asked Vance.

"Some did, but the majority approved."

"I can't imagine such an undertaking," Gary said. "Your ship is nearly beyond description—but something larger? So people who started the construction never saw the completed ship?"

"Most did on the *Velgot* but not on the *Geaalo*. Their life span was just shy of two hundred years at that time. Our life span now averages more than three hundred twelve years."

"Three hundred twelve years?"

"We've had a long time to alter and perfect genes to allow us to reach that age."

"What is your age?" asked Alex.

"In your years, one hundred ninety-seven."

"Wow, you don't look a day over fifty," said Vance.

"I don't feel much over thirty, actually." Oruku smiled. "Your age is greater than ours, all time considered."

Vance smiled. "I guess that's right; it depends on how you count the years. Several hundred by some measure and a couple hundred by others."

Oruku smiled brightly. "You don't look a day over thirty-six."

Vance laughed. "The advantage of being a synthetic."

Oruku nodded and then paused for a second. "While we are on this subject, we Arkell are prepared to offer humans a gift."

"Gift?"

Oruku briefly thought back to the conversation he'd had with the other nineteen councillors concerning the gift he was about to offer the humans. *A few were opposed.* He smiled to himself *But most weren't.*

"Yes, of a somewhat longer life," he said.

"Longer as in more years?" asked Alex.

"Yes. Early loss of life means the loss of intellect and wisdom that the deceased may have otherwise contributed to their societies. The histories of all civilizations, including our own, have lost or have had delayed a great many future advances in countless areas, all due to premature death. Clearly, the advancement of civilizations would have proceeded at a much faster pace had we had the benefit of these intellects for a longer period."

"Without question," agreed Dale.

"How exactly would you provide such a wonderful and far-reaching gift?" asked Alex.

"We have the technology to slightly alter and enhance genes, making them stronger and more durable."

"What does that entail?"

"An individual is subjected to a form of radiation and gene manipulation you're not familiar with. It takes an average of twenty minutes per person, depending on his or her size."

"How many years would be added to their life spans?"

"That depends on the person's current age. The younger the subject, the more benefit will be realized. As many as fifty years for those under the age of full maturity and as few as eight years for older individuals."

"Fifty years! That's mind-boggling. That's incredible," said Dale.

"I can't see anyone objecting to this," said Alex.

"Everyone, of course, will have a choice. I'm assuming those who do not wish to live longer can opt out," said Vance.

"Fat chance of anyone opting out," said Troy.

Oruku smiled.

"How would we proceed?" asked Vance.

"The ideal time will be when your people visit our ship. Each group will pass through our lab decks while on tour. Each person can take twenty minutes out from the tour to undergo the treatment."

"I imagine most Gabrielites watching this are dancing with glee at this moment," said Alex.

Oruku nodded. "Shall we continue the questions?"

Everyone was quiet for a moment.

"Yes, I have question," said Alex.

"We know you do, and it is a great deal more complicated to answer than Dale's."

"Did you send me back in time?"

"We did."

"Why?"

"To do what you did."

"How?" asked Dale.

"Again, the complete answer is lengthy. I recommend we save that discussion for another time, but I will tell you now that it was done within the physics of temporal dimensions and space-time shifts. Nothing ever ceases to exist. It's a difficult principle to comprehend."

Alex nodded. "To know that you did it is enough for now. It is an understatement to say that the who, why, and how have been on my mind for a long time. Now I know the who."

"And the why," added Oruku.

"And the why, yes," agreed Alex.

Vance spoke up. "My question is similar to Alex's. What did you have in mind for me?"

"Our original thought was that a being such as you, with your exceptional genes and Arkell enhancement, would have the intelligence, physical strength, and force of character to make a huge difference in the leadership of Earth. However, you took a turn that we did not anticipate when you joined a fighting force for your country." Oruku smiled. "I did mention that we are far from superior." Oruku's smile faded a little. "We later realized that we did not give enough credence to your Greek and Irish genes. Those genes clearly were not opposed to conflict."

The admission of fallibility caused everyone to smile.

"However," Oruku said, "through exceptional happenstance, you and Alexander got together, and it was a perfect mating of personalities and abilities. The rest is history, as you say."

"That is absolutely remarkable," said Dale.

"We thought so too," Oruku said. "It was wonderful."

"I don't know what to say," said Alex. "Not nearly enough adjectives at my disposal."

There was silence on the bridge for a moment before Dale spoke up.

"Did you have anything to do with my life?"

"No, you were not on our radar, as you would say. You were a pleasant and welcome surprise. Due to your brilliance, we calculate that our goal was advanced by at least sixty years, probably a great deal more. The day that you and Alexander met is legend among us."

"Really?" said Alex. "Our relationship was nearly over before it began. I remember thinking at the time how angry my father would have been if I'd prevented Dale from working at Norman Research. Now you tell me possibly billions of beings in the galaxy would have been upset."

"No, at that time, we were still unaware of Dale's brilliance or his future contributions."

"I see."

"Could you have prevented the destruction of Earth?" asked Vance out of the blue.

"The loss of Earth was one of the most horrific disasters in our history. Our entire race went into mourning for months. It still brings tears to many when they think of it." Oruku paused. "We simply were not in a position to stop the asteroid. We, at the time, were paralleling the *Norman*'s voyage through space. We were, as you were, thirty light-years away when the asteroid was discovered."

"You were able to detect the binary neutron stars merging decades before the actual occurrence and, we now know, redirect a massive comet in both speed and direction in order to prevent the GRB from destroying Gabriel," said Dale. "How was it that you couldn't detect the planet-killing asteroid?"

"That is a reasonable question. And the answer is that we did detect it. But it couldn't have been predicted, as was the GRB. That asteroid was a result of a series of catastrophic collisions in the

Kuiper Belt in Earth's solar system. That cataclysmic chain reaction hurled tens of thousands of comets and asteroids out of the belt. One of the largest, unfortunately, was sent in the direction of Earth. At the speed it was originally traveling, we would have had just enough time to intercede. We turned our ship and headed back at full speed." Oruku paused for a moment before continuing. "Our sensors, at that extreme range, calculated that the asteroid had a good chance of impacting with Jupiter. That would have in itself been problematic but not necessarily catastrophic to Earth. But that is not what happened. The asteroid used Jupiter for what you call the slingshot effect and tripled its speed. We could not—" Oruku stopped again for a few seconds while he gathered his emotions. "We could no longer get there in time."

Vance could see that Oruku was on the verge of tears just from talking about it.

"That answers the question. There is no point in continuing the conversation," said Vance with empathy for Oruku. "We truly appreciate your feelings of great loss."

"It was a terrible thing for us," Oruku said.

Vance could feel the sadness coming from Oruku and changed the subject. "I suggest we take a break and maybe show you around this cave, the *Norman*'s cave," said Vance. "Then we can have lunch."

"Excellent," said Oruku. "We would like that. May I invite seven of my fellow councillors to join us for lunch?"

"Absolutely."

"They, Janos, Nola, and I make up half the governing council on our ship. Tomorrow, with your permission, we would like to bring down the other ten councillors."

"I'm sure we're all looking forward to meeting them." Vance paused for a second. "So let's head out."

Vance, Oruku, Troy, and Gary spent the next hour showing Oruku the interworking's of the *Norman*'s cave. It was much more than just a hangar for the *Norman*. It contained a sizeable hospital, an arsenal, tons of emergency supplies, a large supply of gold in bars of various weights, and a small cafeteria to serve the two dozen or so who worked in the cave.

Oruku was impressed. "You are prepared for just about any contingency."

"With experience grows some wisdom," said Vance.

Oruku noted the size of the cave. "How long did it take the Vout to create this cave?"

"More than fifty years in actual time, they tell us," said Vance. "It contained huge deposits of gold and silver. Interesting to note the floor is flat to within two millimeters from front to back and side to side."

"Remarkable," said Oruku as he looked to the back of the well-lit cave and then up to the ceiling five hundred feet above them. "Remarkable."

About that time, Shem, Jarleth, Nola, and Janos were walking on the boardwalk near the center of Home-Bay.

Jarleth was as happy as she had ever been. Spending the past three hours with Nola and Janos milling with the crowd while giving the Arkell a tour of Home-Bay was an experience she had never had. She was with fellow beings—beings like she and Shem. *I see where Shem gets his strength and intelligence,* she thought as she looked at Janos. The family resemblance was strong.

She and Shem introduced Nola and Janos to everyone they came across, much to the thrill of the humans and Yassi in attendance. The Vout weren't as social as the Yassi, and for them to be absent from the Home-Bay area at any time was not unusual. Jarleth hoped the Arkell would stay on Gabriel for an extended stay so the Vout would be able to meet them.

Shem was the first to spot the second Arkell shuttle descending from the mother ship. "Look at that," he said as he pointed skyward. "I think we should return to the landing site."

"Agreed," said Nola and Janos nearly in unison.

By the time the four returned to the gazebo park, a crowd had already gathered around Vance, Oruku, Troy, Gary, and the seven new Arkell—four females and three males. Vance was just completing the Waoca with the seven, when Shem, Jarleth, Nola, and Janos joined them.

Vance stood back while Jarleth and Shem were introduced to the Arkell and went through Waoca with each. By the expressions on the Arkell's faces, Vance could see they were enthralled with Shem and Jarleth. Shem's demeanor was more relaxed and easygoing than he had ever seen before.

The Gabrielites maintained a respectful distance, not wanting to interrupt the ceremony.

When the formalities were complete, Oruku asked, "Shall we eat?"

Vance nodded. "Right this way."

Vance led the new Arkell to the gazebo.

Once inside, Oruku looked at the seating arrangement. "Might I make a suggestion?"

"Please do."

"I think it would be appropriate to have one Arkell at each table. That way, many will benefit from this historic experience."

"Excellent. That's what we'll do."

The majority had taken seats, when Teddy, Colleen, and Lara made their appearance.

"Hello," said a voice from the entrance to the gazebo.

Everybody turned and immediately laughed, wooed, and clapped as Teddy walked in with Colleen on one arm and Lara on the other.

"Oh my," said Oruku. "It's Teddy."

Vance raised his hand to signal Teddy. Teddy spotted him and started walking toward him, his bright smile lighting the way as the three closed the distance.

When they arrived, Vance hugged Lara and gave her a quick kiss and then did the same with Colleen. He hugged Teddy before turning to Oruku.

"Oruku, it is my pleasure to introduce you to my wife, Lara, and to Teddy and his wife, Colleen."

Vance sensed Oruku was momentarily spellbound and smiled to himself.

"Oh my," said Oruku. "This is a moment to remember. This is wonderful."

He first opened his arms to Lara. She accepted the offer and gave him a warm hug. "The wonderful Lara of Earth and Gabriel. The loving wife of Vance. We cannot begin to tell you what an honor and pleasure it is to meet you. This is outstanding."

"Well, sir, the honor and pleasure go both ways. To meet with a Superior—um, Arkell—is something I would have never thought possible."

"We will talk more soon." Oruku turned to Colleen. "And to meet the absolutely gorgeous Colleen of Earth and Gabriel, the wife of Teddy." He and Colleen hugged. "You are even more beautiful than all of the images we have had of you since the time you went to work with Walter Gabriel."

Colleen smiled brightly. "That is nice of you to say, and meeting you and your fellow Arkell will certainly be one of the highlights of my life. I'm surprised to hear you've been watching me for centuries."

"Well, we could only pick up images transmitted through various means by your media. I can assure you that you have not been singled out, but you are one of the delightful highlights."

Oruku's smile broadened as he turned to Teddy.

Teddy's eyes got big. "I don't know whether to genuflect, bow, or kiss something," Teddy said seriously. "You tell me, sir, and I'll get the job done."

Everyone within earshot broke down laughing, including the Arkell.

Vance knew Oruku wanted to hug Teddy, but he was momentarily incapacitated with laughter. *Teddy never disappoints*, he thought.

"May I hug you?" Oruku finally managed to ask.

"Well, you don't look as strong as Vance, so sure, I can probably take it."

Oruku hugged Teddy for several seconds, longer than normal for men to hug, but Teddy didn't seem to mind.

The fact that Teddy didn't mind hugging a man at length was a testament to the loving nature that Vance perceived Oruku possessed. He smiled to himself. *Had Oruku not been genuine, Teddy would have sensed it quickly, and the hug would have been quite short.*

Oruku released Teddy. "I cannot tell you how thrilled we are to meet you, Teddy. You have given us great pleasure and amusement for centuries. You are wonderful."

Teddy was uncharacteristically speechless for a moment. "Well, I guess I've been jester to the gods. Who'd have thought?"

"A great deal more than that to us," said Oruku. "We cannot answer for the gods."

Teddy smiled broadly.

"May I?" Oruku moved to put his fingers on Teddy's temples.

"Yes, sir."

Oruku placed his hands on Teddy's temples and let them linger for a moment. "Not quite," he said as he moved his fingers off of Teddy's face.

Teddy reached over and put his hands on Oruku's face. Then his face looked as if he were in deep but comical concentration. He smiled brightly as he removed his hands. "I'm not getting so much as a 'Hi there' from your face."

Oruku smiled broadly. "Hi there."

Oruku's humor took everyone by surprise, and they laughed.

Teddy laughed the loudest. "Good one."

"Thank you. To make you laugh gives me great joy."

Teddy nodded. "You feel like a real good person. You feel like Jarleth and Shem."

"Your intuitive genes are similar to what, over hundreds of generations, we have developed in order to give us the ability to send and receive feelings. We have observed that you have consistently used your abilities to make everyone you come in contact with feel better in many ways."

The noontime meal lasted for a full two hours and would become a notable part of Gabriel's history.

When the meal was finished, Vance asked Oruku, "Would you like to take a walk? We'd love to show you around the river and bay."

"We would indeed."

CHAPTER 15

A SUPERIOR WALK

The touring party had grown to eighteen.

Jarleth suggested they split into two groups for the tour. She would guide Nola, Janos, and the seven Arkell councillors while Vance, Shem, Oruku, Troy, Gary, Teddy, Colleen, and Lara were sightseeing.

"Good idea. Thank you," said Vance.

"Excellent," said Oruku.

After the two groups separated, Oruku turned to Shem as they walked. "You and Jarleth are the finest traits of both races. We are so pleased and proud of you both."

Shem was speechless for several seconds. "I am humbled that you would feel that way about us. Your visit has answered most of the questions we have had all our lives. I just don't have the words to express our gratitude."

Oruku smiled. "No words necessary."

In a few minutes, Vance asked, "What do you think of our dear friends the Vout and Yassi?"

Oruku smiled. "The Vout are among the most peaceful, industrious people in the galaxy. They, even in their formative centuries and millennia, were opposed to violence of any kind. They are one of the few races to continue to grow and gain intellect without conflict." Oruku paused and smiled again. "However, their peaceful nature also contributed to a rather unemotional and somewhat lackluster nature. But they remain a wonderful, loving, and loyal people."

All three men smiled in understanding.

"And the Yassi?"

"The Yassi are delightful." Oruku stopped walking as they were in the middle of the bridge and looked upriver. "Oh, this is beautiful."

From that vantage point, they could see and hear the crystal-clear sky-blue river as it cascaded down from the mountains, through the forest of deciduous trees, and over boulders and small waterfalls.

Vance could see that Oruku was taken with the sight.

"What a wonderful spot," said Oruku.

"Agreed," said Troy, Gary, and Shem at about the same time.

"Was it up this river that you encountered the bear?" asked Oruku.

Vance was surprised. "You know about that?"

"Big story on our ship at the time," said a smiling Oruku.

"Wow," said Vance.

"What bear?" said Gary.

"The story is in the archives," said Troy.

"I'll check it out."

"Shall we?" asked Vance as he gestured forward.

The four of them continued to walk toward Vance's home.

"Did the Yassi have a violent past?"

Oruku's eyebrows went up. "You did not want to incur the wrath of the Yassi. They were vicious, but that was a thousand years in the past. Their history is similar to humans'."

"They finally saw the light?"

"Hardly. Their light took a long time to brighten. They didn't have an Alexander, Vance, or Dale. You three, plus Jason, changed the course of human history in what amounted to a cosmic blink of an eye. It took the Yassi centuries to finally shake off the chains of evil and violence. Your way was a great deal easier on your population. It was an incredible action. We Arkell were both stunned and impressed."

"Did you aid that endeavor in any way?" asked Troy.

"No, all we have done over the past millennia to guide progress on Earth, other than the genetic enhancement of Vance and sending Alexander back in time, was to clear a few paths, if you will, and let nature take its course."

"Right up here," said Vance as they came to the walkway leading to his home.

Forty-five minutes later, they were back in the *Norman*'s bridge.

Once everyone was settled in Vance returned to their previous conversation, "What about the Malic?"

"As you would say, Vance, they are 'nasty little bastards' and, I might add, stupid."

Everyone was amused.

"They seem to have gone through a change in attitude and appearance as of late. Did the Arkell have anything to do with that?" asked Alex.

"We have an interesting outcome to something you inadvertently started. Forcing them to wash and cutting off their offensive canine teeth started a chain reaction in their society. Seeing this, we decided to give the ugly little things a nudge along. We altered the genetics of most of their leaders."

"Altered their genetics, did you?" said Vance with some humor.

"We'll get to Shem and Jarleth in a while," said Oruku.

Vance smiled. "Okay."

"The Malic breed quickly and mature at an early age, so the genetic changes spread quickly. The leaders' offspring were born looking different, but that was a bonus as far as the Malic were concerned. The rest of the Malic wanted to look like them. Within two more generations, there were tens of thousands of improved Malic."

"That answers most of the questions," said Dale.

"There is something we would like you to know," said Oruku. "We were unaware of the Malic's attack on the *Marian* and their subsequent attack on Gabriel. We were twelve light-years away when we found out about those events—too far to help. Had we been close by, we would have stopped them, of course."

Vance and the others nodded in understanding.

After a moment, Vance asked, "So the Malic's offer to welcome the Byuse back to their planet is sincere?"

"We believe so, yes."

"What do you know of the Byuse?"

"Little. We have not spent much time observing their race. We know they are a peaceful people much like the Vout, and because of that, they lost their planet to beings half their size and intellect."

"That's interesting," said Vance.

"To change the subject," said Troy, "do you have any knowledge of the other two Earth ships that escaped the asteroid as we did?"

"We do," said Oruku. "We traveled to the other two chosen planets to observe their progress."

"That would have been quite a trip. How long?" asked Vance.

"Forty years."

"Wow!" said Vance. "At exactly light speed, the humans' progress here and on those other planets will have been that same forty years."

"That's correct." Oruku stopped for a moment before continuing. "I'll report that we believe all is well with them now."

"Now?" asked Troy, a bit of alarm showing on his face.

"I'll give you a rundown on what we know. The *Vance* made it to a promising planet that had a large and varied animal population. However, they soon determined that four of the planet's five major continents were too dangerous to inhabit because of the carnivorous and ill-tempered animals. There are some truly nasty creatures there and some very large birds that could be a danger to humans. Their planet, which they named *Isley*, has north and south poles—"

"Wait," said Vance. "They named their planet after Dale?"

Oruku smiled. "They did—quite appropriately. There would be no humans without Dr. Isley's contributions. It is a well-deserved honor."

"I can tell you that there is a very humbled man on the *Norman* right now," said Vance.

Oruku continued. "But to continue the story of the planet *Isley*, even in those inhospitable climates at the poles, there are some extremely aggressive animals."

"Was there no way of controlling those critters?" asked Vance.

"Short of a massive effort to eradicate them, apparently not."

"We are a much kinder and gentler people than when we were on Earth," said Troy, "but I would bet that by now, they have come up with a program to cause dangerous animals to avoid humans or to reduce their populations to a manageable level."

"No bet." Vance smiled.

"We agree," said Oruku. "I can tell you they settled on the planet's smallest continent. It has been isolated from the rest of the planet for tens of thousands of years. It contained dozens of species of herbivores and omnivores not living on the other continents. It had a few carnivores but none that they couldn't control or avoid. Two bearlike creatures, one small and one fairly large, both seemed to avoid contact with humans. There were three small carnivorous species about the size and appearance of your domesticated cats. They were no threat to humans. But this continent was also the home to a large canine similar to Earth's wolf but about ten percent larger." Oruku paused for a moment. "They were a problem."

"How so?"

"Seems they considered humans a new source of protein. Two lives were lost and several were injured before the colonists taught the wolves to fear them."

"How did they manage that?"

"The colonists started hunting them with a very efficient wireless Taser. Not lethal but apparently very painful. We have video recordings of life on *Isley*, which we will share with you."

Vance nodded enthusiastically. "Great."

Oruku continued. "Their continent contains all of the space they will require for a millennium or more, and humans being what they are, they will undoubtedly tame all of the continents before they'll need them."

"That seems likely," said Troy.

"By the time we arrived to observe their progress, they had established a viable and vibrant colony. Their original five hundred humans were more than two thousand and growing. It's interesting to note that their choice of location for their first colony on the continent was quite similar to Home-Bay."

"This is all music to my ears," said Vance.

"Ditto," added Gary.

"We could not see any catastrophic problems in their future."

"That's good to hear."

Troy looked concerned. "What about the other ship, the *Alexander*?"

Oruku's countenance darkened a little. "The *Alexander* did not fare well. Their new planet had a climate that was extremely hostile."

"How can that be?" asked Gary. "Those two planets' specs were nearly identical."

"Volcanoes. As close as we could determine, the planet went through a nearly complete upheaval. Our analysis showed massive extinctions, continental shifts, and weather disruptions."

"Oh my God," said Troy. "That's a nightmare."

"It surely was in the beginning. Fortunately, they chose to land on the only place they could survive. To land at all, in our opinion, was a mistake. They should have turned and joined the other colonists on the first planet."

"Why didn't they do that?"

"A truly bad decision. Their ship was damaged upon landing to a point that it could only serve as a life-supporting shelter. It could never be flown again."

"Are you monitoring each planet?"

"Yes, but the data we get is forty years old when we receive it, depending on where we are in the galaxy. Forty years ago, both colonies were surviving, one well and the other just."

"Are they in contact with each other?"

"Yes, and there is a bright spot here. They were making plans to have the *Vance* come rescue the *Alexander* colonists and return them to Isley."

"Then that probably has already been done," said Vance.

"We believe that is likely the case. Their planets were only four light-years apart, so by this time, all human colonists are now living well together."

"We won't know for sure for thirty more years," said Gary.

"That's correct," said Oruku.

"Is there any way we can get a message to the planet Isley?" asked Troy.

"We will set up a relay. You will be able to get information to and from them as fast as we do."

"How soon can we get that ability?"

Oruku paused for a moment while gathering information from one of his techs. "Two of your years."

"Okay, thank you," said Troy. "I choose to believe that all colonists are now living on the planet Isley and doing well."

"We feel there is a ninety-eight percent likelihood that is the case."

"Agreed," said Gary.

Oruku smiled. "On the lighter side, there was only a small variety of fish in their waters, and most were quite small. We managed to introduce the Vun to several of their larger lakes and two mammal species that will be a benefit to them as the years pass."

"I wonder how long it will take them to figure out that those fish and mammals are not native to the planet," Gary said.

"Being that was forty-six years ago, we assume they have made that discovery by now," said Oruku.

"No doubt."

"I'm sure that caused a whole lot of speculation," said Dale.

Troy smiled. "They're probably still at it."

"How long have you been keeping tabs on us?" Dale asked.

"We have the same number of permanent satellites in orbit around Gabriel as you do."

"What?" said Vance.

Oruku smiled. "When you placed the forty-five satellites in orbit at the beginning stages of developing the planet, three were large command satellites designed to monitor the planet's progress. At the appropriate times, they ordered the seeding satellites to drop out of orbit onto the surface of the planet."

"You knew about those, did you?" asked a bemused Vance.

"Not right away. We discovered them shortly after you left the planet for your first ten-by-a-hundred-year absence."

"Ten-by-a-hundred-year?" asked Vance.

"That's our expression for the time you left the planet. Ten years in ship time and a hundred years in planet time."

"That explains it quickly and correctly," said Gary.

"While you were gone, we took the liberty of attaching three of our finest orbiters to your three command satellites."

"What?" Vance was taken aback.

"We were able to keep close tabs on you without you detecting our technology."

"I'll be damned," said Alex.

Oruku smiled again. "They are still there."

"Of course they are," said Troy.

"I have a question about Waoca," said Vance.

"Please ask."

"It's a perfect way to get to know someone," Vance said. "It takes the guess work out of the process. There can be no hidden agendas or subterfuge."

Oruku nodded in agreement.

Vance smiled. "Will I be meeting all one hundred twenty thousand Arkell in the near future?"

"No," Oruku managed to say between laughs. "We will spread your thoughts and feelings to each Arkell through what you would refer to as a chain reaction. I and my fellow councillors will touch many; they in turn will touch many; and in a short period of time, all will know you."

"Oh, good. I was thinking I'd be doing little else for the next month or two."

Oruku laughed again. Vance smiled.

"Another question along the same lines," said Vance. "I have never experienced that before with anyone. Why?"

"Shem and Jarleth have had the ability from birth because they have a great percentage of Arkell genes. Your ability had to be turned on or given a path, if you will, by me when we touched. Because you're synthetic, we weren't sure it would work, but thankfully, it did."

"Have Shem and Jarleth always known they had this ability?"

Oruku thought about that for a moment. "They, without question, have used Waoca from the time they could put their hands on one another. I'm sure their parents saw them do it hundreds of times but probably wrote it off as an unusual quirk." Oruku paused for another moment; his brow furrowed a bit. "It is interesting that they did not reveal this ability to anyone in all these years."

"Shem performed Waoca on me when he was three." Vance nodded and smiled. "He seemed satisfied at the time but said nothing. I thought it interesting, but until you came to visit, I hadn't given it any thought for the past seventeen years."

"Had you touched Shem in the same way, you may have had the Waoca experience seventeen years ago."

"Really?"

"It's possible."

"That I didn't accidentally preform Waoca may be a blessing."

Oruku nodded. "Agreed. That could have caused problems. You would have been very confused."

"Without question," Vance said.

HISTORY LESSON

All viewers on Gabriel were on, and all Gabrielites were watching. The viewers displayed a beautiful room on the Arkell ship. Sitting in the center of what appeared to be an elaborate U-shaped board table was Oruku. On either side of him were ten Arkell, both men and women. Many Gabrielites recognized all of them; they were the twenty Arkell councillors who had spent the past few days in and around Home-Bay. Oruku was speaking.

"Our civilization had become, for lack of a better word, bored. We had progressed about as far as we could technically, medically, and physically. Your old expression 'An idle mind is the workshop of the devil' didn't fit. But 'Necessity is the mother of invention' did. We began actively looking around the galaxy and found thousands of life-bearing planets in various stages of development. We began observing those that were the most advanced. Earth was of great interest for two reasons. First, it was a beautiful planet, a true gem in the galaxy, much like Gabriel is now. That was the reason for our first visit—just to see the magnificent planet. When we arrived, we found that it was in the process of developing intelligent life. Your first humanoids had appeared several million years after what we determined later was a catastrophic event." Oruku paused for a moment.

"They know more about Earth's development than we do," said Vance to Lara as they sat watching their viewer.

"We knew nothing about Earth's dinosaurs. Their existence and extinction occurred tens of millions of years before we became interested in Earth. We learned of those periods of time when humans themselves discovered their existence and began recording their finds. But that was thousands of years after we became interested enough to place several fairly sophisticated satellites in orbit over areas we deemed to be the most likely to develop over the millennia. There they remained for three thousand years while we watched."

"They had satellites that lasted three thousand years?" said Lara.

"Guess there's no reason satellites wouldn't last that long, other than being struck by a meteorite or other space debris. Their designs and manufacturing are impeccable."

"The word *watching* infers that we had great interest in Earth's development," Oruku said. "That was not the case. A few astronomical historians recorded what they observed, along with observations made for dozens of other planets."

"This is fascinating," said Vance.

"After two thousand years, our historians reported that things were getting quite interesting on Earth. Our curiosity grew over the next millennia, to the point where we returned and replaced the old satellites with more sophisticated ones in order to enhance and continue our observations. As your intelligence grew, you became more interesting. At first, there were only small colonies of simple beings. At some point, which we did not witness, humans began using fire. We observed the first conflicts among these colonies, the outcomes of which generally resulted in a melding of the colonies involved. As the years passed and the colonies grew into towns and cities, we started observing battles of one kind or another. We assumed most conflicts involved control over a given territory, which is more or less the history of most civilizations. The larger the populations, the bigger the battles, and of course, more melding occurred. Cultures blended and progressed. It was all so very interesting to us."

"No doubt," said Vance.

"When your technology advanced to the point of electronic communication, we really became enthralled. Now we could see and hear what you were up to, which caused our interest in humans to grow quickly. We watched and listened to the human evolution. Your technological advancements during the period of your AD calendar were amazing to observe. At some point, you started putting everything in your computers, including literature. Shortly after that, you began transmitting vast amounts of technology, via satellites, around your planet. That included the text of entire books into space. We became totally captivated. We read those books. We know your culture from beginning to end from thousands of points of view. We may know the who, why, when, and where of human evolution better than you do."

"There is little doubt that they do. This is just remarkable," said Lara.

"We have all that I have told you and will tell you recorded in our ship's archives and will be happy to share it with you."

"Wow," said Vance. *Our historians will be jumping for joy right about now.*

"It will be a massive treasure trove of information," remarked Lara.

Oruku continued. "In addition, there have been thousands of books written by Arkell about the humans of Earth." Oruku paused for a second and smiled. "Yes, we will see to it you get the best of them."

He's still reading our minds, thought Vance.

"To understand our evolution and culture as observed by highly intelligent alien beings might be more than just insightful; it could be unsettling," Vance said to Lara.

"It's true that some of what has been written is far from flattering. There are some dark and truly evil periods in Earth's history." Oruku paused for a moment. "As I've said before—and it's interesting to note—many advances in science and technology are a direct result of the horrible conflicts your civilization on Earth and many other alien civilizations have gone through."

No doubt about it, thought Vance. *Trauma care, antibiotics, and other drugs were a direct result of wars.*

Oruku's facial expression darkened, and his voice lost much of its warmth and even displayed a touch of anger. "We were unaware of Earth's various factions simultaneously developing nuclear power. They somehow managed to keep that development a closely held secret. When the first nuclear device was detonated, we were surprised and alarmed," Oruku said. "Then, a short time later, two were detonated over populated areas. We were stunned. Many Arkell were outraged."

"Wasn't one of our finest hours," said Vance.

Oruku took a moment before continuing. His countenance

lightened. "But all of that was in your past. You brought none of that with you to this planet."

The talk lasted for two full hours. It was a historic event, and thousands of recording devices on the planet captured every word.

"Ian Henderson would like to meet you, Oruku," said Dale.

"I'll bet he would," said Vance.

Oruku smiled. "Let us meet this prophet."

"You know of Henderson?"

"Yes, his postulations have been quite accurate."

After Oruku spent a full hour talking to and answering a multitude of relevant questions for an exhilarated Ian Henderson, Henderson politely excused himself and left the bridge of the *Norman*.

After a moment, Oruku turned to Dale's hologram. "I will tell you, Dale, that one of your possible scenarios for our civilization wasn't all that far off."

"Really?"

"Yes. About two hundred thirty thousand years ago, our technology advanced to the point that our artificial intelligence, with our full knowledge, was on the verge of taking over everything. To most, it seemed the logical thing to do."

"What stopped that from occurring?"

"One farsighted, dynamic, and charismatic man was able to convince the Arkell to stop the plunge into irrelevance. Had he not, we might not be here. We might not be at all."

"That's very interesting, if not scary," said Alex.

"That basic scenario was used in an ancient motion picture," said Dale.

Oruku smiled. "Yes, we are aware of that movie. Very clever and entertaining."

"It was a big hit on Earth a few hundred years ago," said Vance.

Oruku nodded. "I might point out, Vance, that you, Troy, and Gary are somewhat like the Terminator as portrayed in that movie. The Terminator was, in fact, a synthetic life-form, a SLF."

All three SLFs nodded in agreement.

"We are certainly aware of that," said Troy.

"You are a great deal more sophisticated than that fictional SLF.

His body was animated by gears, cables, and hydraulics. His brain was a hardwired computer. Primitive in comparison to your Isleium composition."

Gary smiled. "That's been our attitude also."

Oruku looked at Alex. "May I ask why you decided not to use the SLF body that was made for you on Earth so long ago?"

Alex said nothing for a moment. He had rarely thought about the SLF body stowed in a small, concealed room a couple of meters behind the captain's chair of the *Norman*.

"That's a difficult question," Alex said. "Deep down in my heart, I have felt that if my consciousness were to be transferred to a SLF, my soul, if any, would no longer be residing in peace with my parents. I would be yanked away from them."

"I've never heard that explanation before," said Vance.

"I've never given it before."

Dale was pensive before speaking. "I recall that when Vance came alive in his SLF body, his first words were 'I am here, gentlemen. All of me. I'm all here.' And later that night, you told Alex, 'That absolutely would include my soul, if any.'"

Alex nodded. "Those words were one of the reasons I didn't become a SLF."

"Interesting," said Oruku.

Vance nodded slowly in understanding. "Words can have a great impact. I didn't realize that what I said would, in effect, alter history. Had I not told you that, both of us probably would have been seeding the life on this planet."

"Maybe, maybe not. In the first few years of our voyage into the unknown, the voyage that eventually brought us here, I thought a great deal about making the transfer. I reasoned that if my soul resided in my consciousness and my consciousness was already housed in the *Norman*'s computer system, there would be no reason to resist the transfer to a SLF."

"But you still didn't do it."

"No, but to ease your conscience some, that remark about your soul may have played just a small part."

"That's some relief," said Vance.

Alex smiled. "Being housed in a computer, I became complacent, maybe even lazy. Decades passed without my help. I had a minimum amount of responsibility. The huge pressure that I had lived with most of my life was no longer there. I was comfortable and content."

"I often wondered how one man could remain sane with the awesome responsibility and horrific decisions you had to shoulder," said Dale.

"You had the world on your shoulders," Vance added.

"We, of course, were not fully aware of Alex's actions," said Oruku. "We were aware of the results. Your actions ended all wars and most crime and set in motion a population-control system on Earth. One of the end results is the planet Gabriel, and all of the life on it, to say nothing of the continuation of the human race."

"I had a lot of help. A full half of it is on this bridge."

"Three-quarters-plus. You're on the bridge too," said Vance.

"And Jason makes the four," said Alex.

"He would," Dale said, "but back to your decision not to inhabit a SLF body."

"There were times after we arrived on this world when I nearly asked Vance to start the transfer process—times when Vance was working hundreds of hours nonstop to seed this planet." Alex paused. "Had he asked, I would have agreed to transfer—but he never asked."

"Have to admit I thought about it a time or two."

"How could you not?" asked Alex.

"Do you still feel that way?" asked Oruku.

"Not as strongly."

Oruku remained silent for a moment.

Alex smiled. "The last time I wished I had a body was when you arrived, Oruku. I would have loved being out in the open to watch your arrival."

Oruku nodded as he leaned toward Alex. "What if I told you that if you had a soul, that soul would be wherever your consciousness was, no matter how many places that happened to be at the same time?"

"I don't understand."

Oruku nodded once. "Do you recall what I told you when you asked me if we sent you back in time?"

Alex smiled. "Yes."

"I told you that we sent you back in time using temporal

dimensions and space-time shifts. And that nothing ever ceases to exist."

"Yes, I remember that quite clearly. Didn't understand it, however."

"You don't need to know the mechanics of it, but you must believe that your soul, if any"—Oruku smiled—"can and will exist in a multitude of places at the same time."

Alex was clearly mystified. "Truly?"

Oruku smiled broadly. "You can take that to the bank."

All but Alex laughed at Oruku's use of the old Earth expression. Alex continued to look perplexed while they waited for his response.

After a moment, Alex's face displayed a small smile. "Well, given all that, I believe I should become a SLF."

"Yes!" yelled Vance as he quickly stood.

"Outstanding," said Troy, also standing.

"Great," said Gary with a big smile as he joined Troy and Vance.

Oruku joined in the celebration. "Wonderful."

"When do you want to do this?" asked Dale.

Alex thought for a second. "Well, there's a great deal going on right now. Maybe we should wait until the Arkell have departed before I transfer."

"We would be delighted to witness Alexander Gabriel's transfer to a SLF," said Oruku. "It will be historical, an act that will be recounted for decades to come."

"Decades?" Alex said.

"Yes, absolutely."

Alex's normally stoic expression changed to one of deep thought. He remained silent for a full minute, his eyes fixed on the deck in front of him. Then he looked up at Oruku. "Okay, if it's that important to you, we'll start the process."

Oruku's positive reaction was immediate. "Excellent."

Gary came into the conversation. "Might I suggest we transfer your SLF to the *Marian's* lab for the upgrades now? There are a lot of improvements in technology that we should apply."

"And we need to install the uranium core in your reactor," said Dale.

"Now?"

"Not this minute, but maybe before the end of the day."

"Now everything is starting to move fast. Getting a little nervous here," said Alex.

"You'll be pleased. The updates will include taste buds, saliva, and tears. You will be able to eat, drink, and even cry tears, should that emotion ever come up," Gary said.

"I might point out that I had none of those enhancements for centuries," said Vance.

"I noticed that it didn't take you long to agree to those upgrades after the *Marian* arrived," said Dale.

"About a millisecond," said Vance. "I'd forgotten what it was like to eat and drink. I can't tell you what a pleasure it is now."

Alex smiled a little. "That I understand. Dale and I haven't had a bite for quite a while. Fortunately, we also don't get hungry or thirsty."

"Also," said Gary, "we have added a lot of nerve endings in just the right places. You will be able to enjoy the companionship of a woman to a delightful degree."

"I know that all of those things work, but to what extent I have no idea."

"I did my best," said Dale with a naughty smile, raising his eyebrows twice in quick succession, "but there have been improvements."

"Yes, we've managed to make some modest improvements in that area," added Gary.

Vance's smile broadened. "I noticed."

"Being a computer program, I've had no raging hormones, so I haven't missed sex," said Alex.

"Simulated hormones are part of the upgrade package."

"Really?"

"Yes, sir."

No one said anything for a moment.

"Want to take a look at your SLF, boss?" Vance said.

Alex smiled. Vance hadn't called him boss for centuries. "I don't know why, but this is making me quite anxious."

Vance gestured behind the captain's chair. "You're just behind that bulkhead."

"I know." Alex paused. "Maybe seeing it will remove some of the anxiety."

Vance looked at Dale. "Open 'er up?"

"Okay."

"Splendid," said Oruku.

Vance stood up and walked toward the back bulkhead. "Dale, if you will."

Within two seconds, a panel slid to the side as a light came on in the small compartment. There, snug in the middle, sitting on a gurney, was a sarcophagus-like container covered in a thin layer of dust.

"Might want to record this," said Vance.

"Not for public viewing right now," said Alex.

"Agreed."

"Recorders are on," said Dale.

"I would like to record this for the Arkell also," said Oruku. "I will not show it without your permission."

"Sure, that will be fine."

Vance stepped over, bent down, and released the locking mechanism that held the gurney in place. He stood, turned the gurney, wheeled it onto the bridge, and stepped to the side. "Everybody ready?"

Troy, Gary, and Oruku joined Vance at the container.

Vance reached over and flipped up three stout-looking latches on the side; a hiss of air exited the container.

Vance smiled. "Pressure packed." He lifted the lid.

There lay an exact replica of Alexander Gabriel as a young man in his thirties. The SLF was clothed in the same type of body sock Vance used when in stasis.

"Oh my," said Alex, "I'm bald."

"Not for long," said Gary.

"My old friend, you're about to become animated after hundreds of years. I can't tell you how pleased that makes me," said Vance.

"I can't tell you how nervous I am about this. *Scared* might be a better word. Seeing my SLF hasn't helped at all."

"It's a whole new world out there for you to see, touch, smell, taste, and interact with," said Vance. "Trust me; you'll be thrilled."

CHAPTER 16

THE TRANSFER
MO-FIVE 8, 142

That day would be historical, but they decided not to inform the populous that Alexander Gabriel was to become a SLF until the transfer was complete, on the off chance something went wrong.

The *Norman*'s lab was equipped to transfer Alex's consciousness into the SLF body, but it was not nearly as sophisticated as that of the *Marian*, so they decided to make the transfer using the *Marian*'s SLF lab.

Alex's SLF body had been there for upgrades for the past ten days.

Oruku, Gary, Vance, and Troy were on the bridge of the *Norman*, conferring with Alex and Dale.

"First, we'll transfer your consciousness to the computer in our SLF lab," said Gary. "Then we'll make the transfer to your SLF."

"The SLF is powered up?"

"And all systems are now in perfect working order. We tested the reflex, nerve, and muscle coordination protocols that were programmed originally and found them adequate but not up to our present standards. We updated those systems."

Alex was still nervous, and everyone could sense it.

"Guess you can't give me a tranquilizer," quipped Alex.

"Sorry."

"Okay, let's make the transfer."

"You do realize you're going to leave me alone in this computer?" said Dale.

Alex nodded. "I do."

"Are you ready to be transferred?" asked Gary.

"As I'll ever be," responded Alex.

"See you aboard the *Marian*," said Gary.

"Transfer being made," said Dale. "Transfer is complete."

Gary turned toward Dale. "We could possibly, with the Arkell's help, build a SLF for you."

Everybody looked at Dale, who had an unusual bemused expression on his face. Then he smiled broadly. "Okay!"

"Really? Just like that?" said Vance.

"I've thought about it many times but not too seriously. Now, with Alex switching over ..."

Oruku smiled broadly. "Whatever we can do to help."

"We don't have the materials to build a complete SLF," said Gary, "but we have the technology. We have the hardware and software to manufacture muscle tissue, ligaments, tendons, and vessels. And we have two spare power units." Gary paused for a moment of thought. "But we would need help with the skeletal material and construction. If you could produce the skeletal structure using titanium or a similar material and produce enough Isleium in its various forms, we could build a SLF for Dale."

Oruku immediately responded, "We will provide you with whatever you wish."

"This is moving quickly," said Dale. "Now I'm starting to get nervous."

"This is great," said Vance, clearly enjoying the turn of events.

"This is another historical day." Oruku beamed. "You will transmit formulas, specs, and designs to our labs, and we will begin the process."

"You don't even need to know what the process is before agreeing to do it?" asked Gary.

"I'm going to try not to sound superior here, but if you provide a proven technology, we are capable of producing whatever that might be."

Dale smiled. "What the hell am I thinking? Of course you can. In this case, it probably is child's play."

"To an extent, yes."

Vance smiled as he turned to Dale's hologram. "I'm assuming we have an embryo of Aidan Keefe in a freezer somewhere?"

Dale looked puzzled for a moment before understanding took hold. "Colleen's sister?"

"Yep."

Oruku nodded in understanding.

"Of course," said Troy.

Gary took a little longer to figure out what was happening. "Ah, I get it."

Dale smiled. "Give me a sec here while I check the databanks. All right, we have five of them. They are on Faith, suspended in a nearly absolute-zero environment."

"That's right. I remember," said Vance. "Valuable things that we wanted to preserve for an indeterminate time were put in safekeeping deep inside the moon."

Dale nodded. "We're going to have to send someone up there to retrieve an embryo."

"I'll volunteer for the job," said Gary. "You can give me the particulars."

"Perfect. You're the best man for the job," said Vance.

"Consider it done," replied Gary.

"I can't tell you how pleased we are to be here for these history-making events," said Oruku.

"Ditto," said Troy.

Vance paused for a second. "We'll need to find a surrogate mother who lives some distance from Home-Bay."

"Agreed."

"You and Alex did me a great service when you surprised me with Lara. It was very difficult watching my first cloned Lara grow up here; it was a long wait. Maybe we can give Alex the same surprise in eighteen or nineteen years."

"That's what we'll attempt to do. But with the small population here, the chances of Alex running into a young Aidan before she is fully grown are good."

"I know, but the longer we can put that meeting off, the easier it will be for our friend."

An hour later, everyone gathered in the SLF lab on board the *Marian*. There were two lab assistants who, along with Gary, were completely versed in SLF technology. They stood beside Vance, Troy, Oruku, and Gary. Oruku asked if an Arkell technician, their expert in synthetic life-forms, could be allowed to witness the process via a transmission directly to his lab aboard the Arkell ship. All agreed.

Alex's consciousness had been successfully transferred to the *Marian's* computer, but his SLF body was not hooked up to thousands of separate fine wires, as Vance's had been many centuries ago. Rather, it had been placed in a special chamber.

"Want to see your SLF one more time before we make the transfer?" asked Vance.

"Okay, I guess."

A camera moved directly over the transparent chamber, its lens pointing straight down.

"What the hell?" said Alex.

Everyone smiled. Alex's SLF was no longer bald. It had honey-blond hair exactly the color and style Alex had had on Earth when he was in his thirties. It was even sun-bleached, as it had been. In addition, the SLF now had eyebrows and lashes. It looked perfect.

"Damn, I was a good-looking young man," Alex said with some surprise in his voice.

"And rich. You were a double threat," Vance joked. "Are you less anxious now?"

"A bit, yes. So where are the wires?"

"The technology has improved over the past five hundred years. We no longer require wires," explained Gary.

In lieu of the wires, two dozen probes surrounded the SLF's cranium, placed within a few millimeters of the head. An equal number ran the length of the body.

Gary spoke while making a few last-minute adjustments to the computers. "I need to point out that Vance's, Troy's, and my transfers were made with our human bodies and minds as the source, which was an integral part of the process, but your consciousness will be transferred from a computer. There will be no body to assist in coordinating muscles and nerves. This hasn't been done before."

Dale came into the conversation from the viewer. "Hopefully you'll get the kinks worked out before you start on me."

"Kinks?" said Alex.

Gary smiled. "We have thousands of videos of you that were recorded on Earth. Before we're done, your SLF will move all of your body parts exactly as you did in the past. It will just take a little longer."

"I understand."

"We've run hundreds of simulations through the computer for the past ten days. I think we have a good handle on it."

"Think? I don't want to be floppin' around like a fish out of water when the transfer is made."

Gary smiled. "We'll hold that down to a minimum."

"Also," said Troy, "they will be working with small sections of the brain at a time. We'll make sure your brain will recognize and interact with a specific part of your body before we go to the next section. You should only be floppin' in one small area at a time.

"We'll start with the large muscles and work our way to the finer muscles. You will remain as a hologram while at the same time existing as a SLF. Once we get you where you can balance and walk, we'll go to the smaller muscles. Your hologram will smile, and we'll adjust the SLF's face accordingly, and so on.

"Our simulations show that the brain will quickly recognize which nerves are controlling which muscles and adapt quickly."

"Give me an estimate of time here," said Alex.

Gary shrugged a little. "Five hours."

"Oh, well, hell, I thought we may be talking days. Let's get on with it."

"Yes, sir," said Gary as he turned toward the lab's computer.

Ten minutes later, Gary announced, "Transfer is complete."

The chamber's clear lid slid back, and Alex's eyes opened. He looked frightened—and then terrified. Strange sounds came next— garbled, choking sounds. His body began shaking violently.

"Oh shit!" yelled Vance.

"Oh my God," said Dale.

"Can you hear me?" asked Gary in a loud voice.

"Alex, wake up!" screamed Vance. "Wake up!"

A few seconds later, Alex's body stopped shaking, and the choking sounds died away. The room went dead quiet; all eyes were riveted on the SLF Alex. There was no movement or sound—there was nothing.

Vance appeared to be paralyzed, as was everybody in the lab. All in the lab seemed to have quit blinking and breathing.

Please, Alex, wake up. Wake up! Vance's mind screamed over and over.

It seemed an eternity to those in the lab, but it was just more than a minute before Alex's eyes opened again. This time, they looked to be at peace.

Vance was the first to speak. "Can you hear me, my friend?" he said gently.

Alex's head turned toward Vance and then nodded slightly. "I hear you," said Alex in a slow and deep voice.

"Good," said Vance. Then he turned to Gary. "Fix him," he ordered.

"We need to get him up," Gary responded. "Want to sit up?" he asked Alex.

Alex nodded.

Vance quickly moved to the chamber, slid his hand under Alex's back, and lifted him to a sitting position.

Alex's unique blue eyes sparkled as he slowly looked around at the lab and people. His gaze fell on Vance.

"Hello, my friend," Alex said in a deep baritone voice.

"Welcome back, boss," said Vance with tears showing in his eyes.

Alex's right arm lifted jerkily toward Vance before his hand came to rest on Vance's forearm. "Thank you."

Vance's brow furrowed. "For what?"

"I was being destroyed," Alex said with great emotion. "You saved me."

"I just told you to wake up."

Alex nodded. "Yes, that's what you did. That's what you made me do."

Vance was overcome with emotion. He was only able to nod at his dear friend.

"Why don't we get Alex out of there and set him in this chair?" said Gary.

Vance found his voice. "Got it." He slid his left hand under Alex's knees and supported his back with his right. He lifted him up and over the chamber's edge and set him on a specialized chair.

Alex looked around at his friends. His movements looked to be somewhat unnatural. He was sitting as a physical being, containing mass, for the first time in many centuries.

"Hello, sir," said Troy.

"We are honored to be witness to this historic moment," said Oruku.

Alex's movements remained jerky, not at all smooth and flowing.

"Dale?" said a concerned Vance.

"Give us a little time. We'll straighten all this out."

An hour later, Alex was up and walking quite well. His movements were still a little imperfect but were improving quickly. His use of his arms and hands followed suit.

"Let's get started on the small muscles," said Gary.

"Okay," said Alex, "let's start with my voice."

An hour later, all initial adjustments to his voice, hearing, and smell had been made. The testing and tuning went on for another two hours until they had Alex walking, running, jumping, and playing catch with Vance. It was remarkable how quickly Alex's synthetic brain and body became coordinated.

Gary said, "That's it. We'll fine-tune as time goes on, but right now, sir, you're good to go."

Alex again looked around. "This is great. I can see everything so clearly."

"Your vision should be about twenty-ten."

"My vision is different from what I had as a hologram. This is from a singular point of view and requires me to seek what I want to see. Might take a little getting used to."

"It will be completely natural in a short period of time," said Gary.

"Exactly," said Vance.

Alex smiled again as he looked down at his body. "How about getting me out of this big sock and into some clothes?"

"Right here," said Vance as he retrieved a large garment bag from another bench.

"Ahem," said Dale.

Everyone turned to look at his hologram.

"Let's get to work on my SLF ASAP, if you don't mind."

Fifteen minutes later, five men walked out of the SLF lab, down the hall, and into the elevator. When they reached the bottom deck, they exited and walked down the ramp to the surface of the planet.

Vance and Alex were in the lead. Alex was now dressed in black slacks and a short-sleeved blue cotton pullover shirt. He was smiling.

"My God!" he exclaimed as they walked into the sun. His smile faded, and he stopped. He looked around, sniffed the air, and turned his face up toward the sun. "I had forgotten what it's like to be alive."

"I can't imagine," said Vance sincerely.

"I can feel the sun, I can feel the earth, and I can smell the most wonderful scents." Tears began forming in his eyes. "Jesus, I've missed so much."

The men around him said nothing; there was nothing to say. They let Alex have his moment of rebirth.

My God, thought Alex. *This is wonderful.* He looked around. He saw people going about their daily business, sometimes alone and sometimes with others. He saw a young couple walking hand in hand, talking and laughing. *That's beautiful.* Then he had a moment of sadness. *How could I have stayed out of this for so long?* But the moment passed quickly. He again took a deep breath. *The ocean.* He took another breath. *The grass.* He sniffed again. *Wood smoke.* He smiled. *Someone's cooking.*

The four men with him remained silent while they enjoyed their friend's rediscovery of life.

As Alex looked around, he saw people starting to notice his group. He smiled to himself. *They've spotted us.* He could see them talking excitedly among themselves before heading toward them. *Here they come.*

Vance, ever vigilant, quickly spotted them and held up one hand, palm forward. They stopped and remained quiet and still. Vance gave them a warm smile while motioning with his hand for them to disperse. They understood, returned the smile, and turned and went about their business, all looking back in curiosity at least once.

Ever my protector, thought Alex as he turned his attention to his companions. "You mind if Vance and I take a walk by ourselves for a while?"

"Not at all. Take all the time you need," said Gary.

"Indeed," said Troy

"This is your moment," added Oruku.

"Thank you." Alex looked at his best friend. "Shall we?"

"Yes, sir."

They walked west toward the ocean. Their trek through the field took them to the sandy beach a couple hundred meters south of Home-Bay. A gentle breeze was blowing onshore, causing the tall grass to wave gently. There were foot paths leading in various directions through the field, but they took the one that led directly to the ocean. Within five minutes, they were standing on a short bluff overlooking a narrow, sandy beach and the Vast Ocean.

"Jesus, Vance, look what we have. Look at the beauty, smell the ocean, and feel that breeze." Alex looked up and spotted several different species of sea birds. "I'm overwhelmed with it all."

"Sometimes we get complacent," said Vance. "To see and experience all of this again with you is tremendously uplifting."

"I will never get tired of being alive again. Never," Alex responded with joy in his voice.

Vance remained quiet for a couple of moments. "I owe you a huge apology, my friend."

"I forgive you completely."

"Haven't said what I was apologizing for."

Alex smiled. "I feel a little like Oruku here. There is only one thing you would feel the need to apologize for at this moment."

Vance nodded. "I am so sorry, Alex. I should have talked you into this hundreds of years ago."

"I gave no indication that I had any interest at all. Had our roles been reversed, I probably would have done the same."

"No, you're a great deal more sensitive to others' feelings than I am—always have been."

"I feel so euphoric now that all of that simply doesn't matter." Alex turned toward the *Marian* and the *Norman*'s cave. "Let's get the SLF techs to double their efforts to build a body for Dale."

"Absolutely."

As they walked on the sand toward town, Alex's head didn't stop moving. "Look!" Alex said as he pointed to a flight of pelicans skimming no more than a quarter meter above the water. "Pelicans! Wow! We brought them here to this planet from so far away—it's all so remarkable. You should be so proud, Vance."

"I am, but not for myself as much as I am for our team. And you are the leader of the team, you know?"

"Leadership was transferred to you the second the *Norman* lifted off from Earth. From that point on, everything that was accomplished was through your efforts."

Vance smiled. "Sorry, boss, but I can't accept that. I simply followed the protocol designed by very smart people. I just did some grunt work."

"Okay. I'll just say that somewhere in between our points of view lies the truth."

"That I'll accept."

"All right." Alex smiled brightly. "I'm a bit hungry. Let's go into town and have a beer and a burger."

Vance laughed heartily. "Now you're talking."

They continued to walk down to the beach at a leisurely pace. Alex could feel the onshore breeze blowing against his skin and through his hair as he continued to look around; he didn't want to miss anything. After walking on the sand for a hundred meters, he thought, *This is effortless. SLF bodies don't fatigue.*

Fifteen minutes later, the two walked up a short bluff onto the cobblestone street at the southern end of town. Alex's head moved from side to side as he looked at the beautifully designed and built log and stone buildings containing the shops, stores, and restaurants. His smile was continuous as he observed the raised and covered wooden sidewalks. *Reminds me of the old west.* The wooden sidewalks ran the full length of the town on both sides of the street as it curved around the southern entrance to Home-Bay. Alex had seen this street thousands of times on a viewer over the decades, but this was different; now he could feel it, see it in three dimensions, and smell it. Now he was part of it.

Alex spotted a hardware store. He touched Vance's arm. "Let's go in here."

Vance smiled, shrugged, and followed Alex up the three steps into the shade of the covered sidewalk and into the interior of the store.

There were two men and one woman inside. One man, obviously the proprietor, was behind the counter, holding some sort of gadget while explaining its function to the other man. The three looked around as the two most famous people in the history of mankind walked in.

The proprietor dropped the gadget, along with his jaw. The

other man's jaw also dropped but not quite as far. The woman's face suddenly bore no expression whatsoever. They were all clearly—and somewhat comically—stunned at what they saw. No one uttered a word.

"How's everyone today?" Alex asked casually, knowing full well what his appearance out of the blue would mean to these people.

The three remained silent. The two men managed, after a few seconds, to close their mouths. The woman's face remained expressionless.

Alex walked up to the woman and put out his hand. "My name is Alex Gabriel."

The woman remained dumbstruck as she slowly raised her hand to take Alex's. It was more of a reflex than a conscious effort.

Alex smiled. "I apologize. We kind of sprang our arrival on you."

She found her voice. "I don't know what to say, sir. I'm completely flummoxed. I'm Lucy Gonzales, sir, and I'm glad …" She paused for a moment. "I'm dreaming."

"You're not dreaming." Recognition came across Alex's face. "Lucy Gonzales? I know that name. You're a member of Dr. Paco's medical team."

"You know my name? Yes, sir."

"You people have done great work for our folks who've suffered physical trauma over the years."

"Yes, sir. Thank you."

Alex nodded and then turned toward the two men at the counter and introduced himself. They came out of their initial shock and shook Alex's hand vigorously.

"Are you real, sir? We haven't heard—"

"Holy moly. Wait till I tell my wife!"

So it went for a few minutes.

After the greetings, Alex excused himself from the three and took a walk around the small store. He smiled inwardly as he realized he was unfamiliar with most of the tools and products displayed.

All this while, Vance said nothing; he just stood to one side and observed. He normally would have been the center of attention, but he was completely ignored.

As Alex completed the tour of the hardware store, he turned to the three. "You have a nice store here, Sam. And it was nice meeting you three. See you later."

Still somewhat stunned, the three managed to say goodbye as Alexander Gabriel left the store.

Alex and Vance walked across the street and headed east in the shade of the covered sidewalk, heading directly to John Carlon's pub.

"Right here," said Vance as he gestured at a swinging set of doors reminiscent of an old-west saloon. Above the doors was a simple but nicely done sign: Carlon's Pub. Alex smiled brightly. "This is going to be fun."

Shem and Jarleth were holding hands while strolling up a path alongside the Vance River. Every time they were together, they held hands or in some way touched each other. Their love for one another was well known throughout the planet.

After two kilometers, they came to a historical site commemorated with a bronze plaque affixed to the side of a huge boulder. It was the place where Vance had encountered the huge bear more than three hundred years ago. The area had, over the centuries, become a popular picnic and rest area.

"Let's sit," said Shem.

Jarleth sat on a log bench that faced the river, and Shem sat beside her. He turned, reached over, and took both her hands in his, and she smiled as she looked into his eyes.

"We have loved each other all our lives," he said warmly. "Will you be my wife?"

Two weeks later was the day for celebrating Shem's and Jarleth's twentieth birthdays. That day was one of the reasons for the Arkell's visit to Gabriel. Their birthday party would include not only dozens of their friends and relatives but also all twenty of the Arkell's council and Alexander Gabriel.

Fifteen or so minutes after the party began, Shem's and Jarleth's parents and siblings arrived. A few minutes after they had taken their reserved seats at one of the head tables, Jarleth and Shem walked into the gazebo.

Their choice of dress for the evening was not what one might have expected. Shem had on a perfectly tailored tuxedo, and Jarleth wore a stunning white gown.

"Holy shit," said Vance. "They're going to get married tonight."

ALL ABOARD
MO-FIVE 16, 142

Oruku, Alex, Troy, Gary, and Vance were enjoying the day while sitting at a table in the shade of the gazebo. The weather seemed to know that the planet had special visitors; every day of their visit had been nearly perfect.

A couple dozen Gabrielites and a few Arkell were sitting at the other tables. The conversations seemed to be light, as they might have been in a gathering of old friends.

"So we agree," said Oruku. "Tomorrow we will begin to transport Gabrielites to our ship for a tour."

"I can assure you of enthusiastic cooperation," said Alex.

"Excellent. I suggest that you two, Shem, and Jarleth be the first to take the tour. There is not an Arkell who does not want to see all of you in person, and it will have a calming effect to have the anticipation of seeing you behind them."

Alex nodded. "That makes sense."

"I believe there are three other humans the Arkell might like to get a firsthand look at," said Vance.

Oruku nodded. "Of course—Teddy, Colleen, and Lara. I should have realized. I must be getting old."

Vance smiled. "You are old."

Oruku laughed. "Indeed I am."

"It's all relative," Alex said with a smile.

"But to include those three is an excellent suggestion and easily accommodated. Our shipboard transports will carry up to twelve people." Oruku paused in thought for a moment. "My problem is how to limit the number of Arkell on each deck we visit. Seeing all seven of you on our ship at once might cause our streets and roads to be clogged with well-wishers."

"The words *streets* and *roads* in connection with a spaceship seem out of place," said Alex.

"It will seem in place once you see the interior of our ship."

"I'm sure of that."

"One hundred twenty thousand is a lot of people to see," said Vance. "How long do you think the tour will take?"

"The tour we have planned will take five hours for most humans. But your tour, I'm sure, will take considerably longer. Shem and Jarleth, along with five of the most famous humans in history, will slow the process considerably."

"Whatever time it takes to see all of your people," said Alex, "is the time we'll take."

Oruku nodded in thanks. "Tomorrow, after we finish your tour, we will begin shuttling our people down for their tour of your planet. The returning shuttles will ferry Gabrielites up to the ship."

"Good."

"The logistics have been worked out," said Vance. "We have hundreds of volunteers anxiously waiting to guide the Arkell around all of the continents."

"This will be a great highlight of the millennium for our people," said Oruku.

"That will also hold true for we Gabrielites," said Alex.

The following morning, Alex, Vance, Lara, Teddy, Colleen, Jarleth, and Shem walked aboard the Arkell shuttle waiting for them just south of the gazebo.

The men wore clothes similar to what the Arkell men were wearing, but the three ladies were dressed in beautifully designed and tailored jumpsuits that fit their splendid figures perfectly. Lara's flame-red suit complemented her red hair and soft complexion. Colleen's was emerald green, matching her eye color and setting off her lustrous red hair. Jarleth's was made of a black satin-like material that showcased her platinum hair and astounding blue eyes. Separately, any one of the women commanded the attention of anyone within eyesight. Seen together, they were spectacular.

"Oh my," said Oruku as he spotted the women. "Yet another reason the Arkell will be talking about this day for centuries to come. You ladies are absolutely stunning."

"Thank you, sir. We thought we'd clean up a little for the tour," said Lara.

"It's hard to draw one's eyes away from you." Oruku smiled. "The men may not be noticed at all."

"What men?" asked Teddy.

"Exactly." Alex smiled. Alex was paying particular attention to Colleen. His mind flashed back to Earth many centuries in the past. He warmly remembered the original Colleen, Colleen Keefe, who'd gone to work as an eighteen-year-old apprentice at Uncle Walt's stock brokerage business in Inglewood, California. The first moment the ten-year-old Alex had laid eyes on her, his infatuation had begun.

I believe that was 1964, thought Alex. *So long ago.* He remembered his instant crush. *What a beauty. She and Uncle Walt got married a few years later. They were a good match at the time, but now this second clone of Colleen is married to the second clone of Teddy. They seem to be a perfect match. Different times, different planet.* Alex smiled to himself. *But then came Aidan.*

Aidan was Colleen's younger sister. That they were sisters was obvious; they were both stunning in appearance. Aidan was slightly smaller than her sister, and her red hair was a shade darker, but that did not detract one bit from her beauty.

When was it—1979—when I met Aidan? Colleen and Uncle Walt's wedding. Alex looked over at Colleen. *She was the most beautiful woman on Earth that day, as she was most days probably.* Alex smiled at the memory. *Met Aidan at the rehearsal dinner the night before.* The smile left Alex's face. *I screwed that up.*

Alex had been just twenty-five years old and already one of the richest men in the country, but his obsession with amassing an enormous fortune had precluded the possibility of a serious relationship. That obsession eventually had driven Aidan into the arms of a young man who did want to take their relationship to another level.

I lost Aidan in my drive for wealth, thought Alex sadly. *She was perfect for me, but I had no choice at the time.* His smile returned. *It was at one of her company's Christmas parties that I first encountered Vance Youngblood. That was some night.* Alex looked over at Vance. *He looks much like he did then—younger, in fact.* The thought brought him back to reality.

The unique design of the deck aboard the Arkell shuttle was a great deal more than just a design. Oruku turned and moved his hands in front of a panel, and eight lounges emerged from the floor.

"Whoa, this is really nifty," Teddy said with a big smile.

"Nifty indeed." Oruku smiled. "It saves the time and energy needed to move furniture around. Please seat yourselves. The lounges will adjust to your bodies."

Each passenger sat down, and as they leaned back, the lounges transformed their shapes to fit the individual bodies perfectly.

"Ready to go?"

Affirmatives from the seven came quickly.

Without further ado, the shuttle rose quickly and headed for the massive ship 210 kilometers above them.

"If you look at the viewer above, you will see Home-Bay and the surrounding area. Quite a beautiful sight."

The town and bay were shrinking rapidly in the viewer. The shuttle was accelerating at a brisk pace.

"Wow!" said Alex. "This is incredible. I don't feel the acceleration."

"Synthetic gravity—or, in this case, synthetic antigravity. Our gravity remains steady no matter the rate of acceleration or deceleration."

"That's what allowed you to jump to close to light speed nearly instantly when we first spotted you?"

"It is."

"I'll bet Dale would have a question or two about that technology."

Oruku nodded. "He's been talking to our engineers already."

Alex smiled and looked back at the overhead viewer. "Look how blue the water is in the bay."

"All fresh water from the Ring Sea," said Vance. "You can see where it meets the salt water of the Vast just half a kilometer from the mouth of Home-Bay."

The shuttle slowed a few seconds later. The array of large viewers that surrounded the bridge gave the passengers an amazing view of the enormous ship as they approached. It seemed to go on forever. It was hard for their minds to conceive of such a mass being an interstellar ship.

"We will enter the ship on deck two. As you will see, a section of it functions as our hangar and machinery deck. In addition to shuttles, we store many other craft and machines that are used for various functions. Also, there are dozens of workshops and factories and several research facilities."

"Hangar, workshops, and factories on a single deck?" asked Teddy.

Oruku nodded.

The shuttle slipped silently through the hangar opening and slowly continued into the ship's interior for nearly half a kilometer. Vance could see out of all sides via a dozen large viewers. He could hardly believe what he was seeing. In the background, he could hear his fellow passengers chatting with enthusiasm, but he paid little attention. His attention was on the ship's interior.

"Would you look at this?" said Alex. "It's bigger than a small city on Earth. And this is just one deck."

"The area of this deck is just more than seven square kilometers—or, to put it more dramatically, seven million square meters," said Oruku. "This is one of the smaller decks because of its position near the top of the sphere."

"In old-Earth terms, how many acres is it?" asked Vance.

"Acres are an unusual measurement." Oruku paused for a moment while one of his techs gave him the information. "Including all decks, it's more than one and a half million acres."

"This deck is larger than any of our farms on Gabriel."

"And how many decks are there?" asked Alex.

"Five hundred eighty," Oruku said.

"In a spaceship," said Vance. "Astounding."

The shuttle slowed and stopped in a place clearly prepared to receive the distinguished passengers. In front of the shuttle stood at least two dozen Arkell, all dressed in their finery. They were smiling and chatting among themselves.

The ramp slid down, and the hatch opened.

The eight, led by Oruku, walked down the ramp as the waiting Arkell burst into loud applause and good-natured wooing. They expressed surprise and delight when they recognized the seven famous humans. It was difficult for them to pick which one to look at.

All seven celebrities shook hands with each of the Arkell. Vance, Jarleth and Shem took the time to touch the faces and in turn be touched. It was a delightful experience for everyone involved.

After ten minutes of cheerful interaction, Oruku addressed the small crowd. "Due to time constraints, we must continue our tour without the pleasure of spending more time with everybody."

"We understand," responded a distinguished-looking Arkell, presumably the spokesman for the group. "Please enjoy your tour."

Oruku led the visitors to a small open-topped transport about two meters wide and four long. It resembled an eight-seat golf cart without wheels.

Teddy leaned down and looked under the transport. "What's this thing sit on?"

"It has a magnetic drive."

"Of course. Should have known." Teddy flashed his famous smile.

Oruku smiled back. "Please." He gestured into the transport.

They stepped aboard and sat down on the comfortable seats. Once all were seated, Oruku moved his hand in front of a small panel, and the transport accelerated smoothly down a wide lane. He narrated as they passed various points of interest.

The entire tour of deck two only took twenty-six minutes before the transport slowed and drove straight into a large open elevator. After the doors slid shut, the transport quietly spun 180 degrees as they went up to deck one.

"Cool," said Teddy.

"Deck one is the power deck. It houses our generators, converters, engineering facilities, and research and learning center," Oruku said as they drove off the elevator.

Alex looked into the interior of the power deck. "Wow!"

"I'm suitably impressed. Are you?" said Vance.

The deck was vastly more impressive than deck two. For starters, its ceiling height was at least three times that of deck two. A cluster of enormous machines were housed at the center.

"This is beautiful," said Jarleth.

"Breathtaking," said Lara.

Colleen enthusiastically nodded in agreement.

"This deck houses twelve power generators—those spheres in the center." Oruku pointed in their direction. "And twenty-four converters, which you might call engines." He waved his hand from one end of the huge array to the other.

"I thought there would be eight generators," said Shem. "One for each of the ribs."

"That's a reasonable observation," said Oruku. "Eight are dedicated to the ribs, as you call them. The other four are used for other purposes but can be used as a backup for the ribs if necessary."

The huge spheres sat in an immense circle, with twelve meters separating one from the other. Surrounding the spheres were two dozen evenly spaced converters.

Shem pointed past the spheres and converters to a single large structure sitting in the center of the spheres. "I'm assuming that's a collection point, judging from the number of large conduits leading to it from the generators and converters."

"Collection and distribution point," answered Oruku.

The structure was about half the height of the spheres but eighty meters in diameter.

"Those machines must be seven stories tall!" exclaimed Teddy as he stood with his hands on his hips, leaning back to see the tops of the spheres.

"Closer to six. About twenty meters."

The twelve generators were gleaming copper-colored spheres nearly reaching the ceiling. Hundreds of evenly spaced, conical-shaped dark protrusions two meters long covered the entire surface of each. Each of the cones was connected to its adjacent cones by a network of polished silver conduits, almost like a stylized fishing net.

The twenty-four converters surrounding the generators were cylindrical and dome-topped. They were twenty meters in diameter and fifteen meters high. Their surfaces were a flat gray color, in stark contrast to the spheres, and each was identically festooned with a multitude of protrusions of various shapes and sizes. Most were made of a highly polished metal of either a gold or silver color.

The tourists could feel a low hum on the soles of their feet.

"Power source?" asked Alex.

"A form of fusion about thirty generations ahead of what the *Marian* is using. It's quite efficient at producing a substantial amount of power."

"Moving a ship this size would take more power than I can imagine," said Shem.

Alex took his eyes off the impressive power generators to look at the array of large glass-faced edifices encompassing the outer bulkhead. The tall structures stretched out of sight around the massive machines in the center. There were many Arkell inside and outside these buildings, moving from structure to structure.

"How many Arkell on this deck?" asked Alex.

"Probably around a thousand involved in research, maintenance, and development. There are many youngsters here studying as well."

"Youngsters?"

"We do have children on our ship, though not many. Just enough." Oruku smiled again.

"Maybe you will elaborate on that later," said Alex.

"I'd be happy to."

"May we walk around?" asked Lara.

"Yes, please. But I suggest you not touch anything connected to our power source."

"Promise we won't."

"I'll say. I'm going to keep my hands deep in my pockets," said Teddy.

"Come on, silly," said Colleen as she took Teddy by the arm and walked with Lara and Jarleth. The others fell in behind. The shuttle, without a driver, silently followed the group at a constant ten meters. Teddy noticed it first.

"It's like a pet dog. Cool."

Alex smiled as he continued to look around. "I hate to point out the obvious, but this deck looks a lot like a high-budget sci-fi motion picture depiction of an alien power source. It's just stunning."

"Overwhelming," said Vance.

"It is an alien power source," said Teddy seriously.

Oruku nodded. "As a matter of fact, we've noticed the same thing. A tribute to the creativity of Earth's motion picture industry."

"That they were," said Teddy with an inflection of loss.

Oruku paused for a second before continuing. "These machines produce all of the power necessary for the ship's propulsion, as well as its internal functions. Artificial gravity consumes the most power while the ship is in orbit."

"Dale will be more than curious how your artificial gravity is created," said Alex.

Oruku smiled. "Dale has a full list of questions that he's been quizzing our engineers on—artificial gravity is among them."

"You're maintaining one gravity on more than a million and a half acres of surface area at the same time?" asked Shem.

"We are."

"I assume a lot of fuel is consumed in doing so."

"Fuel is plentiful."

"And your fuel is?" asked Vance.

"Hydrogen mainly, using uranium as a starter."

"Starter?" said Shem.

"Uranium produces the energy required to superheat hydrogen atoms. Hydrogen atoms, as you know, begin to bond when superheated."

"I, for one, did not know that," said Teddy in mock sincerity.

Everyone smiled.

"Superheated?" said Alex.

"Hotter than the interior of a star. It transforms hydrogen into an extremely hot plasma. Once the hydrogen plasma pops into existence, the energy produced is self-sustaining—we need only to feed it hydrogen."

"Wow," said Teddy, continuing to look up at the incredible machines.

"What are those protrusions?" Alex pointed at one of the cones on the spheres.

"They produce the magnetic field that contains the plasma. We don't want any of that to get out."

"I would think that would burn a hole right through the ship in a hurry," said Shem.

Oruku nodded. "This ship would explode like a mini-supernova if the magnetic field were interrupted for just two seconds."

"Okay, that's it," said Teddy. "I'm outta here." With that, he turned, quickly crossed the ten meters, jumped back into the transporter, and sat down. "Let's go."

Everyone laughed.

Having accomplished his goal, Teddy climbed out of the transporter with a big smile on his face. "I'm guessing you have a handle on the safety precautions."

"I think we've finally got a handle on it. It's been nearly a month since we blew up one of these things."

Everyone laughed again, Teddy the most.

Oruku turned his attention back to his guests. "While in orbit, we need only keep one generator online to maintain gravity and provide power for all other ship functions."

"Just one of these generators will do that?"

"Yes. As I've said, they are quite efficient."

"I'm guessing you've got a big fuel tank somewhere on this ship," said Teddy.

Oruku nodded. "Between decks one and two."

"It would take a great deal of hydrogen to run this ship," said Vance.

"Water is available to us throughout the galaxy. We will not run out of the raw material."

"Water? I thought you said hydrogen," said Teddy.

"We just separate hydrogen and oxygen from the water. And that is child's play," said Oruku.

"I knew that." Teddy made an amusing face that clearly displayed that he, in fact, had not known that.

"Our processing factory, located just on the other side of these generators, produces all of the hydrogen we require and up to three kilos of usable uranium fuel per day, which we get from semi-refined ore. That's much more than we require. We consume very little while in orbit."

"I assume the oxygen byproduct from the extraction of hydrogen provides the ship with all of the oxygen it requires?"

"Not all but most of it while in orbit. You'll see another source of oxygen later."

"At what point do you require the most power?" asked Shem.

"In the seconds before and as we accelerate to light speed."

Shem nodded. "Creating the thrust?"

"Actually, no. Eighty percent of the power is used to mask our mass."

"That much?"

"Yes. This ship isn't going to move a meter until the mass is completely masked. Once that is done, you could move it with a breath."

Shem understood. "Oh, of course."

"Hold on," said Teddy. "What do ya mean 'Oh, of course'?"

"I'm sure you've blown on a balloon to move it," said Shem.

"Well, sure, who hasn't?"

"This ship will weigh less than that balloon."

"Its mass is completely neutralized," said Oruku.

Physics was as far from Teddy's long suit as anything could have been, and his expressive face clearly showed that. "Well, of course it becomes weightless. Who wouldn't have known that? Jeez."

Everyone laughed again.

Shem again asked a relevant question. "Once light speed is achieved, how much power is used to maintain it?"

"Two generators are kept online: one to maintain our gravity and life support and the other to produce and maintain our shield. No power is required to maintain velocity."

"You no longer have to mask the ship's mass?" asked Vance.

"No, we simply coast at light speed. However, when altering course or slowing, we have to bring our generators back online to mask our mass."

"How far do your shields extend?" asked Shem.

"The shields can be detected at just shy of half a million kilometers, but of course, they are extremely weak that far out. Our shield when we're moving is concentrated into a cone shape. The point of the cone leads the way; the ship follows. This way, we don't just smash mass out of our path; rather, mass bounces off the sides of the cone."

Shem's face showed amazement. "The point is half a million kilometers in front of the ship?"

"The only thing that can be deflected at that range is space dust. But at fifty thousand kilometers, objects as large as small asteroids and comets will be deflected. We don't want to run into anything at light speed."

"Ah," said Shem, "correct me if I'm wrong, but my guess is that you manipulated our planet-saving comet using the ship's shields."

"Yes, that's exactly what we did." Oruku smiled. "We had to blunt the cone some to fit the comet."

"Incredible," said Shem. "And how much power was required to move such a huge mass?"

"In manipulating the speed and direction of the comet, we used nearly ninety-six percent of our power for seventeen days." Oruku paused for a moment. "You might consider the chore equal to a single small tugboat maneuvering a huge cruise ship up a narrow, fast-moving river."

"Seventeen days, when your power source is normally used for just seconds at a time. Did that cause any problems?"

"We'd never attempted anything like it before. It was a strain on the ship, and there were a lot of frayed nerves aboard."

"Was there any danger of damaging the ship or injuring your people?" asked Alex.

Oruku didn't answer for a few seconds. "I don't know how much to tell you." Oruku paused again. "Many of our physicists were convinced we would perish during the attempt."

The enormity of that statement hit the seven like a truck. The Arkell, these ancient beings, had been willing to sacrifice their ship and their lives to save the humans.

Jarleth was the first to react. She stepped over to Oruku, put her arms around his neck, and gave him a long hug. She then stepped back and placed her hands on his cheeks. Tears came from Oruku's eyes as he absorbed and understood the gratitude and love radiating from the young lady.

Shem stepped forward and repeated what Jarleth had done. Again, Oruku was nearly overwhelmed with emotion.

Vance came next and followed the path taken by the first two. Oruku apparently got a slightly different feel from Vance. He smiled and extended his hand. Vance took it, firmly shook it just once, and held it for a long moment.

The four remaining Gabrielites took turns hugging Oruku, all without uttering a word. None were required.

After a few moments, Vance changed the subject.

"We used less than fifty kilos of uranium to power the *Norman* from Earth to Gabriel," he said.

Oruku nodded knowingly.

"But we didn't have to provide power for artificial gravity," said Vance. "As I'm sure you're aware, our gravity is maintained only when we are accelerating or decelerating."

"We had a similar disadvantage when we were at your stage

of technology," said Oruku. "It takes you fourteen of your months, accelerating at one g, to reach ninety-seven-percent of light speed and a similar amount of time to stop. It's very time consuming."

"How long does it take this ship to reach that speed?" asked Alex.

"Eleven seconds under normal conditions," said Oruku.

"What would be abnormal conditions?" asked Vance.

"If we find ourselves in a hostile environment or under threat of attack—that sort of thing—we alter our protocols. We speed things up a bit."

"A bit?" said Vance with half a smile.

Oruku just raised his eyebrows a little and said nothing more.

Shem changed the subject. "We have assumed that the external ribs are an integral part of the propulsion system. Is that correct?"

"They are the propulsion system. They not only mask our mass but also create the thrust drive. Interesting physics."

"Beyond my imagination," said Vance.

Alex nodded, accepting the information at face value. He knew he would not understand any of the mechanics past that; few humans would. Gary and Dale were the possible exceptions.

The transport started moving, and a half hour later, it had made a complete circle around the ship's colossal power plant.

"The next stop is a nontechnical deck," Oruku said as they drove onto the elevator.

After a few seconds, the elevator slowed and stopped, and the door opened, revealing a mind-blowing vista. There in front of the transport was a panorama of plains, forests, mountains, and rivers.

Alex's mouth was open, but no sound came out. He was mute. He stood up, stepped off the transport, and walked slowly down the narrow road, his head moving from side to side. After nearly twenty meters, he stopped and turned back toward the other seven. He raised his arms out to the sides, palms forward, and said, "Inside a ship—holy shit!"

"Ditto on that holy shit," said Teddy as his head went from side to side.

"This is just beyond belief," said Vance.

"I had no idea," said Lara.

"This defies description," added Colleen.

Oruku smiled brightly as he put his hand to the control panel, and the transport moved forward to meet Alex.

"Would you like to take a trek through our rain forest, sir?"

Alex smiled. "We would."

He stepped aboard and took his seat.

"This is our tallest deck, to allow for what we call our mountain range. It's one hundred eighty meters tall."

"It looks to be thousands of meters tall. I can see snow on the peaks."

"An allusion created by clever holograms."

"We could fly the *Norman* in here," said Shem.

"We could?" asked an amazed Teddy.

"With a lot of room to spare."

They drove across a broad plain, heading in the general direction of the mountain range.

Alex pointed excitedly at a group of four large animals. "Are those our elephants?"

"They are. We have many of your large mammals and many bird species here on this deck. I'm told they are doing well."

There were substantial herds of animals on Gabriel's continents, and the Arkell had taken breeding pairs of many, including large species, such as elephants, giraffes, and buffalo. Most, they were told, would not remain on their ship for long. They would be transplanted to other planets known to have the necessary ecology for the transplants to thrive. The Arkell had been introducing all manner of life to hundreds of planets for tens of thousands of years.

Soon they came to a small river with a simple bridge crossing it. They continued over the bridge and into a more heavily treed area. It became denser as they traveled into the interior.

"It's getting humid," said Teddy.

"This is our rain forest. It is home to hundreds of species—birds, reptiles, amphibians, and mammals."

Many species of colorful birds were visible as they flew from tree to tree. Their songs came from all directions as the group moved into the forest.

"Keep your eyes open for some interesting mammals that you will not be familiar with. They're sometimes hard to spot."

"How many acres on this deck?" asked Teddy.

"Just more than three thousand."

"Jeez, it looks closer to thirty thousand."

"This is just remarkable," said Alex.

"Again, the bulkheads are all part of a sophisticated hologram system. It is difficult to distinguish where the real meets the illusion, even from a few meters away."

They spent a full hour touring that deck. Vance and Alex each spotted a number of otherworldly mammals due to their sharp SLF vision. Teddy managed to spot one ahead of the others. It was a small, hairy critter similar to a monkey, with big eyes, hands, and feet. Other than being cute, it was noteworthy because of its antics. When it spotted the transport, it began jumping up and down, clapping its big hands, and making a sound like a child's giggle before shooting up a tree and disappearing into the canopy. It was a humorous display.

"Maybe we should rename that animal Teddy," said Oruku.

"That would make sense," Vance said. "It's certainly entertaining."

"What's its name now?" asked Teddy.

"Grookru," said Oruku. "That means 'clapper.'"

"That's a good name for it," said Teddy.

Oruku nodded. "Okay, we'll leave it as it is."

Teddy smiled. "That was one very cute creature."

"It is. Many think it is the cutest in the galaxy."

"Do they make good pets?" asked Teddy.

"Actually, no. They do not do well in captivity. They require a lot of space."

"Teddy bear," said Colleen, "I already have the cutest creature in captivity."

"Yeah, but I can't climb trees worth a hoot."

Oruku smiled. "We have five other decks similar to this one, each varying in topography, climate, and wildlife."

"Have you come across any environments that provided for life but were so foreign or hostile that you didn't try to duplicate them?" asked Shem.

"Many." Oruku paused briefly. "A good example is a dark planet eighty light-years from here that lies far outside of the Goldilocks zone of its sun, where the sun's light and heat cannot reach. Its volcanic core keeps it warm enough to sustain life for some unusual animals, animals as large as elephants and as small as mice. All are completely blind."

"Really?"

"Yes, but they have extraordinary senses of hearing, smell, and touch. When observing them, you would swear they can see."

"Without sunlight, there is no photosynthesis. Plants can't grow. What do they eat?" asked Gary.

"Very sophisticated forms of moss and mold, some as big as trees. There is little color on the planet, mainly just shades of gray and some dull yellows and oranges—no green. It's fascinating to see, almost beautiful in a way. There are very strange predators that eat the animals that eat the mold."

"You have videos, I'll bet," said Lara.

"We do—of that planet and thousands more. We will provide you with data and videos of all of them."

"That's going to be very interesting to a lot of people," said Shem.

Once aboard the elevator, they dropped down five decks and exited onto farmland.

"Wow again," said Alex.

The deck displayed fields of row crops as far as the eye could see. It was another illusion, but it certainly gave the impression of wide-open space. Off in one of the fields, a harvesting machine moved down a row of vegetables.

"Looks like Kansas farmland," said Vance. "Flat as a pancake and seems to stretch out forever."

"Do you create these illusions to keep your people from feeling claustrophobic?" asked Alex.

"Everyone aboard this ship was born here. Claustrophobia isn't something we suffer from, but in our early years, we found that the illusion of unlimited open space created a calming effect for the majority of Arkell."

"That makes sense to me," said Alex.

"You might find it interesting to know that a small percentage of Arkell suffer from a form of reverse claustrophobia, if you will. They become uncomfortable on a planet's surface. They feel exposed in knowing that there is no ship surrounding and protecting them."

"That's interesting—a form of agoraphobia," said Alex.

"That is interesting," said Vance.

No one said anything for a moment or two. "How often do you find new life-bearing planets?" asked Shem.

"It is our main goal. It is what we do. We explore." Oruku paused while taking in some facts via his earpiece. "I'm told we come across a life planet about once every nine point four years."

"That sounds tremendously gratifying," said Shem.

Oruku smiled. "It is our reward. The pot of gold at the end of the rainbow, so to speak."

Shem nodded in understanding. "After a discovery, how long do you remain on a planet?"

"It depends on the planet. We've spent as little as two weeks and as long as six months. They are all different."

"How often do you find intelligent life?"

"Intelligent life such as yourselves, very rarely—maybe once per century."

Shem nodded. "When you discover intelligent life, do you make contact?"

"Almost never. We will monitor them for a few years to ascertain their level of sophistication."

"As you did with Earth?"

"More or less, yes. After spending a sufficient amount of time monitoring their civilization after the initial discovery, we place satellites in orbit and then leave to continue our explorations. We rarely return sooner than ten years."

"As you've done here."

Oruku nodded.

Alex came into the conversation. "Why did you wait so long to make yourselves known to us?"

"You colonized this planet; you didn't evolve here. We were waiting to see how you progressed on an alien planet and how the planet developed under your guidance. Also, we had planned on waiting until your population was at least double what it presently is, but the discovery of the merging binary stars and subsequent gamma-ray burst caused us to revise our plans." Oruku smiled. "That's when the idea of Shem and Jarleth was originated."

"And the rest is history," said Alex.

"As you would say, yes."

Oruku continued a narrative as he drove. "There are thirty-one decks dedicated to food production. The decks vary in weather, depending on which crops are being grown. In addition, there are two decks for food processing and three for storage."

"Does your diet vary?" asked Jarleth.

"Oh yes. We even have seasonal foods. Of course, our seasons are created, but a change of pace is pleasing and necessary, we believe."

After a few seconds, Vance moved on to a different subject. "Do any of your citizens go into stasis to endure years in space?"

"We no more endure the years in space than you do years on Gabriel. We're living our lives, as you do on your planet. There's little difference."

"Boy, that's hard to comprehend," said Alex. "But from what we've seen so far, your ship is a planet."

"That's right." Oruku smiled. "The difference is that our planet's life is on the inside, not outside. And of course, it's mobile. As we continue our tour, you will get a better idea of why our ship is our home."

"There are gasses created by life's mechanisms. Carbon dioxide and methane come to mind. How do you handle that?" asked Shem.

"A high percentage of the carbon dioxide produced on the inhabited decks is circulated throughout the decks containing vegetation."

"Of course it is," said Shem. "In turn, the vegetation creates more oxygen."

"Exactly. A percentage of the methane is converted into its liquid form and used by our citizens to cook. The byproduct of burning methane is more carbon dioxide."

"You use natural gas to cook with?"

"Most prefer it over electric or wave cooking. All of our restaurants use the gas."

"That was true on Earth too," said Vance. "But that seems primitive, considering how advanced your technology is."

"As you know, we are vegetarians, so we don't have livestock, but we do have lakes, ponds, and rivers to produce fish."

"Lakes, rivers, and wide-open spaces on a ship—hard to comprehend," said Vance.

"It's marvelous," added Jarleth.

"I've not eaten your fish, but I remember the accolades given by those who have," said Alex.

"We'll be having lunch in our main town," said Oruku. "You'll get a chance to judge for yourself."

"Town?"

"The deck the town is on is what you might consider our cultural center. There are museums, art galleries, marketplaces, stores, shops, and executive offices. Ship management, other than emergencies, is run through that deck."

"Of course. Such an area would be necessary to run your ship—your world. I should have assumed you would have a place to gather and socialize," said Alex. "We have a bridge."

"It's a ship. There is no reason you should have assumed that it has a town," said Oruku. "We have other gathering places—restaurants and such—on fifty other decks as well. We'll see a couple of them on this tour. Next stop is suburbia."

The elevator opened to a scene reminiscent of an upscale neighborhood on Earth. The wide tree-lined streets meandered up and down actual foothills. The street they drove onto was lined with hundreds of Arkell, all dressed in their finery and all smiling brightly.

"What the hell?" said Alex.

"Oh my God," said Colleen.

"In a ship!" said an amazed Lara,

"Have I mentioned that the Arkell are enthralled with the human culture?"

"Yes, but I had no idea."

"This looks a little like Beverly Hills of Earth," said Teddy.

"We've never seen Beverly Hills," said Colleen, "but we've all seen the pictures and videos."

"Again," said Vance, "astounding."

Oruku nodded in appreciation. "You're going to be doing a lot of waving while we drive around some of these decks. There are forty-eight decks of housing such as this, but we're not going to visit them all. Certain decks have been designated for your visit, and Arkell from other decks have gathered on them. We're trying to give all a look at you while you are aboard their home. It's important to them."

"We understand," said Alex while he smiled and waved to the onlookers lining the idyllic streets.

They visited more of the residential decks over the next two hours. During their tour, the questions from the humans did not abate.

"How many live on each residential deck?" asked Alex.

"Each deck averages about twenty-five hundred."

The passengers' heads swiveled while Oruku drove and answered questions.

The residential decks varied a great deal. Some contained condos complete with pools, beaches, tennis courts, restaurants, nightclubs, and many other facilities for the active youth.

"This and a few like it are for our younger populous—those under a hundred."

"Under a hundred is the younger generation." Teddy laughed. "Wow."

At one point, they stopped at a sandy beach where dozens of Arkell were sunning themselves under what appeared to be an actual sun, while others were in the water, swimming, wading, or surfing the nice-sized waves rolling into shore.

"You've got to be kidding me," said Teddy.

"You have an ocean on board this ship?" said Alex.

"Again, it's an illusion. The ocean only covers about half a square kilometer. It is three hundred fifty-five meters from the shore to the bulkhead, but it's enough to create the artificial waves for surfing. Again, an activity copied from humans."

"I can see waves rolling in from at least ten kilometers away," said Shem.

"The hologram is in sync with the wave machine."

"Of course it is," said Teddy.

"It appears as big as our Vast Ocean," said Vance.

"Remarkable."

An hour later, their transport exited the elevator onto a street made of beautifully interlocking pavers. The wide street circled up a low hill and into a picturesque town like one found in the foothills of a majestic mountain range on old Earth. Homes were scattered among tree-covered hills above the town. Beyond, snowcapped mountains appeared to rise thousands of meters. Above their heads, along with a sun, wispy white clouds slowly moved across a bright blue sky. Occasionally, a cloud passed under the sun, casting a shadow over the town.

Oruku stopped the transport to give the humans time to take it all in. They stood to get a better view.

"This is absolutely stunning," said Alex.

"I keep telling myself that I'm aboard a spaceship," added Colleen.

"If you didn't know it, you would never suspect it," said Shem.

"Not in a million years," said Teddy.

"My home is up there about half a kilometer." Oruku pointed up and to the right.

"Kind of a middle-aged enclave?" asked Teddy.

Oruku nodded and smiled. "Now that you've said it, I believe you're right."

"It seems the old Earth expression holds true in almost all circumstances in the galaxy," said Alex. "Birds of a feather flock together."

"That's an apt expression."

"Speaking of old, where's your geezer deck?" asked Teddy.

Oruku smiled. "Two decks below, actually."

"That would be those over three hundred?" asked Lara with a smile.

Oruku nodded, "Generally speaking."

They remained quiet for another minute as they took in the sights.

"Anybody hungry?" asked Oruku as he pulled in front of a pretty building that looked like a large private home. The large courtyard held two dozen tables and chairs to match.

Ninety minutes later, after they thanked the proprietors and shook hands with all the Arkell around, they reentered the transport.

"That was, as promised, the finest fish I have ever tasted," said Alex.

"I could eat that three times a day," said Vance.

"Otherworldly," said Teddy with a big grin.

"I've noticed that all Arkell seem to treat all other Arkell as if they were close family," said Vance. "I've detected no status separation as such."

"All Arkell are considered on the same plane. None are considered superior to another. My station as a councillor is not considered any loftier than a farmer, machine operator, or restauranteur. It is simply my job—one that I, along with the other councillors, am well suited to. However, you don't want me treating an illness, building your home, or piloting a spacecraft."

"I like that," said Vance.

Oruku smiled. "You clearly don't realize it, but that's pretty much what you have on Gabriel. Most call you, Alex, Troy, and Gary 'sir', but if they used your first names, I doubt you'd be offended."

"That didn't occur to me," said Vance.

"Me neither," said Alex.

They spent that afternoon touring a dozen more decks, including warehousing, manufacturing, food processing, and the research and medical decks. On the medical deck, Teddy, Colleen, Lara, Jarleth, and Shem were put through the life-extending procedure. They were the first humans to go through it.

When the last of them had completed the process, Oruku said, "I believe we just added an average of thirty years to your lives."

"I don't know about the rest of you, but I feel... I feel great," said a beaming Lara.

"I thought it was just me," said Teddy. "I feel like running and jumping like a child."

"I don't think I've ever felt this good," added Colleen.

Oruku smiled broadly. "Did I fail to mention that the process will have that effect?" Oruku was clearly pleased. "Your genes are now in the condition they were at their peak - as they were when you were young and growing."

I don't ever remember feeling like this," said Lara.

"When you're young you don't realize how perfect you feel, you have nothing to compare it to. The old Earth expression, `Youth is wasted on the young', has a great deal of validity."

"When I see children playing I sometimes think – I wish I had their energy," said Colleen.

Oruku smiled again, "Now you do."

"I don't know what to say," said Teddy. "*Thank you* just doesn't get it done."

"More than adequate," said Oruku. "We will also benefit greatly from your longer lives."

All of a sudden, Oruku's expression changed. "We must get you back to Gabriel right now," he said with considerable alarm.

"What?" Vance said.

"Quickly—into the transport!" ordered Oruku.

A few seconds later, all the Gabrielites were nervously sitting in the transport. Oruku was just about to take his place, when he stood up straight, clearly getting information over his earpiece.

"Too late," he said as he jumped into the transport, made a quick U-turn, and headed for the elevator.

"What's going on?" said Vance.

"We have detected an entity entering this sector—it is the one we were concerned with. And it's heading this way."

Vance instantly went into war mode; his expression hardened. The others looked a little confused and a little frightened, except for Shem, whose face looked composed and strong.

"I am getting you to the center of this ship—to a safe area," said Oruku.

Within a minute, the transport had exited the elevator and sped to the center of the ship. There, a hatch was open, and they passed through into a large chamber. It looked to be at least a hundred meters in diameter.

"This area is self-contained and reinforced," said Oruku. "It's nearly indestructible."

Dozens of Arkell were already in that safe place, and dozens more were entering from eight different hatches that circled the chamber.

"Are you going to stay with us?" asked Lara.

"No, my duties are in the control center and will be until this problem is resolved." Oruku quickly looked around. "The Arkell joining you in here are nonessential personnel in times like this."

"I want to go with you," said Vance. "I'll be of no use here."

"Me too," said Alex.

Oruku looked ready to deny their request, but after a brief pause, he said, "Okay, you two stay in the transport." He turned to the remaining five. "You will be able to see and hear everything happening on one of the many viewers we have in this area. Make yourselves as comfortable as possible."

With that, the transport spun 180 degrees and left the chamber.

Oruku said nothing, but it was clear he was receiving intelligence.

"What can you tell us?" asked Vance.

"We're at half-light speed on an intercept course," said Oruku as the transport entered the elevator.

"Half-light?" asked Vance.

"Didn't feel a thing," said Alex.

"How fast is that ship heading our way?" asked Vance.

"Half-light also."

The elevator shot them up dozens of decks before stopping. The transport then moved them a short distance to an impressive multistoried structure sitting in the middle of immaculately kept grounds.

"Follow me," said Oruku.

They entered the building, and several Arkell joined them as they walked rapidly through two anterooms; none spoke. They entered what must have been the control center.

"Whoa," said Alex.

There were upward of two hundred Arkell sitting at an equal number of stations. All were fully engaged in whatever their responsibilities were. Most startling was the image displayed on the huge viewer in the center of it all.

"Oh my" was all Oruku said as he stopped in his tracks.

There on the viewer was a massive ship that looked like what an old-fashioned Arkell ship might have looked like. The ship was obviously moving at a tremendous speed. The stars in its background were passing by like snowflakes in a blizzard.

There was a lot of anxious chatter among the Arkell in the control center. Nobody was relaxed as far as Vance could tell. He certainly wasn't.

The approaching ship bore ribs similar to those of the Arkell ship but didn't have the featureless gold hull; on the contrary, its hull was constructed with hundreds of thousands of separate panels of various shapes and sizes. Their overall color was a dingy gray, with darker and lighter panels scattered throughout its surface as far as the eye could see. The gigantic ribs were a shape slightly different from those of the Arkell ship and the same gray as the rest of the ship.

A voice came over the sound system: "It is confirmed; it is the *Geaalo*."

All chatter ceased. One could have heard a mouse sneak over a bale of cotton. The silence was ominous.

"It's stopped," said the same voice.

"Stop here, and maintain full alert," commanded an Arkell standing near the center of the control room. "Protocol one," he said calmly.

Vance recognized him immediately as the tactical leader, the man in charge of dangerous situations.

"That's Kilee, our chief sentinel. Wait here, please," said Oruku, and then he proceeded to walk forward and join Kilee.

Vance watched Oruku greet the sentinel and begin an intense but brief conversation. Apparently, Kilee agreed quickly with whatever Oruku suggested. Oruku's voice came over the sound system: "Open communications with the *Geaalo*; translator on."

"Communication open," said a voice.

"*Geaalo*, this is the Arkell ship *Velgot*. Do you understand?" said Oruku.

There was nothing but silence.

A few seconds later, Oruku said, "This is Oruku of the Arkell ship *Velgot*."

"We hear you, *Velgot*," said a male voice. "Why are you on an intercepting course?"

Oruku did not mince words. "We have two reasons: first, we wish to learn about you, and second, we perceive you as a threat to our friends on the planet you're heading to."

There was silence.

"You are Arkell, are you not?" asked Oruku.

After a brief pause, the voice said, "Most are."

Vance could see Oruku's expression change to one of confusion. "Most?"

"There are three species aboard."

Oruku said nothing for a moment. "What are your intentions for this planet?"

"We require gold."

Oruku didn't hesitate. "You can't get it here."

"We will get it here," said the voice flatly.

Kilee spoke up. "We have scanned your ship, and I will tell you that we could disable you in an instant; you will have no defense."

Again, there was silence.

Oruku spoke. "It would not be our choice to harm your ship in any way. We are Arkell, as are you. Why do you feel it is necessary to be aggressive?"

"It's our way."

"That has not been the Arkell way for tens of thousands of years. I've no doubt you know that," said Oruku.

Again, they heard only silence.

"We would like to talk to you. There is much to discuss and much to learn," said Oruku.

After a moment, the voice said, "We don't trust you."

"We have not given you any reason not to trust us. Why would you feel that way?"

"We assume you are going to try to punish us. We did not follow our protocols. We did not continue our voyage to another universe. We failed."

This man is ashamed, thought Vance. *Oruku will know that.*

"Whatever caused the *Geaalo* to cancel its mission would have happened thousands of years ago. You would have had nothing to do with it." Oruku paused for a moment. "We need to talk."

"We have no wish to talk. We simply want gold."

"I will not repeat myself concerning your intentions to take gold from Gabriel. But we will give you coordinates to a non-life-bearing planet that contains as much gold as Gabriel. Would that satisfy you?"

After a moment, the voice asked, "How far?"

"Twelve point two light-years."

"Too far."

With that, the huge ship flipped ninety degrees, allowing its top axis to point at the *Velgot*. A beam of some sort shot out of the *Geaalo*.

"*Velgot* is at light," Kilee reported calmly. "Disable them."

"Holy shit," said Vance. "We just went to light speed before their weapon could reach us."

The view on the large screen was flipping from one view of the *Geaalo* to another every second.

"Holy shit! We are surrounding the *Geaalo* by ourselves," said Vance. "They cannot get a shot."

Alex said nothing, but his expression was of awe.

"Stop here; maintain the distance," said Kilee.

The screen showed the *Geaalo* as it had been before, its axis now pointing ninety degrees away from the *Velgot*. It floated still in space. No exterior damage was visible.

"We just went from the speed of light to a dead stop several times in seconds," said Vance.

Alex just nodded.

I don't see any damage on the Geaalo, thought Vance. *But it's no longer pointing its weapon at us.*

Oruku said something to Kilee and then turned to face Vance and Alex; he waved them over.

Vance didn't hesitate and started in their direction. Alex paused for a full two seconds before hurrying to catch up to Vance.

"Kilee, please meet Vance Youngblood, Shem, and Alexander Gabriel," Oruku said quickly.

Kilee looked older than Oruku. He appeared to be in his mid-sixties. He was slightly shorter than most of the male Arkell but built much stockier. He looked vaguely familiar to Vance.

"A great pleasure," said Kilee as he offered his hand. "A great pleasure indeed." Kilee turned to Alex. "Alexander Gabriel—outstanding." They shook hands as well.

Kilee continued to scan the various viewers and other screens while meeting Vance and Alex. "I cannot spend any time getting acquainted but look forward to doing so a little later."

"We understand," said Vance.

"Agreed," said Alex.

"Have you disabled the *Geaalo*?" Vance asked.

"We have, but they should be able to effect repairs within an hour."

"That is the time we have to convince them to join us in a peaceful talk, leave this sector, or face total destruction," said Oruku. "The latter is not our desire."

"But you have that capability?"

"We do."

"Why would you inflict just enough damage to disable them for just an hour?" asked Vance.

"It is our hope they will see the relatively minor damage we did to their ship and conclude we wish them no harm. Hopefully that will give us a chance to talk them into meeting us and dissuade them from attacking Gabriel," said Oruku.

"Now, if you'll excuse us, we need to get back to the situation," said Kilee.

"There's a sitting area over there." Oruku pointed to what looked like a comfortably appointed elevated lounge fifteen meters to their right.

Vance nodded. "That's where we'll be."

Vance and Alex had not quite reached the lounge before Kilee hailed the *Geaalo*. "You, being Arkell, now know two things: one, we mean you no harm, and two, we have the capability to destroy you if you persist in your aggressive posture."

A full minute passed in silence. Then a different male voice came from the *Geaalo*. "What do you propose?"

Now it was Oruku's turn. "We would very much like to meet with you and exchange histories. We started from the same place a long time ago, and we are now on completely different paths. We want to know why you Arkell have taken such a destructive path."

"Why do you believe we are on a destructive path?"

"We have seen what you have done to other planets you have plundered. The damage and loss of life have been massive in scale."

There was a long pause. The tension in the control center was palpable. Oruku and Kilee seemed collected as they talked quietly to one another. Seeing their apparent confidence had a soothing effect on Vance.

"*Velgot*, we do not wish to meet. We have nothing in common after these tens of thousands of years. We are going to withdraw from this part of the galaxy."

"We are sorry you have chosen not to meet with your species. We believe our meeting would have been beneficial to us both. But this was your choice to make."

Vance could see Oruku's demeanor was of discouragement.

"*Geaalo*, this is Kilee, *Velgot's* chief sentinel. We will let you leave this sector of the galaxy. We now believe you have no compassion, no empathy, and no honor. And we find this very sad. We wish it would have been otherwise." Kilee paused for a moment before continuing. "So this will be the only warning to you. If you reenter this sector of the galaxy at any time in the future, you will be destroyed completely. You have one hour to leave; after that time, if you are still in this sector, you will be ended."

All the technicians in the control center began talking at once. Vance kept his eyes on Kilee and Oruku; he needed to see what their demeanor was. He could see a great sadness in Oruku, and to a lesser extent, the same was true of Kilee. He didn't see any expression of concern.

"*Velgot*, we don't believe we can effect repairs within the hour allotted."

"Fifty-four minutes," said Kilee.

Forty-nine minutes later, the *Geaalo* went to light speed and left Gabriel's sector of the galaxy.

CHAPTER 17

DALE'S SLF

Vance smiled every time he noticed that Alex was still in the process of learning what it was like to be a SLF, a person who was mobile and could walk among and interact with other living beings. He and Dale both noticed that whereas the human Alex on Earth had been quite stoic and introspective, his SLF was clearly not. He was rarely seen without a smile on his face. He was warm and friendly to all he met; he was, without question, a happy person.

That day, Vance, Alex, Gary, and Oruku were together in the *Marian's* SLF lab.

"Seeing how much you are enjoying yourself, Alex, I'm getting anxious to join you," said Dale.

"You are going to be one jubilant being, my friend," said Alex.

"I'm sure that's true," said Dale.

"We are within two days of completing the manufacturing of the Isleium and three days from completing the skeleton," reported Oruku.

"A bit ahead of schedule," said Dale.

"All Arkell are excited for Dale Isley to become a SLF."

"Once we receive those materials, we will get to work putting it all together," said Gary.

"Ten days to finish?" asked Oruku.

"Give or take, yes."

"There is something more," said Oruku. "In addition to the Isleium necessary to build Dale's body, we are producing enough Isleium in all forms to build an additional seven SLFs, plus enough to effect repairs when necessary. In addition, we are manufacturing seven skeletons in various sizes and corresponding power units. Use them as you see fit."

"I don't know what to say," said Alex. "A simple thank-you, as usual, seems inadequate."

"It's comforting to know we will be able to care for our SLFs," said Gary.

"Is that a hint for us to build more SLFs?" asked Vance with a trace of a smile.

"Not now, but we feel that sometime in the future, you may desire to do so. We want you to have that capability."

"That's very thoughtful of you," Alex said.

"You have asked little of us," said Oruku. "It's not your nature, so we try to anticipate what you may need or want in the future."

"And I'm sure that will be the case, considering all your anticipations have been dead on," said Vance.

"All I can offer are my thanks," said Dale.

"Your thanks are more than sufficient."

No one said anything for a few moments.

"I have a request," said Dale.

"You have but to make it," answered Oruku.

"Everyone on this planet has taken a tour of your ship. I wish to do the same when I become a SLF, if you can make time."

Without hesitation, Oruku responded, "You will get a tour like none of the others. We will provide you our top scientists as your guides. You will be able to ask all of your questions while viewing and experiencing the machines that are at the heart of your questions."

Gary raised his hand. "Can I tag along?"

Dale's SLF body was in the final stages of completion. As expected, the Arkell had no trouble producing the Isleium or constructing the skeleton. At Dale's request, they made the skeleton ten centimeters taller than his original.

"No point in being a stub among all you giants."

"You're going to be taller than me," said Vance.

"But not nearly as wide."

"That would take a great deal more Isleium than we presently have," Gary said.

"About twenty kilos more," said Vance with a smile.

Dale's hologram nodded.

"The Arkell made your skeleton out of a material a bit stronger and lighter than titanium," said Gary. "We also incorporated a couple of other tweaks they suggested. They will improve the durability some."

Five hours later, Dale Isley stood on his own two feet for the first time in more than five hundred years. He, like the SLFs before him, appeared to be in his mid-thirties. He was dressed in clothes Vance had made for him, clothes he was famous for wearing on Earth: slacks, a dress shirt, loafers, and a cardigan sweater.

Other than his new height, he looked exactly like the Dale Alex remembered so long ago on Earth, although not the Dale he'd first encountered in his office in Southern California—the Dale who had been a walking trash heap, the young man who had not only looked as if he had been recently dragged heels first through all the plagues of Egypt but also smelled the part. No, this was the Dale Alex had re-met two weeks later, after he had effectively thrown Dale out of his office and told him to clean up or stay away from Gabriel Industries. This was the Dale who had gone through a complete makeover, including hygiene, wardrobe, and attitude. Under the dirt; tangled, greasy hair; and scruffy beard was a good-looking young man. On top of that, Dale had miraculously become stylish. His beard was trimmed to perfection, his hair was clearly styled, and his wardrobe was the latest in fashion. The transition, at that time, had left Alex speechless. Dale, for his part, credited Alex with changing his life in ways he'd never imagined. Before, he had been someone others avoided when they had a choice, and now he was a person others wished to work with and be around socially. From that point on, he held a deep gratitude and affection for Alex.

"Hi, my friend," said Alex.

"Hi, Alex." Dale stepped forward and gave Alex a big hug before stepping back and smiling. "You're shorter than I remember."

MO-SIX 10, 142

Vance looked down the table at the other men gathered. This was to be the final meeting with Oruku prior to the Arkell's departure. The knowledge saddened him.

"We would like to run a thought by you," Oruku said to the other five men sitting in the *Marian*'s meeting room.

"You have our attention," said Vance.

Oruku smiled. "We Arkell thought about asking Shem and Jarleth to join us on our voyage but quickly concluded that wouldn't be the best thing for them. So how would you feel about us taking some of Jarleth's and Shem's DNA when we depart Gabriel?"

Everyone immediately nodded while giving an affirmative response.

"We assumed you would make that request," said Gary.

"You can have your own Shem and Jarleth without traumatizing them or us," said Dale.

"Yes, exactly," said Oruku. "Their genes are superior to ours in some ways. Our civilization would benefit greatly as the years pass by infusing their DNA into ours."

"I'm sure they'll readily agree," said Vance.

Oruku nodded. "In addition, with your permission, we would like seeds, embryos, and DNA from hundreds of other plants and animals."

"Granted," said Vance. "Tell us what you want, and we'll assist you in collecting them."

"The list has just been transmitted to your main computer," said Oruku, "and thank you."

"While we wait for Shem and Jarleth to arrive, I would like to ask another question," Alex said. "Will you ever return to Gabriel?"

Oruku nodded. "You can be assured that we will return to Gabriel every ten to thirty years."

That put a smile on everyone's face.

"Excellent," said Alex.

"Ditto," said Vance.

"Perfect," said Troy.

Gary smiled. "That being the case, can I go with them?"

Troy returned the smile. "No."

Everyone laughed.

The six continued to discuss various details concerning the Arkell's departure, and thirty minutes later, Shem and Jarleth walked into the meeting room. Both were smiling and seemed enormously happy. Everyone stood to greet them.

After greetings, hugs, and some small talk, Vance asked everyone to sit.

"Oruku has a request of you," he said.

"I can't think of a thing we wouldn't grant the Arkell," said Shem.

"I agree," Jarleth said.

"Thank you," said Oruku. "We first discussed asking you two to join us on our voyage." He smiled and paused. "But we were sure you'd decline, so we would like to take some of your DNA with us."

Shem smiled, looked at Jarleth, and turned back to Oruku. "We've talked about that. We thought you might ask us to join your voyage but probably wouldn't because you'd feel we would be stressed over the thought of leaving this planet."

Oruku smiled and nodded.

"We assumed, as an alternative, you would ask for our DNA."

The Arkell were scheduled to leave Gabriel within the next two days, prompting Oruku and the leaders of Gabriel to dedicate the remaining time to answering all questions that had not yet been asked and answered. A delegate from the Vout and one from the Yassi were invited to attend the final meeting. For the first time, Dale sat with the others as a real person.

The meeting was broadcast throughout the planet and to the Arkell ship. It was doubtful a single person in either place was not watching and listening.

"Your civilization is nearly seven hundred thousand years older than ours," Alex said. "At what point in your extensive history did your civilization settle in and remain as you are now, with no internal conflicts or other major social problems?"

Oruku nodded. "If we were to compare our history to yours, it is likely that had Earth not been destroyed, the humans would have had less than a hundred years before they became completely civilized and peaceful. However, had it not been for the WGC, that would not have been the case. We calculate that strife, wars, and violence could have continued for thousands of years."

Vance's eyebrows rose. "That long?"

"That is our calculation."

Alex nodded. "It was our hope and intent that our actions through the WGC would dramatically change our civilization's course."

"It did so," said Oruku.

"Without question," said Troy. "It's astonishing to read the history of Earth prior to the WGC. Our generation had little to contend with when compared to what you four men, the creators of the WGC, had to endure and overcome. It was considered the single greatest feat in Earth's history."

"Oh, we agree," said Oruku. "I refer back to the Yassi." He turned to acknowledge the Yassi representative. "They didn't have the benefit of a movement such as the WGC, and all things being equal, their strife went on for nearly two thousand years longer than Earth's."

"Two thousand years?" Alex smiled. "But they came out of their malevolent ways with shining colors in the end."

"Yes, they did, and maybe even stronger in their resolve to remain a peaceful people. They cast out all things that led to conflict of any kind and turned their energies toward developing beauty in all of its forms."

"Yes, they did," said Gary. "Their planet is like one massive art gallery. The beauty is indescribable."

"They are wonderful beings," said Oruku.

The Yassi smiled brightly. "Thank you."

"I have a big question," said Dale.

Oruku turned to Dale and nodded once.

"Are you the most advanced civilization in the universe?"

Oruku smiled slightly. "That is a relevant question. In the universe, no, it's highly unlikely. This galaxy? We would give a provisional maybe."

"Maybe? There may be other civilizations who are more advanced than the Arkell in this galaxy?"

"We can't rule that out."

"I would like to get back to your statement that you aren't likely to be the most advanced intelligence in the universe."

Oruku smiled. "Yes, you would want to know more about that."

"We all would," said Alex.

"Of course." Oruku paused. "The phrase 'more advanced' may not fit here. We think there may be an intelligence that is completely different from ours. A different thing entirely."

Oruku had everyone's attention.

"Could you expand on that?"

"I will try, but as your old saying goes, we will be attempting to compare apples and oranges—or, in this case, maybe the brain of a flea to a human brain. One contains nothing but instinct, while the other, by comparison, knows everything." Oruku paused for a moment before smiling, "We may be the flea."

"Really?" said Gary.

"Have you any idea who or what?" asked Dale.

"We have a few ideas—and mind you, they are just ideas. Theories. Please don't take them as facts or beliefs." Oruku paused again. "The most prevalent theory is that they reside in, are a part of, or are what you call dark matter or dark energy."

"Dark matter?" asked Gary, clearly surprised.

Oruku nodded. "Again, this is just conjecture."

"But there has to be a basis for such far-reaching speculation," said Dale.

Oruku nodded. "We might suggest, before we continue, a different name for the phenomena. *Dark*, in the English language, can have negative connotations. We don't believe there is anything dark about it."

"What do you call it?" asked Dale.

"We call it *Sharkra*, which roughly translates to 'unknown force' in English."

"That does make more sense than *dark matter*," said Gary.

"The actual Superiors may, in fact, be the Sharkra," said Oruku.

"You're going to expand on that?" said Dale.

Oruku nodded and continued. "One reason for such speculation is that there are many questions that remain unanswered. Where did the original seed come from? What placed the building blocks of life in billions of asteroids and comets, as was hypothesized by

Ian Henderson? The majority of comets and asteroids contain life to one degree or another."

"We assumed it was you who seeded them."

"You assumed superior beings accomplished that, and you believed we were those superior beings. There could be few other assumptions from your point of view." Oruku paused. "But now you know we are not superior—just beings."

"But you believe the Sharkra could be responsible?" asked Gary.

"We don't know. We simply believe it's a possibility that we can't rule out."

Oruku paused for a few moments and looked at each person sitting around the table. "We, with all of our technology, have not been able to penetrate, dissect, or see a single molecule of Sharkra. Yet it exists—of that there is no doubt. We know little more about the Sharkra than you do."

"That's remarkable. That's—" Dale quit talking.

Gary picked up the conversation. "Are you suggesting the Sharkra is an entire race of beings?"

"Again, we don't know. That is just one part of the speculation. Another prevalent hypothesis is that each universe or galaxy may be a single mind, or possibly a cluster of entities acting in harmony."

"You know there is more than one universe?" said Dale.

"We know for certain that there are more than the one in which this galaxy resides. We have been using extremely sophisticated technology to penetrate fourteen universes that border this one. We believe there may be no end to universes. They may be infinite."

"Infinite?"

Oruku nodded. "Maybe."

"How do you know they are separate universes and not simply an extension of ours?" asked Dale.

"They are expanding in different directions. And we have detected slightly different physics in each. They have different characteristics. They are individual."

"As in *individuals*?" asked Gary.

"Some of us believe that."

"Well, that's a ..." Dale couldn't finish the thought.

Vance was surprised at Dale's reaction to the revelation. *He is stunned by this conversation. This theory hasn't crossed his mind.*

Oruku smiled. "As you might have said on Earth, this is huge."

"Couldn't get any bigger," said Alex.

"That's right. It's the sheer size—the enormity—of what you're sharing with us that's throwing me off my game," Dale said.

Oruku nodded. "I understand. But to continue along the same line, I go back to the Sharkra. What if it they were a form of brain matter? What if each universe or galaxy is a massive brain unto itself? What if the universes or galaxies are a collection of beings?"

"That's another astounding concept."

"It is," said Oruku. "It is a thought that has been among the most prevalent in our civilization for thousands of years."

"I have to admit here that I'm completely blown away by this," said Dale.

Oruku smiled. "You are not alone."

"If the universes or galaxies are individual beings, we may simply be a tiny virus, an anomaly," said Gary.

"Certainly a possibility, but we don't think so. That scenario has been batted around for millennia and rejected by the majority of our thinkers. If, in fact, the Sharkra is a form of intelligence, most believe they would have created us for a reason. Possibly for nothing more than amusement or maybe an experiment. Maybe we are pets. We have speculated about everything."

"All of the races are somewhat different and somewhat the same," said Dale. His mind seemed to be catching up to the extraordinary theories.

"Yes, exactly. Almost like testing several formulas to see which worked out the best," said Oruku.

Vance smiled to himself. *Dale's getting with it.*

"Let's assume for the moment that Sharkra are, in fact, sentient beings," said Dale. "They might pick thousands of planets to plant various DNA upon. Then they sit back, if you will, and watch how things shake out. Time may not have any meaning to them—in fact, it may not exist."

Oruku nodded in agreement. "Or they may deposit the same DNA on each world in order to see how the myriad of environments cause changes or mutations upon the DNA."

"Or an infinite number of different DNA, thereby ensuring a myriad of results," said Dale. "That's what I'd do."

"I agree," said Gary.

"Planets evolve. They are forming and developing around new stars constantly. Some are destroyed by one means or another." Dale looked at Oruku. "What percentage of planets in our galaxy are in the Goldilocks zone?"

"Those in the Goldilocks zone that contain the necessary components—water, mass, et cetera—number approximately one in ten thousand."

Vance smiled. "How many planets in our galaxy alone?"

Oruku smiled back. "We don't know exactly, because as Dale says, they come and go. But if you used one trillion as a starting point, you would be in the ballpark."

"At one in ten thousand, that's about a hundred million test tubes to watch," said Dale. "An intelligent being could gather a lot of data over a few million years."

"Do you see a time—sometime in the future—when we will know the answer to the Sharkra?" asked Alex.

"We have technology that measures, weighs, creates matter, changes matter, and sees the past and the future to an extent, yet we cannot see the Sharkra. My personal belief is that we will not know until the Sharkra want us to know—if, in fact, there is intelligence there at all."

"This is still causing my head to spin," said Dale.

Oruku turned to Dale. "Would you be interested in helping us prove or disprove the possibility of the Sharkra being a living entity?"

"I assume you're kidding," said Dale with a small smile.

"Not at all. We believe that fresh eyes and an extremely clever mind should look at these theories, and we all agree you're the one person who just may be able to connect the dots for us."

"Me? Connect the dots?"

By Dale's expression, Vance could see that he was taken aback by Oruku's comment.

"Oh yes, you," said Oruku.

"Well, I'm flattered, but if your efforts have been futile, I can't see where—" Dale stopped talking for a moment, and then he smiled. "Have you tried asking the Sharkra what the hell they are?"

Oruku smiled broadly. "We have, but I will admit we didn't think to do that for a very long time—you thought of it in seconds."

Dale returned the smile. "So what did they say?"

That caused everyone to laugh.

"Good one," said Gary.

"It was," agreed Oruku.

The conversation remained on that subject for another hour before Dale abruptly changed the subject.

"Do you believe it is possible to travel faster than light?"

"No." Oruku paused for a moment. "Not faster. Not with the physics we recognize in this universe. But what if the physics were different? What if, as an example, the Sharkra operate under different laws of physics entirely? What if within Sharkra, there is no need to travel? What if you're already there?"

"Meaning?" asked Gary.

"Thoughts."

"Thoughts?"

"If the Sharkra is a single living entity, a life force, it would be everywhere in a universe at the same time. Its thoughts would encompass the universe, and rate of travel would be irrelevant."

"Jesus," said Vance.

The conversation was getting deeper by the minute, which was not lost on the participants. Everyone had elevated their abstract game.

"According to our physics," said Dale, "time remains constant for those traveling at the speed of light. If one were to travel faster than light, time would, in theory, back up. If your ship were to enter another universe and the physics there allowed for faster than light speed, it could, in theory, return to this universe before it left."

"This is starting to cause my brain to seize up," said Vance.

Oruku smiled and then looked from Dale to Gary. "I'm sure that if you think back to the day of our arrival, you will recall that we appeared and disappeared while at the same time closing the considerable distance between our ship and Gabriel."

"Yes," Dale said.

"Did it not occur to you that if we were traveling at under the speed of light, time would *not* have remained the same on our ship and your planet?"

Dale's jaw dropped. "How in the hell did I miss that?"

"We were surprised you did," Oruku said.

"Are we going to get a little more information here?" asked Gary.

Oruku nodded. "A little. As you are fully aware, the closer an object gets to light speed, the more power it takes to move it even faster."

"Yes," said Dale. "Einstein had it right. When you start moving mass, its weight increases dramatically. The faster you move it, the more it weighs. At a certain point, it takes more power to increase velocity a single meter per second than all of the energy it took to get to that point."

"That's correct. The *Norman* and *Marian* both contain SMPE—synthetic mercury plasma eliminator—which reduces your mass to near zero."

"But not zero," said Dale.

"Yes, and that's the problem. That minute amount of mass left limits your speed to ninety-seven percent of light."

Dale smiled. "And accelerating at one g, it takes a full year to reach just seventy-seven percent of that speed."

"Your magnetic variance accelerator, working in conjunction with the SMPE, cannot provide enough power to accelerate much more than one point nine eight g's."

"Yes, that's our maximum," said Gary.

"At ninety-seven percent of light time passes quickly outside the ship," said Dale. "That allowed us to take our ten by a hundred year trips. Allowed Gabriel to develop rapidly under Vance's seeding."

"That's correct," said Oruku.

"Since our system eliminates mass entirely," Oruku explained, "we reach light in just a few seconds."

"What happens at light speed?" asked Gary.

Oruku smiled brightly. "Nothing."

"What?"

"At light, the time warp ceases to exist. A ship at light speed no longer moves forward in time relative to stationary space."

"That's astonishing."

Dale remained silent for a moment before asking, "At what point does that happen?"

"At the moment light is reached, not a millisecond sooner. You were recording an hour between the times we were visible and the times we disappeared."

"That's right."

"The time it took to accelerate past the approach to light and to achieve light shot you ahead an hour. That hour was about six seconds to us."

"This is way over my head," said Vance.

"Ditto," said Alex.

"It's a bit tricky," said Oruku.

"So all things being equal, at ninety-nine point nine percent of light, things age rapidly in the galaxy," said Dale.

"Oh, indeed, but we are able to accelerate from ninety-eight point three percent of light to light in a quarter second."

"If you lingered for a minute at those speeds, the galaxy would age tremendously."

"Yes, thousands of years would pass," Oruku said. "But at light, time on the ship and for everything outside of the ship remains exactly the same."

"If I were human, I'd be taking a sedative," said Vance.

"We, with few exceptions, always travel at light," said Oruku. "Following you here and staying at the same space-time is an exception."

"Sorry?" said Alex.

"We always traveled at the same speed as the *Marian*. Had we not, we wouldn't have been able to keep track of your current activities. We would have been out of synchronization. When you went on your ten-by-a-hundred-year trips, we matched your speed in order to remain in your time. In so doing, our home planets aged hundreds of years. We are way out of sync with them."

"That's astounding," said Gary. "You've lost communications with your family and friends?"

"No. We have been in a different space-time for millennia. We have been nomads for more than a thousand of your years. Our home planets are fully aware of our existence and would welcome us back as long-lost travelers, but we have no emotional ties as such. It's been too long. Our ship is our home."

"That seems sad in a way," said Alex.

"It has to be that way," said Oruku matter-of-factly, "but other than a few exceptions, we travel at light."

"Well, to resurrect an old cliché, we need to talk about the eight-hundred-pound gorilla in the room. It cannot be avoided," said Alex.

Oruku smiled. "Is there a God, a Supreme Being? And if so, could the Sharkra be that God?"

Alex nodded. "That's my question."

"That, of course, all depends on whether or not the Sharkra is a living entity. If not, then we assume there is no Supreme Being as we understand the concept. But on the other hand, if the Sharkra is, in fact, a life force of some kind, then we, the Arkell, believe the entity could truly be considered a Supreme Being—God."

There was silence in the room for several moments, until Oruku spoke again. "That is, in our opinion, the biggest question still unanswered in the universe."

"It is a question that we seldom even think or talk about," said Alex.

Oruku smiled at Alex. "We believe it is possible that some form of a spirit or life force resides within living beings."

"I am astounded to hear you say that," said Dale.

"Don't misunderstand. We are no more certain of that than you are, but to quote a very old Arkell saying, 'The truth could be missed if the mind is not open.' Our scientists have learned to repeat that to themselves when a solution to a problem seems impossible."

"That's a simple but insightful statement," said Dale.

"That's a practice we can all benefit from," said Vance.

"It's been my observation that the subject of religion has no limits for the believer. There has been no end to the conjecture—history has shown that. At the same time, no provable hypothesis has ever been established. But despite that, I'm going to open my mind." Dale smiled.

"Good," said Oruku.

Dale said nothing for a moment. "It just occurred to me that my mind certainly has been closed. Sharkra as a living entity or deity never occurred to me. Frankly, it should have."

"I don't believe that it should have," said Oruku. "It's a thought greatly separated from all others. Minds do not stray far from a clear path."

Dale shrugged in acceptance.

"You possess a great deal of technology that we do not—technology that would probably make our life on this planet easier. Are you willing to share that with us?" asked Alex.

"Some we will—but not all. We will provide you most of our medical technology because we wish all humans to live long while suffering as little as possible."

"You have already given us the gift of longer life."

"But there is more to life than time. We have cures for every known disease, infection, and common malady that still affects humans, Vout, and Yassi. Those will be yours. We are aware that you have already cured all but a very few."

"That's just one more thing for which we'll be in your debt," said Alex.

"You should never feel that you are in our debt. Your existence alone has given us so much variety in our lives, purpose in your care, and entertainment in your creative actions that we will never be able to repay you. It's certainly not the other way around."

"But you have technology you will not share, such as your life-extending technology," said Dale. "There must be a reason for that."

"Because in many instances, by doing so, we would cheat you out of the joy of discovery. Boredom sets in when there are no horizons left to discover. We, as I've explained, reached that point thousands of years ago. Boredom prompted us to look elsewhere in the galaxy for excitement, entertainment, and purpose. Earth and its humans, over the millennia, helped fill that void for us. Also, despite the fact that you are civilized in most ways, some technology may be beyond your emotional level to grasp or, if grasped, might be used improperly."

"Can you give us an example of what that technology is?"

"No. To do so would remove the joy of discovery."

Alex was the next to ask a question. "Have you guided all of our lives?"

"All in nature take the path of least resistance," said Oruku. "We cleared a few paths for some. You and Vance are examples. Nature did the rest."

Alex smiled slightly. "I don't know that I would describe sending me back thirty-five years in time as merely clearing a path."

"It was a bit more than clearing a path, but it was an unusual endeavor for us. We discussed at great length the outcome we wished to accomplish. We needed someone with your particular gifts to rise to the top of power on Earth. Vance was another avenue we took, but he left the path. As I've related, when you and he came together, all of our hopes came to fruition. We will never forget the date when we found out you two had joined forces. There was a huge celebration on our ship."

"Who'd have thought?" said Vance.

"Can you give us another example of path clearing?" Alex asked.

"We occasionally aided in the field of medicine. Humans were plagued with horrible diseases over the millennia. We didn't like to see the suffering, so we occasionally introduced a thought or cleared a path that allowed a researcher to stumble onto a process that led to a breakthrough."

"Polio, plague—that sort of disease?" asked Dale.

Oruku nodded. "Yes, that sort."

"Again, who'd have thought?" said Vance.

"While we were touring your ship, you mentioned that you had children aboard," said Alex. "Would you give us some information about that?"

"Yes, of course. We maintain a population of close to one hundred twenty thousand, sometimes a few more and sometimes a few less. It is the number of occupants our ship is able to support, and it's the number that fulfills all our needs. When we have an imminent death, a surrogate mother will carry a clone of that person. Normally, the clone will be taught, to some extent, by the aging predecessor until the predecessor's death."

"Makes sense."

"We don't normally plan that far ahead, but we have cloned quite a few to continue spreading their desired genes in the population," said Dale.

"Yes, but we're aware that most of your births are from natural mating. You rarely clone individuals anymore," Oruku said.

"We do it far less than we did in the beginning. Now we do it only when there is a specific reason to do so."

Oruku nodded. "That's the point we reached thousands of years in the past; very rarely do we have natural mating or births.

However, it is our hope Shem and Jarleth will propagate naturally. Their offspring will be wonderful."

"In addition to artificially inseminating a few Arkell women with Shem's sperm?" asked Dale.

"Yes, and we hope to fertilize a few of Jarleth's eggs with sperm from a few chosen Arkell."

"Won't that put you over the ultimate population?"

"Not by many, and it will balance out. It will add greatly to our gene pool."

"How many youngsters do you have on your ship at any given time?"

"About sixty, spanning ages zero through seventeen. New babies are a rarity on our world. They get a lot of attention. All have known them as adults, and most of the time, we have been friends for hundreds of years. It follows that when they are reborn, we are greatly entertained by them and marvel at their actions as youngsters."

"We have found the same thing here when watching the clones of the men in this room," said Alex. "Vance's clone, Youngblood, was of particular interest. His genes were strong—now we know why."

CHAPTER 18

GOODBYE, ARKELL
MO-SIX 21, 142

This is a sad day, thought Vance.

It was a sad time for Gabrielites and Arkell alike. Over the past two months, the humans and Arkell had become as close as family. In Vance's, Shem's, and Jarleth's cases, they were, in fact, family. The humans and Arkell had developed a deep bond and love for each other. The Arkell had supplied Gabriel's citizens with knowledge of ancient human history, adding greatly to their knowledge of their own past. They had also bestowed longer and healthier lives on the humans, Vout, and Yassi.

"I would like to present you with a small gift that is entirely inadequate compared to what you have given me," said Dale.

"We received a great deal of pleasure in providing you with what we could." Oruku smiled. "To see you as a walking, talking, breathing entity again delights us more than you can know."

"That is humbling," said Dale. "As a small token of my gratitude, maybe this will be of interest to you." Dale handed Oruku a package. "We have compiled all of the recordings made of Jarleth and Shem as they grew up on Gabriel. There are thousands of hours of footage."

"Oh my," said Oruku. "That is a wonderful gift. Just wonderful. We will take great pleasure in watching these recordings. This is wonderful." He was genuinely grateful.

"Had it not been for Dale, these recordings would not exist," said Vance. "He insisted on recording these two remarkable people from their beginnings. The majority of the recordings have not been seen by anyone other than him."

Dale smiled. "I had a great deal of curiosity when it came to them—more than most, I suspect."

"We know you must already have a great deal of footage from their lives, such as videos of special events involving them that were transmitted worldwide."

"Yes, we have some, but the total time of the recordings amounts to"—Oruku paused for a moment—"forty-six hours and twelve minutes."

"That's all?"

"Yes."

"While we are on the subject, you've never specifically said why you planted the seeds of Jarleth and Shem in the first place," said Alex.

"Or how you did it," added Dale.

Oruku smiled. "You never asked."

"No, I guess we didn't," said Vance.

"We wanted to see what kind of being would be produced by a hybrid of human and Arkell. We had your father, Vince, to study, but he didn't have as many Arkell genes as Jarleth and Shem do. He did not have the Arkell appearance." Oruku paused for a moment. "We fully expected what was produced, but we wanted to see how beings not completely human would fair in your world. We wanted to see how they would be treated, how they would develop, and how they would be loved."

There was silence for a moment before Vance spoke up. "Being different didn't seem to bother Jarleth as much as it did Shem. I could sense he always felt somewhat out of place. Your visit has put a smile on his face and a spring in his step." Vance paused for a moment. "He now knows who he is and how he came to be."

"That he does, and so do you," said Oruku.

Vance smiled. "I didn't know I was different."

"What made you think the two sets of DNA would be compatible before the birth of Vince, Vance's father?" asked Dale.

"Because the DNA is nearly identical."

"How could that be?"

"That's the big question. How could that be?" Oruku smiled. "The answer is simple."

"Simple?"

"We are related," Oruku said matter-of-factly.

That got everyone's attention.

"Our DNA can be found in comets that are nearly a billion years old. Both of our DNA. The sequence varies slightly, but the evolution clearly went down the same path."

Dale paused in thought for a moment. "Sharkra?"

"That's the dominant hypothesis."

"That's a lot to absorb," said Alex.

"The dark matter is getting a little brighter," said Vance.

"Well said," said Oruku.

After a moment, Vance changed the subject. "How did we do?"

"Do?" asked Oruku.

"With Shem and Jarleth."

Oruku smiled. "We are very pleased. Very pleased indeed."

Vance nodded. "We tried not to treat them any differently than the other children of Gabriel."

"That was our observation."

"Did you think we would assume their mutations were caused by the GRB?" asked Dale.

"We knew that you'd consider that possibility but that their identical mutations would cause you to think otherwise."

"Dale thought otherwise within seconds," said Alex.

"We knew he would."

"They certainly have been an asset to Gabriel," said Vance.

"The combination of human and Arkell has produced an exceptional being," Oruku said.

"So how'd you do it?" asked Dale.

Oruku smiled. "It was a little tricky. We had already identified, using desired genetics as parameters, two dozen humans who fit the bill as parents. Then we waited for the gamma-ray burst to hit."

"Wait," said Dale. "You knew the GRB would strike a sliver of the planet?"

"No, but we thought it was possible. We knew it was going to be close. It was an extraordinary piece of luck that it touched the planet at a location where four of our prospective parents resided. It was another lucky coincidence that the two couples had copulated that evening and that the women had become pregnant, which was unknown to them at the time."

Vance smiled. "There were a lot of copulations that evening."

"No doubt." Oruku returned the smile. "Two days later, while Charlie, Amelia, Clair, and Sonny were sleeping, we put them in an even deeper sleep, removed the fertilized eggs, altered the genetics slightly, and replaced the eggs."

"So you were here twenty years ago?" asked Dale.

Oruku nodded.

"Why didn't you make yourselves known to us?"

"Timing wasn't right. We were here to observe the comet's interaction with the GRB and, if possible, alter some genetics. But the planet had just been saved from destruction, and you had rightfully concluded some outside force had intervened on your behalf. We felt that some time should pass before we presented ourselves."

"Okay," said Dale. "That makes sense."

"So," said Vance, "was it child's play to alter the genetics?"

"No, this took a lot of planning and stealth. We had to drop onto the surface in a shuttle and enter their homes without being spotted. This was made easier because of their remote location. There were just a few people living in the area."

"That's for sure. A hell of a lot more have moved into the area in the past twenty years," Vance said.

"How long did the whole operation take?" Dale asked.

"Thirty-one minutes."

"Just thirty-one minutes? That's amazing," said Dale.

"I can assure you it seemed a great deal longer at the time." Oruku paused. "I would like to turn off the planet-wide coverage of our meeting for a few minutes. I apologize to all of the Gabrielites in advance."

"I'm sure you have a reason," said Alex. "Please proceed."

"There is something we would like to provide you with."

"I can't imagine what you could give us that you haven't already," said Vance.

"We are concerned about the Arkell on the *Geaalo*. As you now know, they are technologically advanced and clearly destructive. And you know you couldn't withstand an assault by them."

Vance could see Oruku's demeanor change. *He is saddened by what the Arkell aboard the* Geaalo *have become.* "That's probably been on many minds since our encounter with them."

"We knew that would be a concern." Oruku paused for a moment. "As you know, we told the Arkell aboard the *Geaalo* they would be destroyed if they entered this sector of the galaxy. To that end, we will provide you with a planetary shield."

"How will you do that?" asked Vance.

"We will place a field generator at each of Gabriel's poles and twelve evenly spaced satellites in geosynchronous orbit above your equator and outside of your moons' orbits. The twelve satellites will provide a strong shield against incoming mass, either natural or created by an intelligent force. The *Geaalo* is the mass we are mainly concerned with."

"Would this shield destroy their ship?" asked Vance.

"Not unless they try to penetrate it. If they return to this sector, they will detect the shield; that will stop them from proceeding to Gabriel."

"What about friendly ships?"

"You will be able to control access to the planet." Oruku smiled. "You will have an off switch."

"Is the shield similar in technology to what you use to protect your ship?" asked Gary.

"It is."

"Powered by?"

"Miniature fusion generators."

Dale said nothing for a moment. "You will be leaving us with some extremely advanced technology."

"We will, but we ask that you not examine it."

"Then we won't," said Alex without hesitation.

"We are confident of that, or we couldn't provide it." Oruku smiled. "However, if any examination were to transpire, the machines would violently self-destruct."

"So there is some doubt as to our trustworthiness?" said Gary.

"No, not at all, but there are other beings, such as those aboard the *Geaalo*, who might try to steal the technology, and we, understandably, don't want them to have it."

"How could they get past the shields in order to steal it?"

"They are Arkell."

"Understood," said Vance.

The group walked slowly through the great crowd, shaking hands and exchanging pleasantries. The Arkell were in no hurry to depart Gabriel. It seemed every person on the planet was there to witness their departure. Most of the Vout, Yassi, and Byuse were in the tightly packed gazebo park to say their farewells.

The massive *Velgot* hovered majestically 210 kilometers overhead as the entourage slowly proceeded toward the waiting shuttle. The Gabrielites looked up every few minutes, taking in the sight. They knew they would not see it again for at least a decade, possibly a great deal longer.

By the time they reached the shuttle, Jarleth's large blue eyes gleamed with tears of sadness. The men remained stoic, but their eyes displayed sadness as well.

Oruku turned and, without saying a word, gave his human friends warm hugs; Janos and Nola followed suit. When they came to Vance, Shem, and Jarleth, they connected via Waoca before hugging them. It was an emotional moment, and tears appeared in their eyes.

Oruku finally turned to Teddy and Colleen. He hugged Colleen and received a long, warm hug from her. "There are now thousands of envious Arkell men aboard our ship."

"Please share my hug with them."

Oruku smiled, "They will insist." He turned to Teddy. "Teddy, we hope you never change. You are a wonderful being."

Teddy's expressive face displayed a myriad of strong emotions. Oruku didn't need to perform Waoca with Teddy to understand his thoughts and emotions; they were right on the surface. Oruku gave him an extra-long hug. When they parted, Teddy looked at Oruku with big, sad eyes and said, "You are Gods to me."

Oruku reached out, pulled Teddy in for another long hug, and then held him at arm's length for a moment before turning and walking up the ramp into the shuttle.

The shuttle rose slowly. As it gained altitude, its size diminished until it became impossible to see against the backdrop of the *Velgot*. Five minutes later, the massive ship started to move. It moved slowly for the first minute, but then, in a flash, it was gone.

CHAPTER 19

MORE SLFS
MO-SEVEN 12, 143

As they had done for years, the five councillors of Gabriel sat at the board table in the *Marian*'s meeting room, discussing the planet's needs, wants, and progress.

Vance addressed the other four. "To change the subject for a moment."

"To?" asked Alex.

"Wives."

"Wives? Please continue."

"I assume you probably have the same thoughts and concerns about our wives that I have."

Alex smiled. "I'm sure I haven't."

Dale shrugged. "Nope, me neither."

Vance smiled. "You will when you find your women."

"I've been looking," said Alex.

One of Vance's eyebrows went up. "I've noticed."

"Hard to miss," added Troy.

"I've also spent time with various young ladies," said Dale.

"I know, but you tend to keep your dalliances under the radar."

"I'm not as flamboyant as our dear friend Alex."

"I'll try to keep my social life a bit more reserved," Alex said sincerely.

"Not necessary, my friend," said Vance. "You are not obnoxious about it. I'm sure nobody takes offense."

Alex nodded. "Thank you, but I'll take it down a notch anyway."

"So, Vance, what are you concerned about?" asked Dale.

"About the fact that our human wives will age and die, and we will not."

Alex nodded in understanding. "That's a legitimate concern."

"My Lara is the oldest at sixty-three."

Gary smiled as he interrupted. "She doesn't look a day over forty or act a day over thirty."

"That's true," Vance said. "Good genes and the Arkell's gift have slowed the aging process considerably, but the fact is that she is biological and will eventually die."

Gary nodded. "I believe I know what you're thinking, and I'll admit the thought has crossed my mind from time to time."

"Clair is fifty-two," said Troy. "It will be devastating to lose her."

"I can assure you that such a loss is devastating—more so than you would think," said Vance. "The depth of my grief took me by surprise."

"I don't want to go through that," said Troy.

"Gary, your Pat is fifty-four, and Teddy, by the way, is in his sixties. The point is that none of us has to ever suffer that loss, because we can do something about it."

"You're proposing to make SLFs for our women," said Dale.

"And Teddy," added Alex.

Vance smiled. "And Teddy for sure."

"We lost that remarkable man to old age before. At that time, I doubt any single death had caused more sorrow and grief, not only on this planet but also on two others," said Alex.

"And for the Arkell," added Vance.

"You're right. The *Velgot* is, in effect, another planet," said Gary.

"If Teddy becomes a SLF, we would have to do the same for Colleen."

All nodded enthusiastically.

Vance smiled. "Prior to the Arkell's arrival, there was no way to create any additional SLFs. We had the software and hardware necessary to make repairs and perform upgrades, but we didn't have the Isleium and skeletons."

"Now we do," said Dale.

Vance smiled. "Imagine a Teddy who is perpetually in his thirties, with all the energy being a SLF provides."

"We'll have to build in an off switch to protect ourselves."

That amused everyone.

"So Teddy for sure," said Alex. "How about your wives?"

"For sure," said Troy.

"Ditto," said Gary.

"You know how I feel," said Vance.

"It's interesting," said Dale, "that you three SLFs have somehow found the perfect women—your kindred spirits. The odds are against that."

"I've noted that Gabrielites tend to stay happy together to a much greater extent than was the case on Earth," said Vance.

"Hold on!" said Dale with a smile on his face.

"What?"

"I've just had a minor epiphany."

He had everyone's attention.

Vance smiled to himself. *Dale's epiphanies are golden.*

"Which is?" asked Alex.

Still smiling, Dale continued. "I'd be willing to bet that the seven SLF skeletons made for us by our dear and seemingly clairvoyant friends will be the exact sizes needed to make perfect copies of your wives, Teddy, Colleen, and Alex's and my future wives."

Vance laughed. "Of course! Don't even bother to check the sizes. There is no doubt you're right."

"They knew. Bless their anticipating hearts. They knew," said Alex.

MO-NINE 8, 143

Vance had the floor. "We SLFs are, in effect, immortal, and you, our loved ones, are not. It's that simple." He was addressing the ten people directly affected by the plan to build SLF bodies for four women and Teddy.

"All natural life-forms will eventually age and die, but the heartbreak of losing a loved one to age or illness is no longer necessary for us. We can do something about it," said Dale.

Vance looked over at Lara and smiled. "We love our ladies."

Lara smiled back. "Ditto, kiddo."

"I'm not sure I would like being a SLF," said Pat. She was nearly as tall as Gary at almost two meters, was slim, and had a dark complexion. Her coal-black hair was starting to show gray at the temples, and some salt-and-pepper locks were visible on the rest of her head. She was a horticulturist and a superb athlete.

"Why is that?" asked Alex.

"Because it wouldn't really be me."

"There is truth to that," agreed Colleen. "We would no longer be human; we'd be synthetic."

"I'm synthetic," said Vance, "and so are four other men here. Do you believe us to be robots?"

"No, not you. You're as human—" Colleen stopped talking for a second before smiling. "Forget I said anything."

"I can empathize with you," Alex said. "As you know, I avoided becoming a SLF for five hundred years."

"I did the same," added Dale.

Vance nodded in agreement.

"I'm glad you two changed your minds," said Colleen.

"Everybody is," added Pat.

"I'm sure the older I get, the better I'm going to warm up to the idea," said Clair. "But for now, I'm happy with my life as it is."

"Same here," said Pat, "but it's possible that when I hit one hundred twenty or so, I'll be changing my mind."

"Vance and I have talked at some length on this subject," said Lara. "I'm the oldest here, but I too feel pretty good—not as good as I did a decade ago but pretty good."

"Can you see a time when you would rather be a SLF?" asked Colleen.

"Absolutely. Quite frankly, I'm kinda looking forward to it."

"Really?"

"Ahem," said Teddy.

"Have something to say, my little Teddy bear?" asked Colleen.

"I do. First, my friend Lara, you are only six months older than I am. And—" Teddy stopped talking for a moment while his face took on a confused expression. "That's it; that's all I've got."

Everybody laughed.

"Okay, my friend, what do ya think?" Alex asked Teddy.

"To be serious for a moment, I think we need to talk about how and when all these changes are going to happen."

"You're right," said Alex, "and we five synthetics have come up with a proposal."

"Which is?"

"We build your five SLFs and put them in stasis storage."

"As was done with you?" asked Teddy.

"That's right. In addition, as a safety precaution, we begin recording yours and the ladies' essences and store the data in the computer."

"Now?"

"Absolutely. If anything unforeseen happens to you, we will be able to transfer your essence to your SLF. In addition, we will occasionally upgrade the computer to include the most recent experiences and memories."

"That's a good idea," Lara said. "I'm already suffering slight short-term memory loss."

"I haven't noticed that," said Vance.

"No big deal, sweetie, just things like forgetting where I put something—stuff like that."

"As I see it, the big question is this: At what point do we switch over?" Colleen said.

"That is the trickiest part," said Alex. "We believe it should be up to the individual. You and your spouse can choose the time."

"The problem is obvious here," said Lara. "What becomes of the human when the SLF becomes animated, a viable being?"

"Again, that will be up to the individual. I'm assuming most of you will want to wait to make the transfer until after your natural death, but it's possible your bodies and minds will deteriorate to a point that you want relief."

"That I can understand. We've all seen the heartache of extreme old age. Not pretty," said Lara. "I, for one, do not want to live long enough to burden my loved ones with a bed-ridden old lady."

"I could not agree more," said Colleen.

"I need to point out a couple of things here," said Alex. "First, we're talking about decades in the future before any of this is likely to take effect, and second, your death will not actually occur. Your old body will simply be replaced with a new young, perfect body."

"I'm the only one who has made the transfer from a wrecked body to a SLF," said Vance. "And I can tell you that it's wonderful. You will be pleased beyond anything I can describe to you." He paused for a moment. "I was truly reborn."

"We other four SLFs can attest to that. You suffer no loss of self. You simply gain a new vessel to contain it," Alex said.

No one said anything for a moment.

"Can we pick the age we'd like to be?" asked Pat.

"Of course," said Dale. "The designers and engineers will come as close to what you want as possible."

"I want to be twenty," said Lara.

"Jeez," said Colleen, "to be twenty forever. That's something to think about."

"Twenty-five," said Teddy. "I was still pretty gangly at twenty."

"You were," agreed Colleen, "but awfully damned cute."

A female SLF had never been created. Aside from skin texture, hair, and size, the main difference was the female anatomy. The planet's prominent female gynecologist, Dr. Jen, was brought in to the *Marian*'s SLF lab for weeks of consulting and designing. The process was somewhat simpler because no reproductive organs were required. Later in the process, she and the SLF techs brought in the four women to consult about their individual physiology. It took three months to complete the designs and four more months to finish building the first female SLF. It was Lara.

"Oh my God," said Lara as a smiling SLF tech pulled the curtain to one side, exposing her completed SLF. The SLF was in a standing position with its hands on its hips, and it displayed a slight smile. Its red hair was shoulder length and framed its face perfectly. Its green eyes sparkled as if alive. It was dressed in a skintight emerald-green jumpsuit similar to the one Lara had worn when touring the Arkell ship. The SLF was perfect—she was beautiful.

"She can stand on her own?"

"Oh yes," said Dale. "She's been programed with all of the physical abilities necessary to become an active person. Her mind is otherwise empty and will remain so until the time you switch over."

Lara slowly walked around her SLF, checking every detail.

She stopped when she arrived back at the front. "This is eerie; I remember looking like this. It's like looking in a mirror forty years ago." Lara nodded slowly and smiled. "I look great!"

MO-FIVE, 147

Dale and a diminutive young lady held hands and walked barefoot on the sandy beach a couple of kilometers south of Home-Bay. Gentle waves rolled in from the great Vast Ocean and washed up around their feet.

It had been four years since five SLF bodies had been completed and stored in the *Marian*'s SLF lab. It had been just two years since Dale and Tomako had met and begun seeing each other on a regular basis. Dale had found his ideal mate.

Even though one of the two remaining SLF skeletons was nearly the perfect size for Tomako, the councillors agreed they should put off building a SLF for a while to be sure the two would want to spend hundreds of years together. Dale argued against waiting but eventually accepted the decision.

Alex, on the other hand, had not found the woman he wished to spend eternity with. He argued that he had all the time in the world. "It may be that my perfect mate hasn't yet been born."

CHAPTER 20

THE ONE FOR HIM
MO-ONE 4, 160

In his eighteen years as a SLF, Alex had not found the perfect mate, but he wasn't consciously looking for one. He was enjoying himself as a bachelor, as he had on Earth many centuries ago. Before he'd formed the WGC, he'd managed to keep his relationships casual and noncommittal. That had been the case until he'd met Aidan at Colleen and Walt's wedding in the Earth year 1971.

Alex and Aidan had had great chemistry right off the bat, and from that point on, they'd never been seen apart at social gatherings. It had been a shock to all who knew them when they'd parted ways. Alex, to his credit, had made sure everyone knew the breakup was fully his fault.

Colleen, at that time, had remained angry with Alex for months. She'd known how much love her baby sister had for him, and she'd known the pain Aidan was experiencing. Vance, Dale, and Jason understood the reason for the split as no others did. It certainly wasn't due to anything Aidan had done. She'd been, in their opinion, perfect for their friend, but they also knew Alex to be a driven man. His preoccupation with accumulating a massive fortune had taken precedence over all other considerations. With time, Vance, Jason, and Dale had come to a greater understanding of and appreciation for that obsession. Had it not been for that singular drive, there would not have been a WGC, a galaxy ship named *Norman*, or a planet called Gabriel, and there would have been no humans left in the universe.

It would be Aidan Connor's eighteenth birthday in three months, and her coming-out party would be held in Home-Bay's gazebo, as had been the custom for the past 138 years. As it happened, in the fourth month of the year 160, Aidan was the only young lady turning eighteen. She was blissfully ignorant as to how her life was about to dramatically change.

For the past seventeen-plus years, with some difficulty, Vance, Dale, Troy, and Gary had kept Alex unaware of Aidan Connor's existence. To aid in that endeavor, they'd selected Aidan's surrogate parents, the Connors, in part due to their location on the planet. Consequently, Aidan had been born and raised in a small hamlet on the east coast of the South Dumbbell. She was the middle of five children, with two natural-born older sisters and two natural-born younger brothers.

Alex had visited all of the communities and towns on the planet numerous times and had seen a young Aidan in her hometown on several occasions. In the recent five years, Aidan had grown and matured to a point where Vance and Dale feared that Alex might recognize her for who she really was. To their credit, her surrogate parents managed, in synchronization with Vance and Dale, to keep the two of them apart.

Aidan's family, like most families around the planet, traveled to Home-Bay at least twice a year for various celebrations and events. Keeping the two apart during those times was particularly tough, but with much management and coordination, they managed.

Alex and Aidan knew nothing of the conspiracy, but at age twelve, Aidan began vigorously questioning why she was unable to see the most famous human in history, when she knew he must be in close proximity. This caused many parent-child tiffs, but all of that was about to change.

Just three months prior to her eighteenth birthday, Aidan walked into the living room of her family's home to find Vance and Dale, two of the three most famous people on the planet, sitting side by side on her couch.

"Whoa!" she exclaimed as she stopped dead in her tracks. "What?" She quickly looked from the two men to her parents and back again. A look of concern came across her face. "Did someone die?"

"No, no. Everyone's fine," said Vance. "We have come to talk to you."

Aidan's brow furrowed. "Talk to me?"

"Yes."

She pointed at her chest. "Me?"

Vance laughed. "Yes, young lady, you."

"Oh my God." She looked down at her body. Fortunately, she was dressed in a clean work jumpsuit, and she'd recently washed her long auburn hair and pulled it back into a ponytail. As usual, she wore no makeup; she looked wholesome and presentable. That was not always the case. She had a substantial measure of tomboy in her, and at any given time, she could look as if she'd just plowed the north forty barehanded.

"You look just fine. Not to worry," said her mom.

Her father just nodded.

"You are a beautiful young woman," said Vance.

"I'm in agreement," said Dale with a nod and a smile.

"Thank you. Wow."

Vance knew Aidan would be a bit overwhelmed by their sudden visit, and he gestured toward an overstuffed chair next to her folks. "Please sit down, Aidan."

She did as Vance directed while looking from her mother to her father for some sort of explanation. She got none. She sat with her back ramrod straight and her hands on her knees. She was clearly ill at ease.

"We're going to tell you a story," said Vance. "A story that is not to be shared with anyone other than your parents until further notice. Is that understood?"

"Yes, sir."

Vance smiled. "I believe this story will surprise you and maybe even shock you, so I ask that you hear us out before remarking."

Aidan nodded once before giving a drawn-out "Ookaay."

"You know you are a clone?"

Aidan nodded once without speaking.

Clones were common on Gabriel. They had been a big part of the population growth since the *Norman* had first touched down on the planet with just twenty humans on board. The use of clones, along with semen and eggs donated by thousands of Earth's least faulty humans, provided the genetic diversity necessary for a robust species.

Though the attitude was discouraged, clones were given a little higher standing than the natural-born because they represented a known and desired quality. Otherwise, of course, they would not have been cloned. At that point in time, more than 60 percent of the population either were clones or had parents, grandparents, or great-grandparents who were.

"You are the first clone of a special woman from old Earth to be born here on Gabriel."

"I didn't know that," she said matter-of-factly.

Vance smiled inwardly upon seeing her interest and curiosity heightened.

Aidan looked quickly at her parents and then back to Vance.

"And that being the case, you don't have any idea of what your station was on Earth."

"I do not, no, but I'll bet you're about to tell me."

Vance paused for a moment. *Feisty. I like that.* He smiled slightly and said, "You were the only woman Alexander Gabriel ever passionately loved."

Her head involuntarily jerked back a centimeter or two. She certainly hadn't seen this coming. She said nothing for a moment. Then her demeanor changed again, and she displayed bewilderment and some anger.

"What?" Her head shot from Vance to her parents. "Did you know this?"

Both parents nodded. "We did," said her mother.

Uh-oh, thought Vance. He knew all about the reaction of Lara's second clone when she'd been told why she was cloned. It was reported that after a few moments of confusion, she'd displayed a tentative acceptance followed by utter joy. But Aidan wasn't Lara, and she clearly wasn't going to follow Lara's path. She was a bit more negative in her reaction.

Her head whipped around to face her parents. "Why wasn't I told about this years ago?" she asked with an accusatory tone.

"Young lady," Vance said, "they didn't tell you because we asked them not to."

Aidan's head snapped back with considerable hostility to meet Vance's gaze. "Why would—" Aidan stopped in midsentence.

Vance's facial expression seemed to say, "Don't even think about using that tone with me."

Aidan was a bright young lady. She immediately toned down her attitude. "Sorry, sir," she said quietly.

Vance nodded and then smiled. "That's why I asked you to hear us out before remarking."

"Yes, sir."

Vance continued. "You've heard the story of me and Lara?"

"Yes, sir. Everybody has heard those stories."

"That's what I assumed, but I doubt the stories include any of my feelings during the time Lara's first clone was growing into womanhood."

"No, sir. I don't recall anything being said about that."

"No, those feelings were only known to my old friends Alex and Dale." Vance nodded toward Dale. "You wouldn't know how much I struggled with watching Lara grow up. It was a very long eighteen years waiting to have her back in my life—back in my arms."

Aidan nodded in understanding.

Vance continued. "When Lara passed away in the year eighty, my grief was so great that I put myself in stasis for twenty years."

"Yes, sir, I know that," Aidan said softly.

"At the beginning of that stasis, my dear friends implanted another clone, another Lara for me. They did so out of empathy and kindness, so I didn't have to again suffer the pangs of waiting for her to grow to maturity. She was there waiting for me when I came out of stasis, fully grown and"—Vance smiled in remembrance—"wonderful."

Aidan paused for a long moment before nodding. "I understand completely, sir." She paused again. "You wish me to be Alexander Gabriel's woman?"

"That is our hope," said Dale.

"Me?" she said to herself, clearly trying to absorb the astonishing revelation.

"We'll give you some time to come to grips with it," said Dale.

"Thank you." Aidan slowly got up and walked to the window. She said nothing for a minute before talking quietly to herself. "Me and Alexander Gabriel. Together. Me." She quit talking and just stared out the window.

The four other people in the room sat quietly. Vance, Dale, and Aidan's father leaned back in their seats to make themselves more comfortable while they waited. Her mother remained on the edge of her seat.

After a minute or so, Vance and Dale, with their heightened sense of hearing, could hear Aidan whisper to herself, "This changes everything—everything."

Aidan turned, walked back, and stood behind her chair, placing her hands on its backrest. She looked Vance in the eye. "We—Mr. Gabriel and I—both had to be kept unaware of this plan to spare him from going through what you had to endure."

Vance nodded once. "That was our intent."

Aidan nodded and turned to her parents. "I am so sorry for all the grief I caused you over the years. You had no choice; you did what you had to do."

"There is no need for you to apologize, sweetheart. From your point of view, you were justified in every case," said her mother.

"But still, that had to be tough on you." Aidan smiled. "It all makes sense now."

"I've got to tell you, young lady, seeing you standing here is bringing up memories long since buried from hundreds of years in the past," said Vance.

"Ditto," said Dale. "You are the spitting image of yourself."

Aidan displayed a radiant smile. "Like a clone."

Dale returned the smile. "Like that, yes."

Aidan said nothing for a moment. "What do you think Mr. Gabriel's reaction will be?"

"That's been the subject of speculation for quite a while," said Vance. "Judging from my own experience, I would guess complete shock to start with, followed by considerable confusion, followed by absolute joy."

"That's the desired outcome for sure," said Dale.

"I can practically guarantee it," said Vance.

"Question is, how are you going to feel about it?" asked her mother.

"I don't quite know yet—it's a life changer."

"You do not have to do this at all," said Vance. "It is entirely up to you."

"Don't get me wrong—I just need time to absorb this revelation."

Dale got up, stepped to Aidan, and handed her a package. "This is everything I could find in the archives of the *Norman* and the *Marian* relating to Alex and Aidan's relationship on Earth. I'm sure you will find the contents useful."

Aidan's eyebrows went up. "Her name was Aidan?"

"Yes. We thought naming you Aidan would eliminate some unnecessary confusion when you two meet," said Dale.

"I can attest to that," added Vance.

Aidan nodded in understanding and then looked at the package in her hand and smiled. "Good. I'm sure this will help."

"In addition, Dale and I will be available to answer any questions that come up," added Vance.

Dale nodded.

"When are Mr. Gabriel and I going to meet?"

"We thought at your coming-out party," said Vance.

Aidan smiled. "As you and Lara's first clone did."

"More or less, yes, but Lara and I were just waiting for the moment. In this case, the only one who's going to be surprised is Alex."

Aidan nodded. "My surprise has already been delivered."

"Well, here's another one for you," said Dale. "Something you need to know now before you dive into the package in your hand."

Aidan asked cautiously, "What?"

"Colleen, Teddy's wife, is your full sister."

"Holy shit!"

Aidan didn't have the luxury of two years to study her predecessor's relationship with Alex, as Lara had in preparing for Vance; she had three months.

Aidan read and watched everything contained in the package Dale had given her. Further, she researched everything she could find on Alex's life on Earth and Gabriel.

Video and audio recordings of Alex on old Earth were extensive and impressive. Alex's speech to the entire world on the day the WGC took over Earth's governments was so dynamic and impressive that Aidan sat awestruck in front of her viewer for a full hour, trying to absorb the world-altering consequences of the words he spoke. *Wow, and I'm about to become this man's woman.*

In her research, Aidan came across an ancient professionally produced video of the wedding between her sister, Colleen, and Walter Gabriel, a.k.a. Uncle Walt, in the Earth year 1971. She was surprised and delighted at the beauty of the affair. *What a wonderful document.* Knowing that her sister was the gorgeous Colleen added greatly to her interest. A camera caught Uncle Walt's expression as he first spotted his bride-to-be coming down the aisle. If there had ever been a more loving expression, Aidan had never seen it. *Look at that woman. She had to be the most beautiful woman in the world.*

Aidan smiled when she saw Alex in the video. He was her present age, just a kid of seventeen at the time, and was tall, skinny, and a bit gangly. However, a close-up of his face revealed dazzling blue eyes that seemed to contain wisdom far beyond his years.

When Aidan saw her own image on the wedding recording, she was pleasantly surprised. *That's me—not bad.* Her hairstyle was one she hadn't considered, and her makeup was a bit heavier than she'd ever applied, but all in all, she felt she looked quite pretty, though not nearly as pretty as her older sister. But then, who was?

Aidan turned the video off and leaned back in her chair. *I'm about to meet Alexander Gabriel for the first time. What if his tastes have changed? What if I don't please him? Will he bring a date to my party?*

ALEX AND AIDAN
MO-FOUR 11, 160

"Alex, we need to move it," said Vance.

"I'm on it." Alex's voice came from his bedroom.

"Don't want to be late, ya know." Vance must have forgotten he was talking to a man who was notorious for his punctuality. On Earth, Alex was known to have canceled important meetings if the other party was just a few minutes late. Consequently, those who wished an audience with the world's most powerful man were never late.

Alex walked into his living room while putting on his tuxedo coat.

Lara smiled. "You look mighty handsome, Mr. Gabriel."

"And this beauty will be wasted because you want me to go stag tonight."

"We have our reasons."

Alex smiled. "I can only assume you and the big lug here are setting me up. A blind date concerns me a little. That's way out of the ordinary."

"That's a reasonable assumption," said Lara matter-of-factly. "So are you ready to head over?"

"I know just about every eligible woman on the planet, you know?" Alex answered as he checked his tie knot in the hall mirror. "Let's go."

There was a knock on the door. "Good timing," said Alex. "That will be Teddy and Colleen."

The door opened, and Alex, Vance, and Lara greeted Teddy and Colleen.

Teddy turned to Colleen. "Told you they would be anxious to see us."

Colleen smiled as she slapped Teddy on the shoulder. "You did not, you fabricator."

Alex laughed. "We were just heading over," he said as he hugged Colleen and gave her a kiss on the cheek. "If you ever decide to dump this fabricator, you let me know."

"You'll be the first."

Teddy ignored the exchange as he looked past the three standing in the hallway. "Where's your date?"

"I'm not allowed a date tonight."

Teddy cocked his head. "You're being set up?"

"So it would seem."

"Well, this is going to be interesting."

Interesting? Oh yeah, thought Vance.

"Let's go," said Alex.

Fifteen minutes later, they walked into the gazebo. They

were a little early, proving that Vance's earlier prodding had been unnecessary.

Dale and Tomako arrived at the gazebo within a minute of Alex's party. Alex smiled when he saw them. They were clearly in love; it was wonderful to see. Tomako was petite and had fine features, not unlike Dale's wife on Earth.

People trailed in at a steady rate and greeted friends as they walked around to find unoccupied chairs to sit in. There was an open bar already doing a lively business as the well-dressed partiers mingled with friends and acquaintances. Aidan's family had, of course, invited everybody from their hamlet, and it seemed they all had come.

Jarleth and Shem sat proudly with their family and close friends at a table to the right of Alex's. Both were now thirty-eight years old, and they had four children. The children's genetics were the strongest anyone had ever seen. They had two boys and two girls; the boys were nearly identical to Shem, and the girls were clearly Jarleth's. There was no doubt they were Arkell.

Alex sat with the other leaders of Gabriel and their wives at a large table in the middle of the gazebo. There were three seats presently unfilled, reserved for the honoree and her parents. The table to their left was reserved for Teddy, Colleen, Gary, Pat, and Aidan's excited siblings.

"The honoree will be here in ten minutes, ladies and gentlemen," said the chairwoman of party committee over the PA system. "If our council members, their ladies, and the honoree's family will please form the reception line, we will get ready for our young lady's entrance."

"That's us," said Teddy with a smile as he took Colleen's hand.

Vance smiled to himself. *Teddy's and Colleen's reactions should be interesting. Big surprise coming for just about the entire planet.*

Earlier in the day, Vance had tasked several partygoers with taking close-up and extended videos of Alex, Aidan, Teddy, and Colleen. He wanted to record the facial expressions and reactions to what was about to be unveiled. He didn't say why.

Aidan's father and siblings were already in place and were obviously excited to see every dignitary on the planet there to honor their Aidan.

Aidan's father would be the first to greet his daughter and wife as they entered the gazebo. Aidan's siblings and their spouses would follow. Next would come Troy, Gary, their wives, Teddy, Colleen, Dale, and Tomako. Last in line would be Vance, Lara, and Alex. Alex was purposely put last in line, which in itself was highly unusual.

Alex looked to his left and made eye contact with Vance and Lara. *What the hell are you up to?* he thought. They just smiled in return.

A few seconds later, the chairwoman came over the PA: "Ladies and gentlemen, please welcome our honoree, Miss Aidan Connor."

Aidan? thought Alex.

Out of the *Norman's* cave walked Aidan and her mother, arm in arm. As was now tradition, the path was lined with well-wishers, including a few Vout and Yassi. All were applauding, wooing, or both. The crowd obscured Alex's view until Aidan and her mother stepped into the gazebo and stopped in front of her father. However, her head was turned, so Alex could not see her face.

Still can't see. Alex took a step forward to get a better look. He still could not quite see her face. *Something's amiss here.* An unusual pulse shot through his Isleium brain, causing him a moment of confusion. *Something's going on. Who?*

After hugging and kissing her father, Aidan turned and looked to the end of the receiving line. *There he is.* Her pulse rate increased dramatically. *There he is. There he is,* she kept repeating to herself. *Stay calm.*

Vance, Lara, Dale, and Tomako followed her eyes to the end of the line. They did not want to miss the expression on their friend's face.

Aidan's and Alex's eyes met at the same moment. She was dressed in an exact copy of the bridesmaid's dress her predecessor had worn many centuries ago, and her hair and makeup were identical.

She stood quietly for a moment or two before smiling warmly. Alex's smile slowly dropped until his expression was completely blank.

Vance and Dale nodded to themselves. There it was, the look they'd expected: shock. It was perfect.

Alex's Isleium brain shut down, just as Vance's had when he'd first spotted Lara III and as Dale's had when he'd realized the comet would save Gabriel from the GRB. All of his thoughts, reflexes, and instincts were disabled. However, unlike Vance's and Dale's states of shock, Alex's shutdown lasted only a few seconds. He shook his head slightly before a small smile of comprehension appeared on his face.

As Aidan's mother took up her position next to her husband, Aidan began tentatively walking past the reception line, not stopping to greet anyone and never taking her eyes off the object of her attention.

Teddy's and Colleen's mouths dropped open as Aidan walked by them. Who was this young lady who looked all the world like a smaller, younger version of Colleen?

Colleen quickly recognized the dress and the young lady wearing it. She'd watched the video of her original's wedding to Uncle Walt many times. "Oh my God," she said under her breath as she realized who the gorgeous young lady was and what was about to happen. "Oh my God," she repeated.

Teddy's head quickly turned to catch the look of recognition on his wife's face. She saw something he didn't.

The crowd began sensing something was askew. Why wasn't the new honoree greeting the receiving line? A silence fell across the room.

Aidan looked neither left nor right as she walked up to Alex and stopped a meter from him. Her warm smile never left her exquisite face.

Alex's smile remained as he looked into her eyes.

"I'm Aidan Keefe," she said, using her maiden name on Earth.

"I know," he said quietly.

Alex turned and nodded at Vance and Dale. "Well done," he said loudly enough for all to hear. He turned back to Aidan. "Hello, beautiful. It's been a long, long time," he said softly.

Aidan smiled brightly as she took a step forward, cutting the distance between them in half. "I've been praying I would be worth the wait."

"There is no doubt in my mind that you are."

It was so quiet in the gazebo that everyone could hear what they said. A brief burst of surprise shot through the room, but silence quickly returned. No one wanted to miss a word or gesture.

Teddy turned to Colleen and whispered, "Who's Aidan Keefe?"

Colleen's eyes never left Aidan. "My sister."

"No!"

Alex's gaze shifted and quickly scanned the whole of Aidan from her toes to her hair before settling back on her striking green eyes. He smiled. "You have come back into my life. This is a magnificent surprise," he said lovingly.

"Hello, Alex," she said as her smile broadened. "May I hug you?"

"Oh yes." He reached over and put his arms around her waist as she put hers around his neck. He looked into her eyes. "You have no idea how delighted I am. This is my happiest moment in a very long time."

"Oh, I do have an idea, sir, because this is the happiest moment of my life."

The crowed jumped to their feet and clapped, wooed, and yelled their approval.

Alex smiled and gave Aidan a soft kiss on the lips that lasted just a couple of seconds before pulling back a couple of centimeters. "Oh yes, I remember you."

"That's your sister?" Teddy asked Colleen.

"My sister, Aidan—look how beautiful she is," Colleen said with a great deal of pride.

"I'll say. She's nearly as pretty as you," said Teddy, "and that is no small accomplishment."

"How in the world did they keep this a secret?" Colleen asked, clearly amazed.

"Oh, everybody knew; we just didn't tell you," Teddy answered seriously.

Colleen giggled and lightly slapped Teddy on the shoulder. "Fabricator."

CHAPTER 21

THE FIRST FEMALE SLF
MO-THREE 6, 192

Vance was as gentle as possible as he helped Lara out onto the deck and onto her favorite soft chair, and then he took the chair beside her. Lara was 110, and her health was failing physically and mentally; it was breaking Vance's heart. He knew she was on the verge of losing her dignity, which was something he'd promised her decades ago he would not allow. He knew it was almost time to make good on that promise.

From that spot on their deck, Vance and Lara had enjoyed the wonderful views for nearly a century. They'd watched the community of Home-Bay grow from two buildings to a bustling town and witnessed the *Norman* and *Marian* coming and going over the decades. From there, they could see the Vance River flowing into Home-Bay and the bay flowing into the Vast Ocean.

"I'm falling apart, sweetheart," she said in a weak voice while her old eyes scanned the goings-on across the river.

Vance took her hand. He knew what she was about to say. He knew her well. He had to fight to keep his voice strong and as detached as possible. "What do you want to do?"

Lara turned her head to look her beloved husband in the eye. "I think it's time."

Despite his efforts to remain stoic, the tears in his eyes gave him away. "Okay, if that's what you want."

Lara squeezed his hand. "You know I won't be leaving you, just switching bodies."

"I know, I know. But ..."

Three days later, after they made arrangements and completed a final upload of her inner self, the transfer was made to her SLF. After the lab techs did a preliminary check of her functions, a beautiful twenty-year-old Lara sat up on her own and looked around. She quickly spotted her husband of ninety years and smiled brightly. "Hi, sweetheart."

Oh God. Vance was having trouble controlling his conflicting emotions. The love of his life had been renewed again, but he also knew that in the next room was another Lara, the Lara he had watched grow old over nine decades, who would soon die. There was only one Lara, but she was, at that moment in time, residing in two bodies. This one was his beautiful Lara who would never grow old and never die. He kept telling himself that to ease his sorrow and conscience regarding what was about to happen. The experience was at once a cause for joy and a cause of great sorrow.

Lara, within a week of becoming a SLF, and her aged human self, without consulting Vance, made their plan regarding how, when, and where the human Laura would die. The decisions were a great deal harder to make than Lara had imagined. Both Laras decided the human Lara would be euthanized, and it was to be done on Vance's island, their island. The time had come.

Vance felt conflicted. A highly pragmatic man, he was, for one of the few times in his life, basing his position on emotion rather than logic. But he had no persuasive argument, and he knew it.

Using the superb Yassi shuttle, the three flew to Vance's island and landed in the clearing of the rain forest where Vance and Lara had first met ninety-two years in the past.

"I changed my mind. I'll wait here," said Lara the SLF. "This is a moment to be shared by you two alone."

The human Lara said, "Yes, that's right." Their thoughts remained the same.

Vance nodded without saying a word, and then he exited the shuttle and walked around to the rear hatch. "Open," he said. The hatch opened, revealing three comfortable picnic chairs. He took two chairs, one in each hand; walked thirty meters; and placed them in the shade of a huge fig tree he and Lara had planted together more than ninety years ago to commemorate the spot where they had first embraced. He returned to the shuttle and gently helped Lara exit to the ground.

The human Lara turned back toward the shuttle, knowing that her SLF would be standing in the hatch opening.

"You take care of our man," she said.

"You know I will," the SLF responded softly.

It was all Vance could do not to stop what was about to happen. "You two are killing me here." His voice was breaking up.

"Stay tough, sweetheart," both Laras said at once. They laughed a little.

The human Lara raised her hand to her SLF and received the same gesture in response. She turned, took Vance's hand, and walked slowly to the shade of the tree. Once there, she turned and put her arms around his neck, as she had first done long ago. "I remember"—her chin quivered a little—"this moment. It was the happiest moment of my young life."

"And mine," Vance said.

"You remember I'm waiting in the shuttle for you—all of me and all of my memories," she whispered in his ear.

Vance could only nod.

"Let's sit down," said Lara.

Vance helped her sit and adjusted the chair's back a little so she could lean back and be more comfortable; then he took the other chair.

"This is our spot," she said with a small smile.

"It is; it will always be."

"Look!" said Lara.

On the far side of the clearing, a hundred or so meters away, a band of gorillas cautiously came into view from the thick forest. They were no doubt curious about the shuttle and the beings under the big tree.

"There must be a dozen of them," said Vance, clearly pleased.

"Seeing me off, I'll bet," she said with a little lilt in her voice.

"That must be it." Vance smiled a little as he continued to watch the gorillas.

"We've had a wonderful, long life together, sweetheart. You've been a perfect husband."

Vance turned back to face his wife just in time to see a vial drop from her hand onto the grass.

"Goodbye, my love," she whispered.

"Oh no. I love you. I love you. I—"

She was gone.

Vance sat in the chair, holding his wife's hand, for nearly an hour before Lara exited the shuttle and joined him under the tree.

She knelt beside Lara's chair and put her hands on her cheeks. Tears filled her eyes. After a few moments, she stood, wiped her tears with the back of her hand, and turned to Vance. "Time to head back to Home-Bay."

Vance stood and took Lara the SLF in his arms. "I'll never lose you again."

MO-THREE 14, 192

Lara had invited Pat, Clair, and Colleen for lunch at the Youngblood home. The four were sitting at the kitchen table, discussing how beautiful Lara was as a SLF.

"Was it hard to say goodbye to your old body?" Colleen asked.

Lara's smile faded as she took a moment to consider her answer. "I thought I had it all figured out, but I didn't. It's very tough. It's, in effect, committing suicide—with a twist, of course."

Colleen nodded in understanding. "Was it the right decision?"

Lara paused for a few seconds. "Yes, it was the right thing to do—the only thing to do. But it was very frightening. Both of my minds were terrified."

"I would think that your mind in the SLF body wouldn't be scared," said Pat.

Lara smiled slightly. "It's the same mind with identical thoughts and emotions. My old body was still mine—still me."

"That's interesting," said Colleen. "I hadn't considered that."

"But you now believe it was the right thing to do?" asked Clair.

Lara nodded. "My body, as you know, was failing in all sorts of ways. My dignity was starting to take a beating. And at best, I didn't have more than three months to live." Lara paused for a moment. "But emotionally, I'm still coming to terms with it."

"Getting better?" asked Pat.

"It is. Time will fix it."

"Your experience will be a great help to the rest of us when our time comes. We'll know what to expect," Pat said.

"Yes, this will be a help to you. It would have helped me for sure."

"But back to the bright side. You look spectacular," said Colleen, changing the subject.

"Well, I am who I always was, but now I've been placed in this pretty package." With that, she stood up and gracefully turned 360 degrees.

The three old ladies cheered and clapped. Clair gave a "Woo!"

CHAPTER 22

BICENTENNIAL
MO-TEN 19, 199

Early Evening

"My fellow Gabrielites," Alex's voice said over the planet-wide broadcast system.

Those in the historic gazebo turned their attention to the raised platform located on the far side of the gazebo. On the platform, sitting behind a long linen-covered table, were all the planet's leaders, their spouses, and Teddy and Colleen. A roaring round of applause, whistles, and woos came from the crowd.

Alex smiled brightly, as did the others sitting at that table. "I have been charged with giving the population of Gabriel a short tutorial as to the state of the planet on this last day of our one hundred ninety-ninth year of colonization. Judging by the activities around me, we are off to a great start in this celebration." Alex looked over the crowd and smiled again. "From my assigned perch here in the old gazebo, I can see quite a number of our fellow citizens began their celebration early."

When the knowing laughter settled down, Alex continued. "We'll see if they can maintain their present pace until midnight." Alex again looked over the crowd, smiled, and nodded before he turned back to face the camera, never saying what his amusement was about.

"Where was I? Oh yes, Gabriel's age. The two hundred years that we have inhabited this planet seems like a very short time, considering how advanced our infrastructure, government, and civilization are. However, it's been six hundred years in planet time since Vance Youngblood first landed the *Norman* just a few meters south of this spot. Remarkable—just six hundred years since this incredible man stepped off the *Norman* onto the surface of a planet that had not yet been named and had not been lived on." Alex looked at Vance and nodded once. Vance returned the gesture. The crowd applauded appreciatively.

Alex continued. "The population at that moment in time was a sparse twenty-one—Vance and twenty colonists who were in a deep and long-lasting sleep, a sleep that was to last an additional four hundred years in planet time from that initial touchdown. The colonists slept while Vance Youngblood prepared the planet for them." Alex paused for a moment while he checked a paper in front of him and smiled. "Interesting to note that our present population, as of thirty minutes ago, is five hundred one thousand six hundred twenty-six. Wow!

"After that initial landing, Vance Youngblood spent those next four hundred years in the company of the holographic forms of Dale Isley and myself. We were ensconced in the *Norman*'s computer, not simply to keep Vance company but also to offer advice and counsel to him on the myriad of challenges that such an undertaking would undoubtedly produce.

"Vance spent decades in real time single-handedly seeding this planet with all manner of life, from grass and mighty trees to fish, fowl, and animals, all brought from our home planet of Earth. As you all know, our home planet was destroyed by a massive asteroid in the Earth year 2540. We learned of this tragedy thirty years into our journey to Gabriel." Alex paused. "It was by far the worst moment in human history."

There was a loud murmuring throughout the crowd.

"But to continue, while never sleeping or resting, Vance alone planted an astonishing variety of life on this beautiful planet. When he felt the planet was capable of nurturing humans, he took our original twenty colonists out of their stasis." Alex paused for a moment. "Actually, nineteen. One, Terri Diggs, was sadly lost, but Vance introduced the surviving nineteen to their new home." Alex smiled. "That's when the clock started running, and it will be two hundred years ago tomorrow—two hundred years since a mostly barren orb in a far-off star system was transformed into one of the most hospitable planets in the galaxy. It is our home; it is our paradise."

Another round of applause sounded.

"Backing up more than eight decades to the year 117, the comet known as Yassi did a spectacular flyby. It caused considerable damage, creating half a dozen new volcanoes of various sizes and levels of activity and adding another pearl to the Black Pearl Islands. But as it turned out, the comet had an important chore to complete. Later that year, Yassi blocked a gamma-ray burst that would have destroyed all life on our world. It was assumed at the time that gods or superior beings sent it to protect us, which proved to be more or less accurate.

"Then, in the year 118, two remarkable people were born in the northwest section of the Vast Continent: the famous Shem and Jarleth. Their story is well known to all Gabrielites, Yassi, Vout, and the aforementioned superior beings, our dear friends the Arkell.

"The Arkell, led by Oruku, visited us for the first time in the year 137. That's when we learned they were the ones who saved our planet from destruction. They gave us Shem and Jarleth. They extended our lives. They provided us with many life-enhancing procedures, and they installed protective shields around our planet. After their initial arrival, they revisited Gabriel in the years 149, 161, 178, and 189, and they are expected to be here for our bicentennial celebration. In fact, they are expected here this very afternoon. It's always wonderful to have them spend a few weeks here. They always bring gifts of great value, whether videos of new planets or life they have discovered, medicines to ease our suffering, or technology to aid us in our everyday lives." Alex smiled. "Yet their greatest gift has always been their love for human beings. We are so very fortunate that we count the incredible Arkell as our friends."

Alex checked his notes before looking up at the camera and smiling. "We have a thriving, dynamic planet. Agriculture and construction are the dominant enterprises. Manufacturing continues to expand to cover the needs of the populous. Each year, we require fewer products from the Yassi and Vout, but both of those wonderful races endeavor to invent new products that appeal to the Gabrielites and earn our gold." Alex smiled again. "And I might add that they have been extraordinarily successful in their endeavor.

"Commerce has evolved over the decades from a predominantly barter system to a currency system. The currency itself is, of course, Gabriel gold in various coin and bar denominations.

"Home-Bay now has a population of approximately twenty-five thousand. There are five other cities around the planet with similar populations. Twenty-five thousand is considered ideal based on extensive social, industrial, and economic studies.

"Bicentennial celebrations are being held planet-wide in all towns and cities rather than in just one location, as was the case with the first centennial. The entire planet's population in the year 100 was just more than seventeen thousand, and it was estimated that more than ten thousand gathered at Home-Bay to celebrate that milestone year."

Alex looked off camera and nodded. "We've just received word that the Arkell ship is about to arrive. You will forgive me if I leave you for a short time. I want to be outside, looking up, when they arrive."

With that, the image on all the viewers worldwide changed to the blank sky. Only the dim view of Gabriel's smallest moon, Faith, was visible in the lower left corner of the screen.

The Arkell ship came in like a fastball. In two seconds, the *Velgot* went from the size of a BB to a massive golden orb stopped 210 kilometers above Home-Bay.

The End

Printed in the United States
by Baker & Taylor Publisher Services